For Brent Mic
18th July 1964–28th

1. GIN

When she woke they had already buried him.

Gin lay in the small white room, watching the doctor's mouth move as he told her. And for once she was grateful to the ancient Hasidic laws, the quick burial that saved her from having to face his father's broken stare, his mother's swollen eyes. She did not have to stand and watch his weeping wife and sons, nor answer unspoken questions, clear the confusion as to why she had been there at all. Was she the reason for his silence in his last two days of life? And if she could have borne to get past the guilt, the rage, would she have been able to so glibly lie? To deny her past, her part in his life, and his in hers? He, who once so savoured honesty, what would he have said? Lie? Protect his family yet again? She would have, for that.

A moot point. *So unusual for a BMW to roll.*

But how would she have been able to stem her own pain and look into his wife's eyes, pretend it was his wife's name on his lips as he died?

Perhaps they could have found some mutual comfort in the truth, the shared pain. But then she realised, with a small shock, that even now if she mentioned Leila there would be questions as to who Leila was. What irony that even at his death, she, Gin, was still the only one who knew. At least she had allowed him honesty at death. She held onto this as the only comfort. Held fast, to silence herself, and any shame.

Gin lay in the hospital room and relished the semblance of peace. She was allowed no visitors in the first days and, indeed, expected

none. Later when, of all people, Viv arrived, Gin said little of conse-
quence, still drugged and uninclined to the weariness of talk while
Viv's chatter assumed an air of desperate cheer. Inevitable that her
family would call Viv, when Gin herself would have been content
alone. She fell asleep, waking to an empty, dark room, lit only dimly
by the lights from the mountain.

The doctors came, and went, and came again, each time with
updates of her progress that she found herself indifferent to. She
lay there, gazing out the window at the immovable mountain. She
would be left with a slight limp, they said, and she thought it inap-
propriate to laugh. Was that all? It seemed obscene that his death
should mark her so little, and she was glad for the news. Her leg
would probably ache in London's winter, they said. Overwhelmingly
she longed suddenly for hard, grey rain and the hustle of a wet Saturday afternoon market. The African sunshine could never capture
that. Lying alone in the small white room, she remembered why
here the irrepressible sun could depress her with its falsity, how it
could burn and be bright when all around was pain and poverty.
In England she would be able to resonate with the coldness that sat
now in her soul.

But for now, she is here, in Cape Town. For now, beneath the mountain's watch, she will slowly repair. Ignoring the hollow ache, the
need to mourn, to cut her hair and rend her garments, to cry and
keen. To kneel over the ashes of all she thinks forsaken, lost, or dead.

2. GIN

It is her fourth day in the small white room, a time twice as long as they had spent together. There is a knock. Light but firm, and unnecessary since the door is always left ajar. Not quite so private a room, it seems.

"Miss McMann. Miss Virginia McMann," says a voice, and it is not a question. He enters despite her silence, her lack of invitation. "I'm Nick Retief."

He is a tall white man, in his early thirties, some five years younger than herself. Hair like hers, more blond than brown, and in need of a trim.

"Detective Sergeant Nick Retief."

She notes a touch of emphasis, a touch of pride perhaps, and wonders at this most peculiar of South African anomalies, a man with an Afrikaans name but an English accent.

He seems unperturbed by her continued reticence to speak. "I'm investigating your –" and here he falters slightly, "accident." He says the word as if it is foreign, as if it exists in a world he seldom inhabits. A world of unconnected incidents and random events, as if his own is certain and assured, where every action is determined exactly by a clear and measured motivation.

Gin blinks at him. Waits. He seems to wait also. Unhurried. Eventually she says, "Yes, Mr Retief?" the question formed in almost exactly the manner in which he has said *accident* to her. And indeed, to herself, her voice sounds thinly accented with an exaggerated Englishness, summoning her years in England so as to separate herself from him, and his Afrikaans name.

He squints slowly back at her, as if deciding something. "Miss McMann," he says again.

His eyes, she notices, are gunmetal grey, but when the light hits them, they opacify to blue.

"Can you tell me what you remember?"

She wants to laugh at him. She has thought of nothing else.

"I wanted a coffee," she starts, and then stops.

Empty coffee houses lined the street; it was too early in the morning. She was longing for the froth of a London cappuccino, but would have to wait instead for the strong black filter of the hotel breakfast. White linen curtains twitched in the breeze, caressing the window. African air was already warm against her skin. And where to now, she mused? Simon was still asleep, an unruly black mop of hair, greying. She was touched by nostalgia and an ache she could call yearning. These moments were just that. Moments, and not forever. Once, a long season ago, she might have dreamed of forever. But time was passing. She tousled the mop and, never an early riser, he grumbled.

"Hello," she said, sweetly. Wanting to brush the hair from his eyes.

He stretched and yawned, ran his fingers through his hair. "You sound so English."

Was it compliment or slur, a reminder of her treachery, or his? Did he miss his wife that morning? She was unused to the duplicity, the complication of feeling. Yet it did not feel like it ought; she was more happy than guilty. As if time were an affirmation. As if she had prior claim.

They drove out early after breakfast, sexual tension sated, an ease between them. He had lied about being here, about being with her, he said. She was strangely moved at his need to protect her as much as himself. She held no illusions, discovering a lightness to her limbs that morning, an unusual joy unfettered by the future, fruit of an elusive search. The sun glinted silver on the sea, its reflection imprinting on her retina, overpowering. They drove first to Rondebosch, the leafy suburb.

He showed her Grove Road, where he had lived, a walk away from the university. She took him over the small hump of a bridge, past the little gallery of shops that in her memory always made her tingle in its proximity to Jonnie. She did not mention Jonnie, wondering if Simon would still be jealous, still feel a kind of fury for the only other man she had ever loved. But she showed him the house in Observatory, its colonial façade intact despite the Cape winters. They walked like lovers ten years younger. Amidst stalls in Greenmarket Square they held hands, secure in anonymity. Had coffee on the sidewalk in Seapoint.

So unusual for a BMW to roll. His hands gripping the wheel.

There is a patter of noise on the window, rain tapping gently on the pane. Detective Sergeant Nick Retief has stayed silent, waiting for her to continue, and Gin turns her head to look out at the mountain. The coffee at breakfast, Simon's face as he made love to her; these are not details that interest this man. The weather has darkened the mountain, and wisps of cloud have shrouded its peak.

Gin starts again. "We drove around the city," she says.

On a whim, Simon took her to Kornfeld and Gold jewellers. She picked a sapphire ring close to the colour of her twin brother Gabriel's eyes, close to the colour of her own.

"It matches your eyes, Ginny," he said as he paid for it. He was smiling.

She felt the thrill of walking into the shop owned by their families, the thrill of no one knowing who they were.

He whispered to her and his voice was full of laughter. "Something to tell the grandchildren," he said. But his eyes were serious and sad.

Years before he had said this same sentence, in a tiny hotel on the coast. Hope had lived full in her chest then.

Today, said Simon, he had something to tell her. Something he should have told her years ago. She was startled, curious.

A white car, heading directly at them. They were already round Kloofnek, ready to sail down the high-set suburb of Tamboerskloof.

"There was a white car," says Gin. She thought the memory was clean and clear. Only now, in the retelling, does she realise how fractured it is. She thinks slowly, stupidly, how unfair it was to have an accident, when they had already rounded the coast, past Llandudno and Hout Bay, safely.

Back in the city, swerving. His hands gripping the wheel. The white car closer, her world starting to tilt. So unusual for a BMW to roll.

"Is that all?" asks Nick Retief.

She hears a caustic dissatisfaction in his tone. Gin closes her eyes. The accident is a blur. She can only remember the urgency in Simon's voice, his eyes.

The mountain tumbling to meet them, his hand outstretched to her. Through heavy-lidded eyes, like a lover, she looked at him, his hand outstretched to her.

"Ginny," he gasped, like a lover, when making love to her. Urgently, his hand outstretched to her.

"Is that all you remember?" repeats Retief, although his tone seems kinder than before.

She cannot bring herself to tell him Simon's final words. What does it matter now if he called a name? So she nods, awkwardly, silently, at this man. Like a child, chastised, instead of a woman of thirty-nine.

Then, "Leila." Like a message.
His hand outstretched to her.

Nick Retief turns to leave. She imagines he is as contemptuous of her faithless memory as she.

His voice sounds harsh again to her now, echoing off the stark walls. "I'll come again in a few days. Perhaps you'll remember more then." A pause. "And you will need to make a statement at the station."

After Retief has left, Gin watches the raindrops increase against the pane till they streak in rivulets down its length.

She did not think of Simon dying, all that loss. It was her soul soaring free, looking down at him. The beach at Clifton, the palm trees at Camps Bay. Hot searing sun. Was it the sun she felt burning her skin? The road, sign-writing itself across the brown earth, the cool mist of foam at the edge of the ocean. Washing-powder-white clouds. The city, sparkling below. Up, up into the blue sky, sapphire-blue like Gabriel's eyes, sapphire-blue like the ring on her hand. Her hand, outstretched to him.

Simon will walk the passages of her soul forever. No bond will be broken now; there is only this eternal longing. And the horror replay, over and over again, with its missing pieces, till it fades in sleep but returns to her restless in dreams. A second time in Cape Town he will haunt her. She wakes to find him her first thought, grief soaking her skin like sweat. It is not as expected. She has waited for the enormity of guilt, but it has not come. Not even with visitors, not even with the flowers from his family, the bouquet of white an offer of forgiveness and understanding, if only she will proffer more than silence, give some sort of explanation. It is as before, as if merely an ocean or a continent separates them, as if a phone call or a plane ride could reunite.

She remembers their first parting, first loss.

His voice was warm and deep. His eyes would not meet hers. Simon had held her so gently. And gently, he had let her go. She had sat for a long time on the three stone steps, sat in the afternoon shade for a long time after his car had pulled from the cobbled courtyard. Something was lost between them. And a week later she herself had left, packed up her battered blue suitcase, closed the door.

He is leaving her again. She is losing him, for the last time.

Perhaps, thinks Gin, the love is there still. Perhaps it could not leave, though the lovers had. It must be there still, in the little flat. On a good day, perhaps it could be glimpsed. Like incense wafting through the air. Like dust in sunlight. At first, this thought depresses her, but later it is comforting. By then she is up and walking, the promised limp more evident with fatigue. The doctors fuss her less, the nurses more.

Nick Retief visits once again, but she is asleep, and she wakes to find he has left a note, and an incongruous bunch of stiff proteas on the table. The note is brief; she is vaguely surprised at the even strokes of black ink, demanding her presence at the station on her discharge. The bouquet lasts the rest of her stay, and when Viv comes to fetch her, when Gin is well enough to leave the small white room with its view of the mountain, she takes the rigid flowers with her.

3. *VIVIENNE*

It is time to fetch Gin from the hospital. Viv stares at the mirror, pulls at the skirt that falls loosely about her angular hips. She has lost more weight, she notes absently. She touches her eyes briefly. Fine lines. So long, so long. So many years since Gin had truly been part of her life, so many years since they had been friends. Viv closes her eyes to block out the thought. What will Gin think of her now? What will she make of her life?

At Viv's first visit, Gin had been drowsy and drugged. She lay pallid and still, those blue eyes glassy, elsewhere. It had been easy for Viv then. Easy to sit in the chair across from the bed. Sitting in shadow, into darkness, while Gin slept. Easy to study this stranger, this scarred ghost, who was once her friend.

Viv pulls the car out too sharply, too quickly. A horn blares behind her, the driver throwing up his hands in exasperation. She waves him an apology and pivots her ankle on her high heel, pushes the accelerator to the floor. At the traffic light, she slows to catch the amber, and lights a cigarette on the red. She rolls the window down to the afternoon heat, and the smoke from her cigarette lifts and coils, sliding out, a cloud in the clear blue sky.

Jonnie. What to say about Jonnie?

A beep from behind. Green. Viv takes off more slowly this time, unwilling to close the distance between herself and Gin, her unexpected guest. It was natural that Gin's sister would call her after the accident. Natural that, as always, Issy remained oblivious to Gin's feelings, still ignorant of any acrimony between Gin and Viv, still unaware it had been years since they had even spoken.

Viv turns into the squat concrete of the hospital car park and stubs her cigarette out in the ashtray. She turns the rear-view mirror towards herself, smoothes at her long brown hair. Lipstick. Somewhere. She fumbles in her bag. Scarlet is all she finds. Appropriate. She waits for the guilt and the hurt to overwhelm her again.

Jonnie.

She smears the colour across her lips. Her mouth feels suddenly dry.

Gabe.

She checks her appearance again, and sighs. Too many people lie between her and Gin. It is bad enough to look into Gin's eyes and see Gabe's eyes looking back at her. Now to meet those eyes again, with Jonnie's name as yet unsaid.

Viv takes a deep breath, and gets out of the car.

On Viv's second visit, Gin had been awake. By then, Viv had packed Gin's clothes from the hotel, the sumptuous Mount Nelson with its palm trees and faded pink walls, set in sun beneath the slopes of Table Mountain. A tourist's hotel, she had thought, settling the bill, sifting through the mundane chores that continue unabated after tragedy, after death.

"Hello, Viv," Gin had said. A hand, stretched out to her.

"Hello, Viv," she says again now.

Awake. But not alive, thinks Viv. Gin's restless eyes search the room, as if she has forgotten something. A mind searching for what is unfinished. She turns to look at Viv. *Help me,* the eyes say, *help me.*

"*Hamba kakuhle,* Miss Virginia," says one of the nursing assistants from the doorway.

Viv watches as the woman grabs Gin's hand, wishing her to travel well with the traditional Xhosa greeting. Gin leans forward and hugs the woman briefly.

"*Enkosi kakhulu,*" says Gin, thanking the woman in the same language. Their hands linger, pale white folded into rich black. Gin's left arm is still bandaged, covering the burns of hot metal, where the mangled car had melded to her flesh. At the edge of white gauze, Viv can see pink skin, healing.

Nurses gather round to say their farewells. Viv stands and waits, holding onto Gin's suitcase. Gin must have been an ideal patient, she imagines. Quiet, compliant, uncomplaining.

Eventually, Gin walks somewhat lopsidedly towards her. Viv is taken aback by the extent of her limp.

"I'm sorry to take so long, Viv," whispers Gin.

Viv smiles at her, trying to convey warmth.

Gin takes her arm. "I need to lean on you a bit, if that's all right – don't let them see," she pleads, her voice still low.

Slowly they wind their way through wide hospital corridors to the car park outside. Gin's gait seems to straighten with the walk. Something bothers Viv about Gin's appearance. It is not age or injury, she thinks, but something vague and undefined.

Viv turns the car into the late afternoon traffic on de Waal Drive. Cape Town sprawls below them through the haze of February heat, a blurred mix of beiged-out buildings, silvered motorways, blue sea and sky. The mountain retreats from them as they drive. The city speeds by, the verdant suburbs of Newlands receding to the brown edge of the Klipfontein plain.

Fruit and flower sellers litter the roads at junctions. Some of them rap at the car window to gain attention. "*Only ten rand, merrum, five joosey oranges!*"

Gin sits quietly, as if absorbing this city anew. Viv, having expected awkwardness, feels relieved. She lights another cigarette, rolls down her window, and switches on the radio.

She is pleased to get home, pleased the girls are away and there is none of their usual mess. They sit in the lounge, drinking rooibos tea while Gin tries to tell her about the accident. Gin's blue eyes darken as she talks. Her gaze flicks from the floor to the framed photographs of Viv's daughters and back again. Viv stays silent, making no comment, trying to make sense of the stumbled recall. She touches Gin's arm when she seems to struggle for breath between sentences, touches Gin's trembling hand as she apologises and starts again. Time appears to have warped oddly for Gin. She speaks Simon's name quickly, lightly, as if to say it otherwise would be to taste it, to feel it on her tongue like salt from tears. Gin's account of the accident itself is garbled and rushed. She shivers violently, and Viv imagines she remembers Simon, beside her in the burning car, dying.

The tea is cold and Viv rises to make a fresh pot. The kitchen is dark, the sun having already abandoned the rear of the house. She switches on the kettle, notes the lack of groceries in the house, but is thankful again for the absence of her daughters. They are with her mother and stepfather on the flat plains of the Klein Karoo. It will be easier for Gin, she thinks; it may give her the time and space necessary to heal, without constant reminders of past pain, past loss. And the presence of Viv's children could not have failed to remind her.

The kettle starts to boil, and Viv busies herself with the new pot. She needs more tea, and the milk is low. Reaching for fresh cups in the half-gloom, she knocks the sugar bowl to the floor. She tenses, shuts her eyes, anticipating the noisy crash of porcelain, yet it falls almost gracefully, cracking cleanly. The crystals hiss out across the terracotta tiles.

She had been saddened by the news of Simon's death, and slightly shocked at his being here in Cape Town, his being here with Gin. Gin's presence in the country was not a surprise in itself. Viv had known she would fly out for her father's funeral. Issy had told her that Alexander McMann had died, had asked if Viv would be coming to the funeral. But Viv had declined, unwilling to upset Gin further, and, she admits to herself now, unwilling to face her.

She sweeps at the sugar. In the immediacy of helping Gin, she had hardly thought of Simon Gold. After all, she had hardly known the man. Even after her brief contact with him, when in desperation she had sought him out for help, she had known him no better for it. There was no further reason to stay in touch thereafter. They lived different lives in different cities. She remembers black hair, grave-dark eyes. He had been courteous to her, and patient while she had tried to explain he was the only doctor she knew who did not also know Jonnie.

Jonnie. His name sits constantly between her and Gin.

Yes, Simon Gold had helped her. Because of Gin. But Viv suspected he would have helped her despite that. There had been a brief spark in Simon's eyes when he asked about Gin. It had flickered out as abruptly when Viv admitted she did not know, and he had not mentioned Gin's name again.

Viv throws the cracked bowl in the bin. Neither she nor Gin takes sugar so it is no loss. She wonders whether she ought to mention her meeting with Simon to Gin. But this will necessitate explanation, and certain pain, suppressed since Viv's divorce from Jonnie.

Jonnie. They must clear this, she resolves.

She takes the pot of tea to the lounge. Gin sits huddled in the armchair near the window that looks out over the lawn's square expanse, the grass fresh and revived from the recent rain. The high walls keep the noisy neighbourhood at bay and the unintentional sparseness of her garden creates a serendipitous serenity. Gin smiles wanly at her as Viv pours and hands her another cup of rooibos. She hugs it between her hands. Looking at her, again Viv finds herself vaguely disturbed by something in Gin's appearance.

"I haven't even shown you your room, Gin. Come, bring your tea. I'll take your things."

Gin follows her. Turning at the top, Viv watches her take the stairs one step at a time, her knuckles white as she grips the banister for support.

"Thanks for this, Viv," says Gin, as she is settled into the spare room. "It reminds me of my hospital room." Then, as if realising the statement might offend, she adds hurriedly, "I mean, it's light and airy… and I can see the mountain."

Viv looks out the oblong of window at the mountain, now a dark purple in the fading light, almost a silhouette. From this angle, it resembles a recumbent woman, the one peak a shoulder, dipping to a waist, the swayed curve of hip covered lightly by a rumple of blanket.

"Have they – my dad, or Issy – kept in touch then?" Gin's voice is hesitant as she talks of her family.

Viv does not turn around. "In the beginning more so. Less when… when I was married." She pauses. She feels uncomfortable for the first time. "Your dad did more so than Issy. But not that much after your mom… since your mom died," Viv talks quickly now, "and not since he got ill." She turns around to face Gin, who is looking at the floor. "Issy rang about your dad. I'm so sorry, Gin."

Gin nods. There is another awkward silence.

"And I'm sorry about Simon too," adds Viv, as gently as she can.

Gin sits down heavily on the bed, leans back, and closes her eyes.

Viv takes a deep breath. "Ginny…"

Gin opens her eyes and looks at her, a direct blue gaze.

Gabe's eyes, thinks Viv, a stab to the heart. "You know, about Jonnie and me…"

Gin looks away quickly. She rubs at her leg. "Viv," she says, exhaling in a sigh, "it doesn't matter. It doesn't matter anymore. It was so long ago. I'm just really sorry it didn't work out for you."

Viv's heart contracts. No doubt the aged pain of Jonnie pales against the raw loss of Simon. But she is relieved. She does not want to talk about Jonnie either, but at least the effort has been made, his name said, the lingering spirit dispelled.

Jonnie. And all for nothing.

They both stare out of the window. Voices of children playing, shouting, reach the room. A siren sounds somewhere. Friday night in the nearby township has begun.

After a while, Viv turns from the darkening view. "I'll let you unpack… I'll get us some supper soon. Is there anything you fancy? Bunny Chow?" she smiles, referring to Gin's old favourite, a scooped-out loaf of bread, the hole filled to overflowing with spicy meat curry.

Gin shakes her head.

Viv senses her displacement, a certain inability to connect. She touches Gin's arm. "Just shout if you need anything. There are towels in the wardrobe. And a phone in the room next door. It's my office."

"Viv…" Gin rises stiffly, grabbing at the headboard for support. She moves forward and hugs Viv. "Thank you," she murmurs, "for everything."

Viv feels her own throat burn with sadness. For a moment they cling together, two wounded women.

Viv goes downstairs and takes the tea tray to the kitchen, closes the blinds, switches on the light. In the brightness, she notices some spilled sugar still on the floor. Reaching for the brush and gathering it up, again she thinks of Simon. They had met in his office, sparse contemporary rooms of high ceilings and designer art, at odds somehow with Simon's manner, she had thought. He had been so kind to her, at a time when kindness had been so lacking in her life. Afterwards, Simon had sent her flowers. Yellow roses, remembers Viv. She still must have the card somewhere, a brief *Get well* followed by the simple sprawl of his initials, *SG*.

She takes a lasagne from the freezer and switches on the oven. She walks back into the lounge and lights a cigarette. The mountain is black now; only a thin line marks the border between it and the descending night. She draws the curtains and sinks back into the couch.

It strikes her suddenly what has been bothering her about Gin's appearance. Gin looks shrunken, realises Viv. Diminished somehow. She draws deeply on her cigarette. It is as if Gin's loss is physical. Yes, thinks Viv. Diminished. We are diminished by death.

4. GIN

A week after leaving the hospital, Gin is summoned to the police station to make and sign her official statement. She walks up the concrete steps and finds it hard to calm her heart. This is the new South Africa, she reminds herself, it is February 2005, and the police are ostensibly no longer the iron fist of an apartheid government, but it is still difficult for her to walk down the cool, green corridor and believe this.

She announces herself to the young black policewoman at the desk. The woman is pretty, despite the heavy blue uniform. Gin waits in the wide sunless corridor with its polished wooden floors. She sits on the hard wooden bench and reads the notices on the board opposite. There are posters with photo-identikits of wanted criminals. Crime abounds, some of it horrific, and she is staring down at her hands, tired of reading about death, when Nick Retief comes to call her to his office.

The room is windowless, and posters similar to those in the hall adorn a huge noticeboard behind his desk. He thanks her for coming and she wonders, with all this crime, why he bothers with a car accident. But he tells her what he requires, what she needs to tell him, and how her statement will then be typed and if she could wait to sign it he will be grateful, it will speed the process some. She wonders what process, but does not ask. An echo far below sounds to her like a cell door slamming. Gin realises she cannot relax in this country. She deals with it as if it is the same place she left almost two decades ago. So she keeps silent, asks no questions.

Detective Retief switches on a tape recorder, and asks for her home address. He seems surprised that she lives in London and Gin in turn feels unsettled by this. Her experience of the police hails from a time when they knew all, before they hauled one in for questioning, when they would use their knowledge as power. She remembers the insults she suffered the last time she was in a police station, waiting for her dead brother's body to be released.

She had kept quiet then too.

"Miss McMann," says Retief, "If you are from London, and Mr Gold from Johannesburg, how come you were both here in Cape Town?"

She had known. Had known the minute the phone screamed after midnight. She had felt her father's presence, like a warm hug as she drifted into sleep that icy night. And the air had chilled further. And she knew. Knew her father was dead before she picked up the receiver to hear her sister Isadore's stuttered falterings. Didn't hear them, didn't have to. The next day she had left London, bound for home. Death had a strong call, reaching out over decades even, grabbing at all she thought forgotten, gone. Unmasked emotions cut through all the mediocrity and mundanity. Daily rhetoric was seen for what it was, made bland and trivial by defining moments such as this.

Landing, landing. Durban's greenness from the air, the white horses of the waves onto sandy beaches, the blur of blue mountains, a humid Englishness. Port Natal, named by Vasco da Gama as he sailed up the coast on Christmas Day, a Portuguese name for an English town in the middle of Africa.

And the day after that, she and Issy stood alone and watched the plain pine coffin grind its way to the fire. It was smaller than she thought it would be, and it registered somewhere how her tall, lean father must have wizened with the cancer, shrivelling away from life, retreating as it advanced upon his body and his brain. As Issy drove her away, she looked back on the valley of Pietermaritzburg, watched the grey-white smoke of her father's body curling from the chimney, and wondered what he would wish of his ashes, that tall fair Scot who let his spirit fly high now above the African veld.

"My father died, Mr Retief," she says, and then thinks she does not know if the *Mister* is appropriate. Perhaps he must be called *Detective* or *Sergeant* all the time.

But he does not comment on her lapse, if indeed it is one. Instead he asks, persistent, "And Mr Gold?"

Simon. Pain now, and she feels a spear of it.

So why then, Simon, why that night to ring her, why then when she was vulnerable again? Condolences about her dad, questions as to how long she would be home for, would he see her. A terrible surge of feeling at the sound of his voice. How long had it been? A lifetime. His face had dimmed, but not the intensity of his eyes, and she found that although the sound of his laugh had faded, she could still recapture the feel of his hair in her fingers, the touch of his strong hands.

Why then? Numbness, and she was tired. Oh, Simon, why then? Was there anything she needed, he had asked. She longed, in her state of fatigue, to lie. Nothing, thank you, no. And yet it was the truth. The truth, that anything she needed from him was a long time before, long before that night, before those words. She must have been quiet for a while, because she heard him say "Ginny?" rather worriedly, and then again, stern. He must meet her, he was insistent. She was so very tired. Nothing I need, no. I left you behind, in an innocence long-gone. An innocence beneath a jacaranda tree, its petals falling slowly like purple snow onto cobbles. Left him behind when she packed the memory of him safely, in the far end of her mind, alongside the jacaranda. Picked up her battered suitcase, closed the door.

"He… I… we, we arranged to meet here, Mr Retief. We knew each other a long time ago. Our families, well, his grandfather and mine were business partners." She coughs.

"Would you like some water?" he offers. He has already risen to get her some before she can reply.

"They owned a jewellery store," she continues. "They were friends," she adds, lamely. She does not know why she feels the need to explain this to him.

But Retief has moved on, apparently uninterested in her family tales.

"Mr Gold is – was – married." He says this firmly, flatly, putting a heavy glass of water in front of her.

Statement, not question. She nods.

He looks at her, an intent gaze. "You were lovers?"

She baulks at this. "A long time ago, Mr Retief."

"But you met up here again, this time, after all these years, in Cape Town," he insists.

She nods again, looks down at her glass of water but he has carried on, relentless. "You stayed together, at the Mount Nelson, in one room." He has been looking at some papers, but he looks up at her now, "Expensive hotel."

She does not know what to say to this, so she keeps quiet.

"Mr Gold was a surgeon, I see. *Doctor* Gold, then."

She does not correct him, does not explain the small vanities of the medical profession that dictate surgeons return to *Mister*, an accolade to their prowess with the knife.

"Plastic surgery. So he could afford that kind of hotel, then." Sergeant Retief says this almost to himself, as if taking notes into the recorder. "His wife did not know he was with you."

Statement again, so Gin does not answer. The way he says it implies that Simon's wife is now aware of this fact. That he, Retief, has told her, inadvertently or otherwise. Gin does not know why he asks her this, what this has to do with their accident. She feels guilty, as if the act of merely sitting here, in a policeman's airless office, and allowing herself to be questioned, means she is guilty of something. Perhaps, she thinks, he is accusing her of causing Simon's death. That, through their adultery, she has somehow caused it.

A week later, after her father's funeral, another airport. She flew to Cape Town, to the city between mountain and sea, to all she still held precious of home. And although the week of mourning had numbed her, she felt a stir of excitement in her blood, as if the sun itself was thawing frozen pieces of her cells and she could feel them melting into the liquid of her veins. Simon would meet her. As Jonnie had once. They flew in low over Paarl valley, the inky lines of roads, the wine farms set beneath the maroon hills, touching tarmac with a screech now familiar to her ears.

Simon. She would see him before he saw her. A catch of breath – the grey, the grey, in that mop of black. Her heart betraying her, lifting to see him. The same heart, stilling to see him. Those dark emerald flecks lighting to see her. He was moving towards her, easily, through the sea of inconsequential others. She was rooted suddenly, unable to move.

And then, those arms around her, that voice again. Words to her, words for her. How long, how long, how long? Her senses, dulled by time and distance, heightened as if emerging from the numbness of hibernation, fresh and raw. His skin on hers, the very taste of him. So many years, so many times, she had longed to rest in the remembered haven of his embrace. Confused, she longed then merely to turn, to flee. But he was taking her by one hand, picking up her blue suitcase with the other, leading her away.

She and Retief spar back and forth for what seems to Gin like hours. Her leg is stiff as she rises from the hard-backed chair to follow him out of the room. She waits in the cold hallway again, while somewhere a clerk types up the words they have exchanged, turning

Simon's last hours into a bleak and formal statement. No doubt their two days together will translate into a sordid little affair, as cheap and worthless as the paper she will have to sign.

"Tell me!" she laughed, tugging at his sleeve as they left the jewellers. His arm was around her and he pulled her against him. An arc of desire between them.

"I'll tell you later," he said, his lips pressed against her ear.

Later. So there would be a later.

When she has limped down the concrete steps and across the street to a compact café, she wonders at what motivated a man like Retief to join the South African Police Force, with its chequered past, its ignoble history. The café is hot, glass windows allowing the sunlight to flood across the black-and-white vinyl tiles of the floor. Gin orders tea while she waits for Viv to fetch her and stares across the road at the imposing building she has just left. Nick Retief is younger than her, but not by that much. It is sixteen years since she left. Gin wonders if even this amount of time would have been sufficient for her to have changed her outlook on the police, on the many government institutions of this country that was once her home.

She remembers leaving. That last day, leaving. Simon.

Simon.

Always Simon. Through him, she is forever bound to home.

5. VIVIENNE

Nick Retief, it appears, has not finished with Gin. He is waiting one day when they return from a drive into the centre of the city.

Gin had taken to accompanying Viv on her daily routine, waiting in the car while she made her rounds. Often Viv's patients had become her friends, and she their unofficial counsellor after she had ceased to be their social worker. Sometimes on these journeys, Viv and Gin talked, sometimes not. Mostly Gin appeared content to see the city pass her by. The constant motion seemed to soothe her, like a child rocked to and fro. Viv had consciously avoided Kloofnek and the scene of the accident, although she knew Simon's car would have since been towed away. Only in the city did wrecks get moved. Outside, alongside the open roads of this country they remained, rusty reminders of a turn too sharp, a tyre too smooth, a driver too careless.

But this day, they had been talking, exchanging fast chatter, until Viv had turned into the bottom of that hill. As Gin's speech had trawled to a stop, Viv had realised.

"Oh, Gin, I'm sorry," she said, checking her rear-view, signalling, making ready to turn off into one of the steep, narrow roads that fall away from the climb of the Kloof.

"No, Viv, it's okay. It doesn't matter." Then Gin laughed. A strange gurgling sound in her throat, a foreign sound.

Viv was horrified. But then she realised nothing could ever erase that day for Gin. It did not matter whether she drove up that hill again or not. Simon's blood would have faded from the tar, would have been washed away down storm drains, but the dark stain of that day had set itself inside Gin's soul.

"It doesn't matter," repeated Gin, her laughter turning to hiccoughs.

So Viv laughed then too, a tiny tinkling laugh. They drove home, taking the long route, talking about the recent rains, wondering at the ridiculous Anglicisation of Afrikaans names around the peninsula.

And there is Retief, waiting, just when they had been planning on opening a Cabernet and toasting their lives. Their lives, so full of sorrow, so full of pain.

Viv opens a bottle anyway, once they are inside. Once Gin, suddenly weary, has slumped into her favoured armchair near the window. The imminent night casts her into shadow. And neither Viv nor Nick Retief, standing near the lit kitchen, can see whether her eyes are open or closed.

6. NICK

Nick watches Viv pour the rich red into rounded glasses. She is tall, almost as tall as he, slim, and definitely attractive. In fact, you could say the woman was beautiful. She hands him a glass without ceremony but when he sips it she looks at him, amusement in her deep brown eyes. He judges her to be about the same age as her friend Gin, and some years older than himself. Nick likes the warmth in her voice, the russet swing of her hair, the palest hint of freckles on her fair skin. On any other day, he might find himself lingering, spending time with her. But it is Virginia McMann who must interest him for now, the quiet woman who sits in the chair near the window, possibly asleep, but just as possibly not.

Nick has seen Gin sleep.

He had sat for a while in the small white room and waited for her to wake. He had watched her eyes move restlessly beneath closed lids. Eventually he had decided he would wake her, especially as she seemed to gain no repose from sleep. Then she had stirred, as if awake, and murmured. Her hand had clenched, unclenched, and stretched out across the thin blanket. And he had the sense of intruding upon a moment so intimate, so private, he had felt obliged to leave.

"More wine, Mr Retief?" asks Viv, and he is surprised to find he has drained his glass.

"My name's Nick," he says.

She swirls the neck expertly as she pours generously.

Suddenly, from the darkness, Gin asks, "Why are you here, Mr Retief? I've told you all I can remember." Her tone, if not for its fragility, would be hostile.

"Well, Miss McMann," he starts, and then, glancing at the woman alongside, "Mrs Kassan…" He stops. He wants to acknowledge this woman, to include her, elicit her help even, in the hope she will draw out lucid details from her recalcitrant friend. He remembers noting Kassan as an Indian surname, noticing that the address Virginia McMann had given him was in Kenwyn, in the predominantly mixed-race area of Cape Town. But this woman is white. For a moment he wonders if she really is Mrs Kassan. Then he finds himself wondering where her husband is. Viv is leaning against the sideboard, glass of wine in one hand, a cigarette in the other. Watching him.

"I go by my maiden name now," she says, "Weetman. But call me Vivienne, please." She waves her cigarette at him, a dismissive gesture.

Again the hidden laugh in her brown eyes. Again he feels in some way mocked.

"Vivienne…" he says, turning back to talk into the lounge. He likes the sound of it. And he likes the fact that she uses her maiden name. He can no longer even make out Gin's silhouette in the gloom. "Miss McMann," he starts again, louder, assertively.

But Virginia McMann interrupts him. "Mr Retief, what happened to the other car, the other driver?"

"Well, *ja*, that's the thing," says Nick, slightly frustrated. "The other driver fled the scene. We have a couple of witnesses, you see."

"Do you mean two, Mr Retief, as they do in England, or a few, as is the colloquialism here?"

If Gin is mocking him also, he does not know. Her voice is without emotion. He ignores the question and continues, "Apparently the car came out of one of the side roads then headed straight for your vehicle." Nick stops and clears his throat. "And another witness says the other driver may have been a woman." He takes a sip of wine. "Your car swerved," he continues, "but glanced off the other car. Your car rolled. Caught fire." He stops, glances at Viv, then back to the dark interior where Gin sits. "The other car, according to the witness, stopped for a moment. Then it sped off again, turned down into Oranjezicht."

Viv breaks the silence that follows. "You mean it was a hit-and-run?"

"Well, *ja*, Mrs... Vivienne." Her slight frown does not mar her beauty. He turns back towards Gin. "There's another thing. What was Doctor Gold's state of mind?"

Gin's voice sounds strained. "Simon? What do you mean?"

"How was he? Did you know he was seeing a psychiatrist? That he took antidepressants for some years?"

"Simon?" she says again. After a slight pause, her voice flat, she says quietly, "Simon was Simon. He was..."

He waits.

"Greyer," says Gin finally. Then she is silent.

Viv moves closer to him. Her voice is quiet, meant for him alone. "Are you suggesting it wasn't an accident?"

Nick turns to her, takes another sip of wine. "It's possible, yes."

7. GIN

Doctor Oldman, who is neither old nor a man, peers at her through thick-lensed spectacles. "You're pregnant."

Gin stares at her. The lenses have the odd effect of making the doctor's pupils small and far away. "I can't be," she stutters. The doctor squints sceptically at her, and her glasses slip down her nose. "I mean –," says Gin, "I thought – ". She does not finish.

Simon's child.

Doctor Oldman shifts the black rims back up her thin nose. "About twelve weeks."

Twelve weeks. Is it only twelve weeks since Simon took himself from her life as suddenly as he had re-entered it?

A white car, heading directly at them.

Gin had returned to England duty-bound, for want of purpose. The faintness in her head as the plane lifted from a tarmac rippled with heat, a nausea only now equated with something other than grief.

His hands, gripping the wheel.

She continues to stare at her General Practitioner. Doctor Oldman is new to the practice. In some ways she reminds Gin of Nick Retief, hiding behind the authority of her position. Perhaps from embarrassment, perhaps out of confusion at Gin's silence, the doctor has started talking at her rapidly, writing notes, making arrangements for regular check-ups, midwife appointments, further tests.

His hand, outstretched to her.

This has been her journey back to London. Dirty, crowded, desperate London. Squashed tubes, uncaring commuters, angry cabs, politics and rhetoric, repressed rage. Lonely London. But dear London, dependable London. Home all the same. Home. She had breathed a sigh of relief to escape her other home, the claustrophobia of Africa's south. The air less free there, polluted with its past. Somehow England's stains have bled with time into the very walls. Somehow they wound her less, somehow she feels less raw. Something endures here. Walking past the sturdy fragility of Parliament, the black majestic statues of Empire, the winter sun is a hazy shimmer of assurance on the other side. Over the bridge, the river beneath is a sheen of rippled glass. Watching the tiny white specks of seagulls soar above the polished gold Westminster spires. But lonely still. And grey, cold London. February, mercifully short given its infinite nights, mercifully gone before her return. March. She walked a lot, hoping Simon's eyes would fade from her mind. The faintness and the nausea ever-present. Simon's death, her father's, these things have changed her.

She had sat, irretrievably distant, as her colleagues lectured at her after her absence. She had looked at them, once her friends, seen them hardened by avarice and changed by commerce. She had enough money to live on, albeit simply; she could survive. Her silence had elicited shock, her resignation recrimination.

Gin leaves the doctor's surgery in a daze, starts the half-mile back up the Portobello Road, past the market stalls, back up to the Gate. The market is busy despite the damp, overcast afternoon. Lights are strung from stall to stall, looped against the dimness. April and its promise of spring. The daffodils have fought their bright and yellow way through the ground, pushing stiff green stems through wet earth with that unknown life force. The same life force as that within her.

Twelve weeks.

The days are longer and lighter now, though still grey. London has a thousand shades of grey. Green-grey, brown-grey, blue-grey; river, houses, sky.

Simon's child. From his last two days of life.

"Can I help you with anything?" says a woman's voice.

Gin, stopped at a bookstall, is staring sightlessly at the hard spines of children's books. She focuses. *Peter Pan, The Famous Five, Nancy Drew, Grimm's Fairytales.* Books from her own childhood, which her dad had read to her and her twin brother before bedtime. Back in the big house, upstairs. And she had always been afraid of the giants and the witches, of the *tokoloshe*, the long-tailed bogeyman that Evelyn their nanny had told them about. The *tokoloshe* was the reason Evelyn put her bed on bricks, as if on stilts. This, she had confided to Gin and a wide-eyed Gabe, was to fool the *tokoloshe*, as he was short. Shorter than them, even, she said. This way he could not reach Evelyn to play his evil tricks on her. They, of course, he could reach, and easily, and Evelyn never ceased to threaten them with the dreaded *tokoloshe* if in any way Gin or Gabriel irked her.

"That's a lovely edition," says the voice again. The stallholder is peering at her, much as Doctor Oldman had.

Gin pulls out the pale blue Barrie, pays for it, continues up the slope. She does not know why she bought the book; on a whim, for her child, but she had always hated Pan, its story sad to her and silly. But Gabe had loved it, had always wanted to play Peter with his swashbuckling adventures, swinging from tree to tree outside the house, outside Dad's surgery, the one their father shared with his partner Jacob.

Gabe, always the leader. And she and their friends, Michael and Hannah, had to join in. Hannah, Jacob's daughter. Michael, from down the road. And Gabe would make Hannah play Wendy while Gin and Michael would be lost boys. How apt, thinks Gin. As if Gabe knew. Knew he would never grow old. Knew Hannah, all grown-up, would marry, have children. Knew she and Michael would be lost, still lost.

| 30 |

Hannah, Michael, Gin, and Gabe.

So long a time they'd been together. Class photos from an Eastern Cape childhood showed them squinting in their poppy-red blazers, absurdly hot under an African sun. Aged nine, ten, class after class, tracing shy smiles to adolescent sulkiness and lank teenage haircuts. Living within streets of each other, they knew the same life. No secrets. There was a sense of belonging to each other, common knowledge, the ability to all laugh uproariously at some jointly-remembered incident, like Sandra de Jongh falling face down in the freshly-delivered horse manure. Or the fearsome hill that challenged their eleven-year-old egos and their bikes. Down Beach Road. Down Southampton Drive. Through the ditch if they could make it, the scars if they couldn't.

A dusty town, a small town, an African town.

The sky has started to spit, and Gin hastens. She is at the top of the hill, the market behind her, where the street turns into Pembridge Road, and soon she will be home. Home, her new house, into which she has yet to move properly. With her father's death, she has inherited the building on Ladbroke Road. It has stood empty for a month now. Her father's estate had been soon settled, his affairs as expected in impeccable order. But Gin has yet to haul her belongings from her rented flat above the music store on Lancaster Road. It is not far, and she has few possessions, but it is the flat she had shared with Michael, and somehow she is loath to leave it.

She misses Michael suddenly, misses his humour and his warmth. It must be thirteen years since he left London for Denmark. Michael, part of her life, always there. Michael to whom she had run when all fell apart, when Africa became intolerable those sixteen years back.

After Simon, Jonnie had saved her. But after Jonnie, it was Michael who had been her refuge. Michael the reason she is in London. London, the natural place to run.

Gin opens the door to the house. It opens into a tiled hall that feels chilly at the afternoon's end. Straight through from here is the huge kitchen with its original Butler sink, its new Aga. To the right is the lounge. She likes this room; it is cosy and has an open fireplace, a rarity in London now. To her left, the stairs mount immediately to the three bedrooms and two bathrooms set over the upper two floors. Below the kitchen is a big, empty basement. A house too large for one, thinks Gin. And then remembers.

Twelve weeks.

Simon's child.

As once before.

She had not told the doctor.

Twelve weeks.

Gin feels a tightness clamp her head, her throat. Oh, God, she had not told the doctor. She moves fretfully from room to room, opening doors, switching on lights, pulling covers off furniture. When she is back in the lounge, she draws the thick damson curtains against the gathering dusk. Gin stacks the grate with paper, cones, and kindling, lights the fire. It smokes and falters but the chimney, recently swept, pulls the ash-grey surge of it upwards. Slowly life seeps into the grate, and with it the house starts to warm, to breathe. I can be happy here, thinks Gin. She remembers her father talking of the place with affection. His summers in Scotland, his school terms here. She feels warmer now, the fire has dispelled the cold if not the fear. She wishes her mother were alive still. Her mother, who would have loved to be a grandmother; her mother, who would have helped.

She wants to speak to Michael. Michael who will understand. Michael who had held her head while she vomited, Michael who had put her in the cab and taken her to the hospital, Michael who had cleaned up the blood and tidied the flat while she was gone. Michael who had brought her back, sat up beside her, and Michael who had lain in the narrow bed holding her to him all night.

But it is not Michael who answers the extended Danish ring. Instead it is his wife Kristina. Kristina who had married him, and Kristina who had taken him away. She never recognises my voice, thinks Gin, going through the motions, asking Kristina how she is. She waits for the woman to clip her usual false pleasantries in reply. No doubt for Michael's sake, thinks Gin. Instead Kristina's tone is brittle.

"Michael's not here." A beat. "I thought you'd be the first to know."

"I've been… away," starts Gin. Her thoughts catch up. Know what? Where is Michael? She feels her breath quicken, shallow. "Know what?"

Another pause. "Try his mobile."

"I don't have it."

Everything smashed or burned in the crash, her own mobile included. She manages to tell Kristina she has lost it, writes Michael's number down with a trembling hand. She repeats it to Kristina.

"Yes."

"Thank you." But the line is already dead.

"Gin!" says Michael, his baritone warm, unchanged. "How are you? Where are you? I've been trying to get you for ages. Did you get my text? I've been a bit worried, actually."

"My mobile. Was. Broken," she says. Then, "Michael, where are *you*? Kristina, Kristina said –". What had she said? Kristina had only given her his number.

"I've moved from Praesto, Gin. I'm teaching in Naestved."

"Teaching? Since when do you teach?"

He laughs. "Since I did a teaching qualification. It's a temporary job. I'm here till June. In fact, I've applied for a post in London after this."

She cannot find her voice. She is longing to see him, to talk with him face to face. Hope is an emotion almost too much to bear.

"Gin? Are you still there?"

She makes a sound like *Yes*.

"How was home?" He sounds concerned now, perhaps remembering her dad.

No one will even have told him about Simon, Gin realises. A desperate loneliness takes hold. "Michael," she says, and it is like a sob. "Michael, I'm pregnant. Mikey, I need you. Please come to London."

8. VIVIENNE

"He was furious, you know," says Viv. The line crackles and Viv holds the telephone away from her ear.

"Who? Retief?" Gin's voice sounds English and far away.

"Yes, who else?"

Viv turned into her road to find Nick leaning against his car, arms folded. Waiting impatiently for her. How long he had been there she did not know. Viv was at first amused, intrigued. He asked where Miss McMann was while Viv unpacked her groceries and her files from the back of the car. When Viv told him that Gin had left, had flown back to London, Retief started pacing in the street. Miss McMann should not have left without telling him, he fumed. Viv had grown vaguely alarmed, then angry.

"Mr Retief," she said, "would you kindly not talk to me in that tone."

He stopped, startled, as if unaware of his rant. "I'm sorry, Vivienne," he said, contritely.

Viv softened. She did not know why. Perhaps it was the way he used her first name, yet so formally, as if determined to pronounce each syllable. Perhaps it was his sudden boyishness, or the dark-blond lock that had fallen across his forehead, making him swat at it absently as he tried to hold her gaze.

"Look, Nick," she said, handing him one of the bags, "help me take these in and we can talk properly inside. I do have neighbours you know, and I don't like them thinking I'm in trouble with the police."

He followed her in.

"Why, Viv?" Gin's voice brings her thoughts back to the present.

"Something about procedure. Part of an ongoing investigation. And now apparently the insurance people are involved. On his back about it."

"Insurance people?"

Viv hesitates. She fears sounding callous. "Simon's insurance, Gin," she says as gently as she can, "his life insurance. You know what they can be like, checking everything."

Nick had said they'd been onto his superior, who had been onto him. Give them what you've got, close it up, move it on, he had been ordered. Nick hated that, he said, hated handing a case over untidied, unfinished. He paced again, this time in her kitchen, up and down, while Viv unloaded the supermarket bags on the sideboard. She handed him cans to slow his tread, and he started to help her unpack, talking all the while. Eventually he stopped and they settled into a scene almost domestic. Viv made coffee and their hands touched as she passed him the mug. Retief reddened at the contact.

"You like him, don't you?" Gin asks, changing the way the conversation is headed.

"Well, yes. Yes, I do," reflects Viv.

It had been ten years since her divorce and it had felt nice, having Nick in her kitchen helping her. They sat, deliberately apart, sipping at their coffee while the conversation drifted from Nick's work, from his apparent obsession with Gin's case to other, simpler subjects. He commented on her garden, green from the rain. Viv listened, surprised, while he told her that hellebore might be good for the dry shady spot in the barren corner, that agapanthus would thrive on neglect if given the sunny space near the front gate.

"I didn't know you gardened, Sergeant Retief," she smiled, embarrassing him.

"Well, ja, *I don't really. Not now, but when I grew up, on the farm, my mom liked to garden. And the lack of water was always a factor, what would grow and what wouldn't."*

He told her about his childhood in the Transkei, about the constant droughts that would threaten the farm, that would bring lines to his father's already weathered brow. About how it had been his grandfather's farm, and his great-grandfather's before that. Viv made more coffee and the afternoon slipped into evening. He told her about his mother, whom his father had met while buying supplies in the Cape, and how his father had brought her back to the farm and the small farming community. He had not told her if his mother, uprooted, had suffered, but instead told Viv how, while his father farmed, his mother had grown vegetables and tried to coax flowers from the hot, dry earth.

"And did they not want you to take over the farm then, Nick?" Viv asked.

They had progressed onto wine, and she had tucked herself next to him on the couch as she handed him the glass. He stayed quiet for a while after her question, and she sensed it was a topic he did not want to talk about. Then he murmured something about not wanting to battle nature endlessly for scant reward. But Viv thought this wasn't a man afraid of a battle, and suspected other reasons.

"I thought he seemed to like you," says Gin, rather absently.

"Did you?" laughs Viv. "Well, *ja,* he's sweet." She tells Gin about the gardening advice. "Anyhow, he said they might call you or something."

"Who?"

"The insurance people."

"Oh."

"And he might need to call you also."

"Oh," says Gin again, without enthusiasm.

They talk of other things.

"How are the girls?" asks Gin, "I wish I'd seen them when I was home. Abbie must be what, seventeen soon?"

"Yes," says Viv, and launches into the recent tales from school, how Abbie is all teenage angst and pimples, while Kayleigh, just turned fifteen, is still full of innocent wisdom. "You know, Gin, I don't know where she gets it from! Not me!" She stops herself from saying: *or Jonnie.*

They laugh, talk some more about the girls, about Gin's move from the flat to the house, progressing slowly. About Gin's pregnancy, her astonishing news.

"It'll be all right, you know," says Viv. She knows what it is like to raise a child without a father. They are silent. Viv knows they are both thinking of Gabe now. "You know you can always come home. Come stay here if you need. I'll look after you, like you looked after me." Viv is solemn.

"Yeah, Retief would probably like that."

They laugh again.

Viv does not mention how, long after Nick Retief had left, she had opened the French windows to the cool of the evening and sat smoking on the porch, long into the moonless night.

9. GIN

Michael finally arrives on a clear summer morning, his teaching stint done. Gin takes the lengthy drive out to Gatwick airport, passing fields still dew-wet, the pink dawn tinting the hills.

It is not difficult for her to rise early; she has lain awake and restless on so many nights that on most days she is up by five. She has taken to walking down to the river on these occasions, walking the miles, crossing through the park. She takes bread for the ducks and swans that dip and preen upon the pond, readying themselves for the coming day. She wanders past the Serpentine, the fountains still silent, through the walk of roses, across the Arch, and down through St James' Park till she reaches the water of the tidal Thames. She likes the cool of the early day, and walks back to the house well before the traffic increases to its morning peak, before the heat hits its height.

Summer, dreaded summer. Its orange twilights are reminiscent of those at home, the sunsets that she had hated. London should not be allowed the so-called good weather of other climes; it is not suited to a hot July. Heat does not become this grand old city; it sweats and smells, steams and stifles. A haze sits, visible, palpable. Gin stays in the house for much of the day, thankful for its old walls, thick with cool. The air is finer here on the hill, high above sea level. Sometimes she swears she can smell the barley from fields a hundred years long gone. Sometimes she dreams of Simon. He is trying to tell her something but the message is lost in the fog of awakening.

Gin exists outside of herself; she feels as if her consciousness hovers above and to the right of her eyes. The accident, she theorises, must have damaged connections to her limbic system. At the oddest times, she has spinal shivers, a sensation of being watched. Perhaps, she thinks, it is herself watching herself. Perhaps there is a part of her truly dead, with Simon, a part that watches herself with his eyes, the same penetrative stare. Then again, perhaps it is his genes she carries now awhile that makes her feel his touch once more in sleep, and lately she sees again his outstretched hand, hears the gasping rattle in his throat. These nights she wakes with a ring of sweat about her neck, her breasts, as if it is toxin she carries. She hopes she will be able to love this child.

Gin pulls the car into the anonymous sprawl of the airport car park.

Michael hugs her as he always does, a huge, encompassing embrace that makes her feel both safe and sleepy. As if she now can rest.

"Gin!" Grabbing her to him. "God, you're so thin. What's happened to you?" He holds her back away from him to look at her. "You're supposed to be pregnant, fat, glowing." Michael's voice is teasing but she can see his worry.

She looks at him and laughs. "You should talk. And your hair!" Michael's glossy brown hair, always worn long, is shaven. Gin reaches up to brush her hand through the spiky shortness. "You look like you're in the Army."

He buys her coffee before the drive back into London, and over it she tells Michael much of what he does not yet know. In a flat tone she relates the trip home, her father's funeral, what she can remember of the accident. She does not mention Simon's final words; she has told no one, not even Viv, and especially not Retief. Michael listens without questions, allows her the space to speak. She tells him too how she has left her job, feeling slightly guilty. It was Michael who had found her the post based at the hospital. He had been working there himself, portering until his psychology qualifications were approved in Britain. Gin herself had not applied to get her own degree recognised, despite Michael's sensible urgings. Somehow she had lost her lust for healing. Instead she had taken the job of technician in the pharmacy at the same hospital. They had left the hotel, moved from Michael's single room, found the flat. It had seemed huge in comparison, the way the house now in turn dwarfed its four rooms.

"I couldn't take it anymore," she tells him. The unit had, during her time there, been privatised. Profit, not patients, had become the drive. Slowly the work she had initially enjoyed had eroded into endless shifts, preparing chemotherapy well into the nights. Syringe after precious syringe churned out, a thankless quest. It had been even harder for her when her father's cancer was diagnosed. He had the best of care, but Gin knew so many in Africa didn't.

"When I came back from Cape Town I saw it for what it was. I just didn't know why I was doing it anymore."

He reaches across the table and squeezes her hand. "I'd love to work in a hospital again," he says wistfully. Denmark has little need of psychologists, he tells her, and especially those who are not Danish. He had encountered a subtle xenophobia that made him always an outsider, especially at the factory where he first found work, where he checked the same circuit on the same board that passed him forty times an hour. And after seven hours of that, his neck and shoulders stiff from peering through the magnifying scope at the rolling rubber strip that carried the neatly laid-out pieces, he went home through the bland little town to his bland little flat. He laughs self-consciously.

"But now you're teaching?" asks Gin.

"Yes, that's why I did the qualification. It was also an attempt to save my marriage. One that didn't work." There is a weariness in his voice.

It is Gin's turn to squeeze his hand. She waits for him to say more, but instead he looks at her coffee cup, still full, the contents cold.

"Gin, I really am worried about you, are you eating?" he asks again.

Gin blinks at him. "Of course I am," she answers mechanically, but in truth she cannot remember when she last ate.

Michael is looking at her oddly. "Are you sure you're all right?"

That last day, leaving. The day she chose to leave her land, her country and her kin. Africa was so very hard to leave behind. Wisps of long-held memories swirled like ghosts in childhood chambers of her brain. The acrid taste of dust, hot days on Transkei roads, the warm stillness of Okavango air, cicadas screaming, the drenching rains of Cape winters. The land was part of her, but she found herself wishing it were not, wishing to escape that heady, hedonistic mix of beauty and of pain.

She had left Cape Town as soon as she could, her only thought to get away from Jonnie, get away from Viv. A sour week at home. She had said goodbye to Zululand, to her sister, her parents, her childhood. A perfunctory week of goodbyes. To Hannah's parents. Promising to see Hannah in Johannesburg before she left. To Michael's parents. Promising to hug their son when she met him in London. Promising to make him write more, phone more.

And trying to say goodbye to Gabe, her dead brother's memory pervading everything. Her mother still seemed unable to part with Gabe's remains. She had stuck the urn of his ashes on a table in the hall. Gin would rather have taken them up to the blue mountains, scattered them among the ochred leaves of forest, and set her brother free. Set him finally free in this land that he also had loved, the land that had been part of him too.

Then, Johannesburg. She would not have seen him, but for Hannah. Hannah, Gin's friend and Simon's cousin, who insisted that Gin see Simon, say goodbye.

Hannah was hosting a party. Everyone, said Hannah, would be there.

Gin did not feel like going to a party. Her leaving was cause for

*sadness, not celebration. And everyone whom Hannah knew, she did
not. Except for Simon. Perhaps, thought Gin, this was Hannah's revenge.
Hannah, denied Gabe by her father. Just like me, thought Gin. Gabe
and I were not good enough, not Jewish enough. Something sullied and
unclean had come between her and Hannah. Gin was wary, reluctant.
Maybe Hannah wanted to show her Simon's wife, his newborn twins,
show Gin how happy Simon was with one of his own.*

Michael is still waiting for an answer.

"Oh, Michael, I'm fine. I promise." But she cannot blame him.
Years ago now, but she knows he can never forget.

*Simon greeted Hannah with a kiss, looking all the while over his cousin's
shoulder at Gin. She could barely look at him. There was a compres-
sion in her chest at the sight of him. But to look away from him was to
take in his life, Hannah's life, Johannesburg life. Where parties with too
much food were thrown while others starved, and young men died for
no reason. She barely listened while Hannah asked after Simon's wife,
why she had not come. Instead Gin walked away, took in the view from
Hannah's high-rise flat, the diamond lights of the city below against
the black velvet of night. Every city was beautiful at night, she mused,
however ugly and however scarred by day. He had come up behind her,
was watching her watching the city. She closed her eyes at the way he
breathed her name.*

Michael is grimly silent. She knows he is remembering holding her
head over the basin while she vomited, remembering the blood of
her miscarriage. The last time she had carried Simon's child.

*She was quiet in the car. They drove around the city while Simon talked,
a streaming release of words that she did not hear. She did not want to
know of his life, his life without her. But slowly it seeped into her brain*

that, with her, he talked because he could. There was a part of him that was still the man she once knew and loved. His thoughts were allowed a certain freedom in her company. With her, it seemed, he was himself. This thought would later open up regret.

He parked the car back in the garage beneath Hannah's apartment. They had been away for hours. Hannah would be angry with her for leaving the party but Gin did not care. She knew no one else at Hannah's party. She owed Hannah nothing.

Simon was silent. Then, "Ginny," he said suddenly, "this man, this Jonnie, do you love him?"

Gin was startled out of inattention. She had not mentioned Jonnie, few even knew about him. Hannah. Hannah must have told him, she realised. But Hannah knew nothing of what had happened in Cape Town.

He turned to look at her. "You know what it's like then, to try to be with someone in this country who isn't white."

Ah, yes, Leila. The enigmatic Leila. The Leila he had loved. But he had discarded Leila too, as he had discarded her. If she, Gin, white but not Jewish, had not been suitable, how much less so Leila. Leila, not even white.

What could she say, wound him further? She wanted to tell him that he had turned away from feelings that were too frighteningly real, and that his world was now a fake world. A world of plastic surgery, substitute brides, and expensive cars. He had a real house in the wealthy suburb of Sandton, had hired a real black maid to save his real Jewish wife's hands. You, my man of ideals, the doctor who would heal the world. Simon, my rock, thought Gin, you are lost to me, to this land, and to Leila, whom you loved.

She wanted to say this to him, but she looked into the brilliant blackness of his eyes, and lifted her hand to stroke his rough cheek. She could not shatter his cherished illusions. Out of love for him, still. She stared at him. They had lost something, and he knew it also.

His hand was on her leg, and he slipped it beneath her skirt. Gin held her breath. He was married; she was leaving. But she thought of Jonnie, felt an odd release, a relinquishing of responsibility. The garage offered seclusion.

"Do you love him?" repeated Simon, "Does he do this to you?" He was angry, jealous.

She wanted to say yes, that she loved Jonnie, that she loved him with an excitement, a newness. But he was kissing her and she could not speak. And she would have continued, told Simon that whatever she felt for Jonnie, could ever have felt for Jonnie, was nothing. Nothing, compared to the love she felt for him, that ancient knowing inside her soul.

She was kissing Simon back. Tears burned in the back of her throat.

Michael is quiet. He does not believe that she's okay.

She leans across towards him, takes his hand. Earnestly, "I promise you, Mikey, this time it's different."

10. GIN

"Did you tell the doctor?" asks Michael, when they are back at the house.

He has explored the house, unpacked his one leather bag, they have had tea, and he is peering despondently into her fridge.

"Yes," answers Gin, but does not elaborate.

Doctor Oldman had sat, thin-lipped and disapproving, while Gin recounted details of her miscarriage that were no doubt in her notes already. Had said to her, acerbically, that Gin should have told her this before. Gin, chastised, had wanted to apologise. She had felt the need to explain. That she had been young, stupid, but that the loss of his child had eaten at her nonetheless. That she had wanted to laugh when they told her there had probably been something wrong with the fetus she had lost. As if it were symbolic of her relationship with Simon. And she had wanted to tell this stiff woman in front of her that she was afraid. Afraid that there would be something wrong again, afraid that she would lose his child again. Like she lost its father. But the cuff was around Gin's arm and the doctor was already pumping up the bulb.

"Gin, there's absolutely nothing in your fridge. Come on, let's go out. I'm taking you to get a good breakfast and then we're going to the market to buy some food for this sad, empty fridge."

They are in the cool of the hall when the phone rings.

"Shall I get it?" asks Michael, already reaching for the receiver before she can say no. As he answers she motions to him that she does not want to talk to anyone. "Miss McMann?" Michael is saying, looking at her questioningly. She shakes her head, mouths at him to take a message. Seamlessly Michael says, "She's not here right now. Can I tell her who called?" He listens awhile, thanks the caller, puts the phone down.

Gin opens the front door to the warmth of the day. "Well?" she says when they are outside, "Who was it?" She locks the door.

"Someone called Nick Retief," says Michael, affecting a strong South African accent as he says the name. He is expecting her to smile. "He said he'd call back."

She starts to shake, so violently does her body jerk that she drops her keys.

"Gin! Are you okay?" Michael grabs for her.

She leans into him, steadying herself against his strength, trying to quell the shaking. Beneath the cotton check of his thin shirt, she feels the hardness of his chest muscles as he hugs her closely. She wants to cry, but no tears form.

Simon, brushing the hair from his eyes. Simon, pulling her to him on the wide white linen sheets.

"Do you want to go back inside?" asks Michael gently.

Gin tries to bend down to pick up the keys, but her action is awkward, her belly in the way. He stops her and picks them up, hands them to her.

"Thanks. No, I'll be okay. It'll be good to walk."

She tells him briefly about Retief as they take the short cut through Victoria Gardens to Notting Hill Gate. The strange feeling is surfacing again, the feeling of culpability she had felt in the police station. How she felt Retief had almost accused her of causing Simon's death. How she felt tainted, whorish. But she does not tell Michael this, reports rather on Retief's visit to Viv. Michael is quiet when she mentions Viv. They walk along the pavement, past the supermarket and the coffee shops and the cinema. It is early, but already the area beside the exit from the underground tube station is thronged. It will be busy at the market later. They cross the road, pass the book-shop and the bank, and enter the café on the corner.

Michael orders a full English breakfast. "But no bacon," he says to the waitress. He looks at Gin, a smile forming, "It's probably Danish," he says by way of explanation.

Gin makes a face at him, orders toast and a pot of Earl Grey.

Over breakfast Michael tells her about Denmark, about how he had tried, faithfully, to fit in. He had learnt Danish, learnt to wrap his tongue around the throaty vowels. "It's a lot like Afrikaans, Gin," he explains, between mouthfuls of egg and beans on toast.

"Do you think you'll go back?" Oh God, I might as well have added *to her*, she thinks.

He puts his fork down, pushes his plate away. "I don't know. I really don't know. Anyhow, this new job's for three months, so I guess I'll just see how it goes." He smiles at her. "The school sounds good, and it's only up the road. And mainly, it allows me some time with you."

Michael, her childhood friend and twice now her saviour, sits back in his chair. "It's been a long time, Gin."

Her heart is too full to speak.

After breakfast they join the tourists heading down Portobello Road. Gin takes his arm. It is a warm day, the sky above so blue it could be Africa. They pass the silver merchants at the top of the road, the china and the antiques, and head down to where the road flattens at the bottom of the hill. Michael buys vegetables in abundance: fat carrots, succulent lettuce, firm peppers, potatoes still ruddy with soil. And fruit: rich red strawberries, spiky pineapple, a curved yellow baseball glove of bananas. Gin feels her appetite return with

Michael's enthusiastic haggling. He barters with the stallholders as if he has never left. They pass outside their old flat. Michael pauses, looks up at the curtained windows.

"You know," says Gin, "I think there's still some of your stuff in the boxes back at the house."

He laughs. "Well, I obviously haven't missed or needed it in all this time." He tucks her hand under his arm again, and they make their way back up against the wash of people. "Do you ever hear from Hannah?" he asks. His voice sounds suddenly strange.

"No," says Gin, a sadness creeping in. She has, for the first time in as long as she can remember, felt happy. Now the strange sullied feeling is back. "She's in Canada now. Has been for years. About as long as you've been in Denmark, I suppose. Three kids, two boys and a girl, I think."

"And are they all healthy?"

Gin looks at him. What an odd question. "Yes, I suppose so."

She wants to ask why, but Michael continues. "She married a lawyer or something, didn't she?"

They emerge from the worst of the crowds into the clearing at the top of the road. Again, his voice sounds strange to her. Or does she imagine it?

"Yes, a lawyer. Remember Mikey, I went back for the wedding. That first year in England, you were still technically a refugee. And you couldn't travel back then."

Hannah's wedding. Seeing Simon.

She was sitting in the fourth row when their eyes locked. Then she turned away. Alive, suddenly. Suddenly alive now he was there. She looked up at the chuppah, the cream tent of it. White flowers, fringed with green, and trailing gold ribbons wound around the four sturdy pillars. She still sensed his gaze. She examined the walls of the temple. It was a modern shul, pale yellow walls reached up to a sloping roof of glass, at the centre of which was a bright blue Star of David. It tinted the sunlight that cascaded through it. Soon Hannah, her childhood playmate and Simon's cousin, would walk down the aisle on Jacob's arm. It should be Gabe marrying Hannah, thought Gin. It should be Gabe marrying his childhood sweetheart. But Gabe had not been good enough. And now Gabe was dead. The prayers started. Finally she chanced a glance at Simon across the bowed heads, above the closed eyes, to find his eyes still open, still searching her out. I wasn't good enough for you either, she thought. She wanted to tell him that there had been something wrong with their child. She wanted to tell him it had died inside her.

"I always thought she and Gabe would get married," Michael is saying. He sounds sad. "It was a pity. You know, about her and Gabe."

Hannah had pushed all of them away at university, even her, even Michael, even Gabe. Between the end of school and the start of university, Hannah had been sent to Israel, to distant cousins in Tel Aviv. Unexpectedly, she had stayed for a year. Hannah had come back changed. She appeared to have embraced her Jewishness, and in the process she rejected them. And especially Gabe. The university was not large, and Hannah had ended up in the same residence as Gin. A year behind now, and separate. Every Friday night Gin would see her leave the residence, those long black curls bouncing in ringlets down her back, off to shul, and afterwards to Friday night dinner, hoping to meet eligible men. Men who were not Gabe.

They are nearing the house now and Gin is glad. Michael seems so melancholy she feels an almost absurd need to cheer him. "I remember when I first knew there was something between them," she says, hearing her own voice full of forced brightness. "I came across the two of them together one day. Wouldn't have thought anything of it, you know, just like they always were, but then they kind of leapt apart, as if they'd been caught doing something wrong. They looked so embarrassed. Hannah went all red, and Gabe just wouldn't look at me."

Michael says nothing. She wonders what he is thinking.

"You know," she continues, "my grandfather used to say Hannah and Gabe reminded him of my mom and Hannah's dad, Jacob, when they were children. He said they were always together, always close."

"Isn't that how your mom met your dad? Through Jacob?" Michael appears to focus again.

"Yes, Jacob studied surgery here, in Edinburgh, where he met my dad. When they qualified, Jacob invited Dad out to South Africa, and they set up the practice together. So that's how my parents actually met."

"So you kind of owe your life to Jacob then," says Michael, with a short chuckle.

"I suppose. I never thought of it like that before."

There is a pause before Michael says suddenly, "Until Viv."

"What?"

"Ah, sorry, I was thinking aloud. I was thinking how Gabe suffered over Hannah. Until he met Viv."

"Oh, yes," says Gin. Then, quietly, "No, even after Viv." She unlocks the door, and Michael brings the bags into the shade of the hall.

"God, that's better. It's so hot out there!" He wipes his brow.

The display on the answering machine shows one message. Gin switches it on as Michael walks through to the kitchen. Nick Retief's terse tones invade her home. Gin had not doubted for an instant that the promised callback would come. Only not so soon, mere hours later, when she is not ready. The car, Nick Retief is saying, may have been a white Mercedes. Can she confirm this?

A white car. A white car.

"Are you okay?" Michael has come back into the hall. He stops Retief's message in mid-sentence with a press of the button.

"Mikey," she says, and she is shaking again, her voice tremulous, "it was a Mercedes. A white Mercedes."

The mountain, tumbling to meet them. Pine trees angled up against the mist over Lion's Head.

"Come on," he leads her into the kitchen, sits her gently at the wooden table at its centre.

His hands, gripping the wheel.

"Tea," says Michael, and fills the kettle.

"You'd think I'd remember a Mercedes."

"Gin, we need tea. Where are the teabags?"

"I've something to tell you, Ginny, something I should have told you years ago." Simon's face, serious and sad. But a light in his eyes as he looked at her.

"Hmm? Teabags... oh, um, in that cupboard over there." She points across the room.

Simon's eyes as they made love. Those same eyes, later. The light in them dying.

"God, this kitchen's huge. When did you last see Hannah then?" Michael is clattering cutlery, his head stuck in a cupboard. Gin comes over, reaches past him to the tin of teabags. He pulls a face. "Even the cupboards are too big."

The kettle whistles. Steam rises from its spout.

"Leila." Like a message.

"So, when was it?"

His hand, outstretched to her.

"What?"

"When was it you last saw her? Hannah." Michael is looking at her intently.

Gin tries to gather herself. "Um, well, her wedding, I guess. And you?"

His voice has that odd tone again. "That Easter in Cape Town. That Easter with Gabe."

11. GIN

Easter arrived. So soon the year had quartered. Her first year without Simon, her first year in Cape Town. Gin hungered to take the long drive north, to the mine-dump that was Johannesburg. Where Simon had gone.

After Simon had left, she had left also, drove the rusty Renault south. Left his flat, its walls already echoing, hollowed by his departure. No fixed plans, an internship somewhere. Somewhere, on the edge of Africa. She found herself beckoned by the Cape, the mountain a keloid scar curling protectively around the fragile skin of coast. By rote, by proxy, anything to not completely sever the tie between them. Here were roads that Simon would have walked while studying there.

Simon. If she arrived on his doorstep, would he let her go again? But while she argued with her pride, Gabe arrived suddenly. Distracted, dishevelled. He seemed so preoccupied, blue eyes troubled. He was loath to talk, yet seemed at the same time to yearn for it.

Gin had found a yellow house to rent, at the end of a T-junction, with a patch of bare grass at the front and a barren apple tree at the back. The sun poured strong into the kitchen, warming the wooden floors. There was a fireplace of blackened iron and two rooms too many, but a cluster of shops sat cheerily across the bridge and it was close to the children's hospital, and the work she found within its gate.

"Gabe," she asked eventually, "why did you come?"

He shifted to look at her; they had both been staring in silence at the flames in the grate. The logs burned brightly.

"Well," he said at last. "I wanted to see you, and I want to see Han... Hannah." His voice caught in his throat, and he cleared it.

Hannah. Always Hannah with him.

Gin felt irritated with him, but was aware it was her own ire with Hannah also. Hannah was there too, in Cape Town. A year behind, she had chosen a shorter course, and ultimately finished at the same time as Gin. But the years of distancing and disapproval had taken their toll, and Gin saw her rarely. This was how it happened, how you lost the friends you thought would last a lifetime. It had stung, and she had felt each of Hannah's deliberate snubs. She realised she did not even know if Hannah was in town that long weekend, so seldom had they spoken. It was Passover also, and Hannah might be away or back at home.

"Where's Viv?" she asked, and did not know whether she diverted his attention for his sake, or her own.

His girlfriend, he said, had stayed on the farm, she was tutoring that year, and had marking of assignments to finish. He hesitated. Then he told her he was thinking of quitting his degree, going to the Army.

He faced the choice of all young white men in this country. In truth, it was no choice at all. Conscription or leave. Here in intolerance there was no room for conscientious objection. They both knew Gabe was more fortunate than most. Through their Scottish father, he had the means to leave, to live elsewhere. But exile was a lonely choice, and long. There was no return. One must leave the land of one's birth, one's family and friends, all one held familiar, to face uncertain futures. By virtue of her sex, Gin was free of this decision. University had allowed Gabe, and Michael, a period of grace, but the Army would not wait forever. She had seen its destructive force, seen it reach out and ruin young men's minds. Knew the stories of brainwashing, of cruelty. How it broke a sensitivity of spirit, turned it instead to an unfeeling, unquestioning obedience of authority. It perpetuated the system, and only the strong or compliant survived. Simon had told her this, his own term done and served. But he had been luckier, sent to the Navy, and based in the Cape. The Navy and the Air Force were both more sought after than the Army. More lenient, more English. The Afrikaners in their hordes ruled the Army. And they denigrated and humiliated die Engelse, *the English speakers, if they could. Irrespective of origin, one was classified by language. Africa, it seemed, this huge and seething land, remained firstly, and foremostly, tribal.*

Michael arrived the next day. He dismissed her surprise. He had changed his mind, he said, decided to join Gabe and see her after all. A simple explanation became fussy, over-elaborate. Gin looked at Gabe; he looked at the floor, and seemed not himself. Her brother was upset at Michael's presence. Something disturbed these men, these friends.

It was an awkward weekend. On the Saturday they took the wine route, driving the meandering roads beneath the mountains of Stellenbosch and Paarl, from wine farm to wine farm, from Dutch-gabled homestead to rolling vineyard. Gabe was monosyllabic, his usual cheerfulness absent. Michael and he smoked incessantly, and drank too much. Gin drove, confused by the atmosphere, and resentful of it. It was an odd intrusion after the many months without them. On their return, dusk lengthening shadows, Michael made an unfamiliar gesture. He ruffled Gabe's hair, and was shaken off with an angry shrug. They drove on in silence.

It was the need she saw in her twin that made Gin swallow any wounded pride and call Hannah. Hannah was surprisingly friendly, effusive almost, and Gin was thrown, vaguely guilty. Perhaps there had been a certain neglect of friendship on her part also. Hannah's voice was shriller, off-key, when Gin mentioned Gabe.

Sunday morning, they met at Camps Bay. Despite the religious holiday, Blues restaurant was open but not yet crowded. They spent a happy day together, the four of them. Any tension seemed to have eased between the men and Hannah was vivacious, ebullient, at her sociable best. She had put on weight but it suited her, gave her face a softness. She had always had a stunning smile and she bestowed the light of it on the three of them like a benediction. Gin noted a shine in Hannah's eyes, not unlike the glint of tears, as she hugged Gabe. Hannah did not cry easily, and Gin felt a fist tighten around her heart. There was a poignancy in the four of them meeting again and Gin had a strange foreboding that it would be their last.

After lunch, they walked on the beach. Gin sat on the rocks with Michael, watching Gabe and Hannah walk along the shore, voices low, for each other only. Even if the wind had allowed it, they made sure they would not be heard, a habit formed from when they were children. As girls, perhaps she and Hannah should have been closest, thought Gin, but Hannah chose always instead to confide any secrets to Gabe. Gin wondered if Gabe discussed with Hannah his dilemma and, if so, what would Hannah say. Would her opinion sway Gabe in his decision? Hannah had always been so steadfastly unconcerned by the politics that raged around her.

Michael faced the same fate, yet unlike Gabe, Gin assumed he had little choice. She realised how little she knew of Michael, these past four years, of how university had shaped and changed him. She knew nothing of the structure of his life. Michael and Gabe had been studying the same course and staying together in the large commune on the farm outside Grahamstown. Gin had been glad of this; at least they had stayed close. Michael had sat quietest, listening, smoking, absorbing Hannah's tales. And, like Gin, watching Gabe's hungry eyes follow Hannah's every move, every gesture, her slender fingers glittering with rings, and nails of immaculate frosted pink, hands fluttering as she talked.

Gin felt guilty again, as if the fault of wayward friendship lay firmly at her feet. Had Simon distracted her so from all she loved and knew? Yet this could not be true. She tried to remember. Had Michael called, and had she ignored him? Had Gabe visited, and had she cut him short? She had no recollection of this. She felt the sharp pain of missing Simon. No one had mentioned him, nor even asked.

A frigid wind whipped off the waves, reached them on the rocks, and she shivered. Michael smiled at her, his crooked, secret smile. She thought it secret because it seemed to hide a knowledge that he would not share.

There was an odd awkwardness between them, and she mourned the loss of closeness.

They returned, Gabe and Hannah, a handsome couple huddled closely as if for warmth. Hannah made to go. She must, she said, be elsewhere that evening for dinner. Such false gaiety, thought Gin, and hated it. She saw pain in Gabe's eyes. He blinked, turned his face to the sea. Gin knew her twin's reactions were like her own. They said their farewells, Hannah kissing air beside Gin's cheek. But as she hugged Gabe, those long nails left marks in his arms. Another sunset. Darkness, always lurking.

While Michael fetched beer from the car, Gabe blurted words at Gin. He had decided to do his army service, "Get it over with." These were the words he chose. This was the decision he had made, he told her, the beach grown lonely and bleak.

Gin could see Michael searching in the boot of her car for something. No doubt the opener was lost. White haze around her vision, around her world.

No more putting it off. No more leisurely years putting off the inevitable. He'd had his chance, his lazy days of being a student, lying beneath the great leafy oaks on the cricket lawns, reading Macbeth and Tennyson. Waiting. The Army had been patient. Also waiting. Time to exact its price, take its toll. It would take him, shave his hair to spikes and dress him like all the others, in sand-soaked brown. It would give him a helmet; it would give him a rank; it would give him a gun. At nights he would sleep on hard sheets in a single bed. The Army would wake him before dawn, make him run, make him sweat, make him suffer, drive him mad.

Would she write to him, he'd like that, asked Gabe. The sun was setting orange on the water. Why did she notice the sand stuck to wet pebbles, a small crab scuttling to the edge of foam? When her world was crumbling, when all she had known was changing, her attention would be caught by the most inconsequential detail, fogging her memory for later recall.

When Simon had left, she had watched the drop of falling purple, jacaranda blossom tumbling to the cobbled courtyard, whisked about to curls of lilac, or sticking wet, smeared indigo on the ground. She heard the hum of a neighbouring washing machine, smelled woodsmoke strong in the spring air.

Would she write to him, Gabe was asking again, he'd like that. The horizon glowed. And that was how she learned to hate the twilight. Beyond yawned the black void, sucking, devouring, taking all she loved, taking people from her yet again.

She took his hand, said nothing, in silence held it fast, linking again with him as they had as children. They sat in quiet communion. Remembering how the summer sun brought freckles to their pale faces. Remembering Michael's perennial pageboy haircut, Hannah's happy laugh.

But what else they spoke of that day upon the water, she would not remember. Could not remember! How it would feel, later, how she would betray his memory, when later she could not remember the last words her brother spoke to her, that fading orange twilight on the beach.

12. VIVIENNE

Viv cannot suppress a flutter of pleasure at the sound of Nick's voice on her answer machine. Retief's measured tone announces that he needs to talk to her, and would she please call him at his office. He recites the number and then repeats it slowly, considerately, as if he imagines her writing it down. It is already late afternoon. The sky has sedimented purple beyond the horizon and a stiff wind heralds a cold night. Viv puts her files on the dining table, as she will have no other use for it tonight. The girls have gone to Jonnie. As always, somewhat reluctantly and under mock protest. Abbie has more reason to resist the fortnightly visits. Jonnie is not Abbie's father but in truth, he is the only father she has known. Viv is grateful that her elder daughter does not wholly object. She knows Abbie goes more for Kayleigh's sake than her own. But however sullenly they traipse off, Viv knows Jonnie will indulge them, and they will return with presents of new clothes, new shoes, and new music.

She doubts Retief will still be there, but he answers on the second ring. "Retief." Abruptly.

He asks if she can come in; he will be working late. His voice has thawed.

Viv is hesitant. She detests police stations, though it is years since she was last inside one.

Then he says, "Actually, there's a good Indian restaurant up in Vredehoek." Perhaps they can talk over dinner. That is, if she is hungry. Suddenly, he sounds unsure of himself, as if he has assumed too much.

Viv stares at the files on the table. She had planned to use the weekend to catch up with two days of case reports, and the endless laundry her teenage daughters appear to generate, but she feels a strange excitement at the thought of seeing Nick Retief again. "I'm starving," she replies.

The sun has fully set by the time she has showered and changed. The car flies along a relatively empty de Waal drive which ribbons through the city. To her right, the lights end in geometric structured shapes, where the harbour buttresses the black sea that merges uninterrupted with the night. To her left, the edge of lights undulate as they meet the uninhabitable ridges of the mountain. The slopes are lit by night, and it looms above her, its shadowy form darker than the blackness of the sky. She swings off the highway into the flat stretch of the city centre, turns left up one of the long main streets and makes her way to Retief's police station.

The Bedouin is set high up on the steep slopes of the suburb. The owner greets Nick by name and leads them to a cubicle at the window. Cape Town glimmers brightly below. Each chair is draped with silk and the tables dimly lit with lanterns of coloured glass. He explains the Indian terms to her, tells her what he thinks tastes good. She realises he is unaware of her own intimacy with these dishes, having cooked for Jonnie during the long years of her marriage. How little about her he knows. But she doesn't tell him. She does not want to talk about her life, her past. Too much pain, long-suppressed.

They spend time ordering. Nick's businesslike tone is gone and he seems at ease.

"What was it that you wanted to talk to me about?" asks Viv, as the waiter disappears with their order. She hopes her nervousness does not show.

"I haven't been able to get hold of Miss McMann. And there's a few things I need to find out about that may help clear up a few details."

"What sort of details do you need to know?" Viv does not allow him time to reply. "And what sort of things do you need to know about Gin? You want me to tell you about my friend and I don't know why; what if it's things she might not want me to tell you about? Things she might not want you to know. And why do you need to know them?"

Nick does not interrupt her. When he seems certain she has finished, he answers. "I need to know about her past, about people she has been involved with, about anyone that may have a reason to want to harm her or Simon Gold."

"Harm Gin?" Viv's voice rises.

"Yes," Nick says patiently, "or Simon Gold."

"I didn't know him. I never even met him." She is horribly aware of the lie. Guilt settles on her chest. Already she feels the weight of lying to Nick. Nothing, she thinks, nothing in our present can be untainted by our past.

"But you knew that Miss McMann – Gin – was involved with him? You went to university together." Nick sounds surprised.

"At the same time, not together. I didn't meet Gin till after university, till after…" Viv stops.

Nick waits again. When she swallows and does not continue, he asks, "Till after what, Vivienne?"

"Nick," says Viv stiffly, "this is hard for me."

The waiter arrives with their food and busies himself with spreading the various dishes around the table, talking all the while, explaining to Viv which dish is which. She inclines her head politely at him, but stays silent. Nick is watching her across the table, and is silent also. When the waiter has left, she sits staring sullenly at the food. She feels like her daughters, sulky and reluctant to talk when upset.

He leans across to her. "I'm sorry, Vivienne," he says, "I know this must be difficult for you. But I promise you, I'm really trying to help Gin, to find out what really happened that day. And why."

"You really don't think it was an accident, do you?" asks Viv, relenting somewhat.

He fills her glass with Colombard. "No, I don't. And the insurance people don't think so either. They're not going to pay out till they know what happened."

"Will that affect Simon's estate?"

"It'll affect his estate, yes, but only in terms of resolving this one insurance payout. From what I've been told, this particular life insurance policy is a large amount."

"Is his family pushing you also?"

"No, not at all. Doctor Gold was a wealthy man, by all accounts. He left his wife and children very well provided for."

Viv is quiet, thinking about Gin and her pregnancy. She has not mentioned this to anyone and doubts that Retief can know.

"His family are also wealthy," continues Nick. "They own Kornfeld and Gold jewellers."

"I know, Nick." Again Viv realises he has no idea of her own past, of her own involvement with Gabe. "Gin's family is the Kornfeld part," she says, "Her maternal grandfather."

"Ah, yes, I remember her saying their grandfathers were in business together. Friends. Is that how she met Doctor Gold – Simon – then?"

"They met for the first time when Gin was at university, and Simon was doing his medical internship in the same town. Although their families were always close. Gin was very close to Simon's cousin Hannah when they were growing up. But I never knew Hannah either." She stops and takes a draught of her wine.

Hannah, the name sits oddly on her tongue. *Hannah*, the unknown. *Hannah*, the name that had haunted Gabe's dreams.

Nick ladles rice onto her plate, hands her copper dishes of spicy offerings.

"That's all I really know about Simon," she says. She sees again

Simon's serious eyes, looking at her. She feels like his biblical name-sake, denying knowledge. Yet it was true, she convinces herself, I hardly knew him. Just that one meeting, two, three even, didn't mean she had been any closer to the man. "And I can't possibly tell you who might want to hurt him. Or Gin, for that matter. It seems absurd to me. Maybe Simon's family can help you more. Have you spoken to them?"

"*Ja*," he nods, refilling her glass. "They had no idea Miss – Gin – and he were in Cape Town together until after the accident. They didn't seem very happy about the fact, though."

"Of course not," snorts Viv before she can stop herself.

He looks at her, curious. "Why do you say that?"

"I just mean, well, you know, they were the reason Simon split up with Gin. You know, he was Jewish, she wasn't. It's difficult, not the done thing. You know how it is."

"*Ja*, my mom had the same problem, being English and marrying into an Afrikaans family." His voice is soft with memory.

Viv has her own experience of trying to fit in, to belong to a culture other than one's own. Jonnie's family had never quite accepted her, and she had been at once hurt and astonished at their rejection of her. Somehow, stupidly, she had assumed only the white people in this country were racist. His mother had tried to make Viv into a good Indian wife, taught her how to make curries, how to wear a sari, and had urged her to convert to Islam. Viv had resisted everything but the cooking. It is a measure of her progress since the divorce, she thinks wryly to herself, that she can sit and eat the food before her without bitterness.

They eat, and for a while they speak of other things. He seems almost relieved when she laughs at something he has said. Over coffee, he returns to Gin's case. "Tell me more about Simon and Gin."

"Well, he ended it quite suddenly when her course finished at uni-versity. I always thought there was more to it than the whole Jewish thing. Anyhow, he left, took a job in Jo'burg." Viv feels relaxed now and speaks more freely. "I didn't know Gin then, as I told you, but she was devastated. She left also, came to Cape Town."

"How come they got back together here after all this time?"

"Her dad died and she came home for his funeral. As you know, their families are connected… he phoned her I think and arranged to see her. I thought she told you this?"

"She did, but sometimes someone else sees things differently."

"You mean, like his wife?" asks Viv.

He looks at her intently, "Why do you think I was talking about her?"

"It's just that you keep wanting to know about Simon and Gin and who would be upset at them. I suppose the only person I can think of would be his wife." She pauses. "You said the driver was a woman." Viv's eyes widen. "Oh my goodness, do you think Simon's wife found out about them and came after him and rammed their car deliberately?"

Nick is smiling at her.

"What?" she asks. "Why are you smiling?"

"*Ja*," he says, "No, you're absolutely right."

"Well?"

He is obviously amused. "Yes, Vivienne, the thought had occurred to me it might be the wife."

"Have you questioned her?"

He is more sober now. "I have. And it can't be her."

"Why not?"

"Well, two reasons. Firstly, the woman that was seen following them was Cape Coloured, or Malay, not white."

"Following them?" interrupts Viv.

"Someone remembered Simon and Gin having coffee outside a café in Seapoint. Said he noticed them because they looked so much in love." He takes a sip of coffee. "Anyhow, the same chap said he noticed a woman sitting in a white Mercedes looking at them also. Said he didn't think anything of it, I mean, they were a striking couple and so obviously wrapped up in each other, that people noticed them. But he says he then saw Simon and Gin leave in their car. The Mercedes pulled out after them, almost deliberately. Hurriedly. It pulled out quite sharply ahead of another car as if trying to follow them. At least, that's what it looked like." Nick stops, spoons more sugar into his cup.

Viv is thoughtful. "You said there were two reasons."

"Hey?"

"You said there were two reasons it couldn't be Simon's wife. What could have stopped her hiring someone, the woman in the Mercedes even… to follow him if she suspected Simon was having an affair?"

He grins at her. "You've a suspicious mind, Vivienne. You should come and work for us."

She smiles weakly at him. "I'm a social worker, Nick. I also see the human condition, the frailties, the cruelties, the worst of people, what they are capable of." Viv does not mention her own experience of tragedy and betrayal.

He looks at her for a moment before replying. "The other reason it couldn't be Mrs Gold is that she totally and utterly lacked motive."

"But what do you mean? Her husband was having an affair, with a woman he had once lived with… isn't that motive enough to want to kill him?" Viv laughs, somewhat harshly. Then her voice rises again, and she looks at Nick in alarm, "Or Gin, for that matter. God, Nick."

"It wasn't Mrs Gold," he says slowly, deliberately, "we've practically eliminated her from the investigation. You see, before Doctor Gold… before Simon even phoned Gin or came to Cape Town, the marriage was over."

Viv puts her cup down hard. It clatters on the saucer. "What?"

"Yes," says Nick, "they were getting divorced."

13. VIVIENNE

Simon's wife, Retief tells Viv, had sued for divorce some months before his death. "It was her decision. She had an affair with one of her partners in her law firm. They were due to be married once the divorce went through. It's by all accounts a successful firm, a very lucrative business. She has no need for money," he continues.

Viv is insistent. "People have killed for less. Perhaps she wanted it all, perhaps Simon was causing trouble, contesting the divorce. Perhaps, despite her own infidelity, she was furious at his. You know, the scorned woman…"

Her voice trails off seeing Nick's placid gaze. It had all been progressing quite amicably, Nick tells her. In truth, even to Viv, it sounds wild, implausible. She can scarcely believe anyone would want to hurt Gin, let alone possibly kill her. They finish their coffee in silence.

Nick is paying for the meal when Viv suddenly grabs his arm, startling both him and the restaurateur. "It's a good thing then, that Gin's gone back to England."

He looks at her briefly, thanks the manager, turns back to her. "Come," he says calmly, taking her arm, "I'll drive you home."

The night is quiet, and she notices it is later than she thought. He will bring her car out to her tomorrow, he promises. Viv thinks perhaps he has had as much wine as she, but she does not argue. She feels tired, and it is pleasurable to sit back for once and let someone else drive. The lights of the city sweep by. Neither of them speaks. The night's conversation has made her feel sad, bringing back moments in her life best left buried.

Gabe shifted in his sleep, moaned. Viv lay awake. Every sound in the night frightened her. She imagined military police already looking for him, already outside their window, ready to storm the quiet cosiness of the farmhouse. She was afraid for him more than for herself. What were they going to do? He had arrived, exhausted, dirty from travel, but clear-headed and calm. Calm when he said he was quitting, leaving the Army. Calm when he said he was leaving the country.

"I can't do it anymore, Viv," he had said, watching her reaction with a steady blue gaze. "It's hell. We kill people. We drive into the townships and we shoot people. Our own people."

She had lit another cigarette. Her whole world was about to change, and she knew it. Whatever he decided to do now, it would affect her. And still he did not know. "Gabe," she had said quietly, "I'm pregnant."

He had been stunned. She had tried to explain their contraception must have failed, but he wasn't listening. In his expression, she saw confusion replaced by a hesitant joy, then doubt. He had turned his back on her.

"And is it mine?" he had asked, in a voice she hardly recognised, "Or Michael's?"

He could not have hurt her more had he hit her. As if he had cause to doubt her. Or Michael. As if she, Viv, had no cause herself to doubt him. As if she had forgotten the times that Hannah's name fell from his lips.

They had argued, coldly, acidly.

"Gabe," she had screamed eventually, frustrated, "Are you mad? Even if you doubt me, how can you doubt Michael? He's your best friend!"

Gabe's back was to her but at that, she saw something soften in his stance. He had turned to her, put his arms around her, and held her closely. "I know. I'm so sorry, Viv."

Over and over he'd whispered he was sorry. And then, instead of talking of what they'd do, or where he'd go, or planning the future of their child, they'd fallen into bed, made love urgently. And then she lay awake, unable to sleep, while he slept, restlessly. He was on the run from

| 67 |

the might of the South African Army. Who would not fail to hunt him.
And there, at the farmhouse, was where they were likely to start.

"Are you okay?" Nick's voice sounds through the darkness of the car.

They are almost home. "I'm fine," she says, but she feels as if she could cry.

He turns into her road, slides the car easily alongside the kerb. They sit quietly for a moment, both contemplating the empty street, dimly lit. Somewhere a neighbour shouts for his dog. A light in the next house flicks on, then off again. Viv looks blankly at the red wooden gate. It is pulling at its hinges. The sea air has done its damage, she thinks, and it will soon need painting. The blocks of cement leading to her front door are under siege from the tough kikuyu grass. But the house looks good; its walls gleam softly in the light of the streetlamps. Inside, she remembers, will still be the mess she left, the girls' clothes and schoolbooks scattered in the haste of their departure. Viv's own files lay strewn across the table. But the lounge will be warm and welcoming. She had drawn the curtains before she had left, and the warmth will not have slipped through the tall French doors. And the grate is freshly packed with pine cones gathered from the side of the mountain. She likes her home, Viv realises, suddenly aware of her life through outside eyes. She had gathered it together through pain, and loss, and heartache, and made it hers. And more than anything, she longs to be inside it now.

"I'm sorry about all the questions," he says gently.

"Well, now you know everything I know, everything I ever knew about Gin. And Simon Gold for that matter." Her voice is angry. She is feeling used.

"I'll bring your car back to you tomorrow," he says. She is about to tell him not to bother when he adds, "I have a dog. I take her for a run on Muizenberg beach on the weekends when I can. Would you like to come with me?"

She shifts in her seat to look at him. He is leaning back against the window, turned towards her, his hands playing with the car keys. "Nick…" She thinks she ought to tell him it is best perhaps if she does not see him again, but stops. It is not his fault the evening's talk has brought back unhappy memories. And she had enjoyed his company.

"Of course, you'd have to drive me home tomorrow. If that's all right," he adds.

As earlier that evening, the uncertainty in his voice touches her. Suddenly her mood lifts. She can think of nothing more pleasant than walking along the beach the following morning. "That'd be nice, yes," she says. "What's her name?"

"Who?" he asks.

"Your wife," she says, and then, seeing his look, laughs. "Your dog. Unless, of course, you do have a wife."

He laughs also. "Manyanga."

"Manyanga," repeats Viv. The name folds itself around her lips. "What does it mean?"

"It's Swahili," he says, smiling. "It means beautiful girl." His eyes are on her, intent.

"And is she?" she asks, for something to say.

His smile, his look, unnerves her.

"Yes," he answers. "You'll like her," he adds, "she's loyal, trusting. Faithful."

"Good qualities in a dog."

"Good qualities in a companion. You see, no wife." Then, suddenly serious, he adds, "Vivienne, I am sorry about making you talk about things from your past that may have been uncomfortable for you. I know that it's your story too."

Viv is too surprised to speak.

"And that," he continues, almost inaudibly, "I'd really like to know more about."

She digests this.

"Of course," he says, and she can hear the smile return to his voice, "I could always interrogate your neighbours about you."

She laughs again, and his smile broadens, and then he gets out of the car, opens the car door for her, and walks her up the cement path to the entrance of her house. For a long moment, she looks at him looking at her. He lifts his hand to touch her cheek. In that gesture, momentarily, beneath the half-light of the street, he has a look so like Gabe it takes her breath. Viv's mouth goes dry, and she turns from him, fumbling for her keys, half-blind with tears.

He is immediately formal. "Thank you for a very pleasant evening, Vivienne. I'll see you tomorrow, about nine."

Viv pushes the heavy door open, steps inside the hall and switches on the light. Its brightness is blinding after the tepid streetlight. She turns to look out after him.

But Nick Retief has already disappeared into the darkness.

14. MICHAEL

The door opens slowly, pushing against delivered mail. Michael picks up the pile of post, puts it on the table in the hall. Gin moves past him, shaking the rain off her mac. She hangs it on the rail, and fluffs raindrops out of her hair. It has grown long in the last month, notices Michael, hanging his own coat next to hers. She files through the assorted envelopes.

"Michael, there's one here for you."

"For me?" His voice comes out thin with surprise.

The stamp is Danish. Gin hands it to him without meeting his eyes, and walks past him into the kitchen. It can only be from his wife. They both know this.

He stands in the hall, turning the envelope over in his hands for a while. Then he walks slowly to the kitchen, stopping in the doorway. Gin turns on the gas, and flicks the switch to ignite the blue flame. She reaches for the kettle and turns to look at him. He shifts his gaze past her to the window. Rain courses down the clear length of it, distorting the view of the garden beyond into a surrealist blur. Gin turns back to the stove, puts the kettle over the flame.

"What does she say?" she asks, her back to him.

He has been here only a month but he has started to feel as if he might stay forever. Kristina and Denmark feel like a part of some nagging leftover dream. Michael leans against the doorjamb, arms folded. Gin turns around to face him again.

He looks away from her, to the blur of roses outside, the apricot yellow, pinks, and ruby that seep across the kitchen window. Then

his eyes meet hers squarely. "I don't know. I haven't opened it."
He cannot tell her he does not intend to; he can barely admit it to
himself.

She gives him a dark look.

Michael smiles wearily at her. "I know you don't like her."

She looks at him sharply. "I didn't mean –," but her sentence dies
unfinished.

He knows he is right; she had never liked Kristina. She finds it hard
to lie to him, he realises. Politeness has never had a place between
them. "It's all right, Gin," he says, "she never liked you either."

Gin does not react. He is slightly bemused by his own confession of it. Kristina, jealous of everyone he knew, but especially Gin.
With no cause, he reflects. Checks himself; least cause, then. His
two affairs had been remarkable only for their endings. Recrimination, regret, reconciliation. But Kristina's insecurities, her constant
need, had meant the geographical distance between him and Gin
had hardened into an emotional one. Banished finally by that phone
call. Michael moves across the kitchen, the unopened letter crinkles
in his pocket. He wants to go to her, hug her and apologise, but
instead he sits heavily at the table. He looks at Gin, staring ahead
into space, notices the lines around her eyes. We have grown old,
he thinks, without noticing. Waiting for life to take on meaning or
purpose. We, marking time. And time, marking us.

He rubs his eyes, looks up at her. The kettle whistles impatiently
and she turns it off, opens the cupboard and takes down two mugs.

"You know, I never liked Simon either," he says suddenly.

Gin turns to stare at him. Her mouth opens but no words form.
She brings a hand up to her mouth, as if astonished at her own lack
of speech.

"Neither did Gabe," he continues, relentless now. He does not
know why he feels the need to shock her. Perhaps it is her listlessness,
her disassociation that ignites a hard, sudden flash of anger in him.

He wants to shake her out of her disinterest, bring her back to life. To the Gin he once knew. Rarely has he glimpsed the Gin he knows, the healthy tomboy he grew up with, the pretty teenager, the attractive woman with a wide smile, emotive blue eyes, and a ready laugh. She seems to him a sepia remnant of herself.

She has said nothing, is still standing there, eyes fixed, her fingers still raised to her impotent lips.

He has no right to bring up Gabe in this manner, thinks Michael, or Gabe's feelings about Simon. Both men are dead, and there can be no resolution for her. Again, he wants to hold her, say he is sorry, sit her down, make her tea, comfort her. He wants to push back the too-long hair, push away the hand still held to her mouth.

Now he is angry with himself for hurting her. It is not fair on her. She is pregnant, and has lost yet another person whom she loved. His hand slams on the table, harder than he meant. She makes a small sound and jumps. Michael is immediately contrite, the violent expression contrary to his nature. He stands and walks over to her, but she flinches away from him.

"I'm sorry, Gin," he says sincerely. He runs his hand through his short hair, rubs the back of his neck. "I'm sorry," he says again, his hands falling to his sides.

Gin nods mutely, but he knows she was alarmed by his outburst and confused at his confession. On some level, he feels glad her state of stasis has been assaulted. Gin turns back, busies herself with making tea. She hands him his mug. As she does so, the sleeve on her arm rides up.

"Your arm's healed nicely," notes Michael, trying to change the stilted atmosphere that has formed between them. He leans against the sideboard.

Gin's right hand reaches involuntarily to touch her left arm, where the burn has smoothed the skin unnaturally. She nods again, a brief movement of her head.

Michael wants to ask her if she has remembered more about the accident, but he is wary now. He wants to ask her also about her nightmares. He has heard her cry out during the night and thought to go to her room to wake her, but somehow he has desisted, afraid it might distress her further.

How happy she had made him when he'd first heard her voice on the phone those few months ago, soon to be replaced by worry. And fear, he realises. Gin seems beyond his reach at times, and he cannot fail to think of Gabe, and the course her brother chose to take. He shudders at the thought. Gabe's death had brought him here initially, to England, Gabe's death the catalyst for his desertion of his homeland; he could not contemplate army service after what had happened to his best friend. They had been like brothers. He finds himself thinking yet again about Gabe's final months. Those months on the run, hiding from the Army, from the military police, surviving where and how they would never really now know.

The crack of the farmhouse's splintering door. The sound of heavy boots racing up the stairs. Shouted commands in Afrikaans. Viv's scream brought Michael running, half-dressed, onto the landing between their rooms. Viv was being hauled out of her room, a soldier pulling her by the arm, slinging her towards the stairs.

Gin touches his hand, forgiveness implicit in the gesture. He looks at her gratefully. She leans into him and hugs him. His arms reach around her fiercely, although he is mindful of the bump of her belly. She is not totally lost to him, he thinks. She cannot be.

"At least you look pregnant now," he says, when he eventually lets go of her.

She smiles wanly at him. Her health, he thinks, has improved somewhat, and her skin has lost the sallow look he had noted on his arrival.

"I have to have another scan," she says quietly. "It – they said the baby was a bit small. Maybe… maybe not growing properly."

Oh, Christ, he thinks. He worries what it will do to her if she loses this baby. On some level he thinks she has barely acknowledged the pregnancy. When he arrived, he had been appalled by her lack of preparation for it. He forced her to go shopping, to buy a cot, clothes, nappies. But he knows her reluctance is also due to fear. A fear of losing Simon's child again.

"Mikey," she says, when they are seated with their tea at the high wooden table in the centre of the kitchen, and then pauses pensively.

He feels his shoulders tense involuntarily, waiting for her to ask why he and Gabe had disliked Simon.

Instead she asks, "What happened that Easter?"

"What do you mean?" The question throws him.

She takes a gingerly sip from her mug. "Was something wrong?"

His brow furrows. "Wrong?"

She exhales, a long breath, blowing at the steam off her tea. "Well, just, I don't know… it seemed," again she pauses, as if searching for the right phrase. "It seemed as if there was something wrong between you and Gabe."

Michael is quiet, remembering.

Gabe shouted at him. "What's it to you, Michael? Where I go, who I see?" Turned on his heel. "Or is Hannah your business too? Like Viv?" Strode out the farmhouse. "Stop trying to control me, Michael." The engine ignited, wheels spinning dust. "Fuck you, Michael."

He has never forgotten. It had been their last, their only, argument.

"I thought there was some tension between the two of you, some anger even." Her gaze goes past him as she focuses on some memory of her own. Then she looks at him, blue eyes direct. "Was it something to do with Viv?"

"Viv?" Her astuteness astounds him. "No, well, yes. There was some stuff with Viv. But not then, not that Easter." He stops. "That Easter was more about Hannah."

"Hannah?" Gin's tone is shrill.

Michael takes a long sip of his own tea. It sears the roof of his mouth. He breathes in deeply, deciding.

And then he tells her.

15. MICHAEL

"Something *was* wrong," he admits. He feels fractionally guilty. This will be Hannah's story also. But Hannah is across the other side of the world now, and out of their lives.

Hannah stood at the university bookstore window on High Street. Her bag was slung forlornly at her feet. Michael's first impulse was to call to her, but something in her stance stopped him. He checked himself. Was it Hannah? The young woman's long hair draped forward, partially obscuring her face. And she looked thinner than Hannah. He stood for a moment unsure, watching her. She continued to stare into the stacked display of books. He found this odd. Only boring tomes on science and statistics lined the window. Then she raised a hand to her face, made as if to wipe at her eyes. Was she crying? His instinct was to move forward, comfort her. But then, he had not seen Hannah for over a year. Not since school had ended. Not since Hannah had gone to Israel. Would she want him to interfere with her obvious sadness? And if it weren't Hannah, what stranger would want him intruding, offering solace? So he stood back, immobile with indecision. Then the young woman sniffed and tucked a thick rope of hair behind one ear. Hannah. Unmistakeably Hannah.

Michael moved forward, closing the short distance between them. He called her name softly, not wanting to startle her. But she jumped nonetheless, a hand went to her heart, her back straightening, stiffening, away from him. But a smile quickly formed and he felt himself heartened by this. He moved closer, stood in front of her. Her hand moved from her chest to his. He liked the gesture; it was easy, intimate. He reached around to hug her. But she did not return the embrace, instead left her hand on his chest, between them. No longer easy, intimate. It was to hold him at bay, rather. But then her smile forced itself brighter. More the Hannah of old. He asked her if she was feeling okay. She nodded, but there passed between them a tacit acknowledgement. That he had seen her weeping. That he knew.

"So we went to the coffee shop across the road," he says to Gin, "you remember – Daisy's?"

Gin nods. He knows she remembers. The bookshop, Daisy's, both were near where she and Simon had lived. Even in this telling he cannot spare her more pain, he thinks. We are all connected, our lives spun together like a web.

Hannah held her mug tightly. Unusually for her, her nails were short and unpainted, her fingers bare except for two simple rings, one of them made of three intertwined bands, each a different colour. Michael found the sounds of the café at first loud and intrusive. But after a while, after they had ordered a pot of Daisy's Kenyan coffee, after it had arrived with cheerful floral mugs and steaming milk, after they had sat facing each other over the table in the back corner, he found the noise a comfort. Something to absorb their silence, and something, he thought, for by then he had no doubt, if she was ever going to speak, something to absorb the starkness of her words.

"Daisy's," says Gin suddenly.

She hugs her mug close to her, much as Hannah had done that day. He is struck afresh by how alike Gin and Hannah have always been in some respect. Gin fairer, taller. Hannah darker, more like Gabe. But then some had thought Hannah was Gabe's twin instead of Gin, he remembers. Same dark hair, same blue eyes. Same bright smile, same happy laugh. But it is Gin, he thinks, who shared Gabe's intensity of spirit, his seriousness of soul.

"Why was Hannah so unhappy, Michael?" asks Gin, bringing him back to the cool kitchen.

Despite the grey pall of rain, it is still light. The long Northern summers still strike him as oddly as the curt dark days of winter's chill. There is a sound of distant traffic that to him sounds like the sea. It is a pleasant house, he thinks. A nice house to live, to raise a child. Gin can be happy here. He laces his fingers with hers over the tabletop and looks at her. Her face is thinned with sorrow, and he regrets the way the conversation has turned.

"I'll never understand why she cut you all off," says Gin slowly. "Especially Gabe. Me, I understand." She stutters here, and pauses.

"You? Why you?" he asks, incredulous. But of course he has known Hannah's reasons all these years. Gin has had no recourse but to make up her own.

Gin takes her hands from his, lifts her mug and swallows hard. She puts it down unevenly, and the liquid slops inside, but does not spill. "Because of Simon," she says, her voice hoarse. It is as if it hurts her throat to say his name aloud. She coughs, and says, more clearly. "Hannah always disapproved."

"Because Simon was her cousin?"

She looks at him oddly, frowning slightly as if he is being obtuse. "No…" she starts, but then she stops as if to think. "Well, maybe. I suppose that could have made it worse for her."

"Made what worse?"

"Because he was Jewish and I wasn't. We only spoke about it once, when I asked why she never came to see us."

"What did she say?"

Gin sighs, traces the pattern on her mug with her finger. "Said it was wrong. Said it wouldn't last."

She looks up at him. He cannot make out the emotion in her

eyes, but their colour has clouded from a clear cerulean to a hue so dark it is almost indigo.

She smiles, a lop-sided grimace with no humour. "Well, she was right, wasn't she?"

He was right about Hannah's words. At first, they came haltingly, staccato-like. Each word a stab, a cut into the air. Michael sipped his coffee and listened. Hannah started by asking him if he remembered the farewell dance of their final school year. He could hardly have forgotten, but he nodded yes. For a moment her look was one of innocent pleasure. Then came a wretchedness to her gaze. When she asked about Gabe, how he was. Michael contemplated telling her the truth. How Gabe had rang her and left messages as soon as he had heard she was back. Time after time, and how her continued silence had hurt him. He felt he should tell her how Gabe drank too much, and smoked too much, and how he went to every party, coming home each time with a different girl. He thought he ought to tell her Gabe's heart was shattered, broken. And by her. Instead, Michael lied and told Hannah Gabe was fine. A long lock fell in front of her face again. Then she asked him if he knew why she'd gone to Israel. The question took him by surprise. In truth, he had never questioned it. He stumbled over an inadequate answer. Experience, he said. To meet with family, he supposed. To study. A cultural break, even. Her laugh was short and mirthless.

Michael stops.

Gin looks at him questioningly. "Well? Was it none of those things?" she prompts.

"Did you know she didn't go straight to Israel?" asks Michael.

Her look is quizzical. "No. Why? Where did she go?"

He reaches for his mug, drains the last of his tepid drink. Then he puts the mug down and looks at her. "Gin, Hannah came to England before she went to Israel. And she came to England to have an abortion."

16. MICHAEL

Gin's mug slams into the table. This time her tea spills from its side. She stares at the pool of it. Outside, the sky darkens to a threatening violet.

Gin forms the words. "Gabe's baby." It is not a question, but a realisation.

Michael nods nonetheless.

She shakes her head. "No."

He knew this would cause her pain, but at least his words are penetrating. "There's more," he says, but gently. Gin stares at him uncomprehendingly. "Hannah changed her mind about the abortion." Her mouth opens. He knows the question and carries on hurriedly, wanting to explain. "Yes," he says quickly, "that's why she stayed the whole year, Gin. She changed her mind. She went to Israel to have her baby."

"You mean –".

He shakes his head, eager to finish. He knows what she wants to know, and does not want her to think the wrong thing. Quickly now, the words rushing. "The baby didn't live, Gin. It was stillborn. There was something wrong. Badly wrong. Hannah said its heart stopped a few weeks before she was due. She had to give birth to –," and here he stops finally, exhales. He does not want to distress her, but he can think of no painless way to say it. "The baby was born dead."

She makes an exclamation. An odd noise emanates from her throat. "Dead?" she says, and it sounds as if she has a cold.

He nods wordlessly.

Gin's eyes glisten. Perhaps she is about to cry, he thinks, and, while he hates the thought of her upset, he thinks perhaps this is the release she needs. But then she sits back, her hands drop to her rounded belly, link across the top of it. Protectively. He knows where her thoughts are.

The rain has become heavy, a hard patter on the kitchen roof. Water rushes into the gutters and the air in the kitchen cools.

After a while she asks, "What was it? The child? A boy or a girl?"

"A boy," he replies.

"Gabe had a son," she says, staring into space.

"Yes." He can think of nothing else to add.

"Poor Hannah, how awful. What an awful thing to have to endure."

"Yes," he agrees. "I think she was very brave, defying her father. You know Gabe had asked Hannah to marry him?"

Her eyes widen. "No, when?"

"Night of the school dance. Before uni."

Gin contemplates this, her face set.

Michael is grim. "He never told me either. But apparently Hannah's father forbade it. Said he would never allow it. That's why Hannah got pregnant."

"It was deliberate?"

"I think she thought then her father would come round, would change his mind, that they'd have to get married."

"But why didn't she?" Gin's voice is high. "I mean, why didn't she still come back after – after – and marry him anyhow? They could have, she could still have children. She has three now. What happened? Why did she cut him off, after all that?"

Michael shrugs. "From what she told me that day, it seems her father was furious with her. Said it was best the baby died."

Gin is aghast. "Jacob said *that*?" Her tone is one of disbelief.

"That's what she told me. He forbade her to see Gabe again. Told her she was better off with someone Jewish, of her own culture, who would understand her. That sort of thing." He sighs. "She went through such a lot. So young, and all on her own. I think it was simply easier for her, after what she went through. A hell of a thing, you know. Just easier for her to cope. She must have been full of anger and grief still."

"Poor Hannah," reflects Gin. "And you never told Gabe?"

And there it is, the stab to his heart. No, he had not told his best friend. Hannah had made him swear to it. And Gabe had died, not knowing. They look at each other, hard rain the only sound.

Eventually he says, "So that Easter, we – me and Gabe – we argued. He was so determined, you know, so set on going to Cape Town to see Hannah again. After all those years. I don't know what got into him…" Michael's voice trails off. He knows now Gabe's state of mind, the decision he faced about the Army, were part of it. "I don't know," he continues slowly, "I don't know. I wanted to protect Hannah, I guess. I thought her seeing Gabe again would bring it all up for her, for both of them. Gabe was with Viv by then, Hannah getting on with her life… it wasn't fair on Viv either. You know, what if Gabe was going to throw it all away for Hannah again? Leave Viv? I suppose I was trying to protect her too."

Gin reaches across and takes his hand in hers. Her fingers tighten. "Poor Michael," she says softly. "Poor Hannah. Poor Gabe."

"Yes." He takes his hand away and stands. He wants a cigarette, a drink even. He walks to the large pantry door at the end of the kitchen. Inside are several bottles of wine and spirits. He picks up a bottle of Australian red, then changes his mind and pulls out a bottle of whisky. Returning to the table, he pours himself a generous glass.

Gin sits impassively, watching him swirl the amber liquid in the heavy-bottomed glass.

After a large sip, he looks at her. "I was so stupid," he says. "I was trying to control things that weren't mine to control. Weren't even my business." He takes another swig and feels it burn his throat.

It is dark outside now. The rain has steadied to a regular rhythmic drumming on the roof.

"I think you were trying to protect Gabe too," says Gin, her voice low.

Michael puts his head in his hands at this. He feels a tremendous weariness settle on him. Ultimately, none of them, no one, not Gin, not Hannah, not Viv, and not even he, Michael, could protect Gabe from himself.

17. VIVIENNE

"Hello?" Viv is harassed. She balances the basket of laundry on one hip.

Nick's voice at once cheers and unnerves her. "Usual time tomorrow?"

She can hear the grin in his voice. The walk on the beach has become somewhat of a routine for them. Every second weekend for the past few months, he had fetched her precisely at nine on the Saturday, his dog Manyanga barking excitedly in the back of his car. Viv had become almost eager to pack the girls off to Jonnie's expensive cream house in the rich area of Constantia. It was ironic, she thought, that her ex-husband, the Indian doctor, should now be living in the formerly whites-only suburb, while she had stayed in the relatively mixed area of Kenwyn, where the houses were smaller and more compact, and the neighbours poorer. But this weekend is different.

"Is anything wrong?" Nick has heard her hesitation.

She tells him. This weekend the girls are staying at home; Jonnie is at a medical conference in Johannesburg. Initially he had said he might take the girls with him, but as the date approached, Viv had wearily heard his reluctance grow along with his excuses.

"Does it matter?" asks Nick, and she is momentarily stumped.

She has not yet mentioned Nick to her daughters. While Jonnie's every girlfriend, however temporary, had been reported back to her in detail by Kayleigh, Viv had stayed resolutely single. Now, after all this time, she does not know how her children will react. But does it matter? Nick has challenged her. She could take the easy way out and say they cannot be left on their own when, in fact, there have been times she had been obliged to do so, in order to see her patients and make her calls. She had never given her address to her long list of dependants; some would not have hesitated to invade her privacy, others she would not want around her home. Abbie, at least, is old enough to be left on her own. Nick will know this also, she thinks. He waits in silence now while she deliberates.

Viv feels a form of release, a knot dissolving inside her.

She agrees to their ritual, already feeling the thick sand between her toes, tasting salt on her lips. Each time Nick had taken a different route, chosen a different beach. Winter has allowed them freedom from crowds, their only company the hardiest of surfers, tackling the cold Atlantic, or other walkers suitably garbed against the freezing wind. Manyanga had been let loose to run ahead of them, occasionally looping back to leap up excitedly at Nick, bark, and then gallop ahead again, stopping to sniff at rocks, and paw at scurrying crabs.

Phone down, Viv hoists the basket onto a chair, and goes through to where Abbie and Kayleigh lie sprawled in front of the television. It feels surreal to her, this confessional. She shakes the discomfort from her shoulders and clears her throat.

He is outside promptly at nine, his knock confident and loud. A policeman's knock, she thinks wryly, knowing she will not get to the door before her youngest. Kayleigh had taken the news somewhat better than Abbie, who had stared steadfastly ahead at the television programme after Viv had told them about Nick.

Sure enough, it is Kayleigh who is swinging open the heavy door as Viv walks down the stairs, impudently curious of her mother's *hot date*, as she had termed it.

Bright sunshine streams into the hall.

"Well, Kayleigh, invite Mr Retief in!" Viv drops the Detective from his title. Her daughter is suddenly coy. "Nick," smiles Viv, moving to open the door wider. "Would you like to come in and meet my children?"

Kayleigh wrinkles a face at her mother. She hates being called a child.

Nick steps inside. The sun, as he does so, turns his dark-blond hair to gold. He looks fresh – and young – she thinks ruefully. The seven-year age gap between them has not bothered her until this moment. Now she is mindful of her teenage daughters. Will he think her too old?

Nick is smiling at Kayleigh, who has recovered her composure enough to ask him what he does.

"Kayleigh, honestly, that's quite rude," chides Viv, but gently.

Her daughter rolls her dark eyes at her, and flicks her jet-black locks behind her ears. Kayleigh looks very much like Jonnie. Inevitable that she should inherit his coffee-coloured skin, but her eyes, the shape of her face, and her expressions are also all her father's.

"That's okay," says Nick. "I'm a policeman," he answers.

Viv shudders involuntarily. For her, the word has remained tainted. But it is lost on her daughter, growing up in a different land, and for this Viv feels thankful.

"Would you like some tea?" asks Kayleigh, emboldened by his friendliness.

He looks briefly at Viv, the question formed.

She shakes her head quickly.

"Another time, perhaps. I've had a cup not long ago, but thank you." He sounds polite.

Kayleigh giggles. They have not moved from the entrance hall. Viv picks up her bag from the table and checks inside for her keys. They are about to leave when Abbie appears. She skulks in shadow. Her eldest daughter, normally so graceful, looks sullen.

"Abbie," says Viv, too loudly, "this is Mr Retief."

Nick looks up. Viv sees surprise flick cross his face, and wonders why. He knows some of her life's details now, if not the finer, rawer points. He knows that her daughters have different fathers. She has told him that Abbie's father is dead, but not the manner of his death. He knows too that Jonnie is Indian, and a neurologist at the children's hospital in Rondebosch, but the details of her divorce she has not found reason to divulge. On those slow and pleasant walks, she had felt unwilling to delve into sadness.

She wishes her daughter had made more of an effort to look her beautiful self. Abbie has her father's eyes, blue and clear, that darken with emotion. And her hair curls wild and unruly, as did Gabe's. But it is fairer, almost blonde in the sun. She stands, stooped, her hair hanging messily in front of her eyes and her slim figure hidden by a baggy jumper.

"Hello, you must be Abigail," says Nick, in that stiff manner of his.

It strikes Viv that Nick feels awkward, that he hides a residual shyness.

Abbie nods, mumbles something barely intelligible; she rakes a hand through her hair in an ineffectual attempt to push its tangles aside.

"Oh, well, we'll be off then, girls." Viv's voice sounds false to herself. "I have my cellphone. Be good. Bye." She moves towards the still-open door.

In the early morning shadow, the mountain's surface looks dark and cold, thin mist haunts its crevices. Nick says goodbye to the girls and follows her out. Kayleigh holds the door open, watching them walk down the cement path.

"Mom!"

Viv half-turns. It was Kayleigh who called, but it is Abbie who has exited behind them. Nick opens the gate, hooks it, and moves towards the car. Manyanga's head lolls out the window. The dog barks with joy at Nick's return.

"What is it, sweetie?" asks Viv, walking back to where her eldest daughter has stopped, her shoulders curved forward, and her finger in her mouth as she bites on a nail.

"Nothing, Mom," she says.

Viv smiles at her, reaches out to push her daughter's hair behind one shoulder.

Abbie suddenly reaches her arms around Viv and hugs her quickly. "Have a nice time, Mom," she whispers. She glances quickly at Retief, her eyes narrowed, and then turns and hurries back into the house.

"*Ja*," shouts Kayleigh, not to be outdone, "have a *lekker jol*, Ma! Bye!" The heavy door swings shut.

Viv apologises to Nick for her daughter's behaviour as she buckles her belt. Manyanga's hot breath is on her neck as the dog strains to greet her.

"No need," he says, and orders his dog to sit down. Manyanga obeys, shifting her bulk onto the back seat, her huge brown eyes meek with chastisement.

They drive out to Hout Bay, the curve of beach sheltered by the mountains on one side, and by the peak of the Sentinel on the other. It is suitably named, sitting strong and silent, steadfastly staring out to sea. Sunlight blurs behind its buttressed bulk, waiting for the lengthening of day that will allow it to slip past the watch of the motionless sentry and seep along the shore.

"She must look like her dad," says Nick, once they are on the sand. He throws a stick for Manyanga, who speeds away from them, her paws spitting sand.

"Yes," says Viv, "she does." People always take an interest in Kayleigh, her brown skin. These years on, after the ostensible end of apartheid, a mixed-race child with a white mother is still an oddity to some. It is Kayleigh's age more than anything; at times Viv can almost see their small minds calculating the year of her daughter's conception. She wonders what Nick is thinking. Manyanga runs back to them, eagerly drops the wet stick in front of Nick, pants in anticipation. He picks it up and hurls it ahead of them on the deserted beach. They are still in the shadow of the mountains. The dog runs off again, her fur rippling.

"*Ja*," he says, brushing sand from his hand, "it's quite uncanny."

Viv sighs with barely concealed irritation. Surely it is not that big a deal to him? He hadn't seemed bothered by the fact she had been married to an Indian. Once it was legal to do so, of course. Apartheid laws had taken time to catch up with each other's demise; at one point it was legal to marry outside one's race, but still illegal to live together in the same area. Viv smiles grimly at the stupidity; she had been officially re-classified as Indian.

Nick pulls something from his pocket. "This was in Doctor Gold's – Simon's – wallet," he says, handing her a small photograph.

Viv gasps softly as she looks at the aged, faded picture. It is a photograph of a young woman, squinting slightly into sunlight, her mouth slightly open as if saying something to the photographer. She stands on a beach, with her hand raised to sweep her long blonde hair away from her face, blown as it is about in the invisible wind.

Viv stares at the face. Now she understands.

Nick was talking about Abbie.

Her daughter, Gabe's daughter, is the image of the girl in the photo, the photo of Gin.

18. VIVIENNE

The sea is stone-grey in the winter light. White waves whip to choppy peaks and then curl to the soft swish of their demise. Long licks of water eddy up the beach; sighing as they are pulled back along the smooth sand, swept back into the depths. Viv gazes out to where the light shifts pink and gold upon the slow swell of ocean beyond the Sentinel. She fingers the edge of the photo. Manyanga has returned, panting, with her stick-offering to Nick, who throws it again into the strong wind. It arcs and slices, bouncing and cartwheeling haphazardly further up the beach. The dog barks after it.

"Why are you giving this to me? To give to Gin?" she asks, finally. "Shouldn't it stay with his wallet? Isn't it evidence of sorts?"

His mouth twitches slightly in a corner, as if amused. But his voice is serious when he answers. "Well, Gold's personal belongings were all returned to his family last week. I saw no reason for them to have this."

Viv draws her thin jersey around her shoulders. Nick seems to have a singular ability to tug at her emotions. She swallows. "That was kind of you." He looks at her and she cannot read the expression in his eyes. They are as grey as the sea, and as dark. It makes her feel uncomfortable and she is not sure why. "Is the insurance all sorted out now?" asks Viv, looking away from him again. She is aware she is making conversation.

He does not answer immediately. "Only that one claim is outstanding."

"Still?" Viv's voice lifts in surprise. "You mean, they won't pay out because they still doubt it was an accident?" Viv crosses her arms. The wind has picked up; her hair billows out about her face.

Nick shakes his head, then says, "Why do you ask?"

She is taken aback by his tone. As if he is questioning her. She looks directly at him. "What do you mean? You told me about it. Why shouldn't I ask?" Abrasively. How dare he question her? He was the one to produce the photograph, talk again of Gin and Simon. The picture must have been taken not long before Gabe's funeral, she figures.

The funeral, the first time she had seen Gin. Her face had seemed a pale reflection of Gabe's, Viv had thought impassively at the time. And Simon, a dark blur amidst the others at the church hall. She tries to remember his face, but she can only see him older, the features of the man who had helped her so many years later. That awful day of the funeral, all she could think about was holding herself upright, and trying not to vomit with morning sickness. And grief. And no one to help her. Gabe's mother clawing at her arm, presenting her to everyone like some sort of bizarre consolation.

Gin had disappeared from the hall, followed shortly afterwards by Simon. And in the corner, watching them leave, Viv had seen Hannah. Simon's cousin. Hannah's face remained the only vivid imprint of that day, framed by her mahogany hair cascading in curls down her back. Even as the image forms, Viv feels a wave of nausea pass over her. She stops, inhales deeply.

Nick comes up to stand beside her. "Vivienne," he asks, his voice low, "why didn't you tell me Gin was Abbie's aunt? Why didn't you tell me about Gabriel McMann?"

Gabe's name sounds odd on his tongue. She finds herself resentful of him saying it, but the question confuses her. "Why should it make a difference? Does it matter how I know Gin? So, she's Abbie's aunt. So, Gin is – was – Gabe's…" she finds herself stumbling over his name, and repeats it, mockingly, the way he had said it, "Gabriel McMann's twin sister." Acid rises. "And Abbie looks like her. Hardly surprising, then. So what?" She says this sharply, angry with him, for saying Gabe's name, for bringing him between them again.

Since that night he left her at her front door, Nick has made no attempt to touch her, to kiss her. She shivers.

Nick is pulling off his jumper. He holds it out to her. Viv shakes her head, but he takes her hand and puts the still-warm jersey in it.

"Put it on before you freeze. Come on," he says.

She relents, lets him help her pull the thick wool of it over her head. She shivers again. It falls too long over her hands but she tucks the ends of it around her frozen fingers. "What about you?" she asks, her teeth chattering now. She makes a conscious effort to relax into the warmth of the jumper.

He smiles at her. He is wearing a thick long-sleeved shirt. "I came prepared."

Manyanga has been gone for some time. Nick whistles, and the dog emerges from behind a rack of rock. She races up to them, her snout sandy, and bounds around them in circles. Nick grabs her collar, and brings the dog to heel.

He turns back to Viv, "Come, it's cold, let's get some tea or coffee." They walk slowly back along the length of beach to the dockside where he has parked his car.

"I mean it, Nick," she says, her voice as icy as the wind, "why does it make a difference?"

He sighs, as if he regrets the conversation. Instead he stops walking, answering with another question, look at her directly, asks evenly, "Vivienne, why didn't you tell me how Gabriel died?"

She blinks, looks away from him. The nausea has returned.

Nothing was ever going to be the same again. Gabe was dead. They had caught him, not the Army, but the South African Police, picked him up off the street like a thief, or a murderer. Slammed him into a cell. No contact with his family, and certainly none with her, or Michael.

And Gabe had hanged himself with his own belt.

Viv closes her eyes. She feels a kind of revulsion at herself, for being able to be here, to be walking on the beach with Nick.

Gabe's face swims before her; Gabe laughing, that deep honest laugh of his, running his hand through his dark hair, but as he pulls his hand away, his face changes, mutates. And it is Hannah's face that stares at her, dark blue eyes boring into her.

Viv's eyes flick open. Nick is looking at her. He looks sad.

"There are two reasons why the insurance company is making such a fuss. Firstly, the policy I told you about… Simon Gold took it out about twenty years ago and never stopped paying it, so it's a huge amount. So of course they are being careful about it, about the circumstances surrounding his death. And secondly, the beneficiary of the policy…" He rubs his forehead, leaving small grains of sand at his temple, "you see, Vivienne, the beneficiary is Gin."

Viv brings a hand to her mouth. "So of course – oh, Nick, that's so silly! What? They're suspicious of Gin? Because she was with him?" She laughs, shortly, harshly. "I guarantee you, Nick, Gin doesn't even know about any stupid policy, and if she did, she probably wouldn't care. She loved Simon Gold."

She looks at him, relieved that the tension between them has diminished. She thinks perhaps she ought to tell him about Gin's pregnancy.

"*Ja*, I know that. And yes, it appears she didn't know about the policy."

"But then why are they still suspicious? It's so ridiculous, Gin was in the car herself, for goodness' sake. She was *hurt* herself, remember!" Viv is incredulous.

She feels the tension between them return, and she feels sick again.

Nick looks out toward the sea. A ship glides on the horizon, a silver mirage.

"Because, Vivienne, you see, it's not that they think she was trying to murder Simon for money, or anything that melodramatic. But they do think there's something odd about it all. That maybe Simon was suicidal, or that Gin caused the accident, you know, grabbed the wheel or something."

"But the other car…" stammers Viv, uncomprehending, "you've got those witnesses…"

"*Ja*," Nick turns back to her. "But there has been some suggestion that their car, the one Gin and Simon Gold were in, may have been the one to swerve. They may have caused the accident."

Viv is shaking her head. "I don't believe it."

"Witnesses get things wrong, you know, mixed up," says Nick. He sounds as if he is trying not to distress her. "You see, Vivienne, it's to do with Gin's family. The insurance company investigators think she's unstable."

Viv is sure she is going to vomit now.

Nick pauses. Then he says, and his voice is hard, "They think she may have been trying to kill herself. Like her brother. Like Gabriel."

19. GIN

Simon is saying something to her. His mouth opens to form words but instead the side of his mouth spills out red. She sees the blood run out of his mouth but it runs upwards, trickles up towards his open eyes. His eyes that are open but that can no longer see. Yet still his mouth moves. Slowly, he speaks, but in a strange voice, a voice not his, but Michael's.

"Gin, it's almost seven," repeats Michael gently, "wake up."

She stirs, opens her eyes. He puts a hot mug of tea on her bedside table. Light silts onto the pine floor beneath the window. Michael sits down on the edge of the bed, cradling his own mug in his hands.

She sits up, pulling the pillow behind her head. "Morning," she says, and hears her own voice croak with sleep.

"Morning," he says, "sorry to wake you, but we've got the scan later."

Gin nods, glad he has woken her from yet another nightmare. Since Michael arrived, she has slept later, deeper. But the nightmares have not ceased. Every night she sees Simon's dead face, his hollow eyes, his hand reaching out to her. On the worst nights, his hand becomes a claw, tearing at her, into her even. As if he is trying to reach his unborn child. Some nights she feels him breathing next to her, and hears him whisper: *I've something to tell you.* But she wakes to find the bed empty, the house cold and dark and silent. In other dreams her world spins and all she is left with is the imprint, over and over. *1989. 1989.*

She takes a sip of her tea. It is sweet. Michael has put sugar in it.

She looks at him. He knows she does not take sugar. "Are you trying to fatten me up?" she asks, stretching her hand out to him, and he takes it. His hand is warm from the heat of his mug.

He grins at her. "It's honey, a super-food. It's good for you. Come on Gin, let's get going."

They wait for over an hour to be seen. Michael is infinitely patient, thinks Gin, although she herself has become inured to waiting. There is something soothing about sitting on the hard-backed chair and watching the hospital move around them. She finds it comforting, and familiar, the bustling business that is England's National Health Service. She had spent her life in hospitals, around them. With her father, or Jacob. With Jonnie.

And with Simon.

Simon had taken a locum in the Okavango, during the long summer months of her university vacation. An outpost, along the Caprivi strip, that jutted into the heart of Africa, to the point where four countries met. How she had loved the sunsets then, the burning orb sinking beyond the river, bringing the blackest nights she had ever experienced, a luminescence of stars she had not seen since. Given the dearth of doctors, they had travelled between ten mission hospitals. While he examined and treated, easing the burden of the Finnish nuns who ran the clinics, Gin had sorted, labelled, unpacked, and re-arranged their medical supplies and medicines. Pitifully short-supplied, they used all they had, whether expired or not. They had driven close to the border. So close, mere hours away from Victoria Falls, they had tried to cross into Zimbabwe. But without their passports, they had failed to impress the guards.

That night, lying hot beneath mosquito nets, a sheen of sweat between their bodies, she could smell the paraffin of the lamps and hear the cicadas, the constant shrill backdrop of the African night. Then the rain had started, the hard, warm rain with the biggest drops she had ever seen.

Her name is called, and she clutches at Michael's arm. Wordlessly, without hesitation, he stands, walks with her into the bland, square room. The doctor who sees them talks to them as if they are a couple, as if Michael is the father of her child. To Gin it is a relief. The scanner, cold with gel, moves heavily over her stomach. She closes her eyes briefly. Fragments of her dream wash over her. It has summoned odd feelings, which she cannot name, and they swirl about her like a mist.

Simon's face looks back at her, he mouths the same meaningless words, "Nineteen eighty-nine."

Her eyes flit open. The consultant is pointing at an image on the screen, talking to Michael, who nods. If they notice her lack of interest, they do not comment.

They drive back slowly through the traffic. A horn blares. People crowd the pavements. The heat is oppressive.

"Well, that was good news, hey, Gin?" says Michael, as they wait at red traffic lights.

She looks blankly at him.

"The scan, I mean. You know, all fine."

Gin watches a bicycle fly through the red light, swerving around a pedestrian.

"What do you want for lunch?" asks Michael.

"Pineapple," she replies immediately and does not know where the answer comes from.

He smiles at her. "That's better. I felt you going off somewhere while we were in there."

Nineteen eighty-nine.

Gin looks out the window. Roadworks clog the street. A bus negotiates the narrow middle pathway, while another idles, waiting for it to pass. She stares out at the shimmering coal tarmac. Will his image never fade? She does not know what his words mean, if anything, although the thought that he is trying to tell her something persists.

"After lunch," says Michael, as they finally pass the bottleneck, "we'll tackle those boxes." He speeds up slightly to catch the amber of the next traffic light, turning right to take the less congested route back, over the bridge onto the highway that junctions with Harrow Road.

Gin looks into office buildings made of glass, sees people working at their desks. Below stretches the canal, straight, deep, and dark.

"Nineteen eighty-nine," says Simon's dead mouth to her, bleeding upwards.

Gin shivers despite the heat.

20. MICHAEL

Michael grills steak and serves it with her requested pineapple, but he notices that Gin leaves the meat untouched and eats only the fruit. They eat in the kitchen. He drinks two glasses of chilled white wine and watches her pick at her plate. It is mid-afternoon before they can face the descent to the basement, to where box upon box is stacked, possessions from their old flat. Michael brings the open bottle of wine down with him. Gin sits cross-legged on the one piece of furniture, an old Persian rug, skinny and bleached with wear. The air is blissfully cold compared to the muggy cloak of summer outside.

Michael starts unstacking the boxes. He lays them neatly out side-by-side on the cold cement. He stands back when they are all at floor level, dusts his hands off.

"You've hardly unpacked anything. How long has this stuff been packed up anyhow?"

Gin bites her lip. "Ages. The removal company did it all. I threw in a few things. It was all such a rush. I just kept stuff out I needed most. You know, clothes and cups and plates and things." She sounds apologetic. "I just couldn't face it."

He makes light of it. "Well, at least it'll fill up this big empty house." He pauses. "Right, you start that end and I'll start this end. Shall we make piles of stuff for where it's to go? Lounge, kitchen, linen, that sort of thing? Maybe once the first few boxes are emptied, we can label them and then put the stuff in there to take upstairs. And maybe a box for the charity store, things we don't need." He finds himself suddenly invigorated by the task.

They sift through, sorting. It is fairly tedious and routine until Michael opens a box that contains a CD player and cases of compact discs. He plugs the player into the wall socket, peers at the discs, pulls one out and holds it aloft, shaking it at her. "Ha! I knew you had my *Peto* CD." He turns it over to read the back.

"Rubbish! That's mine!" she laughs, grabbing it from him with dusty hands. "See… this is mine, it's got a scratch right here, across the spine."

He snatches it back from her, grinning. "You didn't even know it was here!" He sticks the CD in the player and African drumbeats echo through the room. He sings along lustily to the chorus, watching her out of the corner of his eye, glad to hear her humming along softly. Progress, he thinks.

They break for cheese sandwiches and tea upstairs in the kitchen. He feels almost agoraphobic after the closed atmosphere in the basement. The late afternoon has brought a breeze.

"We're almost there, Gin," he notes, as they return downstairs. He slots more African music onto the player. "And now, of course, I've found all my missing CDs…"

Gin thumps him on the arm playfully and pulls another box towards her. The cardboard side of it rips as she does. Books, letters, and jewellery spill out onto the floor.

"Ah," he says, full of mock gravity, "and those will be my missing books."

Gin is picking up scattered pieces of jewellery. "And I suppose these are your missing earrings?" she flashes back, then stops. She makes a small sound.

"What is it? Have you cut yourself?"

Gin cradles one hand in the other, staring down at her hands. She does not look up. Michael starts to move over to her, but she suddenly extends her hand. "I'm okay," she says, but her voice is thick, "Can you put this with the rest of the stuff for the charity shop?"

She turns from him and picks up a fallen book. Michael looks down at what she has given him. Glinting blue through the gloom of the basement is a sapphire ring.

"Gin," he asks, after a pause to examine its brightness, "this is beautiful. Are you sure you want to get rid of it?" He turns from her, holds it closer to the light in the room. Facets fire back at him. "It's probably worth something." There is a brownish mark on the silver. "Oh, hang on, maybe not… it's rusted, I think, so it can't be silver," he says. He scratches at it and the mark crumbles away beneath his nail. He examines the residue and says, pondering. "No, I'm not sure if it's rust. Where did you get it?"

Gin has not made a sound. Michael turns back to where she had busied herself with another box. What he sees horrifies him. Gin is bent double over herself, clutching at her stomach.

21. VIVIENNE

"Van Hunks and the Devil are at it again," says Nick. He makes a vague gesture out of the car window.

Viv is jolted out of a meditative lethargy. They have been driving along Rhodes Drive, alongside the craggy slopes of the eastern side of the mountain, and he is driving to where the road skirts Kirstenbosch gardens. She has been thinking of the work and care it must have taken, to plant almost every indigenous tree, bush, and flower there, and nurture it, make it thrive, in the Cape's Mediterranean climate. From acacias to watsonia, the long-stemmed *kanolpypie* as it is known. She wonders idly if there is a plant starting with the last letter of the alphabet. There must be, she thinks, surely Nick will know.

"You've no idea what I'm talking about, have you?" he laughs.

She shakes her head, embarrassment tinged with relief at his amusement. Jonnie would not have been so nonchalant about her inattention.

Nick gestures up at the mountain again. "You must know the legend," he queries, "about where the tablecloth comes from?"

Viv looks up at the thick roll of mist that is sweeping over the peaks. They are alongside Newlands forest now, heading out onto the highway that will take them eventually to Simonstown. Or, depending on their mood and the turn of the road, to Fishhoek. Manyanga has been banished to neighbours today, but she knows it is actually a treat for the dog, the company of others, and a long run in the park. Nick is at ease in the car, a confident driver, and she sits back. She spends so much time driving in the car herself, to patients, and endlessly fetching or ferrying the girls.

"I thought it was from the Cape Doctor," she says, "I thought it brought the tablecloth along with the gales and drizzle." She does not add that the strong south-easter also brings for her a gloominess that can last for days.

Nick tells her the story of a Dutch pirate, approached by a stranger while sitting on *Duiwelspiek*. He gives Devil's Peak, part of the mountainous backdrop to the city, its Afrikaans name. Viv wonders if he feels more Afrikaans than English. A boasting match ensued between the two, he continues, ending in a smoking contest.

"What Van Hunks didn't know was that the stranger was the Devil himself, come to see who was walking on his peak. Van Hunks won, and the Devil in a rage had him swallowed up in the smoke, and now when the cloud comes, people say they are smoking again," he finishes, smiling.

Viv laughs. "I've never heard that one," she says, musing once more at this man beside her. More and more he reminds her of Gabe. He would also tell her stories like this, she remembers. How Gabe would have loved such a yarn.

"Did he like stuff like that, then?" asks Nick, with a tender tone she has not heard before.

She blinks at him in surprise. "What?"

"Gabe." He snatches a look at her. "You said he would have liked that."

She had spoken aloud without realising it, without even hearing herself. What else would she give away to this man?

But she gathers her thoughts, and says quickly, evenly, "Yes, he did. He used to tell me stories. Myths and legends that his own father had told him. King Arthur, the Greek myths." She pauses, thinking of Gabe's favourite. The quest for the Grail. And only Galahad up to the task. Gabe had written his thesis on it. At the time, struggling with the inequality of the South African social justice system, Viv had thought it irrelevant, self-indulgent even. Now, she finds herself merely thankful Gabe had studied what he had loved, in what little time he had been given. "He liked African stories too," she says, finally. "Did your father tell you them?"

"My mother," he replies, checking his rear-view mirror and signalling to change lanes. "She was a teacher."

"Oh. Does she still teach, or is she retired now?"

"She's dead."

His revelation is unsettling. For the first time in Nick's company, she feels awkward. She supposes she ought to keep quiet, but says instead, "I'm sorry. And your dad?"

"He's dead too." Nick checks his rear-view again and speeds up slightly. She wonders why he has not mentioned this before.

"Oh," she states, simply. This time she stays quiet, but thinks they cannot have been that old.

Again she feels his swift gaze.

"It's okay," he reassures her, "it was a long time ago. They were killed in a car crash just before I decided to come to Cape Town. An Easter weekend pile-up outside Dutywa."

She puts a hand on his arm, briefly. He flashes her a quick smile. As she takes her hand away, the feel of his warm skin lingers on her fingertips. Viv suppresses an urge to touch them to her lips, to touch the taste of him to her mouth.

"Did he ever tell you the one about the Guardians of the Earth?" asks Nick.

"Who? Gabe?" Viv looks out the window, half-expecting to see Gabe's reflection staring back at her. She hardly ever speaks of him like this. You left me, she accuses him silently. You left me on my own to raise your daughter. Your daughter who has your eyes and your thoughts.

"No, he didn't," she says wistfully. It is Nick's reflection in the window that turns towards her again momentarily, then back to the road.

"African legend has it that when the earth was formed, the Earth goddess Djobela turned four giants into stone, into mountains, to look after the four ends of the earth and protect them from the sea dragon. And the greatest of these was the one in the South. Table Mountain."

"What are the others?" she asks, curious now.

"I don't know," he grins, "it's a local legend, after all. But that's the old name for Table Mountain. *Umlindi Waseningizimu.*"

She looks at him questioningly.

Nick slows, "Fancy a tea?"

She nods, and he puts on his indicator, pulls the car off into a broad sweep of gravel that is a parking lot outside a café she had hardly noticed. It is set back from the road, surrounded by the forest. The roof is wooden, and overhangs a wide verandah.

The rain in the air is palpable as they get out of the car.

"What does it mean, the name?" asks Viv.

Nick looks up at the mountain, far behind them now. Viv's eyes follow. It is almost covered in the smoky swathes.

"The Watcher," he says.

His eyes are dark as he turns to her, and to Viv something ominous sounds in his tone. Involuntarily she takes a step back from the car, from him.

"The Watcher," he repeats slowly. "The Watcher in the South."

22. VIVIENNE

When they are seated at a table inside the café she asks him to name a plant starting with a 'z'. The place is brightly lit, with a counter selling sweets and crisps. The table is covered with a red-and-white-checked vinyl tablecloth. On top stand salt and pepper shakers, a ribbed glass container of sugar, and a plastic red tomato filled, Viv presumes, with tomato sauce. Aside from an auburn-haired woman at the counter, they are alone.

Nick shows no surprise at her question, but his look is intent. "*Ja*," he answers after a moment's pause, "*Zantedeschia*."

Her look is questioning.

"The lily," he explains.

A young woman emerges from a door behind the counter. There is no exchange between her and the woman at the counter. She takes their order of two coffees with downcast eyes.

"What makes you ask?" he smiles at her, when the young woman has returned to the kitchen.

Viv shakes her head dismissively. "Just wondering."

Rain splats heavily at the window.

"Not good weather for walking on the beach," notes Nick.

Viv asks if they can just carry on driving. That is, if he doesn't mind. She remembers her daydreams of driving up Africa, Cape to Cairo. At one stage she had even managed to persuade Gin to join her. An impossible adventure, given their situation and the travelling restrictions on South Africans in an Africa understandably hostile to the Nationalist government. They would have been turned back, at best. At worst, imprisoned or shot.

"No, I don't mind," Nick is saying. "I like driving, in fact."

The coffee arrives, steaming, in thick white mugs. Nick sips at his almost immediately. Then he reaches for the sugar container, pours a generous amount into his mug.

Viv toys with her own mug, pushes it back and forth between her hands. It is too hot to hold. "Do you like travelling?" she asks.

He sits back, regarding her. "*Ja*, I do."

She asks him which countries he has been to, determined to keep the conversation light and focused on him.

"Europe," he answers. "Some of the surrounding parts of southern Africa, the usual. And you?"

She takes a sip of the scalding drink. So much for keeping the conversation on him. "The same," she nods.

"Did you like it?"

She takes another sip, although the roof of her mouth burns with it. Europe. With Jonnie. It had been their happiest time. "Yes and no. I liked seeing the place. But I missed the girls." As she says the words, she curses herself for giving him reason to probe further. Again, she has let him in.

Inevitable that he asks, "You left them here then? When did you go? With your husband?"

She wishes suddenly, stupidly, that he'd said *ex-husband*. The way he said *husband* makes her feel as if she is still married. Attached. Out-of-bounds. But she cannot bring herself to correct him. It will sound petty.

When the girls had been old enough to be left with her mother, they'd taken the trip, she tells Nick. She does not tell him it had been her belated honeymoon, replacement for the one they hadn't had, in the euphoric glow after Jonnie's release, and before the awfulness had begun. She does not tell him, simply sips at her coffee, now cool enough to drink, and looks at the window splattered with rain. She realises that she holds an odd and abstract affection for Europe and the places they had been. Except for London. She had known through Michael that Gin was there. And Gin was lost to her at that time. Like Gabe, she had thought. And indeed, it had felt like a death, the loss of her friendship with Gin. Unexpected, and as yet ungrieved.

"Except for London what?" His voice interrupts her reverie.

Appalled, Viv realises she has spoken aloud again, telling him this. I have been too long alone, she thinks.

"I like Europe. But not London," she recovers.

He drains his mug. "Me neither. I just wanted to get home."

"Oh? You've never thought of leaving?"

This time she has surprised him. No, he says, why would he want to leave. How young he is. Leaving had been something so many of her generation spoke of or considered. Like Michael, to avoid the Army. Like Gin, to get away. She wishes Gabe had left, got away. At least he'd be alive. Would her life be different? Would they be together? The infinite unanswerables. She sighs heavily.

"What's the matter?" It is said with kindness.

She looks at him, feeling old and wearied. "Just the rain," she says as lightly as she can. "The mist makes me gloomy." She expects him to laugh. It sounds silly, trite, even to herself.

Instead, he reaches across the table, and takes her hand in his. He holds it lightly, his thumb rubbing her fingers. Her awkwardness rises, but she forces herself to let her hand rest in his for a while before she takes it away and reaches for her handbag and the calming comfort of a cigarette. She flicks the lighter, hoping Nick does not notice the slight trembling of her fingers. She can still feel where his hand touched hers. The imprint burns like the end of her cigarette.

They drive for several hours. Nick takes the slow route around the peninsula. He stops the car on the side of the road past Kommetjie, and they watch the rain pelt waves that are impervious to its assault.

Suddenly he says, "You've never seen my place. Would you like to? It's not far from here."

Viv expects him to turn off into the lower-lying area of Hout Bay, but instead Nick continues, heading up and along the curving tar that will take them back to the city. She is intrigued when he slows outside a Clifton townhouse, one of the compact flats cut into the side of the mountains that lie along the coast, the land plummeting to the churning sea. It is one of the most expensive areas, outside the city. Surely policemen do not earn enough to afford this, she thinks, but does not comment. He turns left into a short paved driveway and parks outside the closed garage door. The smell of the sea is strong as she gets out of the car, brine brought on the breeze. The rain seems spent now, a few errant drops splash her as she follows Nick to the front door. Viv feels slightly disappointed at the lack of any garden. Pebbles, shells, driftwood, lie scattered alongside the sandy flagstones that make up the path. And this from the man whose eyes shine when he talks of plants.

The view from the inside makes her breath catch. The short hallway leads into a large lounge. Huge glass windows on two sides of it look out over the precipitous landscape that drops to the ocean, and ahead is the endlessness of the icy Atlantic. The room is otherwise as she expected. Clean, comfortable. A large woven rug stops the stone floor looking cold, and on the one inside wall is an open fireplace, stacked with fuel. There are two neatly filled bookshelves on either side of the chimney breast. Beneath one of the windows is a couch, the leather worn and cracked into softness.

The rain has stopped, and Nick leads her through French doors on one side, out onto a steep path cutting through the bedrock that is the foundation of the house. It is then she sees the garden, planted between rocks. Red-hot pokers stand stiff and tall, arrowing towards the muted sky. Viv recognises the blue umbels of agapanthus on pillared stalks. In between is a graceful, arching plant, which looks too fragile for anything but a sheltered position. She turns to him in wonderment to find him watching her.

"Nick," she breathes, "this is spectacular. Did you plant this all yourself?"

He nods shyly, that troublesome lock of hair falling across his forehead. "The wind is the enemy of a seaside garden," he says, sounding to Viv like an antiquated reference book. He gestures towards the pokers. "The kniphofias are unbeatable for wind and salt tolerance. Do you know they grow on the most inhospitable coastlines?" He talks quickly, passionately. She wants to laugh at his boyish eagerness. "It's a formidable plant," he continues and then, as if realising she is amused, he ends, "from a gardener's point of view, that is."

He sounds embarrassed, so Viv nods seriously. "What's that flower?" she asks, pointing to the small delicate one she had noticed before.

"That's called the wand flower. Its name is *Dierama Pulcherrimum*. It likes a sunny position."

As do I, thinks Viv. She stretches her arms out, imploring the sky to clear, the sun to break through, luxuriating in the wild openness of this secret garden by the sea. When she puts her arms down, she turns to find him standing right behind her.

"A wild call, and a clear call," he says, his hand touches her arm.

Viv shifts away, hugs herself. "What do you mean?"

Nick leans back against the granite edge, folds his arms, "Masefield," he says, "his poem *Sea Fever*. That's what it says. It's how this place makes me feel. It's how home feels, why I could never leave this country."

Poetry as well as plants. Another legacy from his mother, the schoolteacher, perhaps. What else would he surprise her with, she wonders. "Are all these plants indigenous?"

He nods. "Yup. All African. Just like me," he grins.

This man is far too attractive.

She starts to move past him back to the French doors, feeling exposed, wishing she had not stretched with such abandon. "I hope the sun comes out now."

He follows her inside. "Shall I light the fire? If you're chilly." He does not wait for an answer.

Viv wanders around the room, still hugging herself, peering at the view, at his books. Then she moves to glance into a door off the hallway. The kitchen.

"Have a look around if you want," he says. "There's not much."

The kitchen is square and sparse, the one window looks out onto the front path. Across the hall is the bathroom. White, gleaming. Again there is a spartan feel to it. When she comes back to the lounge, the fire is lit, already spitting heat, and Nick is standing looking out over the sea. She knows the door to her left must be his bedroom and although she is curious to see it, she is reluctant to pry. She peeks in nonetheless, catches a glimpse of another fireplace, another laden bookshelf, a wide low wooden bed, but the full view of it is partly obscured by the door. She looks around to see him regarding her with what appears to be amusement, and walks purposefully into the lounge, stands in front of the fire and warms her hands. It is no good, she can still see his reflection in the rectangle of mirror that hangs above the fireplace. The frame is of whitewashed wood. It reminds her of driftwood.

Nick's eyes meet hers in the mirror. She watches him walk up, stand beside her, still holding her eyes. Her knees feel shaky.

She steps away from him. "Thank you Nick, your place is beautiful. But you know I really ought to go. I've so much work, and now that the rain's stopped I'd better get the girls' laundry done. Would you mind taking me back now?" Her words tumble out, the edges jagged. She keeps her eyes averted, reluctant to see his expression.

"No problem," he says evenly, "I've got to fetch Manyanga soon in any case."

He moves ahead to the hall, and Viv trails after him. Now it is said, she regrets having to leave the rapidly warming lounge with its cheery fire and view of the horizon. It would be nice to curl up with one of his many books, some tea, or wine even, music perhaps, and Nick's steady company. She cannot help but be disappointed at his apparent eagerness to leave, his easy acceptance of her withdrawal.

The weather clears as they drive back towards the city, sunlight shafting through cloud. Nick does not say much, and Viv herself is quiet, regretting the loss of their regular walk. He takes the flyover that skirts the edges of the city centre. The mountain stands with only a brushstroke of mist swept across it. When he reaches her house, he does not turn off the ignition as he usually does, but lets the car idle.

"See you," she says, jumping out quickly, not wanting to detain him. She does not hear his reply, if indeed there is one. Forcing herself to walk slowly up the path, she listens for the sound of his car pulling away. Only when she is at the front door does she hear him leave. She pushes it open and does not look back.

23. MICHAEL

He cannot sleep. Michael paces the house. It feels empty without Gin. He had not missed the consultant's emphasis. Physically, he had said, pausing, Gin was fine. He wanted her kept in for a few days, he said. Michael stayed as long as possible, watching her slip in and out of sleep. He found the atmosphere of the aged ward oppressive, tiled with its malachite and maroon Victorian tiles. Gin lay sapped of colour, her hair spread limply across the starched pillow with its blue stitching proclaiming it property of the National Health Service. He had brought her more of the pineapple she seemed to crave but, unable eventually to avoid the nurses, who were preparing for the night shift and impatient to empty the ward of visitors, he had left.

Two whiskies and an unread chapter later, he is still awake. Restless. On a whim, he decides on a walk. He pauses at the gate of the house, inhaling jasmine. He lights a cigarette and turns right. The streets are still wet from the evening rain. Cobalt puddles shine up at him. Michael smokes as he walks. When he first came to London, he would often walk alone at night. Nights like this, walking the calm streets, so different to their daytime façade.

He had seen Gin and Viv at their home in Cape Town before he left. In many ways it would have been easier not to say goodbye. Sitting at their table with the door open to the late December heat, he had wished he could stay. Wished the peace of the day would envelop the land, and let him live his life out endlessly beneath the mountain. He had envied them their lives, unfettered by conscription, unfettered by the looming choice to stay or go. But he was being unfair. Both women were scarred by Gabe's death. He saw it in Gin's eyes, sometimes when she looked at Viv, and especially when she laughed. She would cut it short, as if by laughing she betrayed her dead brother. And looking at Viv, Michael's heart had ached. Her hands moved constantly, lighting cigarette after cigarette. At night, after many glasses of wine, she stilled somewhat, and finally her eyelids would fall heavily over her beautiful eyes. Her eyes that earlier had darted, flicked, searched back and forth, as if by moving they could outrun the pain.

He lingers near the tube at Notting Hill Gate. A night bus, empty, swishes by. Michael flicks ash into the gutter and turns left down Pembridge Gardens. The trees seem taller at night. Looking up, he notes the insomniac lights in the students' residence. He stops to gaze at the residential building opposite, the place he had found lodgings when he first came to London. He was still living there when Gin had arrived six months later.

He had been up since five. The night porter had nodded wordlessly at him as he left. A friend of a friend of an acquaintance had helped him find the place. The network of the dispossessed, the new diaspora of disillusioned young South Africans had kicked in. A number here, a contact there. It had been light already by the time he had walked the short distance up to the tube, and for Gin's sake he was glad she was arriving in the summer. England's winter had been a shock almost systemic. The dark mornings, the cold unbanished by any amount of heating. Having left the heat of home, of summer's height in the opposite hemisphere, it had added to his sense of alienation, misbelonging. When Gin had called so unexpectedly, said she was coming, his spirits soared. She had told him some of what had happened, a truncated version, he sensed, and while for her sake and for Viv's this had saddened him, for selfish reasons he didn't care.

A breeze rises, sprinkles leftover rain from plane trees as he bears left again. He had thought to merely walk the block as he smoked and return to the house, but now he has a taste for the night. The moon is a waxing ovoid above. Hands in his pockets, he crosses Pembridge Road, heads up past the elegant houses of the rich. He comes to the top of Portobello Road. Deserted, but still quivering with the resonance of its day. As he walks along Kensington Park Gardens, the width of it seems almost exhilarating after the narrow lanes lined by tall houses. He reaches the sandstone spire of St John's, its lawns sooty in the streetlight, the yellow forsythia hedge greyed. Cars filter past him. There's always traffic on the Grove, he thinks. He stops to sit on the bench in front of the church, lights another cigarette. He loves this view. To either side of the road, the stone pavements and high houses slope down the hill. The road looks like a lit runway. Traffic lights change soundlessly at an empty junction. A black cab passes, a lone passenger in the back. He has met no one on the street so far, but out of the shadows to his right, someone approaches. He watches as a woman walks up to him. She is dressed entirely in black. Black jacket, black skirt, black tights, black boots.

"Got a light?"

Michael is surprised at the contact, even more surprised at her voice. It is deep, accented, but he cannot place its origin. He reaches into his pocket, pulls out his lighter. She is holding no cigarette, he realises, so he offers her one from his packet. The woman takes one, leans down to him. Blonde hair falls across her face as she does so. Sultry eyes flick over him. Her hand touches his lightly as he holds the flame for her. She stands back, draws on her cigarette, looks at him. Michael waits.

"Do you want to go for a drink?" she asks. Her voice is coated with smoke.

He considers for a moment, expecting Kristina's image, the guilt. Instead it is Gin who comes to mind, her sleeping figure, soft hair falling across her forehead.

People were wheeling their way out through the double steel doors. He glimpsed luggage labels from Johannesburg, clues of trips to Africa. He was conscious of his heart taken to thumping against his ribs; his hands felt clammy. Soon Gin would walk through those doors, the image of her brother, blue eyes searching him out in a crowd held at bay by chrome bars. And when they at last found each other, others stared as he hugged her, this waif from home, this lost girl. Come from a place where he last remembered life exploding in his veins. He spun her around in delight. He hugged her so hard, her breath was pushed from her lungs. But she did not appear to care, because for her a long journey had ended. Because she seemed happy to see him again, and she was laughing. Laughing, and crying. As was he.

He shakes his head. "No, but thank you."

The woman smiles slightly, her shrug almost imperceptible. She walks on without another word, trailing smoke. He watches her until she disappears over the rise of road to his left, her blonde hair bleached under the streetlight. She does not look back.

He had forgotten the night creatures. People like him, roaming the murky streets, each for their own reason. Gin's arrival in London had changed that for him.

He is back on Ladbroke Road, almost at the house, when he decides to walk on, to find a late-night bar or club and get a drink. Something about the house bothers him when Gin is not there. He feels a darkness descend on it without her. He hopes she is sleeping, and peaceful.

The club is a subterranean mix of loud music and sweaty bodies, not the quiet sophistication he was after, but it is late and his options within walking distance are limited. Eventually he reaches the bar, slides thankfully into one of the slim barstools to one side of the counter. Here are the other nocturnals at play. He sits drinking white wine and watching them. It will not mix well with his earlier whiskies he reflects, but he can sleep late. As long as he gets to the hospital for visiting hours.

Something in a girl's demeanour attracts him. Something familiar, but it is fleeting, nebulous.

"Where are you from?" she asks. Lifting her glass, she gestures aimlessly with it around the room, as if asking rather, "What brought you here?"

She is so young. Michael has a sudden urge to confess all. To tell her about Gabe, about why he left Africa, where he has been, why he is here. About Gin, about Kristina even – *I have a wife* – about the roads that have brought him here, to this night, this bar. He even wants to tell her about the woman on the Grove, with whom, had he been so inclined, he might be drinking now, instead of here with her. The urge passes and in any case he suspects that she is not really listening, is, in fact, not at all interested in why he, Michael, is here. Perhaps it is the way she drinks her wine, just that bit too quickly. Or the absent look she has, the look of someone who is drinking to forget. Someone very much like himself. Perhaps she is on drugs, he thinks, from the slight shine to her eyes. He turns to the barman.

But she persists, leaning into him. "Buy me another," she breathes, insistent. Her breasts push at the yellow neckline of her dress, her ebony curls spill forward, and he cannot resist.

Her name is Cecile and she takes him back to her studio flat in Linden Gardens. It is on the top floor, small but unexpectedly neat. Immaculate even. Michael inspects her bookcase as she pours them more wine, red this time. It is a good Claret and again he finds himself surprised. She is studying, she says, with a measure of self-deprecation.

"What course?" he asks, though from the contents of the book-case he has surmised literature, history, philosophy – the usual, he thinks.

"Oh, the usual," Cecile laughs, "Literature, history, philosophy." She moves towards him, adds, "sex." Her hand tugs at his belt, "let me show you what a good student I am."

He thinks it so gauche as to be charming, and her giggle is infectious. He watches as she unbuckles his belt.

Only when he is walking back to the house, the night sky paling slowly into a muted dawn, does he reflect how he has made love to a girl half his age, merely because something in her eyes, perhaps in the way she flicked her hair, had reminded him of the only woman he had ever loved. The only woman he could never have.

24. MICHAEL

Gin has to spend two more nights in the hospital. She seems cheerful, if slightly frustrated, when he visits. He is pleased to see her face has more colour. Again he stays as long as he can, and sits and reads when she dozes off. The second night on his own in the house Michael manages to fall asleep in front of the television, waking before dawn, the lounge cold and his neck stiff from the chair. The third night, however, he finds himself walking the Grove again. Trying and failing to avoid the club, he returns to its curved counter, its oddly enticing interior. He knows he is hoping Cecile will be there. He sits at the bar, and orders drink after drink, searching the silhouetted figures for her raven hair, for her yellow dress – stupid, she will not be wearing it again, he admonishes himself – and yet still he looks. Once he thinks he sees her, leaving with a man, but he cannot be sure. He knows it is puerile, but he leaves soon after, walks to Linden Gardens, stares up at her flat. The light is on. Is she studying, or with the man? In the end, disgusted with himself, he walks home.

At the gate of the house, he stops, puts his hand in his pocket, in need of his cigarettes. Instead his hand folds around paper. Kristina's letter. Michael unfolds the envelope. It glows a sulphurous yellow in the streetlight.

He puts the unopened envelope on the table in the kitchen, reluctant still to read it. Kristina's rounded lettering has been marked by his pocket and his forgetfulness. He fingers the outside of it, trying to imagine what mood she wrote his name in, tries to decipher from her writing whether she was angry, bitter, resigned. Or simply past caring? Like himself. The thought weighs heavily on him. He knows he could live happily – at this he stops himself, grimacing – well, at least, less unhappily, if he were never to see Denmark again. He could let it slip away from his life without a backward glance. And his wife? Would she be so easily dismissed? He thinks of Cecile and knows the answer.

He leaves the letter and goes upstairs to shower. As he towels off, he wonders what his life would have been like if Gin had given him a different answer that day in the café so long ago.

Gin was staring blankly at him. For a moment Michael wondered whether she had heard him. But then she blinked, looked down at her cup, and took a big sip of coffee. Her eyes were huge as they looked at him over the rim of the mug.

"Michael," she said, eventually, "let me get this right. You want me to marry you?"

He knew he was asking her to make a huge decision, a huge commitment. If they married, he would gain her passport, her citizenship, her inalienable right to stay. Safe. Safe from any deportation. Safe forever from the reaches of the South African Army. Gin did not seem fazed by his seeming unromanticism. They both knew it was not a proposal of passion. Maybe she thought of Simon or Jonnie, of what could have been. In some ways, Michael hoped she would say no. If she did, it meant she had not given up, had not abandoned forever her high ideals. For a while, they both watched the traffic pass outside the café window. Big red buses ambled past. Now and then a black cab turned sharply, careered across lanes to irate horns. Then he looked at her. She smiled, and he smiled, and then they both laughed.

The noise in the café was loud, and her voice was quiet, but clear. "Michael. Darling. No. Never."

Michael tosses the towel on the bed. In a sudden moment, he envisages Gin old, her brow furrowed, her face lined by all the years. He looks in the mirror, rubs at his chin, regretting his decision not to shave. He imagines his own face, aged. He could ask her again, he realises. Somehow he knows if he does, and he tells her about growing old together, somehow she will succumb, say yes, and that would be that. The understanding would be based on the unencumbered companionship they find in each other. It had been like that when they were growing up, and at school. Then, for a while, it had disappeared. At university, she had lived a separate life with Simon. He had hardly seen her. Neither had Gabe. And so the two men had found themselves apart from Gin and Hannah. A lump forms in Michael's throat. He does not want to think about Gabe now. And especially not Hannah.

Michael sighs, smoothes back his still-wet hair. He had been granted leave to stay in Britain, political asylum. And eventually they had travelled, he and Gin. A month, trawling around Europe.

Tuesday, Barcelona. Gaudi's city. Even if, he thought, agreeing with Orwell, that the Sagrada was the most hideous thing he had ever seen, with its grotesque carvings, one couldn't deny the craft of the man. Every statue, spire, or building of his contorted with colour. They gave Michael vivid nightmares but Gin had revelled in it all, the seven hills, the pedestrianised Avenue de Gaudi with its many shops and cafés, its leftover history of civil war. Although she could not face the castle on Montjuic with its tales of torture, and the beggars distressed her. Too much like home, she said. And the weather hot and humid like Zululand. They even passed a hairdresser's called Durban. They walked the city a thousand times, and talked and talked. He knew, for all his wanderlust, the one place he wanted to go was home. The one place he could not travel to. It said so in his temporary British passport. Michael struggled with the most basic Catalan and Gin had teased him about being an Englishman abroad, which made him smile.

"The plight of the refugee," he said, with good humour.

"Don't give me that look, while you suck on that eternal cigarette."
She was playful.

He squinted at her under the relentless sun, happy.

And right then, right there, they had met Kristina, and her friend
Birgit. And they had moved on to Italy as a foursome. In Venice, aside
a stinking canal, Gin had announced she was heading back to London.
They had been standing at the bridge that led over to the Ghettare, the
original Jewish ghetto. It was a short walk to the train station and he'd
walked with her, his head and heart at odds.

He goes downstairs, stares at the table. The crumpled cream envelope rebukes him silently as he pours himself a whisky. He sips at the
strong liquid. Then he hooks a finger under the mangled flap and
pulls. It tears jaggedly. Extracting the folded contents, he is surprised
to find three folded sheets of paper inside. One is hand-written and
short, Kristina's writing, black ink showing through the thin film of
it. He is reluctant to read it. The other two are typed, official. His
first reaction is resentment. Resentful that his wife has opened his
mail, to send it on she must have read it. Michael opens the first
typed communiqué with one hand, the other picks up his whisky.
But as he starts to read, his hand stops mid-air.

The liquid trembles in the glass.

25. VIVIENNE

Viv turns the hot water tap on fully. The water coughs out. Her body aches from her day's work and she longs to soak in a tub of frivolous bubbles. It is not just a physical ache, she realises. Memories of Gabe had risen unbidden throughout the day, thoughts she normally held at bay with her busy schedule and her own perverse will. Perhaps it had been the route she had driven that day to Camps Bay. As she lipped over the rise of road, the sea had stretched out endlessly beyond. It was the colour of his eyes, when she had met him, before they had darkened to a stormier shade. She remembers the intensity of his gaze the night they had met, his eyes lit like blue smoke in the wood-dark students' bar. For a moment this morning her heart had lifted as she watched the rise and swell of ocean and she had slowed the car as much as she safely could. She thinks often of Gin's accident these days, mindful of the city's endless curves and pitfalls. Then her heart had wearied suddenly, the blue had sallowed, washing out like the tide. Blue no longer held any azure happiness for her, she had decided. Now it meant sadness – blue, blue days.

Viv sighs. The tub fills slowly, steam rises, misting the rectangle of mirror on the bathroom wall. She wipes absently at it and then stops, startled by the smudged circles beneath her eyes. Her pallor is pronounced, and she stares down at her body. She is thin, too thin, she thinks. Her hipbones jut out from her concave stomach and she feels almost insulted by their pronounced angularity. She traces the faded whitish stretchmarks that lace across her buttocks and her thighs, faded reminders of her two pregnancies. Her fingers move up, involuntarily finding the slight scar from her Caesarean. From Kayleigh's birth. So easy, lifted from her numb womb, she remembers, her daughter's nutbrown skin smeared with blood. Whereas Abbie had been so difficult, so painful. Viv's own screams had melded with her eldest daughter's first cries. She knew now that she had screamed not from the agony of childbirth but in rage, and grief, for Gabe.

Viv looks in the mirror again, at the lines raying out from her brown eyes. Laughter lines, the great misnomer, she thinks, not without some bitterness. Each one furrowed through hardship and sorrow.

What would Gabe have thought of her now, she wonders, had he lived? She cannot picture him as a man in his forties. His face never ages. Nick's face replaces Gabe's youthful one. Nick would age well, eyes crinkling with his broad smile, on that tanned and weathered face. She imagines he would grey at the temples, without losing his hair, and keep his lean figure. A shiver passes through her.

The tap splutters, and she turns it off. She is about to step into its heat when the phone rings.

Afterwards, she thinks, I could have left it to ring.

The bath is tepid now. Adding more hot is usually futile, but Viv does so anyway.

She feels shellshocked.

She picks up the bar of sandalwood soap, holds it between her hands, lifts it, inhales its spice. Her heart had recoiled at the sound of Jonnie's voice, her body instinctively shrinking into itself. She had drawn the towel up around her breasts, as if he could see her seminakedness, sense her vulnerability. She had tried not to be hostile, worried, foremostly, about the girls. But no, there was nothing wrong. His tone was upbeat, vibrant. In a good mood, it seemed, asking only to keep the girls a little longer, over this weekend as well, if that was all right. As always, his plans took little account of her own, but they had always remained civil about the girls. At times like these he seemed more like the old Jonnie, the man she had loved.

So Viv had relented, but asked him why.

First bombshell. He was leaving Cape Town.

Viv felt a stab of anger, followed by apprehension. Fear even, she admits to herself now, as she soaps the sandalwood down her arms. Whatever his failings as a husband, Jonnie had been a decent father, she concedes, providing always, if largely materially, for the girls. Even for Abbie, not his own. Yet he did so unquestioningly, without making either of the girls feel guilty or grateful. Viv thinks of Gabe again. What sort of father would he have been? Kind. Gentle. Full of fun. She almost hears his laugh now, and sighs. She tries to stop the familiar run of thoughts, but cannot. She is too tired. Would she give up Kayleigh to have Gabe back? It is a useless hypothetical. Viv wants to cry, weariness overwhelming her. Now the inevitable, unbidden thought. The other child, the other one. Viv swallows, concentrates on lathering her legs. She picks up her razor; it rasps against her shin.

Second bombshell. London.

Not just anywhere. Not another hospital here, or near, not even Johannesburg, not even Africa, but London.

Third bombshell. A year, a whole year.

Such a long time in the girls' lives. Abbie will start Matric next year, her final school year. Viv's heart aches. Oh, Gabe. Our daughter, finishing school already. So much to organise, to decide. Abbie must decide which university, what degree. How typical of Jonnie to let her down at such a pivotal time, she thinks acidly.

So, London. He wanted the girls to visit. Viv could not answer. Not yet.

She thinks of Gin. Gin is there, in London. Abbie could see her aunt. Finally, they could meet again. Viv wonders if she ought to tell Gin about Jonnie. But then, she thinks, what would be the point?

Gin no longer works. London is huge. Their paths were unlikely to cross. And still Viv finds it hard to contemplate talking about Jonnie to Gin. A matter she'd broached when Gin was here, but that somehow they'd still avoided.

London. A whole year.

Viv washes off. She pulls the plug, the water almost cold. Jonnie's fault. She knows she is being unfair. I could have left it to ring, she thinks again.

She wets her long hair with the handheld shower as the bathwater drains out. She picks up the shampoo, contemplates its creamy hue. Sighing again, she squeezes out a blob of it into her palm. It smells of almonds. She starts to massage it into her hair.

Leaving. London. A whole year. Viv rinses off her hair, feels the shampoo slide down her neck, between her breasts. She rinses it again.

And then, fourth and final bombshell.

Blithely, almost. Nonchalant, a facile afterthought, an aside even. "Oh, and Viv, I'm getting married again."

26. GIN

His room is devoid of colour, bereft of Michael's presence. She had seen him off at the airport. They had tidied it before he left, pulling off sheets and leaving only the heavy cover on the bed. Gin sits in the chair near the window, looking out over the back garden, the view Michael had loved. It seems as bland as the room to her now, as empty as the house. A dull dolour has settled on her chest since his departure and her leg throbs constantly when she walks. She rubs at her thigh absent-mindedly.

She does not want to be alone when the time comes to give birth. A vague panic grips her as she realises it is only some four weeks away now. Michael had made her feel safe, but now she is alone again. Maybe Michael was right, that she should see someone, talk. She does not feel like talking. He had suggested hypnotherapy after she told him about the dreams. The constant dreams of Simon, his face distorting, bleeding.

Michael had offered to stay. When she got back from the hospital, he had sat her down and told her about the letter and its contents. She felt for him when he said his marriage was over, showing her the one official document that would spell the end of it, if not for him, he said, then very much so for Kristina. The other document aroused in her a poignant excitement for him. He had been offered a position at their old university. Rhodes. In Grahamstown. At home. Junior lecturer in the department of Psychology. A second chance, a chance to start over.

And at home.

The incumbent professor, he told her, was an old colleague, who had emailed him at the beginning of the year. Michael had half-heartedly filled in the application form and sent it back. With no further communication other than an acknowledgement, he had forgotten about it. They needed him there by September latest for a start the following January.

Gin refused to let him reconsider or negotiate. "You must take it, Mikey, it's a great job."

"Come with me, Gin," he urged. "I know you can't now with the baby due so soon. But when the divorce is through, once I'm settled, once the baby's born. Come home, Gin."

Home. She had felt herself retreat.

It is late afternoon and the light dissolves quickly. The room feels bare. Gin rises to draw the curtains, disregarding the roses outside that need pruning. She turns to leave, pulls the door to shut it. As she does so, a last ray shafts into the room between the open crease of curtain, and a flash of blue pierces her eye. Intrigued, she opens the door again, walks across to what was Michael's chest of drawers. Along the silky mahogany finish of its surface, her fingers find it.

She had barely remembered packing it with the pile of her belongings when she left Cape Town, not noted throwing it into her jewellery box, which the removal company would transfer from the flat to the house. Only when Michael had pulled it from the broken packaging had its presence jarred back into her consciousness. Not silver, as he had thought, but platinum. And not rust, but blood. The force of it had made her nauseated. Then the baby had kicked her with something like viciousness. Like anger. That was the moment she had thought: *this is it.* This is when I lose his child again, when the pain rips through my abdomen, and the blood pours down my legs in clotted grief. And then it would be over. Her punishment would be over. And perhaps there would be an end to the nagging state of nothingness, an escape finally from the numbing hell she had lived in since he died.

Gin holds the circle of metal in her hand, feels the smooth ice of it start to thaw beneath her touch. She stares at the stone as if for the first time, its faceted face. Blue, impossibly blue. Even in the dimness it captures what light is left, trapping smalt fire in its core. Four small, cold claws hold the jewel to the ring. The name of its cut escapes her. Emerald cut? No, that is long, rectangular. Cabochon? No, this has a bevelled edge. I ought to know, thinks Gin. The granddaughter of a jeweller ought to know. She should have paid more attention. Simon, Simon would have known.

Anger spits into her chest. She wants to fling this vile jewel across the room. What is she to do with it? She hates it. She sees Simon's face. Twisted, deformed, his mouth bleeding words.

Instead, Gin folds her fingers around the ring, grasping at it so tightly she feels its edges stab into the soft flesh of her palm. *Breathe.* Michael would tell her to breathe. Her free hand reaches to steady herself on the chest of drawers. She brings her closed fist to her mouth and she shudders with the effort to inhale. Once. Twice. Had she chosen it? Or had Simon? She shuts her eyes.

A sense of mischief, laughter. They had almost run into the shop, stopping before the sobering array of choice. Tray after velveted tray. Simon's directions. This setting nicer than that; platinum, not gold.

"It shines against your skin."

The skin that had lain naked against his own, mere hours before.

The light in his eyes as he looked at her.

Then she had seen it. Blue, impossibly blue. The ethereal glint of it had seemed so fragile against the sturdy silver of its setting.

Then, finally, his voice, low, "It matches your eyes, Ginny."

And the light in his eyes as he looked at her.

Her breath is strained and gasping. The ring is cutting into her skin but she cannot unclench her fist. *Breathe.* Michael would tell her to breathe. With agonising slowness, she starts to uncurl her fingers, the pain like unrelenting cramp. Deep red marks striate across her palm. She stares at it, hating it, but she knows now she must keep it. One day she will give it to her child.

One day she will say: *Here, this is from your parents, from the very day of your conception. If you look deep into its depths, maybe you can even see your soul. This ring, this sapphire stone whose cut I do not know, this ring was given to me by your father, in his last few hours of life.*

27. VIVIENNE

The remnants of summer mean the afternoon sun is late in reaching the front door. Stencilled streaks purple the horizon. Nick stands in the doorway, his blond hair an angel's halo.

"You knew Simon Gold," he says. "Why didn't you tell me?"

She steps back, holding her hand to her chest. "Nick –," she says.

"You lied to me," he says.

She backs away towards the door of the living room. "How did you find out?" she whispers.

"It was in his diary." He paces the floor of the entrance, not looking at her. "He sent you flowers, for Christ's sake! You lied to me!"

She feels herself tremble, wills away an image of an angry Jonnie. She turns away from Nick and walks into the lounge, pulls the curtains shut against the glare of sunset. He follows her.

"You had an affair," he says. "That doesn't matter. But you lied to me. That does."

She turns back to him, her eyes wide, her hand still to her chest. "What did you say?" she asks shrilly. "I had an *affair* with him? You think Simon Gold was my *lover*?"

They face each other in silence.

He starts to pace again. Viv recoils. She had dreaded this moment, knowing it would come, eventually. Inevitable that one day she would have to face it. A deep-seated pain twists in her abdomen.

"Where are the girls?" he asks. His voice sounds strained.

"With Jonnie." She pauses. "Nick, I –".

But he interrupts, turning towards her, openly angry. "Why did you lie to me, Vivienne?"

"Nick!" She almost shouts. The pain has spread to her back. "I need to sit down." She sits on the edge of the armchair, her chin in her hands. She breathes deeply, trying to gather her thoughts. The room is dark now with the curtains drawn. Night encroaches. She is trying to absorb his words, his accusation.

Nick stands in the doorway, across the room from her, watching her, arms folded. His fists are clenched.

Inevitable that it should come to this, that he should look at her like that. My own fault, thinks Viv. My fault he looks at me like that. Inevitable.

"Don't look at me like that, Nick," she pleads into the half-gloom.

He stops pacing, runs his hand through his hair. That lock falls back almost immediately. "How should I look at you, then, Vivienne?" he asks. His voice is hoarse.

She has hurt him. The realisation makes her ineffably sad. Her throat feels raw with regret.

Standing, she turns her back to him, moves to crouch before the stone hearth. Her hands shake slightly as she reaches for the brush to sweep away the ashes of the last fire. Taking a fold of last week's *Cape Argus* from a pile of newspapers, she separates a page, crumples it into a ball and throws it onto the grate. She repeats the action. Page after printed page, ball after ball. It is the only sound in the room, the slip and rustle of the paper as she clenches each one in a trembling fist. Piece by piece, the grate fills.

When it is fully layered, Viv moves towards the stack of kindling piled high alongside the hearth. It is so quiet that she thinks Nick must have turned and left. She bends to pick up a load of wood. Her back still hurts and she arches as she stands.

"Here, let me do that." He is beside her so suddenly that she jumps, instinctively moving away from him. If he notices, he does not comment. Instead he takes the kindling from her, lays it neatly over the tightly-fisted balls of paper. He picks up the copper scuttle and scatters coal over the kindling. Viv watches as he lights one of the long matches, holding it to the paper until it ignites sulkily. The thin swirls of grey smoke remind Viv of the mist over the mountain, seeping over the top of its cyanic peaks. Orange flames start upward between the plumes. Nick stands, poker in hand, his outstretched arm resting on the chimney breast, staring intently into the grate, as if the force of his glare alone could light it.

Viv folds her arms around herself. The warmth from her early bath has deserted her, and she feels cold, almost naked beneath her thin T-shirt. Anxiety shivers through her veins. She longs for a cigarette. She does not want to talk.

Nick rubs at his eyes. He looks tired, thinks Viv. The continued silence unnerves her. I should have known it would come to this. The past will always find you out. She still cannot take in his words. She wonders what details Nick has unearthed. An odd forgotten entry here, an unguarded note there? Simon would not have left the truth. He had, after all, been as much at risk as she.

The fire starts to burn with an efficient briskness, the dry kindling catching quickly, feeding the coal. Nick reaches into the battered enamel bucket of pine cones, throws a handful on the shifting heat. Happier days spent collecting them come back to her as she watches them splutter and glow.

Eventually, eyes still fixed the progress of the fire, Nick asks, "What was Simon Gold to you?" He sounds tired.

"Nick, look…"

She starts to speak, but he stabs angrily at the fire with the poker, as if he cannot bear to hear her answer. His face, in profile, is set. He mutters something to himself.

"What did you say?" she asks.

He turns to her, his eyes meeting hers. But she drops her gaze, looks into the flames. Her arms are still wrapped around herself. The room is warming now, but she still feels chilled.

"You told me you didn't know him. That you'd never met him. Yet you saw him, several times. That, at least, is documented."

Policeman. Interrogator.

Viv says nothing. The colourless office, its high ceilings, the uncomfortable chair reform in her mind. She remembers her halting words, stumbling out her story to Simon. His grave, kind eyes. She had never told anyone else. Over the years, she had occasionally managed to forget. At times it had seemed it had never happened. Like parts of her life with Jonnie, that would sink and then surface with a randomness that felt surreal. Now she must tell someone else: Nick. And it is harder, infinitely harder, she realises, than telling Simon Gold.

She clears her throat. "I should have told you." She looks up to see him still looking at her, arms folded again. "What made you think I had an affair with him?" she asks quietly.

He sighs at her words, but his stance does not change. When he speaks, his tone is exasperated. "Vivienne, you met with him. You had dinner, he sent you flowers… you denied knowing him… what was I supposed to think?"

It sounds so ludicrous to her that she starts to laugh, her laughter coming out in exhalations that sound to her like sobs. Only then does she realise she is sobbing, but no tears are forming. All she can hear are the hollow hiccoughing sounds from her throat, and all she can see is that window. That awful day, looking out the window at a sunny Johannesburg sky.

28. VIVIENNE

Viv's heels clicked and echoed as she walked down the endless corridor. Room 311, she had been told downstairs by the pimple-obsessed young man, not long out of high school, and already bored with directing the unending stream of people through dreary government departments.

Her steps fell silent. The lurid poster on the outside of room 311 screamed, "There's no excuse for abuse."

Yes, this was it, this was the right place.

She opened the door, unprepared for the number of women inside. They lined the walls; squeezed onto the benches, they waited. Slowly, one by one, one after another, they entered and exited a small office at the end of the room. Viv queued alongside, trying to settle herself, trying not to feel self-conscious, reminding herself they were all here for the same reason. She moved from wall to wooden bench, a progression of sorts. The wood was worn smooth from the constant shuffle of women. Finally, her turn, her chance to enter the office. Her back felt stiff as she stood. She was nervous, adjusted her skirt, pulled at her blouse, which was stuck to her skin.

Inside, an overweight woman looked up at her impatiently. "Well?"

Viv was taken aback by the harshness in the woman's tone. But then what had she expected? Kindness? Counselling? "I've come to – I've never done this before, what do I do? Where do I start?"

The woman put down her pen, sighed loudly, exaggeratedly. "Just tell me what happened."

What had happened? How did it get to this point? This point, where her husband had finally hit her so hard she could still feel his fist connecting with her jaw. When did it start? That mild summer's night when he had looked deep into her eyes and promised to love her forever? Perhaps when she had told him, with a mixture of excitement and trepidation, that she was pregnant. Or when he walked out of the courtroom that had sentenced him away for political crimes against the State? Maybe it had been prison itself? Or did it start the day he was released? Prison had changed him. But maybe it was from way before then. He had told her once, sobbing, how he had stood, young and alone, watching his own father beat his mother so savagely that the blood spat from her nostrils and her mouth.

The woman sighed again, picked up her pen. "Do you want to come back tomorrow?" she asked. Her voice was flat.

Viv shook her head and started to stutter through the details. She started to tell this stranger how her husband had held her hair and smashed her head against the red tile of their kitchen floor. Again, and again. Viv heard the quaver in her own voice, but the woman didn't appear to notice. She wrote a number on a form and handed it to Viv, then sent her back into the waiting area outside.

"Wait till I call your number," she said.

Back on another bench, now she was a number.

An older woman next to her looked at her and smiled. "Don't worry, girl, you're lucky, you're young. Look at me, I'm fifty-four."

Viv had no words for her.

"You're young," the woman continued. "You can start again."

Viv stared at her, tried to smile, and failed. She turned her attention to the form, tried to answer questions, tried to find words to describe in writing Jonnie's aggression. Once this was done, the law could protect her. The police, with power to intervene, would only be a phone call away. With sudden dread, Viv realised how angry this would make Jonnie. But she just wanted it — wanted him — to stop.

Back in the cramped office, the woman read the form impassively. She wrote something on another piece of paper and handed it to Viv.

"Right," she said, "take this form to the Sheriff of the court, so that it can be served on your husband. It's a temporary order, which you will have to finalise in court after three months. If you don't, it will fall away, and you will have to come back here when he hits you again."

When, not if.

Viv clutched at the paper – her talisman of hope – and walked awkwardly from the office, trying not to stumble. A hundred faces assaulted her. There were so many women, all ages, races, classes. Violence, it appeared, was a great leveller. And so many seemed to be back for a second, third, even fourth time. That failure to follow up, to have him arrested, trusting his promises, trusting his empty words that it would never happen again, taking the flowers, accepting the kisses. A young blonde woman was flipping pages of the register, trying to track down her last complaint. She had a slight scar between her eyes, and as she looked up, Viv noticed a capped tooth in her mouth.

I will never come back here, she vowed.

Outside, in the fresh air, the sun was like a balm on her swollen face. She wanted to stand and let it soak through her, but instead she put on her sunglasses and walked quickly back to the car. She sat inside, lit a cigarette and inhaled strongly. Her ribs ached with the exhalation. She knew it was probably the bruises, but it felt as if she had been holding her breath for the past five years. Had it been that long? Yes, Kayleigh was five. Kayleigh, Abbie. She wanted to cry at the thought of her daughters; they were so small. How would all this have damaged them, she wondered. But this was no time for tears. At least he'd never hit the girls.

She sat watching Cape Town city life pass by. A man smacked at his parking meter. A couple hurried by, the woman berating him for being late. The road stretched ahead of her, wide and tree-lined, van Riebeeck's statue a dark bronze in the sun. Cars coursed through the crossroads.

Viv started the car, moving out into the traffic. She needed to fetch the girls. She had left them with Leila, who did not know where she had been. Viv checked the rear-view mirror. The make-up would hold; Leila must not suspect. Leila was Jonnie's friend also. Panic filled her chest. She must get away from Jonnie before he was served with the order. The thought of his anger terrified her. She must get away. The panic intensified. He was wrong when he said she would never make it without him, that no one would have her. Having children ended any further studies, and she hadn't worked for years. The job market would be tough; she would need somewhere to stay. He would never give her the house, not without a fight at least. Sweat dampened her armpits as she drove. She wished she had the girls already, could keep driving, keep on going, drive up Africa, to the ends of the earth if need be, as far away from Jonnie as possible. How he had changed from the charming, educated man she fell in love with.

Or had he? He was still charming, educated, and he had always been angry, always bitter. But in the beginning it had been at the State, at the government, the police, the system. She'd thought him brave, outspoken, a fighter. When had their marriage become the fight?

Viv tossed the cigarette butt out the window, fumbled in her bag for another. The folded white paper shifted, stared bleakly out at her. What had she done to deserve this? Had she turned the guilt after Gabe's suicide into something external, that she should physically pay for his death? Or had her white guilt reached the point where she could accept the beatings from her Indian husband, whenever he was in the mood?

She pulled off the highway into Steenberg, drove along the barren stretch of veld that was filled with the reddish ochre of the fynbos growing wild. The mountain rose above her, soot-black. The light had passed beyond its summit. Yet it was not menacing, rather she felt its shadow as a comfort. Guardian, not threat.

The road turned left into Leila's drive. A patch of front lawn, freshly tilled and planted with succulents amidst the gravel, led up to the porched entrance. Leila came out the front door as Viv got out the car. As always, Viv was struck by her fragile beauty, her flawless coffee skin, her almond eyes, the perfectly-applied eye-shadow, her lips never without the shine of lipstick. Viv felt unkempt in comparison.

From behind Leila, Abbie ran screaming, "Mommy, Mommy," as if it had been days, not hours, since her eldest daughter last saw her. The blonde head buried itself to her, slender white arms clinging to her desperately.

Viv glimpsed tears in her daughter's eyes. Those blue eyes that, like Gabe's, she'd had to watch cloud with trouble. Her heart tightened as she thought of Gabe. She could not think of him then; her daughters needed her. There was no time for what-ifs, for hypothetical meanderings, wonderings of what could and could not have happened had Gabe lived.

His child looked up at her. "Mommy, can we stay with Aunty Leila tonight?" It was Abbie's way of pleading not to go home to Jonnie.

Viv knew Abbie heard the fights. There had been times Viv had bitten her lip till it bled, trying not to scream and distress her children. Kayleigh was younger, slept more soundly. Abbie had been too young to remember Jonnie's arrival, when Gin had first brought him home. But on his release from prison, the little girl had taken to him immediately. She would sit on his lap, show him her toys, follow him around. But, thinks Viv, that was before it had all started.

Before, before, before.

She became conscious of Leila's watchful gaze. She found the woman unsettling, was never quite sure of their relationship. Leila had been Jonnie's friend initially, and Viv felt cautious in her presence. It was not a natural friendship, not like her and Gin, she thought ruefully. But Leila had been her only friend in the days after Kayleigh's birth, and then especially after Jonnie's imprisonment. She had been so dependable, helping here and there, bringing supper, looking after the girls, one at a time or both together, and often at the last minute. Viv had grown dependent, grateful. So she had made an effort. Perhaps Leila was lonely. She appeared to have no man in her life. Viv had asked Jonnie once; he had been abrupt, dismissive, saying something about an affair with a *white man that hadn't worked out. Viv, not wanting to start him on the road to bitter regret, had not pressed for more.*

In fact, she had always suspected other history between Leila and Jonnie. The woman was exotically alluring; she must be attractive to any man. There had been times she had caught Leila watching Jonnie, the furtiveness of it disturbing.

"Do you want some tea?" Leila asked her.

Viv was torn, wanting to go home, to take her daughters with her. But she was afraid. Perhaps Jonnie would be home. Perhaps, like the last time, he would leave the hospital early, stopping to pick up wine, and flowers, to make it up to her. And he would want to have sex, stroking the same hair he had pulled, touching the same body he had bruised.

She nodded and led Abbie inside. Leila's house was cool, dark wooden floors made darker still by ethnic rugs and heavy furnishings. Viv found it womb-like, restful. She wondered if she should tell Leila the truth about Jonnie. She wondered if perhaps Leila would let them stay the night.

They sipped Earl Grey from china cups, while the girls stuffed in mouthfuls of banana cake. Viv could not face the smell of it when Leila offered her a piece. Leila looked at her oddly when she shook her head.

"Are you all right, Vivienne?" she asked, in that quiet light voice of hers.

"Yes, of course. Why do you ask?"

"It's just that you usually love my banana cake."

Did she? Viv was taken aback. Good Lord, the woman noticed everything. Would she notice the bruises beneath the make-up? Jonnie had never hurt her face before, but yesterday he'd been brutal.

Viv swallowed, "I'm fine. Just a little tired." She held out her plate, "And yes, I do love your banana cake. You must tell me your secret." I'll force it down, she thought. She could not tell Leila; she could not tell anyone, and she could not stay there. Dear God, where was she going to go? Must she go home, pretend all was unchanged, feed the girls, put them to bed, go through the repetition of making up, feign delight at the flowers, drink the wine, fake orgasm?

"Vivienne," said Leila again, "you're hiding something from me."

Viv almost choked on the cake.

"But it's okay," continued Leila, "I understand."

Understand? What did this woman understand? Viv looked at her, alarmed.

Leila smiled slightly, her lilac lips revealing even white teeth. "You forget, my dear, I'm a nurse."

Viv, uncomprehending, continued staring at her.

"You see," said Leila, "I can always tell when a woman is pregnant. I'm never wrong."

29. *VIVIENNE*

"So you see, Nick," she says, her voice without tone, "I couldn't have his child. Not then. Not after what he had done."

Viv is sitting on the couch, Nick beside her. Viv can feel his gaze, intent and unwavering, but she does not look at him. Her hands interlace in her lap.

"I had to get away," she continues flatly. "So, I had a… termination." The word emanates oddly from her lips. She was going to say *abortion* but she hates the sound of it, an ugly word for an ugly act. She wants to cry, to hug herself and rock back and forth. To scream: *I killed my child.* My child, like Abbie, Kayleigh. But I killed it. Instead, her interwoven fingers twist and tighten. Her teeth tug at her bottom lip. Her head drops, her chin to her chest.

Her voice is hard now, her secret out after all these years. And Nick the cause. "So Simon Gold did the op for me."

The fire spits and rustles as it settles in the grate. The wind has come up, an eerie whistle around the house. A window clatters on the floor above and Viv starts, her head darting upward. Her eyelids feel swollen and itchy, as if she has been crying, and she wants to close her eyes and rest.

Nick stands, then stoops to shovel more coal on the fire. He comes back to crouch in front of her, puts his hands on her arms. She cannot look at him, focusing instead on her hands, so tightly clasped her fingers are red, the knuckles white.

Something prompts her to explain further, like a sinner at confessional. "Simon helped me. I didn't know him. I'd only ever seen him once, at Gabe's –" She stops for a moment, clearing her throat. "At Gabe's funeral. I went to see Simon in Jo'burg. I asked him to help me." Her words come out in a rush now. "I couldn't ask anyone else. All the doctors I know here know Jonnie. He would have found out. Someone, someone, would have told him."

Viv looks past Nick, into the fire. *Father, forgive me.* She thinks she hears Nick say her name, but she cannot be sure, so in the silence she carries on talking. "Simon could have got into trouble also. He knew that. He knew the legal implications. Abortion here was still illegal then. He could have lost his career, been struck off…"

Does he say her name again, a little louder, she wonders. Or is it the wind, circling the house, as if seeking entrance? "He helped me," she whispers. "He barely knew me, and he knew the risks. But he helped me. I think it was because of Gin."

Again she is back in that sterile office. "I think he wrote up some story on my notes." Her voice trails off. Nick mentioned a diary entry, the flowers. Perhaps there had been no notes. Perhaps Simon would rather have risked his personal life than his professional one.

Nick is still on his haunches before her, his one hand stroking her forearm. Viv feels herself start to tremble. "I told myself it was the right thing to do. I could not have left Jonnie if I had that child."

"Vivienne," he says, and now she cannot mistake it for the wind. "It's me, Nick."

Confused, she looks directly into his eyes for the first time.

"You called me Father just then," he says, "Are you all right?"

She stares at him then nods briefly, looks down at her twisted hands. The upstairs window bangs again.

"Let me get that window," says Nick, standing.

Viv stares into the fire while he goes upstairs. He switches on the lights in the hall as he exits, and the room lightens. She hears his footsteps above her in the spare room. Gin's room, she thinks. Maybe we have invoked Simon's ghost. It is an uncharacteristic thought and she is frightened by the notion. Had she really called Nick *Father?* The idea unsettles her further. Begging for absolution.

She shakes herself, gets up, smoothes her T-shirt, switches on the table lamp to avoid the brightness of the main lights. Then she goes into the kitchen to splash warm water on her burning eyes. Her body feels hollowed out. Reaching for the kettle, she changes her mind and opens the cupboard, searching instead for wine. Nick returns to find her battling with the corkscrew. He takes it from her. Viv gets glasses from the cabinet. Mutely they return to the couch. He pours full glasses for them both, hands her one. He takes a large gulp of his and leans towards the fire.

"I'm sorry, Vivienne," he says.

She does not know how to respond. Instead she looks into the flames. He sits back, turning to look at her. Viv sips at the dry Shiraz. Its strength cleanses her tongue, washes her arid throat.

"I'm sorry too," she says at length. "I'm sorry I didn't tell you I knew him. I just never thought it was... relevant, you know. It was long ago. I never saw him after that."

He nods briefly. Viv drains her glass. Nick fills it again almost immediately.

"I often wonder about the child, whether it was a girl, or a boy... what he or she would have looked like." And Jonnie had always wanted another child. Her hands start to tremble, and her wine glass wobbles. She steadies herself and takes another sip of Shiraz. "I'm sorry," she says again, and does not know what she is apologising for.

Nick puts his arm around her. His free hand takes her glass from her and puts it on the table. His voice is serious. "No, *I'm* sorry. I shouldn't have been so angry. I had no right. I judged you – and Gold – too quickly." His hand reaches up to touch her face. "I let my feelings for you interfere."

She blinks at him. *My feelings for you.*

Her heart thuds erratically. She feels unsteady, almost seasick.

This time, when Nick Retief leans forward to kiss her, she does not pull away.

30. VIVIENNE

She hears the front door slam.

"Mom, what are you doing still in bed?" Kayleigh leans into the open door of the bedroom.

Viv peers over the edge of the duvet in confusion, looks at the clock. Past midday. It had been a late night.

She kept her eyes closed as he kissed her. She didn't want to watch him watching her. She didn't want to see his thoughts express upon his face. His tongue, tentative at first, deepened with her response. She tasted the wine in his mouth. He leaned into her, pushing her back until they were lying side by side on the long couch. His lips moved to her neck, to the hollow of her throat. Where her heart pulsed. His hair brushed against her cheek as he did so, and she smelled the clean citrus scent of his shampoo. Still she kept her eyes tightly shut. She willed away an involuntary picture of Gabe, touching her as Nick did, his hand reaching down to stroke her thigh. She felt herself freeze, remembering pain. The last time she'd had sex, Jonnie pulling at her hair, and the bruises she'd been left with.

"Mom, it's afternoon already!" repeats her daughter. Then, with concern, "you're not ill, are you?"

She felt his hair graze her cheek again as he lifted his head. She knew he was looking at her. But she could not open her eyes. They felt red-rimmed and sore. His fingers touched her face.

"Vivienne," he asked softly, "what's wrong?"

She could not answer. She might choke, or sob out loud. She wanted him, she wanted Nick, she wanted this man inside her. But all she could think about was how he would hurt her.

Viv sits up, a hand to her forehead. "No, I'm fine."

"So this is what you do on the weekends we're with Dad." Kayleigh's voice is half-serious, relieved.

"Actually, what *are* you doing here?" They were not due back till Monday.

There was no sound but the sporadic shift of the fire, and the low keen of the wind outside.

"I won't hurt you," he had said.

Slowly, she had opened her eyes.

Viv looks at her bedside table for her cigarettes. They lie next to the packet of condoms she and Nick had finally, mercifully, found. Oh, God, oh God, don't let Kayleigh see, she pleads.

But Kayleigh has moved into the hall, calling back, "Oh, Dad's taking us to his club. You know, the one with the tennis courts and the outdoor heated pool. So we just came to fetch our racquets and our cossies." Her voice trails off and Viv can hear wardrobe doors slamming.

Nick had showered this morning, his goodbye kiss lingering, intimate. She had curled up again and slept. Without dreams. Until now. Viv stretches her legs and then jumps up, starts to pull the duvet from the bed. The action knocks both the condom packet and her cigarettes to the floor.

"Hello, Viv, you look good." Jonnie's voice behind her, smooth as silk.

She whips around, one hand trying to cover her nakedness, the other reaching for her robe. He stands in the doorway.

"What are you doing here?" She struggles into her robe, hoping her voice is stronger than it sounds. Damn him. He is not allowed in the house. She stands back, taking in his presence. Her body always betrays her at the sight of Jonnie, the heat that rises from the initial tug in the pit of her belly, followed by her effort to repress it. Then the anger, first at him, then at herself.

He is dressed casually, an open-necked shirt and jeans hugging his swimmer's physique, the broad chest and shoulders tapering to narrow hips and muscular legs. A thin smile lingers on his mouth, a line of teeth showing white against his copper skin. His eyes sweep over her, that possessive look she had learned to detest.

"Thought I'd just pop in to say goodbye. I leave in a couple of weeks." He strolls into the room, laconic. "You remember – London?"

Involuntarily, she retreats, clutches at the front of her gown. Not soon enough, she thinks. Jonnie turns towards her and as he does, his foot kicks against the packets on the floor. They both look down. Viv shrinks inside.

He looks up at her. "Having fun, I see," but his tone does not match the lightness of the comment.

Viv backs away further until she is against the wall and immediately regrets it. He moves to stand in front of her, puts an arm beside her. No route to the door. She resists the urge to close her eyes and scream.

"We used to have fun," he says, quietly. His eyes slide down her body. He puts his head close to hers. "So how about it, Viv? For old times' sake. And we don't need condoms, do we?" He slides a finger down the silk collar of her robe.

Viv finds her voice and rasps. "No, Jonnie. We didn't have *fun*. What we had was abuse." He stands immobile against her. An old fear frissons through her. This time she cannot help but tense, waiting for the sting of the first slap.

Instead he breathes, "Viv." She feels her gown fall open as his hand reaches inside. She bites at her lip, starts to push at him, when he says, "You know I still love you."

His voice is so full of longing and regret that Viv herself feels a mix of yearning and sorrow. The emotion of last night returns. He sounds so like the Jonnie she fell in love with that for a moment her body relaxes. In her hesitation, she feels him press his body against hers.

"Mom, have you seen my – " Viv's eyes flutter open to see Abbie's shocked blue stare, followed by the flick of her blonde hair as she flees.

"Jonnie, get off me!"

She pushes at him and his laugh is short, derisive as he moves aside, letting her pass. The Jonnie she knows best. Viv rushes out the bedroom. She finds her eldest daughter in the sunroom at the front of the house. Abbie sits huddled in the wicker armchair, knees hugged to her chest, blonde hair hanging across her face. She looks so much like Gin, thinks Viv distractedly.

"Abbie…" Viv walks towards her and touches her arm.

Abbie leaps up. "Don't touch me!" She springs across the room.

"Abbie…" Viv sighs.

"You slept with that policeman, didn't you?" interrupts Abbie, still shouting. "I know you did. Your clothes are all over the floor."

Viv stares at her, feels heat rush to her skin. This she had not expected.

"And he's, like, young enough to be your son!"

"Abbie! That's not true!"

Abbie is pacing in front of her now. "And then," she fumes acidly, "as if that's not enough –" She stops for a moment, looks at Viv, her eyes accusing. "The very next day you go and throw yourself at Dad."

Viv is aghast. She had thought to have to explain. That she is unhurt despite Jonnie's molestation. Sluggishly it dawns on her that all Abbie would have seen was her mother, naked under an open robe, eyes closed, pressed up against Jonnie. This is worse, infinitely worse. And Jonnie will be no help, she knows; he will say nothing to Abbie.

Abbie rages on apparently emboldened by her mother's silence. "Have you no shame?" She comes up close now.

Viv can see spittle at the side of her mouth. They stare at each other, strangers.

Then Abbie leans forward. Her voice, when she speaks, has quieted, but the venom of the single word will stay with Viv forever. "Whore."

Without thinking, Viv's hand comes up. She slaps Abbie across the face.

Abbie's eyes fill with tears of shock and pain.

Viv recoils, her hands fly to her mouth.

Kayleigh's voice penetrates through from the hall, as they stare at each other in mutual horror. "Come *on*, Abbie! Where are you? Dad's already waiting in the car! Bye, Ma!"

Viv reaches her hand out again towards Abbie, starts to apologise in a voice strangled with dismay and despair. "Abbie, I'm sorry."

But her daughter turns and runs from the sunroom.

Viv does not follow, stands and stares out at the cloudless Cape day.

The mountain is painted in green.

She hears the front door slam.

31. GIN

Winter descends once more. A chilly October, a fateful October. Leaves falling red, like blood. Gin walks the wet mile down the Portobello Road, named for an ancient sea victory, past pashminas and porcelain, saucepans and silverware, cheap tin trays. The Spanish store is past the bridge, she has a yen for olives grown under the Mediterranean sun, for biscotti baked in clay ovens. The market is crowded and her progress is slow.

She is barely past the flower stall, run by the elderly Lithuanians, when the crowds overwhelm her suddenly. Friday at its worst, a group of Arab women, ubiquitous trolleys, there is an argument of high unintelligible shrieks. One woman pushes another, who spits out what sounds to Gin like a garbled curse. The crowd parts obligingly. In this movement, one of the women appears to lurch at Gin, and she stumbles back, boots finding no hold on the wet road, her leg betraying her. Perhaps her inattentiveness, the numbness, is to blame. Her hand in instinct stretches out towards her perceived assailant, but only dizziness assaults her. Gin is fragmentedly aware of bright eyes behind a heavy veil, staring down at her. She is down on the cold hard pavement, and there is a new pain, unfamiliar.

"Please," she says, to no one. Oh, God. She feels a wetness between her thighs. It must be time. She looks down. Her jeans are soaked. Red. So much red. "Please," she says again, "I need an ambulance. I'm bleeding."

The noise of the crowd intensifies, the flower seller bends over her, two hairdressers rush out of the salon alongside the stall. The crowd gathers. But Gin is falling further, consciousness slipping. Afterwards she will remember only a scent of jasmine, and a siren, sounding through pain, and into oblivion.

They hand her a tiny bundle that is her daughter. For a moment, Gin finds it hard to breathe, hard to swallow. *Simon's daughter.* The father she will never know. The child he will never know. The daughter he never had.

I'm sorry, she thinks, and doesn't know whether she addresses her child or Simon. *I'm sorry you won't know each other.*

There is nothing of me in this child, thinks Gin. She is pure Simon. She looks up with eyes the colour of her father's, and the same intensity of gaze. Skin a smooth olive, and a head already thick with black curls. Fists clenched, already fighting. Maybe this is good, thinks Gin. Her daughter may face so much alone.

She strokes the sooty hair. *I don't know what to call you, little one.* Exhaustion washes over her.

An image forms. Her grandmother, her mother's mother. Ellen, fair Ellen, as fair as this child is dark. Ellen, whom everyone said she, Gin, resembled.

You look like your father. You have his looks. From me, you will have your name. Ellie.

She takes her home, and mother and daughter stare at each other warily. They are surrounded by a chaos of colour, the bright yellow cot Michael had bought, the baby mobile slung with painted wooden animals – a zebra, a giraffe, a lion. *So she knows she's from Africa,* he said. Why, wonders Gin, with all this brightness, does it all feel so bleak?

Gin goes through the motions of motherhood, the newly learned tasks of feeding, and changing, and cleaning, and doing it all again. Her life quickly falls into a routine based around this needy newcomer. She misses Viv most now, Viv's warmth, Viv's expertise, her seemingly natural maternal instinct. She remembers Viv's confidence with Abbie. She rings her once, twice, but there is no reply. Gin doesn't know what to say to the machine, so she rings off with no message. Viv would tell her the same as the midwife. Ellie is what the midwife calls a good baby. Gin supposes it is an enviable thing, the lack of crying, the relatively undisturbed nights, but she finds her daughter, this familiar stranger, unnervingly quiet. Is there something wrong with her, she wonders, or just something wrong with me? Do all mothers feel this way? Did her own mother feel this about her, about Gabe? She finds it hard to relate to this silent little child with Simon's eyes. Seeing Ellie, seeing Simon's eyes and face, she expected it to be simple, for a bond to form naturally. Instead, all Simon's daughter does is remind Gin daily of his death.

She phones Michael one lonely, quiet night. She tries to tell him how she feels, her worries, but he dismisses her concerns.

"Gin, relax, she's fine. Stop worrying." He starts to talk excitedly about his preparations for the course, how good it is to be home again.

He doesn't understand, she thinks. I am alone and no one can help me.

He phones the following week and leaves a message. She listens to his voice. It sounds five thousand miles away. She deletes the message and does not phone him back.

A month after her birth, Ellie fits. Vomits and seizes, her little body alternately limp and rigid. St Mary's hospital is closer, supposes Gin, but whatever the reason – roadworks, bed space, urgency – the ambulance goes to Hammersmith hospital instead. The same hospital they had taken her after her fall, the same hospital Ellie was born in. Inside the white cell of the ambulance, Gin lets the paramedics intervene. How young they seem. They are efficient and soothing, eliciting information from her she otherwise could not have articulated. Again, she finds herself beholden to this country, its systems, structures, people. An hour later, only an hour, Ellie lies flaccid and pale in the brightly-lit Neonatal Unit, four floors above the traffic of west London.

Ellie has settled now into an imposturous sleep. With each fresh ripple that had passed through her daughter's limbs, Gin had felt a wave of guilt. Others are in control, in charge of Ellie's care. Strangers. She sees blame in the no-nonsense attitude of the nurses. They ignore her while they set up Ellie's drip, turn their backs while filling in her chart. They know I do not love this child, thinks Gin. They know I am a bad mother. She searches the small face for its former liveliness. Those all-seeing eyes are closed from drip-fed drugs. The house officer is apologetic. His registrar is not answering his bleep. Gin must please leave her child, go home, wait. The nurses, infinitely better equipped than she, will look after Ellie. Please, she must not worry, come back in the morning. Ellie has the best of care. Nonetheless, a fitful night follows, till muffled traffic louder than the song of birds wakes her before dawn. Gin walks to the hospital to fill the time, yet still she has to wait.

Halfway to a comfortable consultancy elsewhere, the paediatric registrar had obviously mastered the art of hardening his feelings to protect his sleep. Ellie's blood culture is clean, he tells Gin. With no obvious infection, he will call Neurology to consult. He is already onto the next cot, the next infant who lies isolated by illness.

Neurology will want her child to have an EEG. Ellie's brainwaves must be tracked, monitored, inked by a needle onto feinted paper. Magnificent steel machinery will dwarf her daughter. Soft cool gel will attach electrodes to her fragile new skin, to tiny temples still blue-veined and transparent.

And then they must wait again. She and a listless Ellie must wait in the terrible silence of limbo, invaded by the ignorant noise of a busy ward. Every footfall is harsh, each beep of a machine, the radio too loud, a nurse's laugh, staccato and histrionic.

Later it will blur.

In retrospect it will be seamless, unfragmented, but now Neurology is here, they say. Gin's heart is thudding, battering her sternum, an aortic rage building. Her body is quivering. Neurology is here. Crisp, clean, white-coated Neurology walks toward her daughter. She realises she is hallucinating. She tells herself it cannot be him. No doubt it is lack of sleep. It cannot possibly be him. It must be extreme fatigue.

The neurologist is Jonnie.

32. GIN

The past, another country, another continent. Another hospital, on the edge of Africa, five thousand miles and a lifetime away from this.

She looked up from dispensing. There was a man standing at the counter. He had an arrogant smile, she noticed. A misplaced arrogance. Misplaced in this country that would assign him lesser status because he was not white. She noticed the arrogance all the more because of this. So perhaps it was bravado merely. But noticeable all the same.

This is her abiding memory of Jonnie, how she will always remember him, all smiling confidence and charm. A far-off laughter in his eyes, as if he finds amusement in the tragedy of the present, as if he has the benefit of distance, or of time.

It is two decades on since then, and he stands in front of her again, apparently unchanged. She is swathed with emotion. Her child is ill, she needs no further complications. So many questions lie unanswered in this space between them, so many years elapsed, disappeared in the instant of seeing him. There is so much to be said, and yet there is nothing she wants to say.

Ellie.

Ellie, Simon's child, does Jonnie know? Her thinking is blurred, for of course it does not matter, but she has held secrets to herself for so long that it seems any intrusion from the past is a threat. And Jonnie, Jonnie is dangerous. As always. Dangerous to her stability, her fragile hold on normality; he has always been for her a heady nightmarish tumble off the edge.

He is talking to her, saying something in a voice that seems foreign and far-off. That Ellie's scan, her EEG is clear; that there is no sign of epilepsy, that further tests are needed. That they should talk.

They walk, in silence, down through a makeshift underground corridor and up again. It is painted with dolphins underwater, and as the ground rises, they surface alongside. She wants to glance up at him, to see if he is as unchanged as he appears. She can smell the curious hospital mix of him, of antiseptic and aftershave; citrus, spice, and sandalwood that catapults her back to when they met.

The mountain was mauve in the distance across the hazy heat of the Klipfontein plain. She saw him on her ward. He was holding a child, comforting its ceaseless crying. So many lonely children were here, some of whom had been abandoned. He would look up at any second and find her staring. Gin looked out the window. Later that evening a wind would come up from the east, bringing the cloud to cover the mountain with its misty mantle. He was asking her a dose, he was smiling.

Why ask me that, her heart had shouted, rebelling. Ask me the lines of poetry that sway through my head, ask me why the sea is part of my soul, how the warmth of the sand underfoot is a favourite feeling, the easy answers. Paediatric doses belonged in the obscure realm, hard to access, along with why Simon had gone, why Simon had not phoned, nor written.

Still, somehow she managed to pluck it from obfuscated depths, smiled back. And suddenly aware of the truth of the smile, Gin felt it warm her insides like the sun, lifting back a layer of sadness. The first man to make me smile since Simon. A good day.

The hospital canteen is cold, bare, brightly lit. There are few customers, and they sit alone at a table in the corner. The coffee is machine-made and weak, a thin skin floating on top. Brown granules melt into its tepidness. She looks anywhere but at him. Feelings she thought long-dead are scratching at her throat. She wishes to not be here. Why did Ellie fit? Why is her daughter ill? Why is he here? She will not let him enter her life. Enter it as easily as he once left it. The scratch in her throat becomes an ache and she knows if she talks, her voice will break. But his bleep buzzes, and he excuses himself, walks to the phone on the wall.

He was everywhere. On her wards, in the corridors, walking past while it was her turn dispensing medicines from an awkward hatch. Too high for everyone, her chest would brush the loudspeaker. The scratchy static echoed through the waiting area. The regime of the day dictated trans-lation of all African names, so there were endless misunderstandings, repetition, and calling. It was even more difficult identifying patients, swaddled babies bundled closely to their mothers' backs. Gin had learned how to say in Xhosa how many teaspoons a day, but despaired at the lack of communication, the inability to warn of adverse effects. It was easier with the Cape Coloureds, the mixed-race descendants of black and white, for their language was Afrikaans, and she was fluent. Forced to learn it as if a mother tongue, again by dictate of the day.

She was to call him Jonnie, he said. Once they were friends, before they were lovers.

Mohammed Jay Kassan was privately educated. Expensive private schools in Swaziland were the reason for his ease, his confidence, amongst strangers, whites. Mohammed, he told her, was as common as John. So everyone called him Jonnie, he laughed. Jonnie Jay of the black heart, she added. Black heart, "because," he had said, "anyone not white in this country must by virtue of that fact, be black." Be they Coloured or Indian, the struggle was that simple. The struggle was for all, even her, if she chose. He had challenged her, and Gin's world had erupted. She realised how sheltered she had been.

An innocence lost.

They worked late nights in the mobile clinics in the townships. Gin felt the wound of the country open, expose itself to her like a festering sore, rank and stinking as it touched air. To heal it must be seen. Gin wondered at her capacity for selfishness. It was a raw but cherished time. Surrounded by sorrow, she started to find a fulfilment, a purpose, and looking up at Jonnie from her frantic dispensing, knowledge of a heart healing. Ignorant of the meaning of Simon's silence, whether it was indifference or, paradoxically, not, believing in her soul that the closeness between them still existed, needing no letters or phone calls, there remained a certain anger. Anger for lost time, a full swollen pushing tide of unfinished business, and a fear that Simon's life moved on without her, while hers lay stagnant and dying without him. So Jonnie was necessary to break the bond, burst the dam, flood the flow, to wash away, to cleanse her of Simon.

"Hey, Ginnia," he says.

The soft sound of his nickname for her echoes around the hollow she has created. She tries to focus, looks up at him with heavy-lidded eyes, suffused still with a warmth of memory. Unguarded. His bleep, which had momentarily saved her from the immediacy of conversation, has allowed only for contemplation, reminiscence. She feels exhausted and ill-prepared for this confrontation. She feels the need to shut herself off, to barricade herself against him. The sadness of their situation depresses her. She knows her eyes will never look at him again the way they once did. This they both know, she realises, as they sit over the scratched linoleum of a cafeteria table, the clock gone eight hours into a chilly Friday morning in November.

Perhaps she would have known him less. If not for Simon, if not for Gabe. If Gabe hadn't died. If Simon hadn't betrayed her. If not for the silence between her and Simon that sprung such a well of loneliness it had drowned each day her hope.

Night of dark moon. There were so many people. The air was thick with smoke, incense-like. Heady, subversive, hard to breathe. He was intense. His eyes did not lift from her. Asked her strange, probing questions she found difficult to evade or ignore. Conscious of others' eyes and the fact that she was one of the few white people there. It was strangely thrilling for one so sheltered, kept apart in this land of stilted morality and hypocritical Christianity. The room had darkened, the music deepened, marijuana scented the air. He had her trapped.

"Why are you so unhappy?" So, it was palpable then. "What's your favourite colour?"

Did it matter? Colour, yes. Colour mattered in South Africa, yes, think, Gin, what colour? Blue. Blue, the blue of Gabriel's eyes. Fragments of pain. No, green then, maybe, the flecks in Simon's. The fragments melted into a terrible, tangible cohesion. Black, the deepening blackness of yours, she thought as she stared at him, intoxicated. All my life I have waited for you. Simon's face swam in front of her eyes, and she willed it away, his betrayal stabbing.

"I remember you," she said, unaware of whether it was aloud or not. "I know you. I remember you lifting me into your arms, high with delight, and I remember you dying. I put your body on a barge and lit the funeral pyre, and you drifted away from me on the great river, slowly burning. And my heart could not contain the pain of separation, and I threw myself into the water after you, and drowned. And here I am again, drowning again, in the depths of your eyes, and they will not let me go."

She felt afraid then, of this vastness of emotion. He led her outside, into the icy July night, onto the small cement balcony. Trees stood indigo against the darkness. Luscious willows dipped trailing fingers into the deep chocolate of a narrow stream below. She let him kiss her, tasting cinnamon and ash. She let him lift his hands beneath her shirt and massage her nipples and she did not know if they ached from cold or desire.

Maybe she would not have been pushed, and gone willingly, closer to Jonnie. She would not be sitting here facing this dark part of her past once more. Instead they might have greeted warmly, like long-lost countrymen and colleagues, workmates, surprised to find their paths crossing once more; friends once but now strangers. But then perhaps, thinks Gin, our fates are fixed, destinies determined long before we draw our breath, before our struggling meets and chafes against what we think we can control, against the erroneous illusion of choice.

She turns her head away from him and looks out of the window. The canteen looks out over the back of the hospital. The remnants of last night's rain lie pooling on the stretch of concrete alley, and the sky is a leftover grey. Below her is a steel cage, locked with chain and padlock. Inside, cylinders are lined up neatly, black for the nitrogen, blue the oxygen.

"Gin," he says, "look at me."

Something hardens inside her at his tone. Hard like the steel of the cage. She does not shift her gaze. A white van turns into the alley, and two men jump out quickly. They are both dressed in blue overalls. One gesticulates, and the other laughs. He pulls a bunch of keys from his pocket, moves toward the padlocked gate. He shouts to his companion, thrusts the key in the chunk of metal, easily lifting the heavy gnarl of chain.

"Gin," Jonnie says again, but his voice is softer. "We need to talk about Cape Town. We need to talk about Viv."

Viv. The old knot of emotion contorts inside her. Gin sips at her coffee, tasting insipidness.

The man below is lugging a cylinder with ease, passing it to his partner who shoves it into the back of the van. In turn, he takes another cylinder out of the van, hoists it back. This one heavier it seems, the action slower.

Jonnie sighs. "Ginnia," he says again, and now she resents the use of his nickname for her. "Please."

Slowly she turns her gaze back to where he sits, staring at her. It is the first time she has looked at him fully, and she notes now the lines around his eyes, two deep furrows in his forehead, and a weariness in his demeanour she does not remember. His hair is shorter than it was all those years ago, but still it touches the collar of his white coat. And although she notices fine wisps of white, the thick blackness of it is still so lustrous it shines with a tinge of blue under the fluorescence of the canteen lights.

He has not asked of Ellie's father, who or where he is. He has asked her nothing, no personal questions at all. There lies a frozen wasteland between them. She realises, slowly, with a hidden chill, his position of power. As Ellie's consultant, he would have had access to those privileged notes, the medical history denied even to her. Ellie lies in the same gleaming ward she inhabited minutes after birth, and Gin knows the pitifully short tale must read something along the lines of: *Premature baby. Mother in ICU after emergency Caesarean. Uterine haemorrhage, emergency hysterectomy. Father deceased.* In the spidery scrawl of a tired intern, he could have accessed the insides that were ripped from her. She has no such information, no short synopsis from which to infer relationships, deceased or otherwise, in the time since they last met. She feels small and exposed. It is this urgency, this need to be on equal footing that prompts perhaps her question.

"What are you doing here?" Louder than she meant, and harshly spoken.

If he is surprised at her tone, he does not show it. He does not meet her eyes. "I'm locuming here for a year. My wife –". At this, he stops, his eyes flick to her quickly, then he looks past her, continues hastily, "Not Viv, that is. I mean, we're divorced. I've remarried since…" He pauses, restarts, his voice subdued, "My wife thought it would be a good idea."

So he is unaware of her trip home, her reconciliation with Viv; he cannot know of her accident. Nor of Simon's death.

The canteen fills, the nine o'clock shift will start soon. She smells bacon frying. Although he knows less about her life than she had imagined, she finds his answer not enough. She feels petty, childish, but cannot stop. "Do you have children?" She wants to pry, to make him talk.

Again, he looks away, stares down at his coffee, cradled in his lean brown fingers, two hands on the table, as if in vain to protect it from cooling, congealing, decaying. He wears no wedding ring she notices, and then reminds herself that doctors seldom do. She remembers his hands, caressing her, his finger tracing the line between their bodies as they lay together, the line formed between his dark skin and her own pallor. She had wondered then if sometimes he had hated her because her skin was white.

Jonnie shakes his head and for a moment, lost in remembrance, she thinks he has tapped into her thoughts.

"She – we – we're trying."

Gin is vaguely jealous of this small loyalty to his wife. He knows she knows, is but all too aware he has another child, his daughter with Viv, and that any difficulty must lie with his new wife.

"It may not be possible," he says quietly, almost to himself, and Gin feels ashamed.

"Sorry," she murmurs, and lets a second silence fall.

Her next question is prompted neither by curiosity nor malice. It is a need to connect merely, communicate, be honest. This past year since the accident, she has had no need of small talk, preferring silence to social grace, integrity to inanity. Aside from her time with Michael, she has had few conversations.

"And are you happy now, Jonnie Jay?" she asks softly.

This time his eyes flick directly to hers and do not falter. Perhaps it is the tone of softening, the old endearment.

"Happy?" he queries, and contemplates this.

His answer, when it comes, is spoken softly, with an equal mix of surprise and sincerity.

33. GIN

His eyes, the colour of the Okavango River, narrowed as he looked across at her. It had been so sudden.

"I'm in love with Vivienne," he said.

Suddenly, like that.

Ice in her veins. Gin felt the trembling in her limbs, a disconnection from the ground, an inability to feel her feet. Dappled sun shone through the half-glass of the kitchen door, lighting the wood of the table at which he casually sat. At ease, owning it. The light dripped off the table, pooled on the floor. A tiny tumbleweed of dust gathered strength and rolled itself from a corner.

He tapped the end of his cigarette into his emptied coffee cup. "Aren't you going to say anything?"

Even to herself, her voice sounded strangled, choked with shock. "What do you want me to say?"

She could have gone deeper, delved inside her heart, ignited fury. Did he want her permission? Her forgiveness? For betraying her, being unfaithful, breaking her heart? But she could not summon the anger; her system was numbed. The awkward silences were starting to make sense, the furtive looks. Viv, drowning feelings with wine on nights Gin thought she ached for Gabe. The question built.

"And Viv? What does Viv feel?"

She did not want to hear the answer she already knew. He leaned back in the chair, pulled at his cigarette. The smoke mixed with the sunlight, swirled gently outwards and upwards, dissipated into shadow.

Jonnie smiled slightly, "I guess it's what you call a love triangle."

She could have hit him then, could have walked across the barren gulf of the sunlit floor between them and smacked his beautiful face.

It was done, then. In one sentence, it was decided. In those few words, Gin knew that Jonnie had never loved her. He had chased her, wooed her and won her, but he had never loved her. He had reduced her pain down to a geometric shape.

"No," he says now. He lets out a long breath, as if relieved. Absolved somehow, from carrying a long-held source of guilt, of shame.

Gin waits for the small stab of satisfaction. A small payment for the hurt. There is none, only an odd sadness. So much time wasted between them, so much time wasted on him. She wants to reach out and touch his hand, but cannot. Unhappiness drew her to him once before, and its tendrils reach out to do so once again. She feels her story move around in unceasing circles.

"I'll keep Ellie in for another week, for observation, a few more tests maybe."

Guilt nudges at her reverie. She has been so absorbed by the past that for a moment she had forgotten her daughter.

"I miss home," he adds, his voice quiet amidst the growing clatter of the canteen.

She wants to say she understands, wants to explain the knowledge of exile. That this country offers freedom, anonymity, but that the price can be loneliness, and loss of oceans, mountains, sky. That she misses the sea tide as if it were her very draw of breath, those time-less rhythms one and the same. That there are times she would scour London for a simple taste of home, for wine made from grapes raised in a sun-soaked vineyard, for buttermilk rusks to dunk in hot sweet tea. That her heart still yearned for the wide open spaces, the empty run of roads and sweeping cuttings through mountain passes, for the beauty and dust of the Transkei, the warm rains and swollen muddy rivers of the Caprivi, a sunrise that could steal your breath. For the ice-cold sting of Atlantic spray across the rocks of the Cape. And that sturdy rise of mountain, its many moods; an ancient symbol of enduring Africa.

She wants to tell him also that she cannot explain why she shuns familiar accents, repulsed. That she feels the weight of the invisible cord that stretches umbilically across the distance of a continent, and will not be cut.

That last day, leaving. Leaving Cape Town, that city between mountain and sea, her home and her heartbreak. Two months since she left her home with Viv and Abbie, two months since he had said he did not love her, two months since she packed her bags and drove away. Two months since she kissed her sleeping niece and fled, without confronting Viv. What was there to say? Viv, she had heard since through a mutual acquaintance, was three months' pregnant.

A knock at the door of the rented apartment. She padded along the carpeted corridor. The rectangle of the flat allowed for two entrances, one from the car park above and one from the road below, but it was impossible to see anyone approaching.

Sunlight blinded her temporarily. Her eyes adjusted slowly from the dark of the apartment. Jonnie stood outside, bunch of flowers hanging from one hand, ubiquitous cigarette in the other.

"Hi," he breathed out smoke.

Part of her had wished for this moment, if only to wound him, to hurt him as he had her, but now he was here, she found words stuck in her throat. Since that night he said he did not love her, since he told her about him and Viv, since the next morning when she took her stuff and left, she had kept herself busy. The apartment was found within hours, nestled here in Oranjezicht, the mountain looming steeply to her right, as if at any minute to topple onto the boxy houses glinting in the sun below its peak. From the shaded balcony, she could see far below into the basin of the bay, watch the sails far out on the horizon dip and rise. It was this

hesitation that allowed him entrance. He handed her the flowers. Roses,
she noticed, with bitterness. He knew roses were her favourite, and red.
Buds tight, still dew-fresh. Expensive, prized in Africa for their tempera-
mental growth, their sullen reluctance to proliferate as they did in cooler
climes. Playing hard to get, she thought, had its own rewards. It was a
game she had never had the inclination to play. It had always struck her
as dishonest, requiring levels of artifice and cunning she felt lacking in
her makeup. Perhaps this had been her first mistake. If she had laughed
at Simon when he said he loved her, if she had ignored Jonnie's advances,
perhaps they would have valued her more.

    Like roses in a hot, dry land.

    He was inside. She closed the door, smelled the buds in vain for any
fragrance.

    "Thank you," she said, for want of words. "It'll be a waste, though,
you know, I leave tonight."

    "I know," he said, looking out the window of the lounge, and she
wondered how.

    The mountain's surface was clear to see in all its rugged outcrops and
narrow pines. The apartment was dark against the brilliance of the sun
outside, and when he turned, his face was set in shadow, his expression
unreadable.

    "I'll put these in water," she said and left him, went to the tiny kitchen
with its black-and-white tiled floor and retro fridge. She ran water in
the stainless steel sink, laid the roses in the pool that formed beneath the
taps. They would open after she was gone, soft velveteen petals curling
slightly at the edges, for no one to admire. Later still they would fold
and rust, shrivelling to a desiccated end, brown and fragile, crumbling
to the touch. There was a taste of bile in her throat. She was still in love
with him.

She wants to tell him that it took Europe to free her from him. A full
five years before she could swear it was a week since she had thought

of him, and relief washing over her for it. And Michael helping her forget. She misses Michael so acutely now, she feels her chest contract with pain. But she won't call Michael again, she knows. There's no point.

She felt him enter the kitchen behind her, her senses attuned to his presence. She asked him why he had come, watching the tap drip into the steel sink of roses. Click, clock, click, the drops fell. With an echo into the bowl. A watery echo, like the click of Xhosa at the back of a spit-filled mouth.

"We never meant it to happen," he said into the space above her head. "We fought it. Both of us, Ginnia. Especially Viv."

She stood completely still, facing away from him, although she wanted to scream, to turn and throw his flowers in his face, hoping the thorns would tear at his flesh the way his words were cutting into hers.

"We never meant to hurt you, Gin. I'm sorry."

"I'm sorry," whispers Gin now, fleetingly surprised to find she means it. It had all been for nothing. The measure of pain she had endured might have found some balance had she known it was worth it. That her pain was equalled by his resultant happiness. Or Viv's. "I'm sorry you're not happy."

Jonnie grabs her hand like a man reprieved. "You know what I've been thinking about?" An old joviality to his voice. "That Friday, the day the police came! You remember?"

She could never forget. The thirteenth of May, 6.30 knock, the police had come questioning. Questioning her right to words, her right to live with whom she chose. Ultimately it was what irked her most, the final insensitivity. She had lived with the pettiness and the barring of words, newspapers smudged in black blocks of censored sentences, paragraphs of paranoia, line after line inked out of subversive existence. In taking Jonnie's details, the policeman had been unable to spell neurologist. Rage had wintered these many years to a wry amusement.

Jonnie laughs again.

Gin stares down at their two hands, linked now, folded one within the other, her pale skin sheltered within the burned amber of his. It is a good sound to hear, his laugh, and lifts suddenly the mood between them. Odd how they could laugh about it now, when at the time the threat of imprisonment or detention without trial had hung so heavy in the air there had been little time for mirth. And ultimately he had not escaped that.

His bleep spurts again. "I must go," he says, but not before he takes her telephone number, gives her his.

Now there is a renewed connection, now they will see each other again, now they will be friends.

34. GIN

Ellie does not fit again in the ten days that follow, and she is discharged with an outpatient appointment made for a fortnight later.

The day of the follow-up is a particularly cold Tuesday morning. Gin cannot remember such low temperatures for November in London. Ellie is swaddled in bright blue. Everyone, Gin supposes, will assume she is a boy. They wait in the over-heated blandness that is Hammersmith's outpatients department. Patients sit in sickly-patterned chairs welded together in rows of red metal. As expected, there is a delay. Jonnie is seeing patients and he stops for a quick hello. It is odd to see him again, their meeting having melded into the surreal state Gin associates with Ellie's birth and subsequent seizure. He leans in to smile at Ellie, whose eyes fix on him with that curious intensity of hers. The appointment was for noon, but it is two before Ellie's name is called. She is due to be seen by Jonnie himself, not someone more junior, and Gin is surprised.

"I wanted to see her again," he explains when she comments, but from the way he looks at her when he says this, Gin surmises he means her and not Ellie.

She blinks away, uncomfortable at the thought, looks out of the window onto the brick wall of the building alongside. His attention is too intrusive after her self-imposed isolation, and his presence brings memories, unwanted.

Jonnie questions Gin about Ellie's feeding and sleeping patterns while he takes Ellie through a series of tests, weighing her, measuring her wriggling height, examining her reflexes, ocular response, and checking her ears. This last procedure Ellie takes exception to, and begins to cry. Before Gin can respond, Jonnie picks her up and cuddles her with one arm. He tickles her stomach, and Ellie stops crying, her face scrunching up with delight. Jonnie's smile is endearing. Gin wishes she had his ease with Ellie. She holds out her arms to take her daughter from him, thanks him, and says goodbye. But Jonnie leaves the room with them, closing the door behind him. He walks with them to the reception desk, makes another appointment for a month's time with the female clerk, who seems slightly flustered by this amount of personal attention for one patient in particular. He flirts mildly with the woman, who laughs readily, her skin darkening with pleasure. Gin is reminded once more of Jonnie's social grace, the art he has of dealing with people, something she herself had always found difficult to master.

She takes the piece of paper, thanks the clerk and Jonnie, adjusts Ellie's blanket, moves to leave. But Jonnie asks her to wait while he grabs his coat.

"You've no more patients?"

"You're my last for today. Won't be a moment." He grins at her.

This move was deliberate on his part. Gin is unsure of her feelings and uncomfortably aware of the clerk's scrutiny.

Jonnie returns, shrugging into a long leather coat, and throwing a striped scarf around his neck. He leads them to a sliding door and they exit from the heat of the hospital into a drab and freezing afternoon.

"God, I can't get used to this cold. And these short days!" He shivers. "It'll be dark in a couple of hours." He points the way ahead.

"It'll be better after the solstice," Gin consoles. "It's amazing how you notice the days actually lengthening. Minute by minute."

He looks at her with such heat that she feels as if she is inside the hospital again. The pram butts against a misplaced concrete slab.

"I'll push her," he says, taking the pram with one hand. He crooks his elbow, inviting Gin to put her arm in his.

She feels awkward, but is too polite to refuse. Her woollen gloves slip on the smooth leather of his coat. Jonnie wears no gloves and she wonders if his hands are cold.

"Did you come by bus?" he asks as they near the main road that runs outside the hospital.

To their right are the distinctive cream-and-pinkish-brown parapets of Wormwood Scrubs prison. A disorderly queue has formed at the bus stop, waiting for buses that will be held up by the traffic that packs Du Cane Road. Exhaust fumes puff into the wintry air and wither away in the wind.

She shakes her head. "Walked. It's not far."

"I'll walk you back then," he says.

Gin starts to protest, then stops. She will be glad of the company. The first part of the journey back passes a bleak housing estate and although it is daylight, its deserted atmosphere depresses her.

It is a chilly walk. There are few people on the pavement and their path is unimpeded. He does not comment when her leg starts to cramp up, accentuating her limp. But she notices that he slows his pace. Her awkwardness at holding his arm has gone, and she leans on him slightly for support.

"You know what I miss?" he asks, as they veer left and then right.

"What?" queries Gin, hoping he will keep the conversation impersonal.

She is relieved then, when he answers, "Peppermint crisps."

She cannot help laughing at his longing for the sweet from home, slivers of mint cracknel pressed between two layers of milk chocolate. The conversation centres on food while they walk the wide pavement, into the wind. She and Jonnie reminisce about watermelons dripping with juice on summer sand, the firm flesh of yellow peaches under the shade of bluegum trees, and the peppered kick of biltong. He is lyrical in his remembrance; roasted crab on a beach braai, surf sounding into the night, fish straight from the Indian

Ocean served with sloppy chips too hot to eat, drizzled with salt and tart with vinegar, and the green cane cut fresh from the sugar plantations, so sweet it would make your teeth ache. Eventually Gin puts him out of his misery and tells him there are shops selling South African delicacies if he so desires.

"That wasn't the case when I arrived," she continues, "you know, the first Christmas I was here, Michael and I went searching for a bottle of wine from home." They had found one, at long last, but only after the wary proprietor had looked around fearfully while pulling a fine Cabernet Sauvignon from beneath his counter.

Jonnie laughs heartily. "And I bet it cost the earth!"

She nods, then sobers, "I found people just assumed I was a white racist, either way." Some had actively been aggressive, others more circumspect, sidling up to tell her that "her" government had the right idea. A crowded bus passes them, windows steamed. "But on the whole, I've been very fortunate. People in London kind of accept you as a Londoner mostly, irrespective of where you're from."

They walk over the pedestrian crossing and up St Quintin's Avenue, past a nursing home that used to be a hospital, past the roundabout, down St Mark's Road, and up Cambridge Gardens to reach Ladbroke Grove. Trees stripped naked for the season stick black fingers up into a bleached sky. She asks him if he has been to the market that runs the length of Portobello Road and he shakes his head.

"We've seen some of the sights. But I started work almost straightaway. And we've been settling in." He lives further out, he tells her, the other side of the hospital, but within walking distance of it.

"We can go past the market, then," she offers. "It's not as busy as on the weekend." She leads them across the Grove, Jonnie still pushing the pram, and cuts into the market near the canopy-covered Green, empty now on a Tuesday. Come Sunday it will be packed. "Is your wife also a doctor?"

The idea seems to amuse him. "No, she's not working right now. But she trained as a child therapist."

"How did you meet?"

"My mother," he says after a pause. He gives a short laugh. "She finally found me a nice Muslim girl."

Gin wonders how his mother had reacted towards Viv but says nothing. They reach the fruit and vegetable sellers, stalls stacked high with produce, potatoes, parsnips, carrots, curly kale, tomatoes clinging to the green vine, broccoli tinged with purple florets.

Jonnie slows the pram and stops at one of the stalls. "This is great," he enthuses. He buys four avocados, a couple of thick-skinned oranges, and ten red apples. The stallholder wraps them in brown paper bags and Jonnie stacks them on Ellie's pram.

Gin zigzags off the Portobello, passing colourful houses four stories high. Yellow, cream, lime, cream again, white, blue, aubergine, white again, and scarlet.

"Reminds me of the houses in the Bo-Kaap," remarks Jonnie, "only taller."

It is only polite to invite him in to her blue house on the Hill. He walks around, admires the mature garden, says he likes the spacious feel of the house. She makes him tea while he amuses Ellie.

"There's nothing of you in her," he notes suddenly, then reflects. "No, wait, she has the same shape mouth as you."

Gin makes a face at him as she hands him his mug. He smiles at her, and her heart tugs. She had forgotten how beguiling a smile.

"In fact," he says slowly, and his eyes glint, "she's so dark she could have been mine."

She knows he is teasing her, but there is a tone of regret in his words, for time that can never be recaptured. It is a tone like Simon's, that last day.

I've something to tell you, Gin.

A restless yearning forms.

Something I should have told you ages ago.
A yearning that will be endless, now.

35. VIVIENNE

Michael hugs Viv so hard that her eyes water. His delight is obvious as he ushers her and Nick into his flat. It is in the same courtyard complex where Gin had lived. Viv watches the two men size each other up as she introduces them. They shake hands.

"It's a mirror image of the one Gin had," says Michael when she comments. He leads them off the short hall into a square, comfortably furnished lounge. It is cool inside, a relief from the heat.

"I never knew her then," says Viv, "I never saw her flat. I just know it's the one on the end. She told me." Viv sinks thankfully into an armchair. They had made an early start this morning, and it is good to be out of the car.

"It's great," says Michael, "I get to walk to lectures." He heads into the kitchen to make them tea.

Not like the farm, out of town and subject to the vagaries of weather, the steep incline of road. Gabe lurks everywhere in this town for her, she thinks, but especially on the farm. She is glad Michael hadn't moved back there.

There is so much to catch up on with Michael. His move here, the preparation for the coming year, her life, the girls. He sounds excited and Viv thinks he looks younger than when she last saw him. Years ago now. He does not talk about his divorce, and she presumes this is because of Nick's presence. She wishes she and Michael had time to talk properly, and alone. A sense of disloyalty to Nick catches her unawares. It is disquieting, this attachment to the man.

"Anyhow," says Michael, "I thought you'd only be up in the

New Year. Didn't you want to show Abbie around the university or something?"

"Oh yes. I will be back then." She looks quickly at Nick. "This is just a pre-Christmas break. The girls are at my mom's." She cannot tell Michael of that terrible day in the sunroom, nor of the tentative truce she and Abbie had made. It had been a difficult few months. After Jonnie had left, the girls had naturally spent more time at home, and but for that day, she might have let Nick into her life more. Instead she had been conscious of Abbie's antagonism, and time with Nick had become a snatched luxury. It was Nick who suggested the break when the girls went off to her mother's. "Anyhow, since Port Alfred is so close, we thought we'd stop in on you."

"My good fortune then. Good one, Nick," says Michael.

Nick nods his acknowledgement.

It must be difficult for him to sit and listen to her and Michael catching up, but he shows no signs of impatience or boredom. In fact, he seems quite comfortable in the chair opposite her, leaning back with his legs stretched out.

Viv holds her cup out for a refill. Michael pours from a china pot adorned with a pink Chinese pattern. "And Gin? How is she?" she asks.

"Yes, didn't she tell you? She had a baby girl in October."

Viv looks quickly at Nick, but his face betrays nothing.

Michael continues to fill her in. "I suppose she wants to keep news of Ellie quiet. I gathered she doesn't want Simon's family to know." His obvious concern for Gin's health gives his voice an edge. "Frankly, I'm worried about her, Viv. Do you know while I was there she insisted we put her bed on stilts? Something about being afraid of the *tokoloshe*. And she has these recurrent nightmares of Simon. She says his face is almost always distorted and bleeding."

Viv has been aware of Nick's aroused interest and it has distracted her. She wants to hear about Gin, to take in all the details, but she finds it hard to concentrate on Michael's words. She wishes now she had told him about Nick, about how they had met.

Michael is still talking. "She says he keeps saying the same thing over and over again in the dreams."

It is Nick who asks, "What does he say?"

Michael looks at him. "It's a number, or a year. Nineteen eighty-nine. Over and over, apparently."

"And she has no idea what it means?"

Michael shakes his head. "No. Other than it was the year she left. I suggested hypnotherapy. It can help in cases like this."

"Cases like what?" Viv finds her voice.

"I think Gin is suffering from some form of post-traumatic stress disorder. Because of the accident. I think she's stuck in some kind of limbo state." Michael's face sets in a frown. "You know, Viv, she hasn't grieved properly. Not even for her dad. And certainly not for Simon."

Viv stays quiet now, willing him to change the topic of conversation. She feels uncomfortable talking with Michael about Gin in front of Nick.

"What do you mean?" asks Nick.

Still gathering information, still investigating. Viv resents him asking these questions.

"Well, it's just that she hasn't grieved *at all*. I mean, not *once* has she even cried. It's like it's all bottled up inside her still."

Michael offers them more tea, or something stronger, says he hopes they are staying for lunch. "A beer maybe?" he suggests, looking at Nick, who declines as he is driving.

"You're welcome to stay the night," offers Michael.

Nick looks at her, letting her decide. Viv refuses politely. They must head off after lunch. She doesn't want to travel in the dusk. Michael rises, gives them a choice of lunch in town, on him, or his own paltry efforts.

Viv teases him, insists on the meagre option, but as expected, it is more sumptuous than promised. They sit in the oblong dining room that opens out from the lounge, and Michael serves cold meats, salad, fresh bread, a selection of cheese, olives, sun-dried tomatoes, and ripe avocados. He apologises to Nick for hogging Viv and the exclusive conversation. Nick merely smiles and shrugs slightly.

"So where did you study, Nick?"

Viv is about to intervene, to tell Michael that Nick is a policeman. She worries that Nick will be embarrassed by the question. Instead Nick's mild answer astonishes her.

"I came here," he says.

She cannot help herself. "You did?" She stares at him, becomes aware of Michael staring at her in turn. How little she knows about Nick.

"You did?" echoes Michael, "what did you study?"

Viv is grateful he does not ask Nick when. She calculates she must have been in Cape Town, perhaps pregnant with Kayleigh, by the time Nick would have been studying.

"Botany. And some Marine Biology." Nick looks at Viv apologetically.

Or does she imagine it? Should she know this, she asks herself. Should he have told her? Should she have asked?

"Ah, one of the Port Alfred surfers," Michael is saying, handing out more bread. "The marine biologists to a man were always surfing while ostensibly studying."

Both men laugh.

"I'm not too bad on a surfboard," says Nick, "for an inland boy from the Transkei."

Viv listens as the two men chat. She is still reeling from Nick's revelation and it has made her feel excluded from his life.

"So is that what you do in Cape Town?"

The inevitable questions, thinks Viv.

"No," replies Nick easily, "I'm a policeman."

Michael's look is contemplative and not, as Viv would have expected, one of surprise.

Nick is looking at her now. He smiles with affection. Viv feels her cheeks redden. She dreads the talk returning to Gin, but instead Nick reveals he had studied psychology in his freshman year and the two men reminisce about various lecturers. Viv's attention drifts and she studies the painting behind Michael. The other walls are bare, as are those of the lounge. It is a striking portrait of a stormy sea. In the right upper quadrant, a headland. White waves pound at its base. Mist rises above the crash of surf. A bank of rocks cuts across the foreground. There is nothing but the sea. No people, no ships, no birds in the overcast sky. She finds it vaguely depressing.

"So you're happy to be back?" asks Nick. "That's a long time to be away. You must find the country very changed."

"Yes," agrees Michael. "For the better. I feel I missed out on the transition. But there's still a lot of divisive issues here."

"Like what?" asks Viv, intrigued now, and tired of looking at the painting.

"Well, there's a lot of talk about changing Grahamstown's name, for one," answers Michael. "I gather some people don't like the idea."

"Well, I think it would be a shame," says Viv. "The Settlers contributed to this country too. Name changes risk alienating white people."

"Well, there's something very symbolic about it," muses Michael, "but perhaps it's a bit late, I agree. Perhaps the time for that was at the end of apartheid when people were ready for change."

"We can't change history," interjects Nick, "We inherit the good, the bad. We can only try to move forward now in the spirit of ubuntu."

Ubuntu. The essence of humanity. Central to the concept of forgiveness in the new South Africa, the knowledge that oppression diminishes us all, that we are all inter-connected. Viv thinks of Jonnie, of Abbie, and wonders how people can achieve this with strangers when they so rarely can achieve it with those they know, with those they love.

"Maybe something neutral will be least inflammatory," she suggests, "isn't Grahamstown also called the City of Saints?"

"Yes," chuckles Michael, "There's something like forty religious buildings. In a town this size!"

They all laugh.

"You know," says Nick, "there's another story as to how it got that name." Apparently, he tells them, in the mid eighteen hundreds, a group of Royal Engineers stationed here were in need of supplies. "So they cabled the Cape. The message read: *Send Vice.* A cable came back, saying: *Obtain vice locally.* That prompted another cable to Cape Town that read: *No vice in Grahamstown.*"

They all laugh again.

"So," says Michael, changing the subject, "You'll be up again with Abbie. She's thinking of studying here then?"

"Um-hm," nods Viv, her mouth full. She swallows hard. "Yes. Not sure it's the best place."

"Why not?" asks Nick. "It'll be good for her to be away from home. Find that first independence."

Viv looks at him. Part of her wants to tell him to mind his own business, that this is between her and Abbie, while another part has to acknowledge the truth of his words. She has to let Abbie go, let her find her own way. Viv only wishes it could be somewhere else, somewhere that does not hold for her an agonising mix of happiness and pain.

Lunch ends on lighter matters, and they take their leave.

Michael hugs her again and shakes Nick's hand. "Good to finally meet you, Nick Retief," he says, adding with a nod at Viv. "Look after her."

Viv pulls a face at him.

Nick laughs. "I think she looks after herself pretty well."

"I know," replies Michael, looking at her, "but still."

A rush of tenderness for Michael fills her. Once, long ago, he had been infatuated with her, and she knew it had been hard for him to see her with Gabe. In time, she had come to realise that perhaps Gabe's death had hit him harder for it. She turns back to give Michael another hug. Over his shoulder, she can see the flat at the end of the courtyard, the one that Gin had lived in. It looks empty, forlorn even. Do the places we live in hold a remnant of our lives, she wonders.

Michael waves as they drive away.

"I always thought it was a shame that Gin and Michael never got together," she muses, buckling her belt. "They would have been well-suited."

"Maybe it was because of Gabriel," says Nick, turning into the main road. "It's hard to date the sister of your best friend."

She studies his profile. How astute he is. Although something in the way he has spoken makes her suspect he speaks from experience.

She watches the town pass by. I don't know how Michael can stay here, she thinks. "I admire him for coming back," she tells Nick.

"I think he admires you for staying."

Nick thinks she means Michael's return to the country, realises Viv.

"I mean to Grahamstown," she says quietly, "I couldn't live here again." She stops herself from adding: *Among the ghosts.*

36. VIVIENNE

They drive the stretch of road that sweeps up and out of the town, leaving behind Grahamstown, the City of Saints. The City, thinks Viv, of Sorrow. The day is hot and she winds down the window, letting the air rush in and lift her hair, cool her neck. She glances at Nick, who drives on in silence, his eyes fixed on the road ahead. They are high on the hills now, the tar thin. The road is in bad condition and he has to concentrate so as not to hit the frayed edges.

They reach the turnoff. In the distance she sees the giant pineapple, constructed out of fibreglass, steel and concrete. The ground floor is a gift shop selling home-made jams and chutneys, local pottery and T-shirts for the tourists, and the top is an observation deck with views over farmlands that roll all the way to the Indian Ocean. It is also a landmark, how the students learn the way to the coast. The road is better here, but Nick is still quiet. She is sure she knows why. He had known nothing of Gin's pregnancy. Again, she had kept him out of her life.

"I didn't know she'd had her baby," she offers, and is immediately cross with herself. Why should she have told him? What does it matter? And what of his secrets, his past?

He looks at her briefly, a swift appraisal. A quick shake of his head before he turns his attention back to the road. "It doesn't matter. It has no bearing on the case. It's all been settled, now. The insurance has paid out."

"And you? What do you think?" Viv remembers his conviction that the car crash was no accident.

"It doesn't matter what I think," he says bluntly. "It's done."

There is a note of finality in his voice, and Viv supposes there are plenty worse crimes for him to deal with.

The land is parched dry and brown. Viv's mouth feels edged with the dust of it. Endless sky ahead, blue and cloudless. Torrid sun with no hope of rain. Settler's country. How alienated they must have felt, she thinks. There had been evident nostalgia in the names they gave their towns. She thinks again of Michael saying they might re-name Grahamstown. It makes her sad, not hopeful. There are more important things to deal with still, she thinks, like homes and jobs, than worrying about what to call a town.

They reach Port Alfred as the sun sinks. Nick crosses the new bridge, turns left and drives along the river canalways to reach the beachfront, the rolling sand dunes brushed with grass. The sea looks deceptively flat. She knows the waves are bigger than they look, the rocks not as smooth. They simmer in the day's remaining heat, beneath calm shallows. The tide is out. The tides, she knows, are treacherous, the slick dangerous pull that can suck you out in a minute, drawing you out into the depths.

Nick threads his way through coastal bungalows, over roads that deteriorate with their distance from the town. He swerves to avoid a pothole, bumps over a short cement bridge onto a dirt track, lined on both sides with thick vegetation. He turns the car sharply, stops in front of a steel gate, initially hidden by the bush. He winds down his window and taps a code into a square box attached to a pole. The gate slides open, metal grating against metal, and closes behind them automatically.

The thick forest alongside casts the car in shadow. Half a mile down the track, the road ends, widening into a clearing where Nick parks. On the left, tucked amid the milkwood trees and indigenous sea bush is a low-slung cottage. It gleams yellow in the dying sunlight. Crickets scream at the encroaching night. On the side of the house is a round water tank, covered with a roof of corrugated iron. Moss grows around its damp base. Viv can smell the sea and hear the surf. Nick leads her around the front of the house and there, a short distance from the verandah is a path snaking through low dunes, straight to the beach.

Inside, the cottage is crudely but comfortably furnished. Off the sitting room is a narrow kitchen. Open shelves are stacked with tinned food, candles, candlesticks, soap, matches, some paraffin, paraffin lamps, and a torch. But there is electricity, an oven and a fridge. Next to this is a bathroom with a frosted window set high into the wall. She finds this mildly amusing. There is no one around for miles, they are surrounded by a high steel fence, and even if the window were clear-paned and low-set, the bathroom would still be private. The bath is shallow, water is a scarcity. No shower. There are three bedrooms, two large, one small. Viv walks into the largest one that faces the beach, stands at the window, looking out over the dunes. She feels extraordinarily nervous for some reason.

She turns as Nick enters the room, sits on the bed, kicks off his shoes.

He grins at her. "Come over here," he says, patting the bed beside him.

Viv does not move. I know almost nothing about him, she reminds herself. His whole revelation about Rhodes, about studying there, had upset her more than she would care to admit. What else of his past does she not know? He talks little of it, has never mentioned women, and there must be some, he must have had girl-friends. He is too accomplished a lover for there not to have been, she thinks with some amusement.

Viv puts her hands on the windowsill behind her, leans back slightly. He has shifted to sit up on the bed, propped against the wall, his long legs stretched out, crossed at the ankles. His arms are folded and he is still smiling at her.

"So," she says thoughtfully, "you studied at Rhodes."

"*Ja.*"

"Botany." She nods her head as she says this.

"*Ja,*" he repeats. "Come over here. Please."

"Why botany?"

He sighs in mock frustration. "I was still considering the farm then. You know, agriculture."

"And a bit of zoology, marine biology?"

His look is questioning and his smile has faded. "*Ja,* why?"

"So that means you must have spent a lot of time down here, at the sea?"

"Yes. If I answer all these questions, will you come over here?"

She moves two steps towards him, but stays out of his reach. His grin returns.

"So did you bring girls here?"

"Yes," his smile broadens, "You owe me another step."

Viv takes a short step closer. His arms are still folded but were he to stretch, she is within his reach now. "Were there many?"

"Yes," he says, mock serious. "Lots. Several. Sometimes all at once."

Viv stifles a laugh.

Nick continues in a rueful tone, "In fact, this was my den." He gestures around the room. "A positive lair of lechery, and the seduction of innocents…" His arm swings back and he is up, grabs Viv to him, falls back with her onto the bed. "Got you."

She bursts out laughing. He has her pinned under him.

He lifts his head back to look at her properly. His eyes are blue and direct, his voice tender. "But none of them were as beautiful as you."

She does not know what to say, her throat feels full.

He strokes her hair away from her face. "None of them even came close."

Later, he is hungry and unpacks food she had not even noticed he had brought. They sit out on the verandah, side by side in pastel-green Adirondack chairs, eating cheese on toast washed down with beer. Under the white orb of African moon, she can make out the roll of the dunes and beyond a black strip that is the sea. Stars radiate across an infinite heaven. Nick's hand rests on her forearm, his thumb trails rhythmically along her skin, but she can tell his mind is elsewhere. He sips his beer and stares out into the night.

Her curiosity resurfaces. "So if you went travelling after studying," she says, "that would mean you only joined the police after the change of government?"

There is a pause before his answer. "Yes."

"Why did you become a policeman?"

Another pause. Then he says, "It's a long story. I suppose by then I knew I wasn't going to farm, Mandela was a man to believe in, get behind, and I knew the country was going to need a new police force, forward-thinking, you know, someone to keep law and order." He takes a sip of beer.

"And you were that someone?"

Another sip. "Yes." It is said self-deprecatingly. Another sip. "So I sold the farm, came to Cape Town, bought the townhouse, joined the force."

Ah, she thinks, the money for the townhouse explained. He makes it sound so simple, but she suspects a deeper history. "Just like that?"

"Um-hm. Just like that."

"And girls? No one to leave behind?"

"Still on about that?" His amusement is evident.

"Seriously, there must have been someone." Viv is determined.

He sobers, is silent for a while, as if deciding something. "All right, there was. A long time ago now."

She waits. She feels his eyes on her in the darkness.

"But she wouldn't have me." A lighter tone again that she does not believe. Even in the poor light, she can see his face enough to see a sorrow settle there. A regret.

"Who would?" Viv teases back quickly, with a joviality she does not feel.

That night she lies awake listening. Listening to Nick's even breathing beside her. Listening to the surf thundering outside, beating away at the shifting dunes, moulding them into shapes that will be changed again by tomorrow's rasping wind, as air and water battle each other continually for control of the earth. Even now the air is restless, and the branches scratch repetitively at the window, emaciated fingers trying to get inside. Nick's hidden history has left her with a sense that he too had suffered, has left her with a sadness she cannot shake.

She wakes to an empty bed the next morning. The day is already dazzling. Viv takes her tea and toast outside. Nick is walking back from the beach, bare-chested, wet-haired. He kisses her and she tastes salt. He grabs a bite of her toast.

"Did you know you talk in your sleep?" he asks, affectionately.

She feels herself blush, wondering what she had said, what secret thoughts she has divulged to him now. "Is it safe here?" she deflects.

"To what? To live?" He moves inside to the kitchen, puts two slices of bread in the toaster and pours himself some tea from the pot she has made.

She stands in the front room. "To swim." *To be with you.*

"There's a bit of an undertow, but it's fine if you're careful. We're safe here otherwise. The fence is electric."

It disturbs Viv that the presence of an electric fence is necessary, and disturbs her further that she feels safer for it.

"So it's only me you have to worry about," smiles Nick, coming back into the front room with his mug of tea. He puts it down, reaches for her. The toaster pings, and is ignored.

They swim in the afternoon. The beach is deserted, the water cold. Nick tries to get her to venture further than waist-deep. He treads water further out, then swims to her, circles her. "What are you afraid of?"

"I don't know. Sharks. Drowning."

"It's only a rogue shark that'll actively go for you. Most bites are mistakes, or curiosity."

"That's comforting." Sarcastically.

He laughs, flicks his wet hair back from his face with a shake of his head. "And you won't drown," he pulls her to him, holds her, moves until they are chest-deep.

Viv looks nervously at the water. She was raised inland and, although now she loves the sight and sound of it, the sea has always been a stranger. Nick takes them even further out until the sandy bottom falls away beneath her feet. She inhales sharply.

"Just hold onto me." He keeps one arm around her, the other spread out across the surface. "The water holds you up if you let it."

Viv exhales and lets him guide her out. It is an eerie feeling, to be in deep water, and far from the comfortable safety of the beach. She is not sure she likes it, but when they reach the shore again, she finds she is exhilarated.

That evening he starts the fire for a braai. He covers it with the grill and they leave it to burn down to orange charcoal. They walk on the beach into a glow of sunset. The sand is warm silk beneath their bare feet. Nick is visibly relaxed, his jeans rolled up. The day has done them both good and her limbs feel tired but invigorated from the swim.

"Have you never feared the sea?" she asks.

He looks out at the ocean in question. "I've always loved it, but I respect it too," he replies. "You know, I was swept out once."

"Swept out?"

Nick leans down to pick up a stone, stands, rubs it absently between his fingers.

"What happened? How old were you?"

He plays with the stone. "Fourteen. I was at the Wild Coast, with family and some friends." He pauses. "Mdumbi beach. It's this lovely stretch of beach set below headlands. I went too far out, basically." He tells her how he had swum beyond the waves that swelled and rolled and crashed, and swelled and rolled and crashed again. To where the gulls cried and swooped for food. "I stopped swimming, found I couldn't touch the bottom. The beach was way back, farther than I thought." Nick stares out across the waves as he talks. "It looked a bit like a mirage, shimmering in the distance."

"Were you afraid?"

"Not at first. I'm a strong swimmer. It was only when I turned back that I felt the current against me, tugging at my legs. It had taken me out." His first instinct, he tells her, was to try to swim against it. "But then I remembered my dad telling me that that's what exhausts you, tires you out. And you drown."

"And then?"

"I was floating, treading water. I could see my dad on the beach. He'd realised what was happening, was heading for the boathouse. But up on the headland above the beach I saw a group of Thembu women. I was far out, but I could see them swaying, and I could hear them singing."

"Singing?"

He nods. "I couldn't hear the words. The wind swept them away, but I could make out the music of their voices. Afterwards, I asked my dad what they were doing, what they were singing. And he told me they were singing to the sea. Asking the sea to bring me back." He looks at her, drops the stone. "And it did," he says, "a bit farther down the beach, the current brought me in."

Nick takes her hand, and they turn back towards the house. "You see, Vivienne, you don't have to be afraid. And you don't have to fight it. The sea will always bring you home."

37. GIN

Jonnie visits her once a week, ostensibly to check on Ellie, although Gin suspects it is to check on her as well. But she is pleased for his company, and it allays her worries about her daughter. They walk with Ellie down the lenient slope to Holland Park, and Jonnie wheels the pram along the barren ground as they weave beneath the trees that are all mottled bark and naked branches. He helps with Ellie and Gin feels both grateful for, and yet resentful of, his obvious expertise with children. He stays late sometimes. He brings with him a laughter and an irreverence; it is a feeling she has missed.

He does not mention Ellie's father again and Gin tells him only that he was killed in the same accident in which she had hurt her leg. They mention neither Viv nor his new wife. On the odd late evening when he stays to share some wine, Gin wonders what he tells his wife, or whether he still flouts his religion by drinking wine at home, but she does not feel inclined to ask. In fact, she does not care. Jonnie talks of work, of patients, of how he is finding this new country. He speaks often of home. Politics is a frequent topic of debate. Their conversations alternately exhaust and enliven her.

It is his effect on Ellie she notices most. Ellie, who seems to have an earnest temperament not unlike her father, brightens in Jonnie's presence. She gurgles with delight at his appearance, and in turn Jonnie seems inexplicably drawn to this child. Tiny fingers curl around his with steady hold, while she stares at him with eyes that could penetrate one's soul.

One evening he arrives with bagfuls of ingredients for supper,

"Courtesy of your market," he says, "for a *proper* chicken curry. And because," he adds, "you don't eat enough."

Gin, bemused, sits at the table and watches while he unpacks chicken pieces, rice, tomatoes, an onion, yoghurt, spices, and a single, vibrantly green lime.

"You've got oil?" he opens cupboards without waiting for her reply.

"In the one above the kettle."

Jonnie takes out the bottle and switches on the kettle. He grabs a frying pan from the drying rack and puts it on the stove, adding some oil. Gin has to help him light the gas with matches. He takes a sharp knife and pierces the skin of each tomato, pours boiling water over them. Their skins curl back from their scalding, and peel away easily. Jonnie chops the flesh of them, piling it all on a plate. He pulls a match out of the box and starts to chew on it. Gin's look is quizzical.

"It stops your eyes watering," he explains, dicing onion. He tosses the pieces into the pan, and it spits. "See, no tears," he says, discarding the match. Ginger, garlic, and chillies get chopped and added to the sizzling pan. Spices are next, coriander, cumin, turmeric, stirring all the time to stop them sticking. A dash of salt, freshly ground black pepper and the tomatoes follow. "I tried to teach the girls. Kayleigh would be quite a good cook if she could pay attention long enough." He laughs. The sauce boils and he turns the heat down to let it simmer.

Gin takes this apparently unguarded comment as a cue to ask him about her niece. "What's Abbie like, Jonnie?"

He responds by looking at her briefly, eyes narrowed. "She's lovely." He pauses, smiles at her. "You know Gin, she looks a lot like you."

Gin feels afresh the old guilt. Her lack of contact with Gabe's daughter had always bothered her. But the circumstances were such that she had felt no contact was better than some. And Abbie had been so young when Gin had left, she was sure she would not remember her. But her sister had kept in contact, albeit irregular.

"I know Issy kept in touch."

"Yes, I remember. We met her a few times. She always sent Abbie presents on her birthday. Made Kayleigh quite jealous." Jonnie reminds her that Abbie had spent some holidays with her grandparents. "Less so after your mom died, but your dad, well, he adored her." Her dad, he says, had also commented on Abbie's resemblance to her aunt.

Dad. Gin cannot speak, seeing her father's face in front of her again.

Jonnie adds the chicken pieces to the sauce. "Good, we'll leave that for a half hour or so." As he cleans and tidies, washing bowls, stacking the drainer, he talks more of the girls, telling Gin about their schooling, their favourite subjects, and more of what they are like. They are good students. Abbie excels at languages, Kayleigh at mathematics and biology.

It is apparent to Gin that he misses them more than he cares to admit.

"You like children, don't you, Jonnie?" she observes. "You're very good with them." She cannot bring herself to say he is good with Ellie. It is too close, too much a reminder of her own failings as a mother.

Jonnie checks on the simmering curry. "Yes," he says, covering the pan again, "I do like children. I'm not sure I'm that good with them, though." Steam volcanoes out of the pot of rice and he adjusts the heat.

Gin wonders if he and his wife are still trying to conceive, but keeps her curiosity to herself. Instead she asks, "Did you and Viv want more kids?" It is the first time she has mentioned Viv's name openly like this.

He shrugs as he adds the yoghurt into the saucepan. "We had problems in our marriage by then." The sauce bubbles gently and Jonnie scoops some up in a teaspoon, blows it cool, tastes it. He cuts the lime in half and squeezes it one-fisted into the pan. The juice dribbles over his hand.

"Well, you must have been a good father. You raised Abbie as your own."

He smiles, chops fresh coriander leaves. "That was easy. She's easy to love." His smile widens then and his tone turns playful. "She's like you in temperament too, you see…"

Gin laughs despite herself. She brings out a bottle of Sauvignon Blanc while he serves up the curry, sprinkled with the chopped coriander. They sit in the kitchen to eat. The room is warm from his cooking and the air still fragrant with spice. The flavours hit her tongue and burn her mouth. Hotter than she remembers.

"You adopted Abbie, didn't you, Jonnie? So she's Abbie Kassan now?"

Jonnie nods as he swallows. He takes a slow sip from his wine glass. When he speaks, his tone has lost its humour, and he is reflective. "I may have been a good father, but I make a crap husband."

She does not miss his use of the present tense.

38. GIN

It is Jonnie who makes the effort to decorate her home for Christmas. Gin teases him about his obvious enjoyment of the process, but nothing she says shifts his determination. Late December, he hauls in a tree one morning, leaving a trail of pine needles in the hall, and stands it in a corner of the lounge.

"It's her first Christmas, Gin, you have to."

Jonnie's enthusiasm is catching, and they spend the rest of the morning hanging baubles and trailing tinsel on the pungent branches. Ellie is captivated by the glitter and the rustle of the tree. Come the afternoon, Jonnie takes Ellie out for a walk. Picking up Gin's keys from the table in the hall, he leaves, telling Gin to rest. She looks in the mirror after he has gone, sees for herself the face etched with fatigue that must have prompted his instruction. She feels like a fraud. Her nights are disturbed not by Ellie, but by the unrelenting dreams of Simon.

She runs a hot bath, heaps in a turquoise mix of rosemary and sage bath foam, and soaks in the bubbles. Her exhaustion ebbs out with the bathwater. She wraps herself in a towel, squeezes water out of her hair. Then she cleans out the bath, and rinses it.

Laughing, window open, sea-breeze strong, Simon's sure hands on the wheel.

Then it blanks again, car towards car, the curve undone. Why can she not remember? She can remember his hands. Those long fingers and tender hands. Remembers them on the wheel, remembers the sweep of road that took them up and over the hill. Remembers those hands on her body, touching her. She can see Simon's dead face, his shining eyes lost to life, dull in death. They were stuck open, fixed in their last unyielding stare. She cannot bear to think of his pain. She remembers them wheeling her away, her consciousness slipping. In her vague and unfinished memory of the crash, she knows there was a time before he died that she had watched him struggle to focus through the pain. She knows he fought against death, he would not have let himself slip away without a fight. And he was trying to tell her something, but her memory fails again, blurs into a red mist, like blood, tainting clarity, as her own injuries drew her away from him, as he struggled for every breath. As he fought.

"Leila." Like a message. His hand, outstretched to her.

Gin dresses, makes tea, watches the afternoon creep towards an early dusk. The doorbell rings. It is too soon to expect them back and anyhow, Jonnie took her keys. She opens the door to a ghost.

In the years since she last saw him, Simon's father Isaac has aged. His face, never young, has creased. The hair, never thick, has thinned. He wears it combed over his head, parting low over his left ear. Oiled strips plastered over his shiny scalp reach the other ear, ending in curls, whiter than the preceding streaks of grey. Tendrils pull out above the rest, wave helplessly atop his head. Isaac was always taller than his brother Jacob, but now he seems bent, shrivelled. There exists no sign of robust health.

Stunned, Gin invites him in, gives him a hasty embrace. She is thankful for Ellie's absence and now in dread of Jonnie's imminent return with Isaac's granddaughter. It is possible, though unlikely, that Isaac has heard about Ellie. Gin has contacted no one, only her sister and Michael, and she hopes, albeit vainly, that he knows nothing.

Isaac walks stooped, his left shoulder lists off lower than the right. He is apologising to her, apologising for arriving like this. Unannounced.

Gin barely listens, surreptitiously checking the room for signs of a child, for signs of Ellie. None are obvious in the large lounge and she seats him there, beside the gaudy Christmas tree, offers him tea or coffee in a voice that does not sound like her own. Stalling for time to gather her thoughts, she brings tea, apologises for no biscuits or cake.

No, no, he insists, it is he who should apologise.

They circle each other with polite talk. She asks after Isaac's wife and then feels the horror of having to ask about Simon's wife, Simon's sons. She stumbles over the words, falls mute. Isaac saves her, launching into how everyone is. His niece Hannah – *you remember Jacob's daughter? Simon's cousin?* – is home for the holiday season. She is taking Simon's son to have a look around Rhodes University, he says. Simon's son is keen to read his degree there, the year after next.

Gin swallows hard and then sips her tea. She does not know how to respond. She searches for the flint that burned once in Isaac's eyes, the ever-present hint of a smile on his lips, a readiness to laugh heartily and often. There is none. His eyes look dulled and crescented with grey. Simon's death, no doubt, has robbed them of their light.

Eventually they exhaust the family news. Gin stands and turns on a side lamp to throw light into the darkened room. Where is Jonnie? Surely he will be back any minute. Gin prays he is delayed.

"Virginia, my dear," says the old man sitting in her lounge.

She turns slowly to face him, cold seeping into her body as she does so. Her arms and legs start to freeze, stripping her of feeling, numbing her till there is only the core of her left. Her heart, still beating.

His hand, outstretched to her.

"I expect you're wondering why I'm here."

This she had not expected. She had thought it obvious. Surely he wanted to ask about Simon, about his son, about Cape Town, about the accident?

"Gin," he had gasped, like a lover, like when making love to her. His hand, outstretched to her.

Isaac puts his cup down with some force, sits forward in the leather armchair. "I'm here," he says, with obvious effort, "about Simon's will."

"His *will?*" The words are out before she can help it. "His will?" she repeats, more calmly. Then she asks quietly, "What has that got to do with me?"

His son, explains Isaac, with infinite poignancy and patience, has bequeathed her some things. Gin sits down on the couch opposite him and watches while he pulls out some papers and a package. She listens as Simon's father tells her that his son has left her the flat in Grahamstown. The little flat in the cobbled courtyard, beneath the sun. Where love had lived. Gin feels her legs start to shake uncontrollably.

Simon, you sentimental fool. To put it all at risk, for me.

"So you'll need to sign there," Isaac stabs the sheet. "And then there is the money."

Gin is still trying to absorb the flat. "Money?" she breathes.

A large amount, substantial. A policy Simon took many years ago, as if this explains it all. Gin's hands are trembling. Isaac must be wondering why Simon had left all this to her, but he carries on nonetheless, passing form after form that later, he explains, Gin must sign. She sits and stares at him and the pages, brilliantly white, that pile up in front of her.

Eventually Isaac looks up. "There's one more thing. He also left you this."

Carefully he hands her the package that Gin must find a way to take from him without convulsing. She knows what it is.

Inside is a book. The book is oblong and pastel blue. The top right hand corner of the cover is well worn, with a fold from use. The title is written up along the vertical axis, in a yellowed script that, when new, was white. *Somehow we Survive.* It is underlined by part of a drawing, the line which forms the outer edge of a prison bar. The subtitle *An Anthology of South African Writing* is written parallel, so that it too is underlined, but by the line that is the inner edge of the bar. Wrapped around the bar is a man's hand, sketched in charcoal. In striations, a man's face, with closed eyes, large nostrils, and open-mouthed in a scream, or perhaps, Gin had always imagined, more hopefully a song. Lines run alongside his mouth, into his throat, where the clavicular ends are large, grotesque even, his bones protruding through the thin skin.

Simon, you sentimental fool.

In its day, deemed subversive, the book had been banned. Simon had smuggled it back from San Francisco after a medical conference. Saved it, as a surprise, for several months. Wrapped it plainly for her birthday, that first year. Wrapped it plainly, but with obvious care, in neat folds of cream-coloured paper, the Sellotape cut with surgical precision. Found, he said, at the back of a bookstore in the Heights. Writings of exile, of longing, of love. And in the front, inscribed to her, incongruously, Yeats' poem: *When you are old and grey and full of sleep, and nodding by the fire, take down this book...*

He had been the man who loved the pilgrim soul in her. When he gave it to her, smuggled and illicit, South Africa had been in a state of emergency. Now, her country is free, struggling with its new-found freedom, but free nonetheless. Now, Simon is dead. Yet the book's relevance endures. Now she knows for herself the meaning of exile, of longing, of love. Now she knows that, despite death and destruction, somehow we survive.

Simon. You sentimental fool. What were you thinking?

Gin clasps the book tightly to her chest, her knuckles white. She stares at Isaac, words trying to exit her strangled throat. All she can think of is how, even after his death, he has risked their secret coming out. For her.

Simon had kept the book, though she had left it. The sentimental fool.

"I'm sorry, Virginia. I've upset you."

She shakes her head, wordless. Isaac starts to say something but is interrupted by the sound of the front door opening.

Jonnie. Ellie. Home.

"Gin?" Jonnie calls from the hall. She knows he will be hanging up his coat, folding up the pram, one-handed as he always does, Ellie clasped to him with his free hand.

She stands up as he enters the room. Jonnie stops at the sight of Isaac. Ellie is held to his chest, her face obscured, her curls covered in a crocheted yellow hat with pink flowers. Isaac stands too. They are both looking at her now.

Gin wills herself to talk. Her voice squeaks out. "Isaac, this is Jonnie Kassan. Jonnie, this is Isaac Gold. He is a very dear family friend."

The men shake hands.

"And who is this?" Isaac peeks at Ellie, then steps back, his mouth slack.

"This is Ellie, Isaac," says Gin, "Ellie is my daughter."

Isaac turns from staring at Ellie to look at her. He runs a pale tongue over dry lips. She does not know if he is about to say something or is merely astonished by Ellie's existence. *Oh God,* she thinks, *he knows. Ellie looks too much like Simon. No, she's mine. I will not lose her, I will not share her.* She looks across to Jonnie. Her eyes widen, willing him to play along with the lie she is about to tell. He cocks his head slightly, frowning, not understanding.

Isaac opens his mouth. Desperate to stop any words, she adds swiftly, before he can speak, "Jonnie is her father."

It is Jonnie who is slack-jawed now. He recovers admirably, although his eyes slant dangerously at her and she can see his mouth tighten with disapproval.

Please, please. She begs him with pleading eyes.

Still holding Jonnie's gaze, she directs her words to Isaac. "Jonnie's also a doctor, Isaac." Then to Jonnie, "Isaac is a surgeon."

"Retired now," corrects Isaac. His voice is strained but polite. He looks at Jonnie. "My son was also a doctor."

Jonnie's eyes flick to Gin then back to Isaac. "*Was?*"

Isaac looks as if he might crumble. "Yes, was. He's dead, you see. A car accident."

Both men look her way.

She looks away from them, her eyes finding the pine needles scattered below the tree. Her hold on the book tightens, and her knuckles start to hurt.

A white car, heading directly at them.

"I'm sorry," says Jonnie in a voice weighted down with an emotion Gin cannot identify. He shifts Ellie to the opposite arm. Ellie sticks her fist in her mouth and closes her eyes.

But now Jonnie is saying something much worse. He is asking Isaac if by any chance his son was called Simon. Gin steps backwards, feels the couch hit the back of her knees, and she sits down heavily, listening to Isaac exclaim in the affirmative, listening to Jonnie tell Simon's father that yes, he knew his son, that they had studied together in Cape Town, at medical school. Gin feels her world contract.

She sits, watching her life unravel before her.

39. VIVIENNE

It is a sunny afternoon and the clothes will dry quickly. Viv packs another load into the washing machine and takes the basket out to the line, starts to peg up the clothes. Through the slits in the back fence she can see the neighbours' children playing, kicking a ball, chasing each other emitting high shrieks of laughter. Her neighbour emerges onto her back step, calls to one of the children. As they go inside, the woman turns, sees Viv, and waves. Viv grits her teeth and waves back. She hangs up Kayleigh's favourite striped shirt. She ought to get over her resentment of the woman. After all, it wasn't the woman's fault she had witnessed the fights, heard the arguments.

"Does he drink?" The woman's brown eyes were full of concern, full of pity.

Viv hated her. Why had she arrived home then, and seen it all through the gap in the fence? If he drank, maybe they could understand. Maybe Viv herself could understand.

"No, I'll be fine, thanks." She could feel her face flush with shame.

He had not stayed out long. He stood at the door, sheepish, lost. Jonnie was always irresistible. She reached out her hand to him and he came to her, buried his face in her neck.

"I'm so sorry, Viv. I didn't mean it to get out of control."

She had heard it all before.

Viv hangs up the final two pieces of clothing and goes back inside. She blames last night's dream for her reminiscence. She had spent the night with Nick, beneath cool sheets, the windows open to the warm summer air, but she had dreamed she was still married to Jonnie.

They had moved into a new house, with no lawn. The house was one of the new-build developments, everything shining and pristine. The lawns, although laid, had yet to grow, and the house was surrounded by bare earth. Rich and brown, but bare. She had gone walking into a forest, green and shaded. The path disappeared and she found herself walking on sticks and leaves. They crunched underfoot and suddenly with horror she had realised she was walking, not on undergrowth, but bones. Human bones. Looking down, she had recognised them. Gabe's rib, Gabe's spine, Gabe's skull. She woke, heart pounding, the horror sublimating to gratitude. I am awake, I am here, there is no forest, no bones. It is morning.

Viv dumps the laundry basket on top of the machine, goes into the kitchen. She will have to go shopping again. Her teenagers are like locusts, but she is grateful they are healthy and, she reckons, well-adjusted, despite the awfulness of her marriage to Jonnie. But they'd been so young, she tells herself, and she'd hidden it well. And besides, it hadn't always been awful.

Gin had taken her in, given her somewhere to stay, and Viv realised, something to live for. Her world had died with Gabe. She was so alone, with Gabe's child to care for. She hated people's pity. Gin had not pitied her. Gin had lost him too. Instead they had laughed a lot together. They had given each other an odd sort of courage. Things she would not have done on her own, Viv found she could do with Gin. Chores that were overwhelming became bearable. She was healing. And then, one night, Gin had brought Jonnie home. It was the first time she had met the man Gin was clearly in love with. Viv sat across the table from him, this enigmatic stranger. And then, he had looked at her.

She could not have described the look, other than to say it had gone right through her, like an X-ray to the white opacity of her bones. It was a look that said: I know you, I know who you are, and what you are, and what is more, I know exactly what it is you want. And I can give it to you.

Viv opens cupboards, noting what is needed, makes her list for the supermarket. She had never wanted to hurt Gin but she had forgotten everything. Forgotten Gin, even Abbie. And for some terrible moments, she had even forgotten Gabe. Mostly when she and Jonnie were making love.

She will go later to the supermarket, she decides, and tries to settle to some work, but finds her attempt fractured constantly by memories of Jonnie. She cannot let it go today. She puts her head in her hands, gives herself up to her thoughts. They had become a somewhat celebrated couple, in the last throes of the old government, others eager to affiliate themselves with the dashing Indian doctor and his pretty white wife. She used to see the other wives looking at him, at her, envying her. She used to wonder which of them had fucked him.

She slumped in the chair, her thin red dress no defence against the glacial shock. Thinking about it then, it was almost laughable, the inevitability of it. She had not seen it, had dismissed the late nights he said he was working. She had dismissed Leila's mild comments that all the nurses fell for Jonnie. Now the odd phone calls, the short conversations, made sense. How clichéd, she thought, that she would find it in his jacket pocket.

Viv shakes herself. His affairs had hurt as much as the beatings, if not more. Prison had changed him. The anger, the violence, had stemmed from that. Which is why she had let it go on for so long, she understands this now. Had forgiven him, over and over, because of what he had been through. She had even initiated sex after the fights, something it had been hard to understand in herself. In the end, it had felt less shameful for her to cite his violence rather than his infidelity as reason for the divorce.

The sun has dipped below the mountain. Her work has been a write-off. She might as well go to the supermarket now. Viv sorts her files, leaves a note for the girls, picks up her keys. She is on her way out of the door when the phone rings. It is Nick.

"I'm about to go to Pick and Pay," she tells him.

He will meet her there, he says.

They walk at a leisurely pace down each aisle, talking and laughing. He puts food in the trolley that she has to take out, knowing the girls will wrinkle their noses at it in distaste. When it is piled with all the essentials she needs, she heads for the queue. There are not enough cashiers and each line distends with people.

Nick has forgotten something. "Back in a sec," he heads down one aisle.

Viv, bored, looks around. A familiar face is studying a rack of magazines. She hesitates. She has not seen Leila for some time. Friends were split in the divorce, and although she and Leila had tried for a while, the woman had been Jonnie's friend foremost, and it had petered out. Viv feels she ought to greet her now, but the supermarket is crowded and she will have to relinquish her place in the queue. Nick is nowhere to be seen. Mostly, she is not sure what to say. Perhaps Leila will not notice her. Guilt wins, and Viv pushes her trolley over to where the woman stands, a half-filled basket slung around her forearm.

"Leila?" she says, peering at her face.

Leila looks up. "Viv! How are you?"

Her voice is the same husky honey, she wears the same lilac lipstick, but something has changed about her. Leila's eyes, once so alluring, appear apathetic and unfocused, and circled by heavy rings. Her hair, once lustrous, seems thinner, almost unkempt. And Viv detects a nervousness in her demeanour. The woman's free hand plays with her hair. Maybe, thinks Viv, she has as little to say to me as I to her. Yet they spend some minutes catching up. Viv fills her in on the girls. Yes, says Leila, she is still at the hospital, still living in Steenberg. They avoid the subject of Jonnie.

"Well," says Viv, at a loss for anything further to talk about, "it was lovely to see you again."

"Yes," agrees Leila, but there is no liveliness to her tone. Again, the nervy touch of her hair. Perhaps she is aware of her own dulled appearance.

Leila, the exotic flower, has wilted. Leila, whose many kindnesses to her when she was pregnant, when Jonnie was in prison, had helped alleviate Viv's loneliness. The memory fills her with an unexpected rush of warmth and she asks, with genuine concern, "Leila, are you okay?"

Leila's eyes widen briefly, then narrow again. She seems to shrivel. In a voice that is devoid of feeling, she asks, pronouncing each word alone, the briefest of pauses between, "Why. Do. You. Ask."

Viv regrets her question. She was about to explain that Leila looks ill to her, but changes her mind at the coldness of Leila's tone. "You look… tired," she manages.

Leila's eyes drop away. Again, the jittery fiddle with her hair. "I've not been sleeping well," she offers. Her eyes flit up to Viv's, and then away over Viv's shoulder. Her expression changes. The woman's face twists in a kind of terror, so much so that Viv looks around to follow her gaze.

Nick is standing in the aisle, not looking at them, but at the shelves. It cannot be Nick, thinks Viv, what motive would Leila have to look at him with such loathing? If he were in uniform, perhaps it might make sense, the leftover dislike for the police. There are three other people in the aisle so it must be one of them or something else, she reasons.

She turns back, "Leila," she asks again, gently, "Are you okay?"

"I have to go. Bye." Leila moves away quickly.

Viv, too taken aback to speak, can only watch as Leila scurries away, dropping her half-filled basket near the exit as she leaves the supermarket.

How odd, thinks Viv, how very odd.

40. GIN

Isaac phones and leaves a message, a number where he can be reached. He would very much like to see her again, says the machine, and adds after a pause, "And Ellie."

Gin cannot bring herself to phone him, and she deletes the message. She cannot face it, cannot face Isaac, and talk about Simon. Not now, not after what Jonnie had told her.

The inevitable post-mortem had followed.

"What the hell was that all about?" Jonnie, as expected, had demanded once Isaac had taken his leave.

Gin, out of politeness, had asked Isaac to stay for a drink but he had demurred, apologetic. He was, he said, meeting old friends for supper. She suspected that but for Jonnie, he might have accepted. She was thankful. She did not want to talk about Simon.

But then she had to face Jonnie and his ire.

Eyes downcast, she had to apologise. For putting him on the spot. For the lie. She felt she ought to explain further, but she was still digesting the fact that Jonnie had known Simon, that Simon had known Jonnie, and before she had known either of them.

"Tell me," Jonnie asked, "Simon was Ellie's father, was he not?"

Gin nodded glumly, her throat too thick to form the words.

His voice had risen, he had pointed at the door. "Then why must that old man go away, not knowing his granddaughter?"

She found her voice along with the reason. "Simon is – was – married."

"I see."

But from the way he said it, she knew he was wondering what dif-
ference it would make. She could not explain it all to him, the need to
protect Simon's family from the truth. What could she have said, that
they had been through enough, that surely her affair with Simon, the
existence of Ellie, would make it worse for them, not better? They had
lost him and, she reasoned, having had more of him would mean their
loss was more than hers. And besides, she thought finally: Ellie is mine.
All mine. Mine alone. I will not share her, the way I always shared
Simon. Even, it seemed, with Jonnie.

"You knew him." She tried for it not to sound accusatory, and failed.
She fiddled with the edge of her sleeve. She wanted then to talk about
Simon, wanted to know every exchange between them. It came upon her
like a thirst.

Jonnie was silent for minutes. "Yes," he said finally, but with a harsh-
ness that unnerved her. As if the day had not been unsettling enough.
"Yes," he repeated, "I knew Simon Gold all right. I'm sorry, Gin. I know
he was Ellie's father and I know you must have loved him," here he
paused before adding angrily, "but the man was an absolute bastard."

She still cannot believe what Jonnie had told her. Not Simon. A
traitor. He must have had his reasons. The man Simon whom she
had known and loved would have had his reasons.

But had she known him? There is so much about his life she did
not know. His life, before and after her. Detective Retief had said
Simon had taken antidepressants, had seen a psychiatrist. His life
after her she had accepted, but his life before her? He had told her
about Leila, some of it. She shakes her head. No, she *knew* Simon.
Simon was Simon, and she had loved him for it. She wants to cry.

That day, and its turn of events, had its effect on her and Jonnie.
She does not see him for a month. Christmas arrives and leaves,
and New Year is spent alone with Ellie, and a muted television programme. Ellie becomes alternately fretful and lethargic. She seems

less interested in feeding, but she does not seem feverish, or ill. Gin cannot sleep. She lies awake, listening for any sound from her daughter. If anything, Ellie is even quieter. Gin gets up often to check on her. Sometimes Ellie lies so still that Gin shakes her gently; even then Ellie does not cry, only grumbles. She looks at Gin with doleful eyes, and Gin feels irritable. Surely a child that young could not miss someone so, enough to pine. Gin can barely acknowledge that she herself has missed Jonnie.

He knocks one morning in January, brings a draught of cold air inside with him. Not entirely from the weather, Gin decides.

He sweeps past her to Ellie, picks her up. Then he turns to her. "Gin, are you feeding this child enough? Do you have enough milk?"

He asks this roughly and Gin is at once astonished and offended. But then she realises that Jonnie is paying her scant attention. He is entirely focused on Ellie.

"Yes," she says, moving to stand next to him. "Why? What do you mean?"

He looks at her, a frown furrowing his brow. His fingers edge along Ellie's forearms, first one and then the other. He pulls her blanket aside, and examines each of her legs in the same intense manner.

"What, Jonnie? What is it? Tell me."

His frown deepens,

"Tell me, Jonnie! What's wrong?" Panic sets her voice high. "You're making me worried."

Jonnie's face is serious, his tone concerned. "I think she's losing muscle, Gin. I'm going to have to admit her for more tests."

41. MICHAEL

Saturday in Grahamstown. Michael showers quickly, humming to himself, but does not shave. It'll do, he thinks, pulling on old jeans and a T-shirt. Flip-flops. January is too hot for shoes. The weather is scorching, African summer at its height. Michael loves it, thrives on the sun hitting his skin. So different to Denmark, to London. He is happy to be home. He still feels it, four months on, and is relishing the imminent start of the academic year.

He stands for a moment at the window of his bedroom, looking over the shaded back garden that has been allowed to run wild. Ivy and vine have slunk their sinuous way between thorny stems of dog rose. Tendrils of jasmine reach like fingers then stop, mid-air, wavering hesitantly, not knowing where to go. He leans forward, his head touching the cool window-pane.

It had been great to see Viv. She seemed happy with Nick, if somewhat nervous. It is Gin he has missed most. And he worries about her, about how she is coping. When he'd phoned, she'd been distant, or not there. He had left messages, but there had been no reply as yet. But it had been good to spend time with her, good even to see those brooding British skies. The autumn had come early after a lacklustre summer full of warm rain. At least the weather meant something there, compared to Denmark. He had not wanted to go back to Denmark at all, to a Denmark headed dark and cold for winter. A Denmark with its uninspired landscape, its flat sea, its constant smell of pig farms. And a wife he no longer loved. A wife he had never loved. He thinks of Kristina rarely and is grateful for this small mercy, because when the thoughts come, they bring with them a guilt that is apt to depress him. Guilt had almost incapacitated him.

Michael trails a finger across the pane. Fortunately, he has had a busy time so far, and his intellect has started to come alive again. Denmark, he realises, had stunted him. Having missed the transition to democracy, he had thought adapting to home would take some doing. Instead, the euphoria of change and the relief of a bloodless revolution had dissipated such that he finds the political tension much the same as before he left. But he appreciates anew the fortitude of South Africans, of all races, their resolute determination to survive. Beyond oppression, beyond corruption, beyond suffering, beyond hope.

Michael had found himself in a minority of optimists.

He shifts himself from his reverie. He has a lot to do.

He stops at the chemist, the library, the supermarket, Grocott's Mail, the off-licence. On his way back up High Street, he drops in at the university bookstore.

The bookshop is crammed with the year's intake of students, some having evidently arrived early to search out their prerequisite reads. Michael edges towards the counter at the back of the store. He nods at the assistant, who seems unusually frazzled.

The man nods back, recognising him. "Yes? Can I help you?"

"I ordered a book. I've paid for it already." says Michael. "*The Primal Child.* Arthur Janov."

The assistant's face screws up with concentration. His eyes, already close-set, approximate somewhat alarmingly to Michael. "I'll just check," he turns with a petulant flounce.

A voice behind him, the faintest of accents, "Michael?"

Years melt away as he turns.

She stands, her head cocked to one side. Her hair is cut shorter than when she was a girl, but it is still dark and glossy, and it still curls. She is wearing a cream linen suit and a wide white smile on a perfectly made-up face. Flawless as ever. Michael is suddenly conscious of his unshaven face, his thin T-shirt and torn jeans.

"Oh my God, it *is* you," she says, moving forwards, full of joyous surprise.

"Hannah." He breathes her name as he hugs her. She smells like summer, he notes. Like an English summer, fresh and fragrant. She moves back to look at him, taking in the sight of him. He wishes he had shaved.

"Michael, what on earth are you doing here?"

He fills her in briefly, the job offer, the move. He wants to tell her about Gin, about his marriage, his divorce, but finds he cannot. Instead he asks her the same question.

"Oh," she says, "I'm just home, visiting family, friends." As if realising he is one of those friends she might otherwise have looked up, Hannah adds, "I didn't know you were here, Michael. Last I heard you'd gone to – where was it? Sweden?"

"Denmark."

"Yes, that was it. How *are* you?" With emphasis.

"Fine," he says. The truth of it hits him and he repeats, "Yes, fine."

"So you're living here now?"

"Yes, just around the corner. The same complex where Gin stayed."

Hannah's face changes, and he kicks himself. He wonders whether to expand, to add that he has seen Gin, to update her, tell her about Ellie. But Hannah is Simon's cousin, he reminds himself. Gin would not want her to know. How Gin can keep it from Simon's family forever, he does not know, but in any event, it is not his secret to tell.

The assistant interrupts, "The book you ordered, sir." He hands Michael a packet. "If you could just come and sign for it, sir."

Michael, irritated, forces himself to be polite. He pushes his way to the desk and back again. "Now that you're here, can we have lunch? Dinner? Can you stay?"

"Oh, Michael, I'm so sorry, I can't. I'm not staying. We're only here for the day."

We. "Is your husband with you?"

"Oh no, he stayed in New York – we live there now." Hannah updates him briefly on her life.

It sounds rehearsed, thinks Michael, a well-practised version for people like himself.

Then she says suddenly, "You remember my cousin Simon?"

She is watching him shrewdly.

He cannot bring himself to lie. "I heard he was killed in a car accident. I'm sorry." For a moment he imagines she is going to ask him about Gin.

Instead, she says simply. "I didn't know if you knew." She looks around the shop as if searching for someone.

A young man is standing to one side, peering at the books. There is something familiar about him that Michael cannot place. He is tall, broad-shouldered, with curly black hair.

Hannah beckons him forward. "This is the real reason I'm in Grahamstown," she says to Michael. "I'm showing him around as he's thinking of studying here next year." She reaches an elegant arm out to draw the young man to her. "Aaron," she says to him, "this is my very dear friend Michael."

The young man nods at him, extends his hand. He has dark eyes flecked with green, notes Michael, shaking hands.

"Michael," says Hannah, "this is Aaron. My cousin Simon's son."

Simon's son. The pieces fall into place. Taller than his father. Same eyes. Michael thinks of Gin, alone in London with this young man's half-sister. "So, you're coming here next year?"

"If I can. If I'm accepted. I like it here."

"Good. Well, I'll give you my number. You'll have to look me up if you do."

Aaron thanks him, excuses himself, and walks away to look at the books again. Michael turns back to Hannah who is watching him.

"That's nice of you, Michael. Thank you. Simon's death hit him hard, as you can imagine. I appreciate it. He needs a father figure."

Michael doubts he will even hear from the intense young man, let alone become a father figure to him. "Do you have any time at all?" he asks, "for some tea perhaps?"

She shakes her head, her sleek curls swinging. "I'm so sorry, Michael. I just can't."

Can't or won't?

"We must go," she reiterates.

"Let me give you my number," he says. Adds quickly, "For Aaron." He pats his pockets in vain for pen and paper.

Hannah smiles, opens her handbag, an orange suede, and hands him a leather-covered notebook and a pen. He scribbles down his name and number, closes it and hands it back to her.

She is looking at him with something like fondness. "You look the same, Michael."

He laughs self-consciously, runs a hand through his hair. It is long again now, like it was when he was a student. "You haven't changed either."

"Rubbish," she waves her hand at him, a slight blush to her cheeks.

"No," he says, and it is the truth. She looks much the same. "No, Han," he repeats seriously, "you're beautiful."

The blush deepens with pleasure. "You old charmer. I bet you say that to all the girls! And I bet the freshers all fall in love with you, Prof."

"Not Prof yet."

Aaron hovers nearby. Hannah leans forward and hugs Michael again. Her hold is brief, but tight. Michael inhales her heady perfume once more, enjoying the moment, trying to commit it to memory.

He had not told Gin, but he had always known about Hannah and Gabe, long before Gin had.

He had not meant to eavesdrop, had simply planted himself down in the shade of the school building, on the welcomely cold cement that dipped down to form a shallow gutter. Leaning against the red brick wall, their voices had reached him through an open window. He recognised Hannah's high pitch immediately and after a moment, Gabe's, still cracking with adulthood. He did not hear the beginning, just those few lines, and he had not stayed to hear the end.

"You know I will, Gabe."

"Promise me, Hannah. Swear it."

"I promise."

Hannah steps away from him. He wants to ask her what they had promised each other that day so many years ago, but neither of them has mentioned Gabe. He looks at her, is about to say something when she puts her hand up to his lips, the merest of touches. Her hand drops away so quickly that afterwards he will wonder if he imagined it. Her eyes are bright.

He watches them leave the bookshop. Hannah turns and looks back at him when they are outside. She gives him a little wave. She is haloed in sunshine.

Michael raises his hand in reply, although he doubts if she can see beyond the reflective glass of the bookstore window. He watches her walk away and he does not go after her. He does not go after her and tell her. He watches her walk away from him and he does not tell her he has loved her all his life.

42. GIN

"I know what autosomal recessive means, Jonnie," she says, harsher than she feels.

He backs away slightly and Gin feels bad. No doubt he is used to the venom of parents, knowing how they must blame him for the bad news he so often has to bear. But for her anger, she realises, he must be ill-prepared.

She had arrived early, caught him poring over Ellie, checking her chart, adjusting the patterned rose blanket over her daughter's frail body.

His words penetrate further. She thinks slowly, her mind dulled. *Autosomal recessive.*

Ellie has a genetic disorder. She and Simon both carried a gene, defective. A chromosome, mutated. And their daughter has inherited one copy from her, one copy from Simon. So now the disease manifests. Gin closes her eyes.

Simon's eyes, watching her.

This is what it means, she thinks distractedly, the sins of the fathers. Oh, Simon, what have we done?

"What's going to happen to Ellie, Jonnie?" Her voice is strong and direct.

He takes her arm. His grip hurts her, but she welcomes the physical pain. Jonnie leads her into the square room behind the nurses' station, the square room meant for the doctors, the matron. The square room meant for bad news. He pulls out a chair for her and shuts the door. The nurses will know the sign. The worst of news.

"It means, essentially, that Ellie cannot make an enzyme, which breaks down an acid." He pauses. "So the acid accumulates in the brain and it interferes with the formation of myelin." Jonnie stops, and looks away from her. He rubs the back of his neck.

Gin's gaze does not waver. She sits and waits.

"Gin, Ellie can't make the fatty lining to her nerves. They're eroding away."

"That's why she's lost muscle," mutters Gin.

He nods, his voice drained. "The brain tissue is disintegrating. Even the most elemental signals aren't getting through."

"What else is going to happen?" she asks, and her voice is clear again.

She listens while Jonnie tells her how Ellie will never hold her head up, how she will go blind, and lose the ability to swallow. She listens while he explains that Ellie will require feeding tubes to stay alive, and eventually fall into a vegetative state.

Not now, God, she begs. Not now, when Ellie means everything to me.

She listens while Jonnie destroys her world.

He stops talking, rubs his neck again. Sounds from the ward seep through, the constant beeping of machines, the nurses' talk, the busy insistent ringing of a phone. It strikes her anew how noisy hospitals are.

"Gin," says Jonnie. She looks at him. He looks away, and then back at her, but his eyes askance, not looking at her directly. He clears his throat. "The earlier this manifests," he speaks slowly, as if to choose his words, "the worse the prognosis."

She speaks then, her voice stark. "How long has she got?"

He swallows, and hesitates. Then he tells her there are going to be more seizures, and worse, before it is over. But Ellie is going to die. And soon. "Not long, a couple of months at most. It's bad, Gin. She may only have weeks." He looks out of the window that spills light into the cramped room.

Gin hears a sound escape from her own throat. Suddenly the

room is shifting. Her arm is burning, her leg on fire. She tries to get up, to open the door, but it warps away from her and she feels herself slide sideways. She hears Jonnie call for a nurse, for some water. His voice is very far away and she wonders why. She tries to sit up, but his hand stops her.

"Lie there for a minute," he orders. "Wait."

The pitted oblongs of the false ceiling line her vision. She closes her eyes. This then, is her punishment.

Simon's arms close around her from behind, his cheek rests against her hair, his lips brush her ear. She feels his breath on her face. He holds her to him tightly, as if by gathering her up to him he might stop her from falling apart.

This time Jonnie lets her sit up. He offers her some water, putting a glass to her lips, but she pulls her mouth away.

"Are you okay?" he asks, worried, and, when she does not reply, "Ginnia?"

"Yahrtzeit," she murmurs.

It is only a fortnight till the anniversary of Ellie's conception, the anniversary of Simon's death. *Yahrtzeit.* This date Gin has dreaded, watched it loom ceaselessly ahead, inexorably creep closer. She has tried to give it neither form nor substance but despite her effort it had grown, energised and fed by her repression. Become huge.

Yahrtzeit. Would the dreams stop, she had wondered. Would he leave now? Would he finally leave now, take his presence away from her, away from her and Ellie, his unknown family?

His presence that has never left, not for a moment has she felt him gone. Now, in these moments, she realises he is going. Simon is finally leaving her, and he is taking his daughter with him.

"Are you okay?" Jonnie asks again.

She wants to laugh at him. She is never going to be okay again.

43. VIVIENNE

No one is at the high wooden desk. Viv peers over the top of it and into the empty office beyond. She looks around. Nick's office can't be that hard to find. The corridor ahead stretches into darkness, but it is either that or back the way she came.

She starts to walk along the corridor, her heels click hollowly into the gloom. Windowless doors alternate on either side of her. No light slats from beneath them. She assumes they are daytime offices, locked now for the evening. They are numbered, but she can see no names. She glances back towards the desk in the hope that someone has appeared, but it is still unmanned. She carries on towards the end of the corridor. There is a faint bang. A door shutting somewhere, perhaps. It is followed almost immediately by a distant shout, angry, like a curse. Another bang, louder. Like a cell door slamming, she thinks. Viv shudders, unnerved at the thought, and angry with herself now for coming. She has never liked police stations. She stops at the end of the corridor. To her right, another corridor, shorter, with a faint light at the end. She peers down it. A movement to her left startles her. Instinctively she steps back, swallowing a cry, her hand to her throat. Her reflection in the glass of double doors looks back at her, wide-eyed and pale. Viv sucks in a few breaths. Afraid of my own shadow, she thinks, her heart thudding. Again she turns to look hopefully back at the desk, a reassuring beacon of light. Again she can see no one. I'll go right, she thinks, it must lead somewhere. She braces herself for the sight of her own reflection again, preparing to grimace at herself for her stupid nervousness. She turns, but it is not only her own face staring back at her.

Someone is standing behind the glass, watching her.

This time the cry escapes her throat. She steps backwards, half-stumbling, her heart slamming against her ribs.

One side of the double door opens and a woman in police uniform appears. "I'm so sorry, ma'am. Did I give you a fright?"

Viv nods, then laughs in relief.

The woman smiles broadly, and then laughs too, showing even white teeth that shine against the blackness of her skin. She is young, and pretty. Her name badge says Grace Mathebula. "I'm sorry I frightened you. It's happened to me too. And it's worse at night. Unfortunately the women's toilets are some way from the desk, and I have to go through here."

The explanation for the empty desk. Viv nods again, afraid to speak, in case her voice quakes.

"Is there something I can help you with?" asks Grace. Politely, but obviously back on duty and wondering who this strange white woman is, walking down the unlit and deserted corridor.

Viv tries her voice. "I'm looking for Sergeant Retief." She tries to sound formal, aware of trying to protect Nick's personal privacy among his colleagues.

"Is he expecting you?"

Viv pauses, not quite knowing how to reply to this astute young woman with the steady brown eyes and genteel manner. She can hardly explain to her that no, she and Sergeant Retief had not arranged to meet tonight, but that she had found herself unexpectedly free, with the girls on an impromptu sleepover with friends, and so, yes, she had dressed in the little red skirt Nick loved, put her high heels on, and come down here to meet him after work, for her own impromptu sleepover.

Her hesitation must have said it all, for Grace is true to her name, and says diplomatically, "Sergeant Retief is out on a case still, madam. But he'll be back soon. So if you'd care to wait in his office, I'll show you where it is."

Viv follows her gratefully, and then is mildly irritated to find she was but two turns of the corridor away from Nick's office, the door marked with his name, and would have probably found it unassisted soon enough, and without the subsequent embarrassment. But she thanks Grace, who wishes her a good evening and returns, Viv presumes, to her desk.

She has never been in his office. A bit nervous now of surprising him at work, of arriving like this with no warning, she sits upright in the chair in front of his desk, imagines him sitting behind it. The office has no window, she notices. There is a noticeboard on the one wall, strewn with messages, notes, photos, wanted posters and the like. It is the only untidy piece in the room. Everywhere else she sees evidence of Nick's organised mind. Everything in its right place.

After a while, she relaxes, and goes to sit in his chair, swivels in it, looking around again, this time from his daily perspective. She realises that he has an unimpeded view of the door and that anyone sitting across from him is positioned so as to be in the fullest, clearest light possible. Bored, she pulls at his desk drawers. All except one are locked, and that offers nothing of interest but sheets of paper and official-looking forms. Across from the desk on the far end of the room is a steel-grey filing cabinet. On top of this are some neatly-stacked books and two piles of folders in trays, one considerably larger than the other.

She goes over to the cabinet. The books appear to be legislative, with black and red spines, and gold lettering. The tray with the larger pile of folders is labelled *Open*. The other tray is predictably marked *Closed*, and she presumes they are recently so, and due for filing. Viv picks up one of the folders from the *Closed* pile, opens it and starts to read about a case in which the man of the house had chased two young burglars onto the street, brandishing his golf club and screaming loud enough to wake his neighbours. The scene that forms itself in Viv's mind is initially amusing, until she reads how between them, the neighbours had managed to beat up one of the thieves so badly that he had died from his injuries. No one had been brought to justice it appeared, since no one knew who had struck the fatal blow. Viv is upset by what she reads, and wonders how this case can be so casually closed. She puts the folder back in its pile, but in doing so, she knocks several folders from the larger pile to the floor. Annoyed with herself, Viv starts to pick them up. The files are labelled, she notices, not with case numbers, but names. She wonders whether they were stacked in any kind of order so she goes to the folders that remain in the tray, lifts them out and shuffles a few of them to determine any kind of chronological or alphabetical order. One of the labels has peeled and curled up on itself. Viv trails a finger across it, unfurls its length. A quick intake of breath.

Gold/McMann.

Viv stares at the brown folder, unwilling to open it.

She puts the folder onto Nick's desk, unopened, and neatly stacks the fallen folders back on their tray. Then she walks around the desk again, sits down and looks at the folder. The intrigue is too great and she opens it. Inside are photographs, statements, reports, forms. She reads quickly. At one point, she pulls her eyes away. Had Simon not died, would she and Gin have met again? Have mended their friendship? She brings a hand up to rub her eyes, and the folder starts to slip from her lap. She stabs at it. Another, slimmer folder falls out of it, lands at her feet. Leaning down to retrieve it, she sees the name.

Weetman/Kassan.

44. NICK

She stands with her back to him.

Nick's day has been long and harrowing. Two murders, two rapes, and an armed robbery. He still has reports to file and the night stretches ahead. To find Viv in his office is a welcome surprise. They had not planned on seeing each other tonight, but now he can think of nothing nicer. His eyes trail the length of her, the arch of her back beneath her blouse, the curve of her hip resting against his desk. She is wearing that figure-hugging red skirt that shows off her shapely legs.

"That skirt could get you arrested." He says this quietly, but in the silence of the office, his voice reverberates.

Viv spins around with a small exclamation.

"Sorry," he grins, "I didn't mean to startle you." He moves towards her, but stops at her glittering look. "What?" His gaze is drawn to the folder in her hand. He feels the grin vanish. *Shit.* "Vivienne –".

The atmosphere in his office has a feeling of static, the air before a Highveld storm.

Viv points the folder at him. "You kept a *file* on me?"

"Vivienne –".

"You kept *notes* on me? My family? Jonnie?"

"You know I had to." Nick stops, remembering her anguish that day on the beach when he had spoken about Gabriel McMann's death. He is dog-tired, the day has worn him out, and now this. This is all he needs, today of all days. He tries to explain. "Look," he starts, exasperated, "your name, Jonnie's name, it came up as part of the Gold investigation. It was routine stuff. Gin was staying with you, then it turned out your husband had been involved with her before he married you…" He trails off at the fury in her eyes, repeats firmly, "It was part of the Gold investigation."

She takes a step toward him. He can see she is shaking. "*Routine?*" she says, her voice like thin ice. "I trusted you. You let me tell you about Jonnie, the reasons for my divorce, his – his abuse – when all along you *knew?* So tell me, Nick, was *fucking* me part of the *routine* Gold investigation?"

He has never heard her swear.

"Vivienne –"

She throws the folder at him. It flutters in the air and does not hit him. The contents fly out, papers, forms, photographs, gliding almost gracefully to the floor. Viv steps on them as she walks past him, heading for the door behind him.

Without thinking, Nick reaches for her arm to stop her. But Viv wrenches her arm away. She steps backward, moving away, closer to the door. She clasps her arm where he had grabbed her as if hurt.

"Don't touch me!" A whisper. "Don't touch me."

Exhaustion washes over him. He rubs his forehead. "Vivienne, look, let me take you home. Let's talk."

"Don't call me. Don't come to my house. I don't ever want to see you again."

Then the woman he loves pulls open his office door and lets it slam closed behind her. All Nick can hear are the sharp sounds of her heels running down the corridor. Fading into the darkness. Into the night. Away from him. And out of his life.

45. GIN

It is a strange day, driving to the airport, wondering if the snow, so unusual for London, will allow for take-off. It is icy on the roads, and Jonnie is taking it slowly. She doesn't care. She does not mind if she makes her flight or not. How long since she has been home, how long since her father's funeral, seeing Simon, the weeks in the hospital? Thinking of Simon will lead her to thinking of Ellie, and this she does not allow herself in her waking hours. Instead she thinks of Gabe. How long to get over that one, Virginia? Anger still ready to flare.

The car has stopped. Heathrow already. Jonnie locks the car, takes her arm in one hand and her suitcase in the other. Her ears throb almost immediately from the short exposure to the wind, and Gin wonders again if the planes will leave. Soon the shops will envelop her in their seductive splendour, soothing, distracting, enable a type of normality. She checks in, feeling stuporous while she answers the farcical questions. Lack of food and sleep has exacted its price, and a sense of unreality, a strange feel to her skin, takes over.

Jonnie buys her coffee and waits with her until it is time to board. They say little. She wonders if it is odd to him that tomorrow she will see his ex-wife, his daughter and stepdaughter. For her part, perhaps she ought to be more curious about Abbie and Kayleigh, but she feels nothing, just the constant coldness in her body.

When the gate for her flight flashes up on the lurid screen, he walks with her as far as he is allowed. She is thankful he does not kiss her. Instead he rests his cheek against hers, holding her in an embrace so asthenic it is as if he fears for her fragility. Gin supposes she ought to feel grateful to him, for the past three months, and especially this last one. For his company, his care, for the desolate nights that he has lain next to her, for the use of his body as comfort.

She had wanted to walk back from the crematorium. There were only the two of them. The cemetery was on Kensal Rise, set beside the canal, and they walked against the wind. The high walls of the cemetery had buckled over time, bowing out over the pavement. One day, thought Gin, they will fall, spilling bricks and exposing the graves behind. The walk was about three miles and her leg hurt. Jonnie had made a pot of tea when they reached the house and they had both gulped it down, eager for its heat. She had dreaded him going, leaving her alone in the dusty house.

"Don't leave me," she whispered.

"I'm not going anywhere." Taking her hand.

"Help me, Jonnie." Nothing more than a faint moan. "Help me."

He had pulled her to him and helped her the only way he knew how.

Perhaps she ought also to feel guilt, but there is none. She suspects that Jonnie in his own way had made use of her too, and so by her reckoning they owe each other nothing. It seems that whatever it was that lay unfinished between them is now complete. Her journey with Jonnie is over. Her journey home has yet to begin.

Despite the weather, the planes fly. The sense of unreality deepens till she sleeps, exhausted. Frazzled dreams of home, England. Jonnie, Simon, Gabe, and Dad. Dearest Dad. How she has missed her father, his wise countenance, the shock of grey hair, his kind eyes behind his glasses, and his solid advice. And then Ellie. Ellie, always Ellie, dreams that tear at her until she is awakened by the sound of her own strangled sobs.

The plane is dark, humped figures attempting some kind of sleep, the only sounds the persistent hum of the engines and a fretful child. It had been a late booking, an unpopular seat, with no personal television, but Gin does not mind. The seat next to her is unoccupied, allowing some privacy. Panic attacks threaten to overwhelm her, the old claustrophobia surfaces. Constantly she arranges and re-arranges the scratchy tartan blanket around herself.

The woman across the aisle intrudes on her solace. Could Gin watch her daughter while she nips to the washroom, she asks. Gin is too polite to refuse, and anyhow, what can she say? *No, please, because my daughter is dead?*

Gin looks at the infant and looks away. Her breasts start to ache. Occasionally, despite the tablets meant to dry her milk, her nipples weep. As if her breasts mourn for the tug of Ellie's perfect little mouth.

The woman returns quickly, thanking her. She is Dutch, she tells Gin, and her daughter is three months old. *Ellie's age, the age she will always be.*

This is the first daughter, the woman continues, in her husband's family for three generations. Her husband is South African, and she is going to meet his family. Given the transient nature of meetings like these, they do not even exchange names, but the woman confides further that her husband, an engineer, will join them later. A map comes up on the flight screen, and she asks where Gin is bound. Gin points to Cape Town.

In that peculiar, pleasantly heavy accent, the woman exclaims, "It looks like the end of the earth!"

Gin sleeps and dreams again.

She stands on the edge of a precipice. Gabe is calling to her, calling. She turns back from the wind that wants to lift her from where she stands, turns back to look for him, but he is lost, lost in a wood, and try as she might, she cannot make her way through the tangled branches of its verge.

Awake, she watches dawn breaking over central Africa, orange in her porthole. *Africa, ah, consider Africa.* All its contradictions. It is Africa well enough. They land in Johannesburg and Africa assails her. The heat, the dust, the very blood in the air hits her as she steps off the plane. Even the feel of the air on her skin is unique to this continent of suffering and survival. Nothing changed. Governments, maybe, but it is all so recognisable, frighteningly recognisable.

Yet she feels nothing for this fast, brash city set in the brown veld. This is where Simon had chosen to make his life, pursue his career, set upon his path, away from her. A mild curiosity interests her in shops, their shiny newness testament to almost two decades of democracy, tempting tourists to this still troubled land. Impressions of her new country bombard her. The danger during the time she lived here was probably far worse than now, but a fool would disregard personal safety. A fool like her, she knows. Is Michael right, does she court death in any welcome form?

She allows a man to carry her bag, knowing if he runs with it, she has no chance of catching him. He knows it too, her leg is troubling her, and she limps alongside him. He has no interest in stealing her belongings, however, and deposits it safely beside her after the hot, tedious walk to the domestic terminals.

He smiles broadly in anticipation of payment. Everyone, it seems, is so polite. *Ma'am this, ma'am that.* Then it hits her. This is what it was always like. It is not politeness, but the legacy of apartheid, of slavery and deference to a white skin. This, it appears, still part of the journey. Introspection, retrospection, change.

"Stop running away, Gin," Michael had said. "Time to come home, Gin," he had said. She knew he meant time to grieve.

She drinks a cappuccino while waiting for her connection to Cape Town. She will see Michael soon, she hopes. Viv had promised a trip up to Grahamstown, to the university where he now teaches. Abbie, said Viv, is considering studying there next year. Gabe's daughter, already old enough for university. She has missed Michael so much, his sense of humour and his earthy laugh. He had always felt at home here, owning his presence here, owning his country somehow, owning it well, embracing it for all its sins and sadnesses. Unlike her. And yet she had not been able to exorcise her feelings for her homeland. She had found England alien and lonely. She had tried, succeeded some, used the liberation offered her, but she was always haunted by home. Home, and the ghost of Gabe. Gabe had felt about this country the way she did, disgusted with the discarding of humans on such a huge and awful scale. Perhaps their history made them so, perhaps their grandfather's story had been bred down in them, his early exit from a Nazi Germany, a lesson forever learned, instilled into their very genes. Gabe, like Michael, had hurt to leave. Unlike Michael, he never did. It would have saved his life. How different it might have been. Perhaps now all three of them could have been here, making this slow pilgrimage together. She, Michael, and Gabe. Instead she must make it alone.

Impossible to imagine another life. Perhaps she can find it within her to finally let her brother go. She doubts the possibility of healing fully, doubts Michael's optimism, his enthusiasm about this trip. And now England is tainted too. How can she return when only Ellie's ghost awaits her in the house on Ladbroke Road?

She orders another coffee. The prices here astonish her. She divides her pounds by ten and finds her cappuccino still cheaper than London. She feels fresher now, calmer. Tired, but settling, waiting for the domestic transfer. Passing time, she enters Viv's name and address in a competition to win a car, wills herself to quell the lingering suspicion that any information she supplies will be used to malintent. Is it Africa, or London, that has made her so edgy, so nervous of others and their intentions? Is it strangeness or familiarity that breeds this paranoia? The Dutch woman had remarked on her lack of accent, and now she finds herself adjusting to the heavy gutturals of home.

It is time to board. Gin struggles to stand, her leg numb and awkward. People look at her, the way she stumbles. After a while, movement will increase its flexibility. She finds herself trembling slightly at the passport checkpoint. Cape Town, its ghosts, lies ahead. The Dutch woman's words come back to her: *the end of the earth.*

The flight seems to take forever. Was it only yesterday she left London, only yesterday Jonnie held her like brittle glass? They fly in low over the green plains, the ridge of mountains. She cannot but think of the last time she flew here, on her way to meet Simon.

Simon, making his way through the crowd. Simon, green-flecked eyes alight to see her. The same light in those eyes, dying. His hand, outstretched to her.

She wants to scream, to cry, to climb out her seat, smash the window, and breathe fresh air. Instead she sits, dumb, frozen.

Only when she has collected her suitcase from the rolling rubber rail, only when she has walked the length of the tiled arrival hall, only when she has exited through the automatic doors to see Viv standing alone at the barrier, only then do her eyes start to burn, and only when she is enfolded in Viv's welcoming embrace does Gin start to shake uncontrollably, her body wracked with soundless, heaving sobs.

46. GIN

Issy's house is in the valley beside the Nahoon River, as it weaves to the beach. Viv turns off the highway onto the old Nahoon Road that hugs the hill and crosses the narrow bridge.

After Gabe's death, Gin's parents had moved to Zululand, eager to get away from the Eastern Cape and its unhappy memories. But Gin's sister Issy had stayed on in the coastal town where they had grown up. It is strange to see it again, this place she once called home. She knows Viv had suggested the trip as a form of therapy, for her to see Michael again, but it is also for Abbie. It is so Abbie can see Grahamstown, have a look around the university but, Gin suspects, Viv is also keen to have Abbie spend time with Gin and Issy, and reconnect with her father's family. In the fortnight she has been back, Gin has interacted little with her niece. This long weekend is not only about Abbie's future, but also her past.

They turn into Issy's wooded drive, the sun unable to penetrate the canopy of conifer, and the ground is dark beneath the branches. Issy's home is a large, double-storied house, with two outhouses, and a broad green lawn that slopes down to the river. Issy rushes out at the sound of the car, her face alight with welcome. She has cut her hair, her thick auburn curls are gone, replaced by a feathery cut that frames her face and highlights her freckles.

Over lunch, Issy explains that the children at the clinic had kept pulling at her hair and eventually the only solution was a radical one. Her sister is full of news and questions. She seems happy and Gin is relieved to see her so. There had been a time when her sister's health had waned, and leaden circles had formed under her aquamarine eyes. Now she appears content, married to one of the radiologists at the hospital attached to the clinic.

"I thought Abbie might want to see some stuff of Gabe's," says Gin tentatively after lunch. She is well aware that the family burden has always fallen on Issy. It had been left to her sister to sort through their parents' home after their dad's death.

There is also the awkward question of their father's ashes.

"I hope you don't mind, Gin," says Issy, "I put them in a wall in the cemetery where Mom is." She sounds unsure, as if her actions are questionable.

Gin hates the thought of her father walled into some hole. She would rather have taken his ashes back to Britain and up to the Highlands; she would have brought her father home. Instead she says that this is fine, and thanks her sister for taking care of it.

Issy looks nervously at Viv, says loudly, "I kept Gabe's ashes, Viv." She chews her lip. "I thought," and here she flicks a glance at Abbie, "I thought Abbie might want to decide what to do with them."

Abbie has been sitting quietly through lunch but now a look of alarm crosses her face. She looks at her mother, and Gin is reminded how young her niece is. So young to already be thinking of heading off into the world, to make her own choices, of career, of life, of loves.

Viv's previously composed face contorts with conflicting emotion. She reaches a hand across the table to Issy, who takes it between two hands. "Thank you, Issy."

They prepare to leave the next morning after a breakfast that neither Gin nor Viv can touch. Abbie and Issy in contrast eat heartily, aunt and niece chatting easily. Abbie tells her about school, about how she wants to study English literature and psychology at university.

"Michael's there now, Issy," interjects Gin, "don't know if you knew."

She tells her sister about Michael's appointment.

"Well," says Issy, lathering marmalade on a piece of toast, "Abbie may end up as one of his students then."

Abbie nods, forks more scrambled egg onto her toast.

"It'll be good to see him again," says Gin, looking at Viv, who sips her tea and smiles agreement. Gin imagines it must be hard for her to be surrounded by Gabe's family, his two sisters, his daughter, and not be plagued with memories. The previous evening, Issy had pulled out photographs of Gabe, and memorabilia, from his life before Viv that must have hurt. Hannah is in so many of the photographs. Gin is unsure of how much Viv knew about Gabe and Hannah.

As they pack the boot of the car, Issy produces a cardboard box for Abbie, filled with Gabe's albums, trophies and certificates. At last, thinks Gin, something for Abbie of her father. Then Issy brings another box.

"Some of your stuff, Gin," she says, "From before you left." Issy squeezes her sister's arm.

They had spoken alone the night before, an upsetting conversation about Ellie.

Gin cannot think what she had left behind. The box is closed with tape, marked in felt tip pen with her name, and she is not going to open it now. She packs it in the boot beside the suitcases. They exchange hugs, say their goodbyes, make promises that will not be kept, and make their way back out through the shadowed driveway of gnarled and ancient trees.

Once they have wound their way out of the built-up areas, Viv puts her foot flat on the accelerator and guns the stubborn old car inland. Abbie slumps sleepily on the back seat, her box from Issy beside her. Gin relaxes after the unfamiliar roads of exit. The new highway is not the road she remembers, but soon the tar fades to a familiar hue, and the countryside is once more unchanged from twenty years before. Past the outlying shantytowns, sun gleaming off tin shacks, past the shiny hospital where her sister works, and onto the sliver of road that will take them to King William's Town and then beyond. Beyond to Grahamstown and her past.

Once in King, again the wind of road directing them out of the town is unfamiliar.

"They built a bigger bridge and a different road," explains Viv, "the floods washed the last one away a few years ago."

They cross the new one. Gin can see the remnants of the old further down the bank, a broken frame of rusted iron. Beyond it, there is a turnoff, signposting a memorial to Steven Biko.

"Isn't it amazing, Gin, that now there are memorials to men like Biko. Amazing! And there were times we never thought we'd live to see the day. And I have to remind myself sometimes that Mandela has *already been* president," she pauses, continues, "I saw him once." And then she glances in the rear-view mirror and stops, seemingly reluctant to continue.

Gin wonders whether it is something in Abbie's expression that has stopped her, but says nothing. The rise of the road towards Grahamstown has already brought an ache to her throat and she cannot speak.

They make good progress and soon the russet hills give way to the high plateau before the downward drop to the Great Fish River, the age-old border between the British settlers and the Xhosa tribes. Everywhere, thinks Gin, everywhere are parts of my history. She feels the blood tie of her birth reach down into the core of this land, deep into the earth below, beyond these immovable mountains.

"Viv, can you pull off at the top, before we go down to the river?"

Viv glances at her, slows, waits till they are past the prickly-pear sellers before she idles almost to a stop, pulls the car gently off the tar. Even so, it rattles and bumps and red dust rises.

Gin leaps out the car, almost runs to the bend of road, to the edge where the road starts its plunge towards the river, cut beneath the shadowed bank on one side, the steep fall on the other. There has been rain recently, and the river swirls a full and muddied brown. Normally flat and sluggish, now it thunders its way over the rocks, along its tortuous path to the Indian Ocean. Her gaze follows the course of its muffled roar to the curve of its disappearance between the distant hills. A long time ago she had climbed the ridge opposite, with Gabe and Michael, Hannah tagging along behind as usual, on some school hike to the coast.

Waiting for Hannah, they had fallen behind, until Gabe had seen a short cut through the clinging brush to where the rest of the team steadily climbed their way to the crest. It had been slippery and sheer. She had turned to pull Hannah up over a smooth boulder and had never forgotten the sight. The view behind, beneath, had filled her with fear, yet also a type of elation, a headiness at their height, pitted up against the mountain's edge, at the overbearing blaze of sun above, the generous expanse of sky, and the rush of the river below.

"*Merrum*, are you okay, miss? Have you broken down?"

Gin turns. A motorist has pulled up near the car. Viv sits smoking, the driver's door open to the heat. Abbie appears to be sound asleep in the back. Viv waves her cigarette amiably at the man, shakes her head, thanks him, exchanges pleasantries. He drives off in a puff of dust, his *bakkie* expelling gusts of black smoke. Gin watches him descend the winding road to the bridge below.

His reference had been to the car, yet she thinks with a kind of harsh humour how she had thought for a moment he was referring to her, how she could have answered: *Yes, I have*. Inside she is broken, healing scarredly.

She turns back to the car, her limp suddenly cumbersome to her step.

47. GIN

Viv drives with an unusual caution, following the now-distant *bakkie* to the concrete bridge. After the narrowness of the road, it feels huge. Wider and longer than Gin remembers. Shifting to a low gear, Viv urges the car up the steep rise of the other bank, into what Gin always thinks of as the home strait. She is glad it is still early. Too many times she remembers taking this stretch against the blinding sunset. Her eyes burn from memory.

There are buck alongside the road. One of the herd lies dead, has been laid to one side of the tar, cleaved gut spilling carrion for flies and vultures. She had forgotten the cruel wildness of this land.

Once they are past the uphill heave of it, the road rises to Gin's favourite part of the journey. Here the tall trees and verdant farmland are testament to a lusher rainfall. But ahead of them they see a thick smoke rising. The rain has not been enough to dampen the easy flare of bushfire and the fog of it envelops the road.

Viv drives slowly and they do not speak. Emerging from the worst of the smoke, fine wisps of grey still caressing the car, a sudden elation takes hold of them both, and they chatter away madly, happily. Their noisiness does not wake Abbie or if it does, the girl pretends to sleep still. Laughing, Viv speeds up.

A mile or so later, after a slow bow in the road, their mood disintegrates as a uniformed man steps out ahead of them, his hand raised. Abbie sits up as Viv brakes, cursing. The lone policeman is black, and Gin is suddenly acutely aware of a new and alien vulnerability. They have been speeding, he informs them, officious to the point of rudeness. She finds herself wondering if he relishes this power over a white motorist. Can he jail them? But Viv appears calm as if for her this is an everyday occurrence. So Gin stays silent and watches Viv's beauty beguile the man, listens to her mellifluous voice talk him out of issuing a fine, or worse. A car behind squeals to a halt, caught by the bend. The policeman relents, smiling, either at Viv or the thought of another victim. Gin lets out a huge sigh as they ease off. Viv gently chides her nervousness, her foreignness, and soon they are laughing again, their good mood restored by relief.

It is not long before they reach Grahamstown. Yet again, she is unfamiliar with the road to reach the centre. A huge highway unfurls before them, and a concrete curve of it swings into the old Port Alfred road. No longer do they enter through the winding Raglan Road she had taken all those years before, that last time with Simon. Viv and she had exchanged glances at the turnoff to the farm. Viv's slight shake of her head enough to signal to Gin: *no, not yet.*

Instead they sweep in through pretty houses lined with bougain-villea and thick trees, with shaded verandahs and painted walls. Down the road to her beloved Cathedral. They are all silent now, Abbie looking out of the window, obviously intrigued by this part of her own history, while Viv and Gin are quiet, invaded as they are by the inevitability of memory.

They turn into the gaunt lane. Gin's heart pounds against her ribs. She is afraid. A few feet ahead lies the turnoff to the flat. This is the haven, the home that exists in her mind. There before her will be the purple jacaranda, the three stone steps to the wooden door. Her safe place, her sanctuary, where she travels when all else overwhelms her. She has not seen it since the night of Gabe's funeral, the night she drove here with Simon.

And inside, meaning to her life. And inside, love.

Viv takes the corner into the uneven cobbled driveway, parks at one end of the courtyard. Gin gets out the car and walks deliberately to the opposite end.

She can hardly breathe. It is not as she remembers, nor even as she saw it last, that terrible day. She stares up at the sandy yellow of the building in front of her. It is changed. Gone are the white linen walls, refuge against the African heat. This desert colour makes it look parched. Once it had a leafy promise of shade, of respite. Her throat catches. The jacaranda tree is no longer there. In its place, a fronded palm unequal to its height.

Oh, Simon.

Images are shifting, memories moving like lava in an uneasy growing heat.

That last week, that last week together, Sunday afternoon. Desperation in the love they'd made.

She stares up at the bedroom window, no longer overshadowed by the lilac leaves, no longer bathed in dappled light. No purple droplets, like wine at a papal offering. A pall of emptiness descends.

He had cried the short, strangled sobs of men who do not weep.

Simon, she thinks, I let you go with an acquiescence that outwardly, to you, must have merged with indifference.

It feels oddly right that the tree has gone. That, like Simon, it no longer physically exists. Perhaps it is fitting it was part of their time only, as if it could not go on, living another life without them. Yet there is sorrow also at its passing, unnoticed. Its presence might have been a comfort, a blessing almost, standing there still like some sort of unchanged monument, steadfast and unforgetting. A testament to their existence, to their lives, to their love.

Africa, as ever, moves slowly on.

She is aware of Viv and Abbie, patiently waiting outside the car, outside what must be Michael's flat. How long she has been standing there she does not know. It could be minutes, but it feels like years. Years on hold. Standing on the outside, looking in.

And inside, once, meaning to her life. And inside, once, love.

To the left of the entrance, the lounge in cream. They would drink the semi-sweet white of a summer dusk with the French doors flung wide to the warm evening, or the dry dark red of a Cabernet before the grate, drapes drawn thick against a winter night. It had been her world, their world, a whole new world.

If one followed the wave of sun as it broke in the morning to fill the lounge, then by afternoon one would be through the sliding doors to the darkened dining room, where the light would splash lightly in one corner. Come the evening it would retreat like foam off the wave to the beach of garden at the rear of the flat. How well she remembers their dinners at the oak table. Was it still there?

To the right of the entrance, the yellow kitchen. Afternoon light would stipple the counter. She remembers mess, and happy evenings, how he would put his arms around her from behind, and hug her tightly to him. And then the wooden stairs.

Round and up they travelled to the three rooms and the pale bathroom. Her study had lace curtains and sitting at her desk she looked over the lush garden, stone-walled and thick with jacarandas, a pagan-orange coral tree and a green cane-shooted bush.

"The far end of your mind, Ginny," he had said to her once, "lives there."

She had been so soon his.

She could go inside now, the flat is hers, her gift from Simon. But she needs to preserve the interior intact, at least for now, for a while. The exterior so changed, barely recognisable, disturbs her. Whether she will live to regret this inaction, she will not know. For now, the outside is enough. The three stone steps are still there.

Gin walks back. She looks at Viv, who returns her gaze with compassion. Gin knows Viv's own memories must be surfacing. Gabe is never far away. There is a solemn heaviness in the air.

"Shall we go in?" asks Viv, "or do you need more time?"

Simon, laughing. His deep, delightful laugh. Simon, cooking. Smiling at her, pouring her a glass of wine while they talk. Simon, smoking in the chair. Simon, standing naked from the shower, drops of water on his chest. Simon, deep in a book. Simon, strong hands on the wheel.
   Simon, dying.

Time, thinks Gin, is all I have left.

48. VIVIENNE

"How is she?" asks Michael. They are walking in his back garden, along the stretch of lawn, smoking. The day is settling into evening, the sun has already deserted this part of the house although its warmth remains.

Viv casts a glance to where Gin and Abbie sit inside at the kitchen table, going through Abbie's cardboard box from Issy. The door is closed, and they cannot hear her conversation, but Viv hesitates nonetheless before replying. "Okay, I think. She slept almost solidly that first week, as if she couldn't get enough. I think she's truly exhausted by everything that's happened over the last year."

"Only a year," grimaces Michael. "God."

"Yes," says Viv. She stops, strokes the bark of a tall conifer. Nick had loved Michael's garden, she remembers. She does not want to think of Nick.

Viv had taken Gin home, put her in the same small room with its view of the mountain, and had helped her unpack. Clothes, a toiletry bag, a book. Viv read the title Somehow We Survive. *How very appropriate, she had thought, picking it up. She opened it, stopping at a random page, a random poem. Oxford, January 1965.*

...in this Godforsaken place,
my soul lies naked, and alone.
What words can fill the emptiness?
What words can take me home?

It tore into her. What words could fill her emptiness? There were none. Not after Gabe, not since Jonnie. Once, she had thought Nick's words could. *No one as beautiful as you*, he had said. *Not even close.* But these words in front of her, these words as old as she, had reminded her that words can also tear us apart.

She tells Michael of the day she had taken Gin up to Rhodes memorial.

They drove up the side of the mountain, up the well-wooded path. They ate egg on toast swallowed down with tea while the sun climbed overhead. The city was a haze below, a submerged Atlantis. After breakfast, Viv bought a cheesecake heavy with Cape gooseberries to take home for the girls, and they walked beneath the shady branches, admiring the Roman columns of the memorial to Cecil Rhodes, the British imperialist, coloniser of continents, who would claim and name a country, a man whose shadow was said to fall from the Cape as far north as the Zambezi River.

Gin put her hand on the smooth curves of the carved lion, stroked its stone mane. She started to talk, her face away from Viv, held up to the sun. She told Viv how everything was muddled inside her head. Times, dates, places. Everything felt wrong, she said, inconclusive, and it was all she could do to get through the day. She pushed food down, and it stuck in her throat. Everything, even the slightest thing, felt too much. She described to Viv how her house in London had got dirtier and she had to leave it, letting the dust settle into the corners. She could only keep herself clean, Gin explained, but no amount of scrubbing helped and she would leave the bathroom feeling grubbier than when she went in, and the next day she had to get up and do it all again.

Viv did not know what to say. What words could fill the emptiness? After Gabe, since Simon, since Ellie? She wanted to say she was sorry about Ellie, how awful that must be, how she knew something of what it was like to lose a child, but Gin had started to speak again, her voice faint.

"They say the dead can still hear. If that's true maybe I ought to speak to them. Maybe I should speak to the walls, into the air. But if I were to speak aloud, to Gabe, to Simon," she kept quiet for a second, *"what would people think?"* She looked at Viv. *"You'd think I was mad."*

Michael draws deeply on his cigarette. "She's not mad," he says, "just grieving. It's good she's telling you these things, starting to get it out. Is she still having the recurring nightmares?"

"I don't know," replies Viv, "probably. Sometimes I hear her crying in the night."

"Yes, that happened to me also in London. Sounds like she's still having them. Did she tell you about Simon wanting to tell her something, before he died?"

Viv nods. "Yes. I thought I knew what it was."

He looks at her, surprised. "You did?"

"Nick told me Simon was getting divorced. I thought that maybe it was that – I told Gin."

"When?"

At Miller's Point they had sat on the rocks washed with foam, watching the fishermen bring in their catch.

"I don't know why," said Gin, as she spoke of Simon, "but I always believed we'd last."

Viv, reminded, had told her what Nick had said. Gin had put her head in her hands and wept. Viv sat and could only wonder whether they would live their lives again, knowing what they would be given, knowing how the moments of happiness, so brief, seemed unequal to the pain.

"But then she said it couldn't be that, because he said it was something he should have told her years ago."

"Ah, pity," says Michael. "But still, that must have helped her. To know, I mean."

Viv shrugs. "Maybe, I'm not sure. It could make it worse, you know, knowing they maybe had a future after all."

Michael nods. He looks sad.

"But maybe you're right," she adds, "I did notice that after that she started wearing a sapphire ring."

"Yes, I saw it. You know, she wanted me to get rid of that ring when I was in London. I'm glad now I didn't. It must have helped her, Viv. And hopefully this trip will help her too. It was good of you to come. I take it you had to pull Abbie out of school?"

Viv nods, stubs her cigarette out on the wall. "Yes, but it's only for a bit. I thought it would do us all good. To see you, get away. For Abbie too." She tells Michael of their time with Issy.

He listens, smoking quietly. When his cigarette is finished, he lights another one for himself immediately, offers her one. Viv starts to decline, then shrugs, takes another one, lets him light it for her. She inhales, blowing smoke into the air. It seeps into the air, slips away through green fronded branches.

"Abbie's a lovely girl," he says. "She looks a lot like –"

"I know," laughs Viv, "everyone thinks she looks like Gin. So much so, when we've been out and about, everyone thinks she's Gin's daughter, not mine."

Michael chews his lip, and suddenly Viv has a sense it was not Gin he thought Abbie resembled. Maybe he was about to say Gabe. She regrets interrupting him.

As if following her train of thought, Michael asks, "Have you been out to the farm yet?"

"No, I thought tomorrow maybe." Abbie has made progress, she says, telling him of how before the trip she would always refer to Gabe as *my real father* whereas only yesterday she said *my dad*. "I think he feels more real to her now, you know?" She waits a moment before admitting to Michael that it is possibly harder for her to go to the farm than it is for Abbie.

He puts his arm around her shoulders, gives her a quick squeeze. It is so dark in the garden that the light from inside the house is bright. "Shall we go in and see what those two are up to, then?"

Gin looks up as they enter, gives them a small, sad smile. Abbie sits with her face fixed on the table, seemingly uninterested in their entrance. Her mussed hair straggles in front of her face, a hairslide doing little to hold back its thick fall. She is sorting through photographs spread out across Michael's kitchen table. Viv sits down next to her daughter. Things have not been easy between them. Viv had tried to make reparation for that day in the sunroom, but Abbie had remained recalcitrant. Jonnie's departure meant the girls inevitably spent more time at home. And they were alone more often, given the increasing time Viv had spent with Nick. It had been time she was reluctant to curtail. Until that day in his office.

Again she must turn her thoughts away from Nick. It still hurt. To her credit, Abbie had shown no delight at the break-up. Viv wonders about her and boys. Kayleigh, although younger, is already popular. Already, suspects Viv, a heartbreaker. But Abbie does not talk, does not give up information willingly, and Viv had tried to respect that. If she is honest, she knows she feels uncomfortable with the subject, and it had been easier not to push or pry.

She puts an arm around Abbie, who shifts slightly but does not shrug her off.

They have been talking about Gabe, realises Viv, the reason for the sorrow in Gin's smile. She wonders what Gin has told her. About his decision to go to the Army, about his decision not to leave? Perhaps it would have been better had Gin left Abbie with what she already knew. Must she subject Gabe's daughter to what torture he must have endured, enough to make him take his own belt, attach it to the bars of his window, and pull it tight around his own neck? Must Gin tell Abbie how she and Issy had to go and fetch his body from the police? How it had to be released, like an exhibit in a court of law? Viv had always wondered what had become of the belt, the strip of leather that in desperation had become his release.

Gin leans over to pull her own box forward from beneath the table, tears off the thick tape that Issy had sealed it with. She starts to pick it up.

"Here, Gin," says Michael, "that's too heavy for you. Let me get it."

Gin already has it halfway in the air. As Michael reaches for it, it slips in her hand, and tears, the bottom pulls apart, and its contents spill across the table and the floor. They all start to help pick up the scattered items that Issy had set aside for Gin.

Gin kneels on the floor, files through some envelopes, sorting them into one pile. Michael kneels beside her. One envelope is grubby and stained, with no markings on the outside.

"Gin, what's this?" he holds it towards her for her consideration.

Gin looks up and her eyes close briefly as if from pain, but when she speaks her voice is steady. "That's Gabe's suicide note." Her eyes meet his directly.

A terrible hush.

Michael's hand drops and he sits back heavily on the floor. He runs his free hand through his hair. For a long while he and Gin look at each other, saying nothing.

Eventually, Gin speaks. "You can read it if you want, Mikey."

Viv sits, frozen. Her concern is for Abbie, who is looking at Michael with a weird expression on her face. Michael rubs at his eyes, blinks hard, looks down at the envelope. Gin shuffles over to him on her knees, sits herself next to him and leans against him.

"I miss him," he says quietly. He looks up at Viv and then back at Gin.

She nods. They both look at the envelope. It shakes slightly in Michael's hand.

She touches his forearm. "I'll make us something to drink."

"I'll do it," Viv says, rising from the chair, eager to have something to do. "Tea or coffee?"

"Coffee… strong," says Michael. He stands, leaves the kitchen, taking the letter with him.

Gin stands also. She comes over to Viv, touches her arm. "You can read it too, if you want, Viv. There's not much to explain it."

Viv turns to her, and hugs her tightly. For a while they hold each other. I must not cry, thinks Viv, for Abbie's sake, for Gin's. I have shed too many tears over Gabe, *I must not cry*.

Viv is scooping rich Brazilian roast into the cafetière when Michael appears at the door of the kitchen. They all look up at him. His face is streaked with anguish, and his eyes narrow against the light in the kitchen. In his hand he clutches the letter.

"What?" says Viv, seeing his expression, the spoon of coffee in the air.

"Gin, Viv… this isn't – this isn't what you think it is."

49. GIN

That day, remember. That day, a Monday. A Monday as blue as his eyes. With the phone down, the silence was as intense as its siren moments before. Moments, long enough to change a life, but not a love. Bring back a love, but not a life. Back into the kitchen, she watched the dinner burning, those moments on. Since then, since him, before those moments. A slow anger began to burn. Burning like the dinner, slowly.

Gabriel.

Wednesday, she sat waiting. Waiting on the hard pine of a police bench. Waiting for her sister Issy to exit the room behind the door in front of her. Beyond its heavy varnish lay the pale body of their brother, dark purple bruises around his neck. Somehow, Gabe, her brother, full of life, was dead. Dead, he could be released. Alive, he had been a prisoner of the State, an Army deserter. A dissident, a dissenter, a disgrace.

The door opened. Isadore stood there, framed in stillness. Ashen, bereft, despite the illusion of calm; long, auburn tresses held in check, with wisps twisting, writhing free to stand out stark, Medusa-like, against the pallor of her face. Gabe had nicknamed their elder sister Isadorable, and she could deny him nothing. Issy it was who had to call, to organise, look after things, cover for their mother's eternal incapabilities, their father's devastation. And Issy who must take him home.

Thursday, they sat together on the plane, with no words for each other. They sat, staring ahead, two sisters whose thoughts lay with the coffin below them in the hold. Above the clouds, the sun still shone. They descended through the puffy mist of them, hanging over their home-town. From the air it might have been pretty. If passing over, one might have imagined it peaceful, idyllic even, this untouched town banking up against the dunes, great swathes of sand meeting the tumult of ocean spray. Red rooftops baking on any other given day, heat spilling upward from the tainted tar of roads edged with dust. But not that day. That day it sat cold, bleached of colour, shunned by the sun. As it ought. Fitting that the life be withheld from that airless little cesspool. Fitting that her brother's death took with it the light.

Friday, his funeral, and she felt grief stir inside her. A chilly Friday morning. The whole town would be there, thought Gin. Scandalised in their small-mindedness. Come ostensibly to grieve, commiserate, but voyeurs all, come to feed like vultures off another's pain, to add some snippet of delightful gossip, barely masked as shock or sympathy, to their dinner parties on sticky evenings after days unchanged for thirty years. Unheeded, the revolution sat dormant but growing, on their doorstep, feeding off their ignorance and blinkered self-indulgence.

The church on the hill lent no atmosphere. Stark-white, with stand-ard spire, it sat apart, opulent with newness. The wind off nearby dunes blew harsh and unforgiving. Below in the damp hollow shrouded by trees, lay her grandfather's grave. It depressed Gin, the thought of his body lying there, rotting in the moss. They were all alike, the graves. All slabbed with the smooth white pebbles of death, and many adorned with flowers encased bizarrely in round bowls of glass, as if with preservation of the blooms to deny the decay of bodies beneath. All things must of nature change. But here, this town, like so many others, sat, resisting progress or evolution, stubbornly stuck in its way of life. Adventure may have brought their ancestors to that country, that town, yet any lust for change seemed to have been bred out of their blood.

The church was large, yet full. Irrespective of motive, there was a hush to any petty whisperings as they filed in. Gabe had been so young, so full of potential.

Gin watched her mother greet the crowd, like an actress taking an encore. How could she? Rachel McMann was starchedly beautiful, a dark rose on display, her thick black hair pulled severely off her fore-head. A fat diamante cross dripped from a necklace. She leant heavily on Jacob's arm. As always, Jacob, her refuge and her flight from pain.

Gin's father, stooped, walked behind his wife, with Issy on his arm; his son's death had aged him in a day. They entered the church ahead of her.

Somehow, she was detached, held from them, outside still. Someone was talking to her now, and she had to be polite. There was a while yet before the service would start, the organ still hummed its mourning drone.

And there he was. Simon.

This was what it took to bring him back to her.

A year, almost a full year of silence.

There must have been rage against him inside her, but she could summon none. He looked thinner, in a suit that would once have shifted unfamiliar on his frame, but he wore it well, used to the big city, the hospital meetings with registrars and consultants. Gin must have stopped to stare. As if he felt her eyes on him, he turned from the two young women at his side. They had been at school with her and Gabe, but their names walked with them into the church. A certain catatonia had hold of her limbs. She looked down at her arms, as if they did not belong to her, willed them to move.

Gabe was dead.

This was Gabe's funeral.

A scream of denial built in her chest, some kind of truth finding pur-chase on her mind. No dream of horror, no nightmare.

Almost all were in the church; a few late cars rushed up the drive, then halted, driving more slowly at the gate, mindful of the presence of death.

A blonde woman stepped out of a champagne-coloured car, pulling at her skirt. Her skirt too short, her blouse too tight. A man, overweight, followed; he had the look of a businessman, thought Gin. His lips, she *noticed absently, were thick and wet. He licked them, looking pointedly at Gin. Gin was openly staring, and rude with it. She was trying to remember the woman's name, her mouth moving soundlessly around unknown syllables. They had been in the same school year, she recalled vaguely, but she could not remember her name. The woman gripped Gin's hand.*

"I'm sorry, hey," she said, with an Eastern Cape accent.

Gin looked at her blankly.

It was Simon who answered, who had come up to them. "Thank you," with sincerity. It was Simon who shook the man's hand, steered him in the direction of the church door. They murmured pleasantries in parting. The woman was smiling. She was smiling. Flicking her hair flirtatiously, looking up at Simon, eyelashes thick with mascara. Gabe was dead. And yet she smiled.

It registered suddenly: Sandra de Jongh, the girl who had fallen in the horse manure.

Gabe, thought Gin, would have laughed aloud.

The drone had stopped, the service started.

Gin turned her back on the church. She wished to walk away. The hands that seconds before would not move had now formed themselves into fists. She stared across towards the coastal road, to where it disappeared beyond the sand-hills, back to the Cape. Closing her eyes, she lifted her face to the strong breeze. This paltry little church was not worthy of her brother. Gabe's spirit could not be communicated through, should not be represented by, this blandness. Only the wildness of the wind did him justice that day. Not even the sky could capture the colour of his eyes. The sun could summon not the brightness of his smile. For the first time in her life, she was without him, her twin. The soul that had met this life together with hers had gone. Gone on, alone. And she had failed him on their journey.

Simon reached his arms around her from behind, his cheek rested against her hair, his lips brushed her ear, and she felt his breath on her face. He held her to him tightly, as if by gathering her up to him he might prevent her falling apart. Her limbs that moments before were rigid were threatening to collapse, so loose and unconnected did they feel. Wordlessly, he took her hand, as so many years later, he would again.

Late, they squeezed into the back pew. The minister blinked his disapproval. Slowly, theatrically, his sermon started. In a high indignant monotone, he urged them all to pray for the dear departed soul of Gabriel Alexander McMann. In the manner of his death, in riotous self-annihilation, her brother, it seemed, had denied himself the comfort of eternity and a place at the side of God.

Gin sat, appalled. Her angel Gabriel, fallen. She would never forgive her mother. This was her doing, her religious fervour. Where were the hyped and overblown tenets of forgiveness? Why did they all sit there so silently? In that moment she learned to hate the Church. She wanted to stand and shout, tell them of the man that none defended. He whom they had come to honour, they instead defiled. Where was Viv, whom he would marry? And Hannah, whom he loved? Michael, his best friend? Rage quivered through her system, made her physically shake. She felt Simon's restraining arm, saw his warning glance. Only that kept her from shouting, screaming, leaving. He had heard it too, the slur, the stain on Gabe's eternal soul. But it was not his brother, his church, his faith, nor his turn to talk.

After the unforgiving fire of the sermon, dull dirges followed. They filed out. Her mother stood outside, greeting all, the actress still on stage. Gin could not look at her. Her father was shaking hands, intent on thanking those who had come to pay some sort of homage to his son.

Later, at the incongruous party that came with the service of death, she stood dazed amidst them all. Her mother was holding court with the minister, one thin bejewelled hand grasping Viv's arm.

Viv, suddenly skeletal in a week; her pregnancy accentuated by her thinness. Michael stood to one side, alone, red-eyed, worn. He looked frequently across to Viv, who seemed to avoid his eyes.

Isaac stood with his brother Jacob, Hannah's father. Gin's father joined them. No doubt they spoke of patients, golf. A group of women, Jacob's wife Shirley amongst them, stood nearby. With a start, Gin saw that Hannah was with them. She seemed eerily, icily distant. It was Hannah Gin sorrowed for most. Perhaps Viv deserved it more, who bore Gabe's child, holding the obvious part of his heart, wearing his ring. Or Michael.

So many people. Everyone had loved Gabe. Teachers, pupils, friends. But Hannah, especially Hannah. Gabe had been one of the boys, cheerful, popular. She, Gin, quieter, plainer. People had mused on how unlike they were for twins. And some had thought Hannah his twin, both with their dark hair, white smiles, and so often together. Hannah had seemed special to him. Even when they were younger, with Hannah always lagging behind, it was Gabe who would stop them to wait for her, help her lug her bike over fences, put plasters on her knee, haul her up with a hand, check she was okay, see her home.

Gin was about to move towards Hannah when the minister approached, blocking her path. Unconsciously, Gin felt herself stiffen, her eyes searched the room. Simon stood, head bent low over Issy in the far corner, but as Gin's gaze reached him, he turned and looked across at her.

"My dear," crooned the minister, "your mother tells me you need comfort."

Numbness was replaced by a slow burning sensation to her skin that later she would recognise as rage. Reptile, serpent of lies, she thought.

"Leave me alone," she whispered hoarsely, words catching in the dryness of her throat. "You dishonoured my brother. My brother. He was a fine man. You. You stay away from me, and go back to your shitty... petty... angry... little... God."

She spat each word like venom at him, lucid then.

The two girls who had been outside the church were standing nearby with a former teacher; she recognised him as Gabriel's school athletics coach. They stopped talking, looked at her. Gin's hands were shaking, her teacup rattling, china roses wobbling dangerously on the bone saucer. It was Simon who took it from her, who had come up to her again. Whatever would pass between them afterwards, for that moment, she would always be grateful.

The minister had recovered, he seemed to bristle, opened his mouth. Simon raised his hand. The minister looked affronted. Gin turned her back on her mother's man of God. Perhaps, later, in that moment, she would find something with which to forgive herself for her silence in the church. Perhaps she redeemed herself, she thought. Perhaps after all, Gabe, I did not fail you in the end.

She hated them all, felt a baseline anger. Hated her mother for betraying her own son. Her father for standing by, knowingly, wittingly, letting her mother hold sway. She hated Hannah for rejecting Gabe, Viv for not making him leave the country. Hated the Church for denying him salvation; the Army, for all of it, for driving him to run away. And prison, for driving him to hang himself. And she hated Simon, for the past year. But most of all, Gin realised, she hated herself.

She left, walked out of the church hall. She craved the fresh air, the sanity of aloneness. She needed time to think. She suddenly longed to talk to Jonnie, longed for her own life, the life she had made away from her family, these families, this incestuous town. Cape Town, her home there, seemed clean and far-removed from the weight of it all, the complications.

"Ginny, wait." It was Simon's voice. Plea, not command.

She turned. He stood frowning at the door.

"Wait," he said again, gently.

She watched him turn back inside, through the open door, saw him say something to her father. Her dad turned to look at her, raised his hand in a slight wave, a half-hearted gesture of greeting. But Gin felt her face set, unsmiling, unforgiving. She turned away.

They took her father's car; he had given Simon the keys. It was sleek and smooth, her otherwise-spartan father's only indulgence. It could get her back to Cape Town by the morrow, she thought. But Simon had headed inland, cutting through the mountains of the Fish River valley. She said nothing, tilted her head away from him. Aloes lined the road, flame-haired soldiers, standing to attention as she passed. He drove fast, enjoying the strength of the car, its speed. Cold air cleared the cigarette smoke of the church hall from her lungs, her hair. The sun was setting ahead of them, the shine off the windscreen blinding. The screen was thick with dust and the blood of small insects that had foolishly strayed into its path.

She knew where Simon was going, and felt furious. She hated him for anticipating her need. Like a wounded animal, she needed refuge. So he headed for all that was left of their home together, her home with Simon. It would not be there anymore, she knew, but she had to see that for herself, stand outside, and watch the shadows of others as they passed behind lit and curtained windows. Accept its loss, and move on. She would have to do the same with Gabe, but too soon then, she thought. Too much was tearing at her heart to think of Gabe. One loss at a time, and slowly.

Three roads led into the hollow of Grahamstown. The east was the least attractive. This was the way he approached, the day's heat rising off the tarmac. The land stretched thirsty all around, shrubby bush alternating with plastic packets, pollution of a world too worn to care. Simon pulled the car over, in a haze of dust and gravel, at the turnoff to the farm, the commune Michael, Viv, and Gabe had shared. Gabe's home.

They sat awhile, engine running, darkness silting up the horizon, as if the sun had sunk into the town itself, and the night was burying it. Black soil on a coffin. She stared down the gravel road, perilous to suspensions, down towards the farm with its crude plumbing and cranky lights. Shook her head. No, she had no need to see it again. Her brother was not there.

Slowly they rode instead the winding Raglan Road into the town. She saw it all with new eyes, hating the Casspirs, the army tanks, which sat *there — still, ominous, silent. Hated them for what and whom they represented. Especially then. Since Gabe. They passed the long stretch of tin huts that at some point melded seamlessly with the poorer parts of town, differences that at night would be hidden, if not for the lighting. The shantytown had candles, the town electricity. They could have turned right at the first traffic lights, taken the dip and up again that would have led them to the Grand Hotel, but she wanted to see the length of High Street, and that tall cathedral spire hold sway above the trees and lights. When he reached the square, he turned left, then left again. The corner-shop was lit. It was early still, barely seven.*

Then, the little road so easily missed, and turning right into a courtyard of cobbles, he stopped. She wanted to weep.

They sat in silence.

The sky was fully black with night when Simon drove her up and out the town again, through the campus still busy and bright, up the steep incline past the residences, the lesser-travelled road up to the Motel. Nothing had changed in this town at all. It was to Gin both a solace and a curse. In that moment, she realised that she was where she was meant to be. For whatever reasons her brother had so brutally taken himself from a life he found too painful to endure, she knew that. Knew it as Simon checked them in to the Motel, as he put his arm around her shoulders, leading her, tired and stumbling, down the long and low-slung corridor, with its faded red carpet and gold patterned wallpaper; knew that everything was as it should be. Knew it as he unlocked the door to their room, as they stood together at the window, watched the simmering lights of the town below. As so many years before.

They would make love again. And there was not enough each of the other to satiate. They would sleep till sunlight reached them through the open window. The morning still crisp with dew, breakfast over, the revival of coffee and sleep complete. This then, thought Gin, was her brother's final gift to her. He who could no longer live, his death had brought Simon back to her.

Just then, with hope replacing pain, he took her hands in his.

"Gin," he said, "you know this – we – can't be. Nothing's changed."

She stared at him, uncomprehendingly. Gabe was dead. Everything had changed.

Why, she wanted to ask. Did it matter so much to him what people thought? What religion she was? Would people stare at her, point at her, note her Christian name?

"Gin," he said again, and she thought she heard a sound inside her own chest.

He was silent for a long while, and she also, not wanting to hear it, knowing she could not stand it.

"I'm engaged to be married. She's... Jewish. My parents are very happy."

And you, Simon? Are you happy?

That sound again. Her heart, she realised. Breaking.

50. GIN

Coffee grains litter the counter.

"What do you mean?" asks Gin, her voice a whisper. She swallows hard.

They all stare at Michael. He moves across the kitchen floor, takes the spoon from Viv, pulls out a kitchen chair and makes her sit at the table with Abbie and Gin. He switches off the kettle and pours water into the cafetière, stirs it, puts the lid on. He takes four mugs from the cupboard behind them, puts them on the table. Then he scoops the spilled grains off the marbled surface, dusts them into the bin. He sits down in the chair across from Gin.

Gin looks at him. "What do you mean? Didn't Gabe write it?" she asks again. She remembers the letter, its distinctive backward slant of words to her. She shakes her head in confusion.

Michael puts his hand over hers. "No, no, I'm sorry Gin. I didn't mean he didn't write it. I meant he didn't write it just before he died. I meant it wasn't – it couldn't have been – his suicide note."

He pushes the plunger down.

Gin watches the grains compress against the side of the hot glass. She shakes her head again, trying to clear her head. "I still don't understand."

Michael pours steaming coffee into a mug painted with pink roses and passes it to her. Then he pours one for Viv, one for Abbie, in white mugs edged with gold. Finally, one for himself, spoons two sugars into the black heat of it. He sips at it gingerly. "Gin, Gabe wrote this – he showed it to me – he wrote this on the farm, the day before he left, to say goodbye, before he went AWOL."

The kitchen window, open to the day's oppressive heat, bangs shut suddenly. They all jump. Viv exhales. Abbie giggles nervously.

Michael rises to shut it, hooking its silvered catch to the white wooden frame.

AWOL. Absent without leave. Gin remembers how the expression had reverberated around her brain. Gabe had fled the Army, left before his stint was up. And the innocuous-sounding phrase had taken on a meaning that was both sinister and frightening in its consequences. It had meant her brother was a hunted man.

A bright flash illuminates the room. Gin starts in her chair. Viv gives a small cry, puts her hand to her throat. The heat has brought an evening thunderstorm. Rain starts to pelt down, its drops hard on the jutting kitchen roof. Viv takes a gulp of coffee. A snarl of thunder makes Gin jump again.

"He meant you to have the letter, to explain why he had left," continues Michael.

Three months, almost four, after his death, had come the note. Gabriel's note. To her, to Gin. He had left no other. Initially she was tempted to throw it away or to burn it. Angry with him. Angry at her dead twin. Why me, Gabe? Why try to explain to me, and not to Mom, to Dad, to their sister Issy? Not Vivienne, his girlfriend, nor Michael, his best friend. Not Hannah even, Hannah, the love of his life. She, Gin, left to stare at the grubby envelope, re-sealed after the police had taken their notes, had read, re-read, and analysed her brother's final precious words to her, his twin. His final, private thoughts. She stared at it, put it on the mantelpiece, lit the fire, ready to burn it unopened, unread. But then she hesitated, went outside and got into the little yellow Renault, churned her gears and raced up to the off-licence on Main Road. She bought three bottles of expensive Shiraz and one of cheap brown sherry. Back at the flat, she had poured the sherry over ice. Glass after glass, staring at the letter. Glass after glass, swirling the pungent liquid in her mouth, sucking at the ice cubes. Eventually, drunk and numbed, Gin had opened it, summoned the courage to read the backward slant of her brother's last words. To her.

She had not been able to drink sherry since.

"He gave it to me, to give to you," Michael is saying, "only…"

"But…" Gin stammers, interrupting, "but then I still don't understand. Why did I only get it after… after…?" She looks at him helplessly.

"I meant to give it to you. Gabe put it in his rucksack, his army togs, left them with me. And then, you know, he left that evening. And the next morning, it was barely dawn… they came."

Michael stops, looks at Viv, who sits hunched, her arms drawn across her chest. She and Abbie have stayed silent, listening, absorbing. Abbie puts an arm around her mother. Viv does not move.

"And they took it, they took the bag and all his stuff at the farm, and they left, and then, of course, when I remembered the letter afterward, it was too late. And they got him so soon after that, I never thought to ask about it. You know, by then, he was in prison, and a goodbye letter didn't seem to matter anymore." Michael's words stumble over themselves and his voice is high with emotion, guilt.

"It's okay, Mikey," says Gin, and her voice is calm. Thoughts whir in her brain. The tone of the letter, the words, had never seemed right to her. The promises he'd asked of her. The promise he had made: *Bye, Gin. I'll see you again.* She'd thought it cruel, ironic. Now it made sense; he had written it earlier. Then it strikes her.

"But Michael, if they had it, if the military police had it from the farm already, why on earth, how on earth… did I get this letter as a suicide note?"

Michael is nodding at her words. They stare at each other, a grim realisation forming simultaneously.

Michael is the one to try to form the words. "Do you think this means that… that maybe Gabe didn't –".

The storm is almost directly overhead now.

Gin shivers violently.

"Dear God." It is Viv's voice that rings out clearly above the storm, "They killed him."

51. NICK

The man's bitter tone bites through the night air. "*Ja*, I'll tell you about Simon Gold."

Nick sits back in the wooden chair and waits. The verandah is dark, illuminated only by a window of the house. The lights of Cape Town shine beyond the wide curve of black that is the bay. He knows the mountain rises above that, but it is invisible, inked into oneness with the night. The man's features are blurred in dimness, but Nick can still make out a brow that has known difficulties, irises like wet soil that have known hopelessness, a face that has been pitted with despair.

"At first, man, you know, when he first came along to our meetings…" The man pauses, his forehead furrowing. He draws on a self-rolled cigarette, inhales, and then lets out a long greyed exhalation. The smoke shrinks and recoils, as if burned by the night.

Nick nods encouragement.

"Well, we thought he was just another honky with a conscience. No real commitment, you know how it was." The man looks at Nick, appraising him briefly. His mouth curls at the edge. "*Ja*, well, maybe it was a bit before your time, *laaitie*." The curl becomes a short laugh, which degenerates to a cough. He taps the end of his cigarette. Ash falls limply off its end. "So I guess we gave him a hard time at first. We wouldn't tell him things that were important, you know? But then we thought, why not test him? You know, see if he was working for the Afrikaners, or the cops, your lot." The man looks at him again, assessing any reaction.

Nick suppresses an urge to smile.

Apparently satisfied, the man takes another pull at his cigarette, and continues. "*Ja*, so like, we told him stuff that was wrong, you know, just in case. But nothing ever came of it. So he seemed safe. And man, he was dedicated. Punctual, efficient. *Ja*, you know, he was smart." Another puff of smoke. Another cough. Phlegm rattles his emaciated chest.

Again, Nick nods and is silent.

The man is more voluble now. "So, you know, we kind of learned to accept him, trust him even. Over time. And he seemed to care, to really give a shit, you know. I mean, he would be up all hours, working in the squatter camps, treating people."

"Treating people?" Nick is intrigued.

The man's turn to nod. "*Ja*, Simon set up a regular medical clinic in the township. Every Friday night, he'd be there. Paid for a lot of the medicines himself, and got donations here and there. But then, he could afford it, rich whitey like him." The man stops, looks at Nick again.

Nick keeps his face impassive.

"The other students came and went, along for the experience. But it got quite organised. We all helped now and then. But it was mostly Simon, and Jay and Leila, of course."

"Jay and Leila?"

The man's eyes run over Nick, narrowing. Another cough shakes his pinched frame. Then he shakes his head. To Nick it seems as if he decides something.

"*Ja*," he repeats, "Jay and Leila." The man puts his cigarette out. He rubs his hands together, then reaches into his pocket to pull out a crushed pack of loose-leaf tobacco.

Nick watches as the man takes a red cigarette roller and a square of cigarette papers from the rusted table between them. He inserts the paper deftly into the roller then squashes some of the honey-coloured tobacco inside, snaps it shut, and rolls it once, twice, leaving only an edge of white paper showing. He brings it to his dry lips, licks the strip, and rolls it again. He unclamps the roller, pops out a taut roll of cigarette. The man puts it in his mouth, flicks a plastic yellow lighter and the cigarette ignites, burning unevenly until the man sucks at it. The whole of the circular tip glows and the man leans back in his chair, sighing as another grey stream leaves his nostrils and mouth.

"*Ja*, man, they did good work in the townships, those three. And it was Simon who fixed me, stitched this." The man fingers a blanched line near his right ear. "Got it on a June sixteenth rally," he says. The nicotine soothes his voice to an almost nostalgic tone.

They sit in silence for a while. A train whistles in the distance. A wind visits the verandah, chilling him. The man smokes, blowing silken rings into the darkness.

"So what happened?" asks Nick, when the minutes have ticked by.

"*Ja*, so we finally reckoned Simon was for real, you know. I mean, *ja*, he was a privileged white Jew-boy, but he seemed really genuine, you know? So he was one of us. And anyway, by then, he and Leila were a thing."

"A thing?"

"*Ja*, a thing, man. An item." The man looks pained at having to explain. "Lovers, man."

"And Jay?"

"Ah, *ja*, Jay. Man, that was a weird relationship. He never liked Simon, you know. Made no secret of it to us. He would call him a dirty Jew, fucking honky, the whole lot. But only to us. I think in a way Jay respected Simon, his work, his knowledge. They certainly worked well together. But I know Jay never got to trust Simon."

"Why not?"

"I think mostly 'cos of Leila. Jay used to warn her that it wouldn't last. That Simon would dump her. Told her rich white Jews didn't marry Christian Coloured girls."

"And Leila? How did she take that?"

"*Ag*, she'd laugh at Jay. Tell him he was just jealous. Teasing him, you know. But she was quite obsessed with Simon. I mean besotted. Really a bit too much, you know, like not healthy. And she was a nice, smart girl, you know. Shame what happened."

"What happened?"

The man snorts, a harsh sound full of mucus. He coughs again. "Jay was right, man. Right about Simon. Simon, you know… *ag*, man, the bastard. He betrayed us all."

Only the scant wind moves across the verandah. Far away, a car's horn, a shout, a siren. The man finishes his cigarette. Then he pulls out his roller again. Nick follows the ritual of rolling another one until the man shoves the new cigarette, gleaming with spittle, into his mouth. He jams his tobacco back in his pocket.

"Tell me," says Nick, watching the end of the cigarette smoulder limply between the man's lips, "what did Gold do to you?"

The man shifts in his seat. A sigh escapes with his smoke. "*Ag*, it was terrible. Terrible, man. What he did to them. To all of us. But especially to Leila."

Nick waits.

"Your lot," the man spits, "your lot. The police, man. Seems they got hold of Simon." He sighs again. "I suppose we should have seen it coming. The man was visible, you know. Right there, in the townships. Stuck out a mile in his white skin. They would have known him. Known his politics. He was probably being watched. You know, a suspected dissident. Seems they got him one night. Leila went frantic. She knew, you know. Knew when he wasn't home. She was convinced that's what had happened, that it was them. All over the place, she was. Screaming, crying, begging us, begging Jay, to do something…" The man looks out into the night, searching for something he cannot see. "What could we do, man? What could we do? You know what it was like then?" He does not wait for an answer. "*Jislaaik*, I suppose I can't blame the guy. God knows what they did to him."

"To Gold?"

The man starts slightly, as if he had momentarily forgotten Nick's presence. He scratches his scar. The hard tone returns. "Well, whatever, he must have told them all right. Everything. *Ag*, he's been gone two, maybe three days at the most. The next thing we knew, we were raided. Arrested, all of us."

"All of you? Jay and Leila as well?"

The man is derisive. "*Ja*, especially them, man. What do you think?" After a momentary reflection, he says, "Christ, those guys knew what they were doing."

"What happened?" asks Nick, certain he knows the answer, or part of it. He waits with a heavy weariness for the inevitable.

The man spits out some tobacco. "The usual, man. You wouldn't believe…" He stares sightlessly into the blackness. His cigarette dangles loosely in his hand. A while passes, and the man moves, tapping the ash off his cigarette and drawing on it again, sucking at it as if for breath. "Those boys knew how to get what they wanted. I got off lightly. It was worse for them. For Jay and Leila. Much worse. I saw Jay's back, you know, afterwards. The guy will carry scars till he dies, man." The man pauses. "We all will."

"What about Leila?" Nicks steels himself for the man's reply.

"Poor girl. Poor girl, hey. *Fok* knows what they did to her. She was *waarlik* beautiful, you know. Before. *Ag*, they didn't let anything show. Nothing on the outside that you could see, you know. But if you knew her before… and then saw her after, after, you know, you could tell she was different. But that's the thing, man. It's what they do to you on the inside…" His voice trails off.

"Did you see Gold again after that?"

"*Ag*, no, man. Never saw him again. Just as well. I think I'd have wanted to kill him if I had. That's if Jay hadn't gotten to him first."

Nick absorbs this. "What about Leila? Did she see him again?"

"I don't think so, man. Simon just disappeared. Must've left Cape Town, I suppose." The man exhales heavily and stays quiet for a long time.

Inside the house, someone turns on a radio, there is a clatter of crockery. Nick can hear the start of a news bulletin. "What happened to Leila and Jay after that?"

"I didn't see a lot of them after that. And you know, our group was pretty much ruined after that. They had their eye on us. So things kind of folded, we went our separate ways. Jay and Leila stayed close, I think." The man laughs, a short rasp. "Anyhow, they had futures, man. They had their studies to finish. Doctors, you know. At least, Jay definitely finished. Actually, I'm not sure now about Leila. Poor girl. I remember something about her quitting. Shame, man. So I guess Simon took her career from her too… I suppose I can't blame the guy. I mean, they probably tortured him. Anybody would have folded, given what they do to you."

Nick wonders if the man is talking about himself.

"But it's hard to forgive him for Leila, hey. She really loved him, you know. Girl was a mess." The man leans forward. "Jay told me she would never be able to have children after what they did to her."

Something twists inside Nick's chest. Again, they face the night in silence.

Finally, the man adds. "Jay stayed active, you know. In fact, he went to prison later. Couple of years, as I remember. I haven't seen him since. I heard he married a white girl. Thought that was funny, you know, given his feelings."

After a pause, Nick asks, "What was Leila's surname?"

The man thinks for a bit. "Leila Koning, she was."

"And Jay?"

"Kassan."

The name shivers down Nick's spine.

The man elaborates. "His full name was Mohammed Jay Kassan. I called him Jay. But almost everyone else called him Jonnie."

52. VIVIENNE

Before them the Cape Flats extend till the mountain rises in the distance, unchanged for centuries. It has taken two days of travelling from the Eastern to the Western Cape, from the rainforest and grassland of the coast, through inland scrub with its thorn trees and deciduous bush, to the wide savannah and shrub. They drive the straight road into the city, squatter camps spilling from behind thick green bush. Viv stops to pick up Kayleigh from her friend's house in Wynberg. Her youngest, full of energy and tales and non-stop chatter, changes the subdued energy in the car. By late afternoon, Viv pulls up outside her home, relieved to reach it before nightfall. The last rays of sun finger over the lawn, touching the house with an orange glow.

Kayleigh bounds out the car and she and Abbie, already arguing, slam into the house, traipse upstairs. Viv and Gin stop in the hall. The house has that peculiar bleached-out feel, having lost some of its vitality while unoccupied. She dumps her suitcase down with a sigh and while Gin fetches the rest of the luggage from the car, she rifles through the mail, places it to one side. Nothing urgent that cannot wait till morning. The light on the answer machine is blinking red. Seven messages. Viv switches it on. One from her mother, three from patients, two ring-offs. Gin returns, puts one case down on the tiled floor, takes the other towards the stairs. The last message starts to play. Nick's voice is husky on the machine. Viv stands rooted, noticing that Gin too, has stopped on the bottom stair, listening. The sound of his voice slams into Viv's every cell, and every cell is perfused with the memory of him. Please call him. A pause before clicking off as if perhaps there was something more he wished to say, but had changed his mind.

They are all tired and hungry and Viv orders takeaways. The girls open the boxes eagerly, spreading fish and chips onto plates. Viv opens a Chardonnay for herself and Gin. Her daughters tuck in to their food, but Viv can only pick at hers, and Gin, she notices, barely touches anything. Instead Gin cradles her wine glass, eyes fixed on the heavy curtains drawn against the night.

Kayleigh's energy is infinite. Her time away from them is dissected in detail, her voice animated. Finally she pauses to eat, stuffing sloppy chips into her mouth.

Suddenly Gin appears to focus. She puts her wine glass down on the table and leans forward, addressing Kayleigh. "You look like your dad," she says.

"You know my dad?" exclaims Kayleigh, her intrigue and delight evident.

"Kayleigh," says Viv, "don't talk with your mouth full."

Her youngest chews hard, swallows, and takes a swig of Coke.

Gin sits back, as if bewildered by her own observation. "Yes," she murmurs, "a long time ago." Her eyes meet Viv's across the table.

Viv smiles at her, raises her glass in mock salutation ever so slightly before she puts it to her lips. *Jonnie.*

"Oh my God!" shouts Kayleigh, "I can't believe I forgot to tell you all." Her eyes are wide with wonderment. "Dad's new wife is pregnant!"

Viv and Gin look at each other. This time it is Gin who raises her glass, "Well," she says to Kayleigh, "I think that deserves a toast, don't you?"

Something has changed in Gin's manner, thinks Viv as she lifts her wine. Indeed inside herself something feels different also. She puts her glass down with surprise. *Guilt*, she realises. *There is no guilt. It's over, it's finally gone.*

After supper, the girls go to their rooms, and Viv stacks the dishwasher before she and Gin move to the lounge. It is a mild night, but the lounge feels oddly cold. Gin takes the armchair at the window and tucks her legs beneath her.

Viv brings the bottle in and refills both their glasses before she slides onto the couch. She sighs with relief. "Long day, long journey. It's good to be home."

"Thanks for driving, Viv," says Gin, "It was wonderful to see Michael again."

"Yes, wasn't it. But," says Viv, thinking of Gabe, "well, all that. Just don't know what to say, or do."

"It may turn out to be good for Abbie," manages Gin, understanding what she means. "It may make it easier." She pauses. "It helped me, I think."

Viv sips her wine. As yet, she cannot take it in. It is, after all, only an assumption. It will possibly simplify matters for Abbie. Her daughter may make some peace with Gabe's death. For her, she does not know. Gabe is dead. She will never see him again, never hear his voice or his laugh again, never touch him again. She will live on, skin turning fragile, hair going grey. But Gabe will never age. In the end, she wonders wearily, does it matter how he died?

Inevitably, she thinks of Nick. Nick and his message, short and to the point. She had not heard his voice for so long, she had almost forgotten its effect on her, the controlled heat within its cadence. It must be the wine on a relatively empty stomach, tiredness after the journey, but the thought of Nick sends a sexual shiver through her. She gulps at her wine now. He had wrapped himself about her in this very room. She puts the glass down and takes out a cigarette.

Gin says, "You're thinking of that Nick Retief now, aren't you?"

Viv laughs with a mirth she does not feel. Gin knows her too well.

"Abbie said you'd been involved with him, but that you'd broken up," continues Gin. "She said she felt responsible."

Viv is astonished. "Abbie said that?" When, she wonders, had her daughter and Gin spoken about this? She shakes her head vehemently. "No, no, that's not true."

She starts to tell Gin about Nick. The wine lubricates her speech and it spills out. How it had evolved, what he is like, his good company, their walks, his house, the day in the sunroom, but before she can get to the real reason the relationship ended, before she can tell Gin about the files and what she learned that day in Nick's office, the phone rings. Viv stops, drains her glass, and rises to get it.

Kayleigh yells, "I'll get it." Her daughter is already running down the stairs.

Viv sighs, sitting down again and looking at Gin, who shrugs in amusement.

Kayleigh's muffled greeting can be heard then a pause before she appears in the doorway. Disappointment flattens her voice, "It's for you, Aunt Gin."

Gin looks up in surprise, "Me? Who is it?"

"Dunno. Some man." Kayleigh disappears back into the hall, can be heard labouring up the stairs.

Gin looks at Viv with raised eyebrows and stands, goes into the hall. Viv lights another cigarette, and pours herself another glass of wine. She is exhausted. She cannot make out Gin's conversation, can only hear the monotone notes of her response.

A few minutes later, Gin reappears at the doorway.

"What?" asks Viv, stabbing out her newly-lit cigarette. "Who was that, Gin? What's wrong?"

Gin turns her face to where Viv sits but Viv can see her focus is elsewhere. She talks into the space between them, each word emanating as if from an abyss inside her.

"Simon's father is coming to Cape Town. He wants to see me. He says I need to know why Ellie died."

53. *VIVIENNE*

She had never seen Gabe without his watch. Only at night would he unbuckle the thick tan strap, put it beside the bed. Once showered, on it would go again the following morning. He'd had to replace the strap once where it had weathered, the leather creasing and finally tearing where he fastened it on the second hole.

She had teased him about it being like the farmer's axe, and he had looked at her nonplussed, and she'd had to explain.
"You know, the farmer's axe, the one he's had for forty years, but in that time the handle's been replaced six times and the blade four..."
Gabe had rubbed the watchstrap thoughtfully as she spoke.

Viv rubs her thumb over it now, much as he had then. Of course it had stopped, so many years unwound, but as she winds it now, it starts to tick again, the gilt hands moving gracefully around the off-white face of it. The watch had absorbed his very essence, thinks Viv, so much so that she had only finally realised he was dead when Gin had given it to her.

She walks out of the bedroom. It is time to give it to Gabe's daughter.

Abbie's eyes widen in initial surprise, then fill with unexpected tears. She takes the watch and stares at it as if it is her father's face she sees instead of the cream countenance, the worn copper-gold surround. She massages the strap between finger and thumb and then puts it around her left wrist, pulling the strap tightly. Even on the last bucklehole it still hangs loosely, and the face covers almost the width of her wrist.

"Thanks, Mom," is all she says.

They set off in sombre mood. The journey will take up most of the day. It is Abbie's choice, albeit a strange one. Viv herself would have taken Gabe's ashes inland, to the farm maybe, or the mountains of Zululand that he had so loved. But she respects her daughter's wish to do what she wants, and in some way she understands that for Abbie, this is perhaps a way of keeping her father's memory close, here in the Cape.

They take the Ou Kaapse Weg to Noordhoek, turning right onto Main Road at Sun Valley, which will take them to Kommetjie and its surfer's waves. About five kilometres after Scarborough, Viv turns into Plateau Drive, and after twice that distance, they reach the entrance to the nature reserve with its wild game, its resplendent fynbos. Antelope, baboons, zebra, even ostrich call this park home, but they see only a shy buck peering at them from the bank of forest.

You have to go to the bleak beaches of Cape Agulhas to reach the most southerly tip of Africa, but to Viv, Cape Point always feels like the end of the continent. The rocky promontory set at the end of the Cape peninsula has two other names, each ostensibly from Bartholomeu Diaz, the explorer. *Cabo das Tormentas*, Cape of Storms, he called it on his first voyage, trying to open a trade route between east and west. The second, the weather kinder, he dubbed it *Cabo de Boa Esperanto*. The Cape of Good Hope. She wonders what Diaz must have thought as he rounded the point on his third and final voyage. Perhaps his first impression the more accurate, as the storms took his ship down, all hands lost along with him. Perhaps both names are apt. I have known both, thinks Viv. Perhaps it is an apposite setting that Abbie has chosen after all.

The park is relatively quiet, with few tourists, and their path up the steep and windy walk to the top of the cliff is unimpeded. Ahead is the most powerful lighthouse in the southern hemisphere. A cormorant swoops and dips on the air current, its cry carried away on the wind. Abbie walks ahead of them, clasping the urn to her chest.

"It must be hard to let her go," says Gin, walking beside Viv.

She has echoed her thoughts. "Yes," mutters Viv. She is mindful that Gin must be thinking of Ellie, who will never grow up. Gin has had to let so many people go.

"You never finished telling me about you and Nick Retief," says Gin.

Nick. Viv's heart lurches at the sound of his name. She sees again the scattered folders on the floor of his office, his stricken look.

I promise never to hurt you, Vivienne.

But he had. "It's a long story," she says, and then remembers Nick saying these exact words to her, that moonlit night at the coast.

"I think," Gin is saying reflectively, "that whatever happened, you should try to repair it."

Viv is surprised. Gin had never liked Nick. "Why do you say that?"

The wind is chill, and Gin pulls her cardigan closed, folds her arms across her chest as they walk. "Just because, well," she stops, starts again, as if the words are forming as she thinks. "There've been too many unknowns in our lives. You know, what might have happened if Gabe had lived, what could have been had Simon and I not had the –" she exhales, continues, "accident." She pronounces the word oddly, accented almost. "If Ellie hadn't died."

Viv, distracted, stumbles, goes down on one knee.

Gin reaches for her belatedly, grabs her arm. "Are you okay?"

Viv brushes her knee, nods. Abbie, ahead in her own world, does not look back. "Just a graze," says Viv, but it has already started to throb. Her stocking has laddered, bloodied.

They start up the incline again.

Gin's lips are pursed, her brow furrowed. After a while, she says,

"You should call him, Viv. See what happens. The thing is, Viv, you don't want to spend the rest of your life wondering what might have been."

Abbie has reached the top ahead of them. She stands at the edge before a stone wall. Without looking back at her mother and her aunt, she opens the lid, tips the urn, letting the wind gather up her father's ashes and whip the grey swirl of them far out over the ocean.

Viv and Gin hang back, letting Abbie have this moment alone. They stand huddled together.

"She chose the windiest spot in the Cape," says Viv, arms tightly clasped around herself.

"I'm not sure I'd like that," muses Gin.

"What?" Wondering if Gin too would have chosen elsewhere for her twin.

"I'd have chosen the mountain. It makes me feel safe, its strength, its solidity. I guess the thought of Gabe – oh, I know it's not him, really – but it kind of bothers me, the thought of him drifting aimlessly out there, amongst the sharks and the wrecks and the drowned."

The drowned. Like Diaz. Viv contemplates this for a while. Then she links her arm with Gin's. "The current will bring him in, Gin. Somewhere he'll land safely on a beach. Up the coast." She looks far off into the distance as she adds, "Don't worry, Gin, the sea will bring him home."

54. NICK

Captain Bernard Strydom is standing in Nick's office, idly leafing through the folders in the tray marked *Closed*. The filing is behind, the archives stuffed to overflowing, and hindered by the new computer system. Nick is catching up on paperwork. It is his day off, but since Viv, he has had little inclination to spend it alone.

Nick had ordered flowers for Viv, but they were returned, still in the box. He had written, but the letter came back unopened. His phone calls went unanswered. He knew he could check up on her officially but he did not want to hurt her again. He drove to her house one weekend, to find the door locked, the garage empty. The neighbours told him she was gone. A fist clutched around his heart.

"Gone where?" he queried, to be told she was visiting friends, she was out of town.

And there is always paperwork.

Suddenly Strydom says, "McMann, that's a name that brings back bad memories."

"What do you mean?" Nick stiffens but keeps his voice relaxed, his manner casual. Strydom is a relic, a dinosaur left over from the time of apartheid, kept on in the spirit of reconciliation. *Ubuntu*, thinks Nick. Strydom was not as bad as some of them.

"*Ag, ja,*" sighs Strydom. He rubs at his moustache thoughtfully.

Nick waits, saying nothing, continues writing his report. But he is alert to the older man's every move.

Eventually Strydom sighs again and says, "*Ja*, man, there was some business back at the TRC."

The Truth and Reconciliation Commission, thinks Nick, had exposed unimaginable horrors. Tales of torture and miscarriages of justice had made him ashamed of his race and more often of his profession. The truth had not set him free, he reflects. He stops writing, sits back in his chair, and looks across at the Captain intently.

Strydom seems barely aware of Nick's regard. He has folded his arms and is staring off into the distance, remembering. "There was this fellow in the police, worked with me on a few cases, Du Plessis – we called him Doep – he was pulled up in front of the Commission for alleged abuse of prisoners." He sighs again, as if his own words cause him pain. "*Ja*, anyhow, seems the fellow making the allegations – I forget his name – said that at the same time, there had been a white chap in the cell next door to him. And that Doep had tortured him too. They thought the chap was mentioning him in the hope that they could find the white guy to back up his story."

Nick feels an old feeling rise inside him. He knows what Strydom is going to say. "And did they?" he asks, although he is sure he knows the answer.

"*Ag*, no," says Strydom, not looking at him. "The guy was dead. Committed suicide, apparently. But then the chappie complaining to the TRC said that Doep had tortured the white oke as well, that Doep had murdered him, made it look like suicide."

"And what was the white guy's name?" he asks, but he knows. He asks only to prolong the interlude of innocence, to delay hearing confirmation of something he already knows.

"*Ja*, that's the thing," says Strydom, so quietly it is as if he talks only to himself, "the chap was called McMann. *Ja*, that's it. Gabriel McMann."

In the silence that follows, neither man looks at the other. Nick closes his eyes briefly at the name, opens them to stare down at his unfinished report.

McMann. Gabriel McMann.

He imagines her chestnut eyes looking up at him as he starts to tell her. And he will have to tell her this now. Even though it is apparent she never wants to see him again, he will have to see her and tell her. He, Nick Retief, will have to watch as his words rupture her world.

"What happened after that?" he asks, eventually, when the silence has solidified, thickened the atmosphere in his office so much he imagines he can taste the acridity of it.

"Well, they couldn't really take it any further about the McMann boy. Seems his family never knew, I mean, never suspected it may have been anything other than suicide. So no one had come forward to the Commission asking about McMann. Anyhow, they didn't find any direct relatives."

Because, thinks Nick, they were either ill, abroad, or dead. And nothing obvious to make the connection with a Vivienne Weetman, a Vivienne Kassan. And, he supposes, little incentive, what with so many cases to pursue. He says nothing.

Strydom is stroking his moustache again. "*Ja*, bad business, that."

"Did Du Plessis say anything about McMann?" Nick is surprised at the evenness of his own tone.

"*Jussus*, I can't exactly remember now," says Strydom. "Not officially, no. It was something like he said he hadn't killed him but he knew there had been some sort of cover-up about the guy's death. Said it was an accident or something, that in any event there was enough stuff to suggest McMann had killed himself."

It was incredible that they could sit and talk about this man so dispassionately. A man had been tortured and killed, whether accident or murder, yet it had been passed off as suicide, and everyone went back to work the next day as if nothing had happened. He feels an ancient anger rise in him. He suddenly has a desperate need to walk out of his office, breathe clean air, drive home, run on the sand. He longs also to see Vivienne, take her in his arms one last time, before it will be over between them forever.

But he stays seated in his chair, picks up his pen, turns it slowly in his hands. "And did he name any other men?"

"*Ag*, I can't remember now. If he did, it would have had to be investigated separately. And you know, it would have depended on other people corroborating the allegations. Don't know if anything could be proven. And McMann had left a note as I recall."

"What happened to your colleague, Du Plessis?" he asks Strydom.

"Doep?" says Strydom, with a start. He sighs again, a big hearty outlet of breath. "*Ag*, man. The usual. Acquitted."

55. GIN

Every night, eyelids sinking into sleep, it has been Simon's eyes that flashed before her, like a northern aurora across the darkening horizon of night. But it was not Simon she dreamed of last night. Instead she glimpsed her brother's shadowed form slipping away from her through distant trees.

Gin ran after him but wood had suddenly grown thick and dense around her. She cried his name soundlessly into the approaching night. She knew they hunted him, she knew he was hurt. She saw the blood on the forest floor, mingling with dying leaves. Her damaged, bleeding brother was lost, lost in the wood. Then she heard him calling to her from across a river that led to the sea. She walked towards him, but he was gone.

She knew she must cross the river, but she was afraid of its slow-flowing murkiness, almost stagnant with weeds. Sticks lined the surface, clotted with brown foam. She waded in and suddenly then it was wide, deep, with a strong undertow pulling at her legs. The far bank became a cement wall. Clambering to reach it, she was struck by an overwhelming thirst but heard Gabe's disembodied voice telling her not to drink the river's water. Desperately thirsty, she trailed her tongue along its surface. It was clear, sweet and cold.

Gabe knelt on the cement bank opposite, still imploring her not to drink. Eventually she reached the edge, but he was gone. Instead before her was a steep mountain and he sat at its summit, on a white horse; in his hands he held a cup of water for her. But her way up the hill was barred by an iron gate and fence so that she had to hike around. When she finally found herself standing on the mountain, she could no longer see her twin, but she heard him call to her again. She knew he was then far down below on the other side of the mountain, on the beach. At the river's mouth. She started to run. Then she was there, standing on a black salted rock, staring across the thrashing waves. She called for Gabe, but he did not answer. A wave washed up to the rock and the cup he had been holding was drifting on its swell. Reaching down, Gin picked it up. It was full of seawater but her thirst was such that she drank from it.

Then she shouted into an empty sky, in a voice that exited her lungs only as an undertone: The sea is my blood, these rocks are my bones.

She brakes sharply at a stop sign that looms at her without warning. Cape Town's roads have become unfamiliar to her.

Isaac is staying with a friend. The flat in Vredehoek is large, plush. The hall opens up to the left, two broad steps take her down to a rectangular lounge, doors leading to a flat patio with a plunge pool. The mountain dips below, riddled with other plush houses, patios, and pools that glimmer in the sun. To the right, a dining room, the table already set for dinner. On top of it, a menorah. Friday night Shabbes. Prayers, gefilte fish, and chollah. She feels the old stab of exclusion in her chest.

Isaac shuffles off to make tea, buying them both time, their roles reversed since their last meeting. When Ellie met her grandfather, without either of them knowing it.

Ellie. My little Ellie.

Gin sits on the edge of a white leather-effect couch, trying not to sink into its softness. The carpet is Persian, red and blue dyes woven into intricate shapes. It is worn slightly in one corner beneath the step. At the end of the lounge is a stone fireplace, filled with a vase of dried proteas instead of a grate. On the wall above it hangs an oblong watercolour. A seascape, with a mottled headland falling into a stormy ocean. It reminds her of the one she had seen at Michael's. She had felt drawn to it, its isolated feel.

She waits for Isaac to bring her tea she will not drink. She sits, twisting the ring on her finger. And while he talks, the painting will ingrain itself into her soul, the rocks cutting into her as if at her flesh, the sea that batters the headland battering also her bones, and the mist that rises into the overcast sky is the same colour of the cloud that Isaac's words will cast over her life.

She stares at the painting while he talks, while he tells her the truth of her life.

He stops, his tale finally told.

She looks at him with sudden comprehension.

The old man nods. "Your mother and Jacob came to me when she found out she was pregnant."

His rheumy eyes stare into space, and Gin imagines he sees in front of him her mother, the fragile Rachel, beautiful and weak.

"Simon and you," he continues, and his voice cracks with grief. "Simon and you. We thought it wouldn't last. We thought it best to take its course. You were both so young. It was Gabe and Hannah who worried us all more."

Gin feels fire in her chest. Of course. Hannah. Gabe's sister. *Her* sister.

"Jacob managed that one. Not well, but he managed it nonetheless. Then when Simon came to me, that last year you were together, said he wanted to marry you at the end of university, I had to tell him."

She stares at him. "Simon *knew?*"

Isaac nods then sniffs, reaches into his pocket, bringing out a white linen handkerchief to wipe his nose. He puts it back in his pocket. "Simon wouldn't tell you. He said it wasn't fair. He knew your relationship with your dad."

Dad. The man who had raised her.

"Did my father know?" she can barely bring herself to ask.

The old man shakes his head. "I honestly don't know. Does it make a difference to you? All I can say is, Virginia, knowing your father as I did, I don't think it would have made any difference to him."

Dad. Not my real dad.

There is little comfort in the old man's words. I have done the same, she thinks. Secrets. So many secrets. Secrets and lies. How could I have stopped this man from knowing Ellie? It had been his only chance of knowing Simon's daughter, his granddaughter. Too late. I am as bad as my mother. My mother kept her secrets, and so have I.

Tears start to course down Isaac's hollowed cheeks. "Simon thought you would move on, forget him, marry someone else. It almost broke him, Virginia. You didn't have to watch him as I did. And then, to see you, and know what you thought of him, what he did, what he was, to think perhaps it was because you weren't Jewish, or good enough for him, in some way." The handkerchief emerges again. "God knows, I blame myself. You would have all led happier lives. But it was not my secret to tell."

Isaac's words come out in short exhalations. "My son," he says, "my son, he loved you."

He loved her. Simon had loved her enough not to tell her. He kept the secrets, told the lies. And I have done the same. For I, I am Jacob's daughter. I am Simon's cousin.

In these moments, clarity. The dream, a portent. Ellie's death was no coincidence of random genes. She and Simon shared blood, enough to kill a child.

Simon's face, serious and sad. I've something to tell you, Ginny, something I should have told you years ago.

56. VIVIENNE

She looks out at the mountain while she dials, pressing each number with deliberation. It is one of those distinctly African days, an uncompromising blue sky, the lightest touch of breeze to lift air that lies as thick as velvet on one's skin. Only the mountain gullies hide green and dark from the searching Midas rays.

He answers on the third ring and he must have recognised her number on his display, because he speaks before she can. She can hear his hopeful urgency.

"Vivienne, I've been trying to reach you."

"I know." She paces the floor of her lounge, worry skimming over any other emotion. "Nick –"

"Vivienne, I have to tell you something. It's about Gabriel. He –"

She interrupts, "Nick, I think I know what you're going to tell me." A slight hesitation. "But that's not important right now. It's Gin." Viv checks her handbag again as she talks.

"Gin? Why, what's wrong?" Detective, now.

"You see, I told her about the files I saw in your office." Viv swallows. The silence is uncomfortable.

Gin had returned from seeing Isaac. Viv had made tea, waited for her friend to talk.

Instead Gin had asked if Viv had called Nick yet. "It's important, Viv."

Sensing that maybe Gin needed time to assimilate the morning, Viv had tried to explain, had told her about the folders, names typed neatly onto white labels. Told her about them, falling. Told her about the one with the curled tag: Gold/McMann.

Inside, a statement signed by Gin. A statement from the hotel manager, two accounts of the accident from witnesses. Simon had swerved violently, the full force hitting him. A note in Nick's handwriting. Was Gold trying to protect McMann? A photograph of the crumpled BMW, the driver's side crushed, paint peeling from fire. A photograph of the interior, cream leather dark with blood. An autopsy report with a photograph of Simon's dead face pinned to the top.

That was when she had pulled her eyes away.

That was when the other folder had fallen out.

Weetman/Kassan.

The shock of it remained.

It was all in there. Everything about her, about Jonnie, the girls, copies of her marriage certificate, the restraining order, her divorce. Matters of public record, she had reminded herself, but there was even a copy of her reclassification as Indian, all those years ago. A letter from the university, detailing Jonnie's years there, his exam results, first class; his prison record, exemplary, and a copy of his sentence: four years for political activism. There were also files on him from before she knew him. She read about his activities as a student, his political affiliations. She stopped at one. It had a list of his known associates and fellow students. She scanned the list. Leila's name was there. No surprise. Jonnie had known Leila from way back. The surprise was that Leila had been studying medicine with him. She must have given up, or failed, and gone into nursing instead. But then, the other name.

Simon Gold.

Statements from a man whose name she did not recognise. She had not known Simon and Jonnie had studied together, or of Simon's political leanings. She had no idea they even knew each other. The very realisation had brought a chill.

And then Nick had entered the office.

"And something happened to her. I mean, when I mentioned Leila, she kind of blanched, went really white, and really quiet. And then one of my patients rang, and I've been on the phone, and when I'd finished talking, she was gone."

"Gone?"

"Yes. Nick, she's taken my car keys. And my address book. I don't know why, or what's going on, but I think Gin's gone to see Leila. And Nick, I'm really worried. I've just got this horrible feeling that something's wrong."

57. GIN

Gin drives along the tarred strip of road edged with fynbos. She does not know Steenberg. She slows Viv's car, checking house numbers. The mountain silhouettes against the Cape sky, stands steadfast and watchful above her. *Help me*, she begs silently, *help me*. One last secret to be revealed today.

What would Gabe have made of Isaac's tale? What would he have said? Would he have made peace with it, or, like her, feel instead rage roar into her being? She wonders what it will bring for her. Will it take its toll in more tortured dreams, when she claws at her mother's beautiful face in unspent anger? Will she look for her father and, like the unceasing dreams of Gabe, never find him now? And what of Jacob, still alive somewhere? Her biological father. And Hannah? What about Hannah? Did she know? Should she be told?

A car hoots angrily, and passes her. Gin, alarmed, pulls off onto the hard shoulder. Her hands grip the wheel. *What am I doing?* Maybe she should turn around, go back to Viv. Ask Viv to come with her. Maybe they should call Retief, although the thought unnerves her. And say what?

"Leila." Like a message.

A message. He *had* been trying to tell her something. Gin spins the wheel, ready to turn back. And there, in front of her, with its gravel drive, its stone-walled garden, is number eighteen. At the end of the driveway, under the roof of a lean-to garage, a white car. It is an old Mercedes, winged bumpers and a rounded bonnet, one of the older, shorter Cape Town numberplates, CA 6861.

A white car, heading directly at them.

She gets out of the car, compelled now to walk up the path, scanning the house as she does. Her shoe catches on the gravel, her leg crumples, and she is down, feeling the grit press into her bare arm. The driveway's surface is rounded, the edges forming a gutter for drainage in the heavy Cape rain, and Gin cannot stop herself from rolling into it. She lands on her back, staring up into the cloudless heaven. She lies still for a moment, stunned, checking herself mentally for injury. A sound behind her. Her eyes flick up. She sees no one, but in her upside-down line of vision, the white car, and its numberplate, 1989.

Simon's face, bleeding upwards.

1989.

Gin reaches out her hand, raises herself to a sitting position and struggles to her feet, brushing dust and gravel off her clothes, her skin. There is another sound. Gin looks up.

A woman is standing to one side of the porch step. She is petite, with coffee skin and almond eyes, lips tinged with lilac.

Her voice reaches across to Gin. "I know who you are. You had better come inside."

58. GIN

Light slats through blinds. A radiant day, the Cape headed for autumn. In England, thinks Gin, spring will be emerging from its long hibernation. Magnolia will be insolent with upturned optimism, marshmallow-pink cherries cheerfully shedding blossoms like snow, forsythia will be graphic yellow, and everywhere, she thinks, everywhere, will be rich, resplendent green.

The green flecks in Simon's eyes.

She looks across the kitchen at Leila. They stand facing each other. Leila's eyes have a haunted look. She speaks in a low husk. It might sound honeyed, thinks Gin, but for its absence of feeling.

Leila's words are simple "You know."

Gin wants to tell this woman she understands, that Jonnie had told her what Simon did to her; that although she, Gin, cannot imagine what horrors must visit Leila in the night, she knows something of what it is like to feel pain and loss, and how it is to live scarred.

Leila carries on, as if oblivious to Gin's presence. "I saw you," she says, pronouncing each word, one at a time. "I. Saw. You. Together. I. Had. Not. Seen. Him. In. All. These. Years. Saw. You. He. Looked. So. Happy."

She looks up at Gin now, aware of her. "I followed you. I watched you. I hated him."

What words have I for this woman, wonders Gin. Leila holds her hand to her mouth, turns her back on Gin and bending over the kitchen sink, she retches into it. Her back heaves with spasms. Gin goes over to her, puts her hand on the woman's back.

Leila leaps away from her, mucus flying from her mouth. She puts a hand out towards her, her palm raised to keep her away. Gin stands still. Leila wipes her mouth, staring at her with wild, unfocused eyes.

"I hated him," repeats Leila. "And I hated you." Leila's hand reaches behind her back. Gin is almost curious to see what the woman grabs. She steps back, afraid of this woman for the first time.

It is her leg that fails her again, giving way as she retreats. The knife is so sharp she does not feel at first the slide of it between her ribs. Only a short ache, like the beginnings of a stitch, a sudden difficulty breathing. She looks, not at Leila, as the blade goes in again, and again, and again, but at the warmth of blood spilling out of her chest.

A hot Friday night, late January. He was standing near the entrance.

Illumination, a light switching on inside.

"Oh," he said, "Is Hannah not here?" No disappointment in his voice. He looked at her with something like recognition, something like expectation. "You must be Virginia."

She might have been surprised, but wasn't. It seemed right that this man whom she had known before, a thousand lifetimes, knew her also. It seemed right that his voice knew its way around her name.

She nodded, continuing to stare.

A sound like rain on a roof, but it was her heart, thrumming against her ribs. A drop of water in a pool, forever rippling outward. Her breath.

A still, small voice inside her that whispered, simply, "Yes."

Gin gasps for breath and opens her eyes. The kitchen looms huge above her but she cannot see Leila. There is an abundant agony when she inhales. She lifts a hand to her side where it is wet and warm.

"I'm Simon," he said.

The connection was made. Simon, Hannah's cousin.

"I'll tell Hannah you came by." She could think of nothing else to hold

him there, to keep him talking in those resonant tones, to keep looking into the pools of black, his eyes that flashed with an odd green brilliance as he spoke.

She opens her eyes again. There is a man kneeling over her. For a moment she thinks it is that policeman, Nick Retief. Viv's man. He looks, thinks Gin, a lot like Gabe. An older, wiser, blonder Gabe, eyes grown greyer. Gabe. She tries to smile. He is saying something to her. As always in her dreams, she cannot hear Gabe's words. His hands are pressing on her ribs, her chest.

Simon will go down those steps, she thought, and she will have to watch him walk away from her, but she knew she would stand there after- wards, forever somehow changed. Yet he stood there still, as if loath to go. She must appear strange, she thought.

Simon started to say something, checked himself. "Thanks."

Then he walked down the steps, and she watched him walk away, and she stood there afterwards for a long time, forever somehow changed.

She must warn Gabe, tell him about Leila, she thinks, focusing sud- denly. She opens her mouth, but can only feel froth bubble in her lungs. No words form. She wants to tell him she understands now. She wants to tell him she knows. She wants to explain to Gabe that Leila rammed their car, that it was Leila who wanted to hurt them, hurt Simon. That Leila herself was hurting, hurt.

"Simon," she says. *Like a lover.*

She wishes Gabe wouldn't press so hard on her chest. It's painful. So much pain. It is hard to breathe. She must warn Gabe.

Dad. She can hear her father's voice through the white mist that is starting to enshroud her vision, like the mist of Isaac's words, like the seaspray in Michael's painting. Michael. Michael would tell her to breathe. But it hurts to breathe, Michael. It hurts, so very much.

Dad's here. I must tell Gabe.

She opens her eyes. Leila stands behind Gabe, her arm raised. She holds the knife.

"Gabe," shouts Gin, "Leila!"

Like a message.

In the end, realises Gin, it prevails. *Love.* It is all we have, and do not lose. And all we take. There is only an orange twilight, fading fast, to darkness. And then to dawn. She hears her father's voice, her daughter's happy gurgle.

Through the mountain's mist, someone is walking towards her, and her heart will know him before she can glimpse the emerald promise of his eyes.

59. NICK

He crouches over her, trying to stem the bleeding.

"Gabe," says Gin, and her lips, dry with effort, form a faint smile. Her breath comes in short gasps. Then her eyes widen and leaning in close, Nick can hear her whisper, "Leila."

Like a message.

He turns swiftly, sees the woman behind him. His left arm is raised against her as he tries to stand. The knife slices across the back of his forearm, and he stumbles back, losing his balance on the slippery floor. Leila's scream is a lost wail. His elbow smashes down on the tiled kitchen floor, pain shoots into his right shoulder, his right clavicle.

Afterwards he will wonder why Manyanga disobeyed his order to sit, to stay. He will never know what made his dog leave her post outside, what made her race through the open back door, attacking his attacker.

Down on the floor, he watches Manyanga leap, teeth bared in a snarl, for Leila's right arm. She turns as the dog jumps, the knife held straight in front of her, stiffly, and Nick hears his own shout as the blade slices across his dog's chest, the fur splitting in a thin red line. Manyanga's snarl becomes a howl, yet her trajectory is such that her open jaws clamp down, not on Leila's arm now, but her throat.

Woman and dog fall together to the floor and he cannot distinguish one's rasping breath from the other.

He tries to rise, his shoulder searing in agony, but his feet slip again on the pink foam that has spewed from Gin's lung and he lands on his side, beside her. Gin's eyes are closed now. She looks asleep, he thinks distractedly.

He manages to get to his knees. Holding his right arm with his left hand, bleeding copiously from the flesh wound on his forearm, he shuffles over to where Leila and Manyanga lie entangled on the floor.

Leila is dead. He can see the woman's vacant eyes fixed on a point beyond the room.

Manyanga whimpers as he reaches her, she pants rapidly.

He sits on the kitchen floor. On tiles stained red with blood. He sits on the floor and cradles his dying dog in his arms. *Manyanga. Manyanga, my beautiful girl.*

Sunlight slices through slatted blinds.

60. VIVIENNE

Kneeling on the cold grass, Viv tips the box of ashes onto the ground. She stares at them for a moment, watches the breeze start to touch them, lift them. Suddenly she wants to sob, to lay her cheek against the hard soil and feel the bristle of grass scrape against her face. Instead she sinks her hands into the ash, expecting it to feel grittier than it does. She feels only the soft disintegration beneath her fingers as she mixes it into the dusty earth, as she rubs the blood and bone of her friend back into the land.

You're safe now Gin, the mountain will hold you. I have put you safely here in its arms and it will watch over you forever.

Hot tears drop onto her hands as she works. Finally, she sits back, looks at her dirtied hands, wipes them on the moist grass, the brown rock. *You're home now, Gin.*

She takes out her cigarettes and lights one. She looks out across to Robben Island, watches a yacht on the horizon, white sails flung to the wind.

Later, she thinks, she will drive past vibrant Greenpoint, into Seapoint, through its somewhat dishevelled façade, its high European buildings, its necessarily narrow lanes, hugging the rugged coast, until the bay opens up before her, palm trees lining the promenade, until the road swings up and out towards his house. She will drive towards his house on the steep cliffs above the African ocean.

I will go and see Nick, Gin, and whatever happens, I promise you I will not wonder what might have been.

The end of her cigarette glows the same colour as the sunset. The peach sky has ruddied to a bruised and bloodied crimson, sedimenting slowly to the sea.

Viv draws on her cigarette. She tucks her jersey around her shoulders, sits back cross-legged on the mountain.

Watching the sun ebb away.

Waiting for the long shadows to journey into night.

Acknowledgements

Sincerest thanks to the following people:

- Maggie Hamand and Shaun Levin at the Complete Creative Writing Course
- Gary Pulsifer, Daniela de Groote, James Nunn, Angeline Rothermundt, and all at Arcadia Books
- Atalanta Miller, Julia Weetman, Rosie Rowell, Tree Garnett, Rochelle Gosling, Laurika Bretherton, Alison Nagle, Jennifer Nadel, Elspeth Morrison, Sarah Sotheron, Ruth Hibbert, Donna Collier, Filipa Komuro, and Rosemary Furber
- Kerry Barrett and Tarja Moles
- Jo Humm, Jean Macpherson, Kelli Kalb, Fauziah Hashmi, and Lisa King
- Sean Sweetman and Karen Baxter and colleagues
- Elizabeth Haylett-Clark and The Society of Authors
- Jenny Lalau-Keraly, Susan Turner, and all at Leinster Square
- Joy Goodwin, Jenny Ewing, Mandy Jevon, Arthur Crage, Bruno Bucher, and Peter Wood
- Yula Viedge, Katherine Hill, Debbie Kowarski, and Nicola Meyer
- Lorraine Mann, and the Lansdowne ladies
- Ion Loader, with love

This novel was written over a number of years while attending the Complete Creative Writing Course in London. The insight, inspiration, enthusiasm, guidance, feedback, and faith of the tutors and fellow students proved invaluable.